## "You're supposed to be dead."

Her voice had a raw, uneven tone, the shaking in her hand growing to an alarming wobble as Sin stared down the muzzle of her Glock.

"You didn't blow yourself up," she muttered.

"Says who?" he asked.

"You're wa FBI."

"I'm not  sagreed. "Dead, yo

Her moutou're not dead. And yo

He couldn't hold back a grin at her serious expression.

"This isn't funny." Moving more quickly than he thought she could, she grabbed the Glock he'd taken from her and swung it back in front of her. This time, her hands didn't shake nearly as hard.

Fear battled with grudging admiration. She was tougher than she looked. "What are you going to do, shoot me?"

"If I have to."

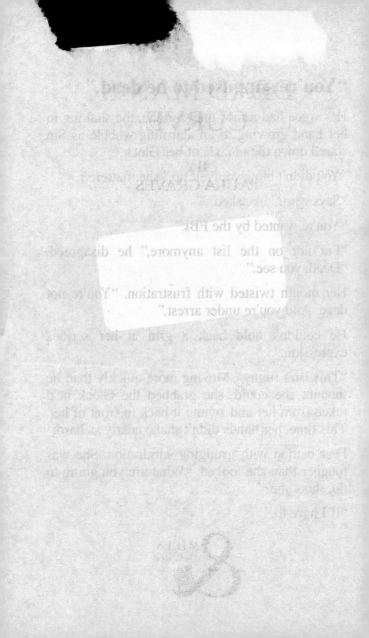

"I'm not on the list anymore", he disagreed. "Dead, you see."

Her mouth twisted with frustration. "You're not dead. And you're under arrest".

# DEAD MAN'S CURVE

## BY
## PAULA GRAVES

MILLS & BOON

Published in Great Britain 2014
by Mills & Boon, an imprint of Harlequin (UK) Limited,
Eton House, 18-24 Paradise Road, Richmond, Surrey, TW9 1SR

© 2014 Paula Graves

ISBN: 978-0-263-91371-2

46-0914

Harlequin (UK) Limited's policy is to use papers that are natural, renewable and recyclable products and made from wood grown in sustainable forests. The logging and manufacturing processes conform to the legal environmental regulations of the country of origin.

Printed and bound in Spain
by Blac

Alabama native **Paula Graves** wrote her first book, a mystery starring herself and her neighborhood friends, at the age of six. A voracious reader, Paula loves books that pair tantalizing mystery with compelling romance. When she's not reading or writing, she works as a creative director for a Birmingham advertising agency and spends time with her family and friends. She is a member of Southern Magic Romance Writers, Heart of Dixie Romance Writers and Romance Writers of America.

Paula invites readers to visit her website, www. paulagraves.com.

For Gayle Cochrane, who knows just how many
ways I owe her my gratitude.
Thanks for all you do!

*Chapter One*

Special Agent Ava Trent took a slow turn around Room 125 of the Mountain View Motor Lodge, studying everything, even though the Tennessee Bureau of Investigation had already given the place a thorough once-over that morning before the locals had called in the FBI. She doubted there was much they'd missed, but she liked to walk through a crime scene while it was still relatively fresh.

She wasn't going to pretend she could put herself in the head of either the victims or the perpetrator—she'd leave the hocus-pocus to the Investigative Services Unit. She just wanted to get a good look at the setup. Get a picture of it in her head. Most people in law enforcement had their own rituals. Taking a good, long look around a crime scene was hers.

Unmade queen-size bed. Suitcases open, partially unpacked, on the luggage stand helpfully supplied by the Mountain View Motor Lodge. Two toothbrushes in the bathroom.

Blotches of blood on the torn green comforter hanging off the bed.

"Married couple. Gabe and Alicia Cooper." Cade Landry, the agent assigned to investigate the possible kidnapping with her, strode up to her, all broad shoulders, square chin and no nonsense. He was new to the Johnson City, Tennessee, resident agency and, if his gruff demeanor was anything to go by, he wasn't going to turn out to be a favorite among the other agents.

She didn't care herself. She wasn't looking to have her hand held, and if she wanted conversation, she could call up her mother or her sister and get all she could handle. And unlike the female support staff at the resident agency, who all found Landry's rock-hewn features and sweet molasses drawl irresistible, she certainly wasn't in the market for a romantic entanglement, especially not with a fellow agent.

"Plenty of signs of a struggle, but not serious injury," Landry continued. "Blood on the bedspread looks incidental. Bloody nose, maybe. Busted lip in a fight. If the Coopers are deceased, it didn't happen here."

"Why were they here in Poe Creek?" she asked.

"Three-year wedding anniversary, according to the motel staff," Landry answered.

"An anniversary trip to Poe Creek?" She took another look around the motel room and shook her head.

"The husband's a pro fisherman. Seems his idea of an anniversary trip included fishing on Douglas Lake," Landry explained, referring to a lake northeast of Knoxville, Tennessee. It was a fifteen-minute drive from Poe Creek, depending on where they'd planned to put their boat in the water.

"Where can I get me a romantic man like that?" she murmured.

It might have been her imagination, but she thought she spotted a hint of a smile flicker over Landry's stony features. Just a hint, then it was gone. "Not an angler?" he asked as he followed her on her circuit of the room.

"Actually, I'm a very good angler," she answered. "But

I don't reckon scaling fish ranks high on my list of things to do on an anniversary trip." Not that she'd ever had an anniversary to celebrate. Unless you counted six years with the FBI.

"Maybe he does all the fish-cleaning. A woman might find that romantic." Pulling out a pen, Landry nudged a piece of paper lying on the bedside table. It was a note, written in a lazy scrawl. "'225 Mulberry Road.'"

"Locals already checked it out. It's a bait-and-tackle shop on the way to Douglas Lake. They're getting the security video for us, in case the Coopers made it there."

"May have nothing to do with their disappearance." Landry's tone of voice was one big shrug. She was beginning to wonder if anything interested him at all.

But not enough to ask him about it. Taciturn and antisocial was just fine with her. She wasn't exactly Susie Sunshine herself.

"We don't have a lot of time before the family shows up," Landry warned a few minutes later when they emerged from the small motel room into the late afternoon gloom. An early fall storm was rolling in from the west, advancing twilight despite the early hour. Rain would be on them soon, making the drive back to Johnson City a gloomy prospect.

"The family?" she asked.

"The Coopers. As in Cooper Security. Ever heard of it?"

"Oh. Of course." Anyone in law enforcement around these parts had heard of Cooper Security, the private agency that had brought down a major-league global conspiracy involving some of the previous administration's top people. "I thought you said this Cooper was a fisherman, though."

"He was. But Mrs. Cooper works for Cooper Security.

They'd have been informed by now, and they have access to helicopters, hell, maybe even private jets, which means they can be up in these mountains before you can say 'civilian interference in an official investigation.' No way will they stay out of this, not with both an employee and one of their own cousins gone missing."

She tried to gauge whether Landry found the thought disturbing or not. For her part, she didn't like the idea of civilians, however skilled and resourceful they might be, getting up in her business on a case. It cramped her style, if nothing else.

"Why don't we see if we can get a couple of rooms and stay here for the night?" Landry suggested, surprising her. She slanted a sharp look his way. "Territorial rights," he added with another ghost of a smile.

She smiled back. "Stake our claim?"

"Somebody's gotta do it. Might as well be us."

First sign of life she'd seen in Landry since they'd arrived. She wasn't sure if she liked it or not, but at least it suited her own intentions.

She called the resident agency and talked to Pete Chang, the Special Agent in Charge. "Do you think the case will benefit from your staying in town instead of commuting?" he asked.

"I do," she answered with more confidence than she felt.

"Approved. Just do the paperwork."

She hung up and nodded to Landry. "Go take care of getting the rooms."

His eyebrows lifted slightly. "Where are you going?"

"Just want a look around." She wandered across the parking lot, where a crowd had gathered in the deepening gloom. Onlookers were ubiquitous at any crime scene, though in a town this small, the crowd wasn't as large as it might have been in a bigger place.

She let her gaze run across the crowd, just out of habit. It had surely taken more than one person to overpower and abduct two able-bodied people, especially if one of those people was a Cooper and the other one worked for Cooper Security. Not likely they could spare someone to see what was going on at the crime scene.

But it wouldn't hurt to give the onlookers a little extra scrutiny.

Most of the people in the crowd came across as tourists rather than locals, though Ava couldn't put her finger on what, exactly, gave her that impression. She wasn't a local herself, though she was close. Her hometown was Bridal Falls, Kentucky, not far across the state line up near Jellico, Tennessee. She knew her way around the mountains.

Some of the people in this crowd weren't dressed for the mountain climate—too many clothes or not enough, depending on where they came from, she supposed. Some wore socks with sandals, which every self-respecting Southerner knew to be a big, flashing sign of an outsider. As she wandered closer to the gathered crowd, she heard a few northeastern and Midwestern accents as well, mingling with the Southern drawls.

Apparently, Landry had followed her, for his deep drawl hummed near her ear. "Is this some sort of FBI magic trick? You listening for the voice of J. Edgar or something?"

"Go get us some rooms," she repeated.

She couldn't see him, but she pictured his shrug. After his one brief moment of liveliness, he was back to the guy who didn't quite give enough of a damn about anything to put up much of an argument. He would have bugged the hell out of her last case partner, an uptight blue flamer from somewhere in the Pacific Northwest.

Didn't bother her a bit, though. A little objectiveness about a case was usually a good thing. Better than sweating every detail until you started seeing things that weren't there.

She turned away from the crowd and looked back at the motel. It was picturesque, she supposed, in the way small mountain motels were. The facade was pure sixties kitsch, complete with a space-age neon sign starting to glow bright aqua in the waning daylight. To a certain type of traveler, she supposed, the Mountain View Motor Lodge might prove too much of a temptation to resist.

Which one chose the place? she wondered. Probably the wife. This was a wife kind of place.

She noticed a truck and a high-end bass boat parked near the end of the lot. The husband was a fisherman. The boat was probably his. She pulled out her cell phone and made a note to check whether forensics had taken a look at the vehicle and the water craft.

Slipping the phone back in her pocket, she turned toward the crowd, letting her gaze slide across the faces again as she pondered the obvious question nobody had yet asked.

Why would someone kidnap a fisherman and his wife? Was it the Cooper name? Was it the wife's job at Cooper Security?

As she reached for her phone again to make a note to check into the wife's open cases, her gaze snagged on a face in the crowd.

He stood near the back, a golden-skinned face in the middle of a sea of various skin colors. Dark hair worn longer than the fashion these days lay thick and wavy around his angular features. He had a full lower lip and deep brown eyes that, back in her foolish, romantic youth, she'd thought soulful.

Someone in front of him shifted, blocking him from her view. She edged sideways, impatient, but when the space opened again, he was gone.

The electric shock coursing through her body kept zinging, however, shooting quivers along her nerve endings and sprinkling chill bumps down her arms and legs. A tidal wave of images and memories swept through her brain, washing out all good sense and replacing it with a tumble of sensations and wishes and the time-worn detritus of shattered dreams.

*It's him,* she thought, her heart racing like a startled deer.

Except it couldn't be him. How could it be?

Sinclair Solano was very, very dead.

UNTIL THAT BRIEF, electric clash of gazes with the woman across the motel parking lot, Sinclair Solano had almost lost touch with what it meant to be alive. He'd forgotten that something other than caution or dread could animate his pulse or spark a flood of adrenaline into his system. That his skin could tingle with pleasurable anticipation and not just the fear of discovery.

But as soon as the sensation bloomed, he crushed it with ruthless intent. He had no time for anticipation. No room for pleasure. His sister, Alicia, had disappeared from her motel room earlier that day, and while Sinclair could offer no evidence to support his theory, he knew deep in his gut—where the worst of his regrets festered—that she'd been taken because of him.

Someone in Sanselmo had discovered the truth. He hadn't died in Tesoro Harbor, as the world supposed.

And if he had not, then his former comrades would

assume only one thing: he had been their enemy, not their friend.

And enemies were not allowed to live.

The crowd shifted, and he darted back toward the woods across the sheltered road, grateful that summer's thick foliage hadn't yet surrendered to the death throes of autumn. He'd dressed today, as he had since coming to these mountains, in olive drab and camouflage, an old habit from his days with the rebels in Sanselmo. Blending into his surroundings had become second nature to him long before his "death," and nothing he'd experienced since that time had given him a reason to change.

Home these days was a lightweight weatherproof tent in the woods. He was able to pitch the tent in minutes and disassemble it as quickly as the need arose.

The only question now was: Had the need arisen again?

She'd seen him. But had she understood who she was seeing? When he'd known her, he hadn't yet crossed the line. He'd been a young man adrift, not long out of college and on a mission to find himself. Twenty-five years old, possessing a law degree but no career, a steady supply of his parents' money and a restless yearning to change the world, he'd bummed around the Caribbean for a while. Haiti for relief work. The Dominican Republic to teach English to eager young students.

The trip to Mariposa had been an oddity. A real vacation, downtime from the poverty and sadness he'd faced every day. And the pretty corn-fed college girl with her Kentucky drawl and pragmatic view of the world had seemed damned near as exotic as the Mariposan beauties.

They'd clicked, in the way opposites sometimes do, and though the smart, practical girl from Kentucky had at first been wary about being alone with a stranger on an island, they'd connected soon enough. It had been the best week of his life, a fact which had confounded him, since neither of them had done a damned thing high-minded or selfless.

Confounded him and made him feel guilty. Especially after talking to his parents one night and realizing, with dismay, that some of the things he'd found most charming about Ava had left his parents appalled and speechless.

It had been his father who'd told him about Luis Grijalva. Luis was doing amazing things in the Caribbean and South America, politically. Organizing workers, fighting for social justice, all the things that mattered to the Solano family.

The things that had mattered to Sinclair.

What was one last day with a college girl compared to meeting the great man himself and learning from his experiences?

He reached the tent, his heart still pounding, and zipped himself inside, wrapping his arms around himself to hold back the shivers. The day was mild, not cool, despite the coming storm, but he felt chilled from the inside out. He dug into the pockets of his trousers and pulled out his latest burner phone. There was a little juice left, but not much. If he didn't run in to town in the next few days, he'd be completely cut off from even the hope of communication.

He stared at the dimmed display, wondering if it was time to make contact with Quinn again. Just a call. A couple of carefully memorized code words. He hadn't tried it yet, but things had changed. Alicia was missing.

He hadn't checked in with Alexander Quinn in almost eight months. He couldn't trust that Adam Brand, the FBI agent who'd recognized him, would keep quiet. There were limits to even Quinn's influence, and enemies more powerful and ruthless than the government who'd once listed him as one of the FBI's most wanted fugitives.

But Sinclair hadn't left the mountains, either. He supposed, in a way, they were as close to a place to call home as he'd found in years of running from his past. He'd always lived in hilly places, from the rolling streets of San Francisco to the volcanic peaks of Sanselmo, the home of his heart. Even on the tiny Caribbean island of Mariposa, where he'd spent a couple of years before the call from Quinn, he'd gravitated to the mountain that filled the center of the island.

The Smoky Mountains were an alpine rainforest rather than a tropical one. But they'd felt like a place of refuge ever since he'd arrived.

Until now.

THOUGH SHE'D GROWN UP in the mountains, it had been a while since Ava had spent much time in the middle of unfettered nature. She'd been living in cities for several years now, where hiking meant leaving the Ford Focus at home instead of driving it downhill to the grocery store when she had a few things to pick up.

But she'd stayed fit, thanks to the demands of her job, and she found some of her old childhood skills coming back to her as she picked her way through the thickening forest.

The land sloped gently upward, making her calves burn as she hiked, but she shrugged the twinges away, concentrating instead on trying to follow the trail through the gloom. Rain had started to fall by the time she reached a fork in the forest trail, turning her hair to damp, frizzled curls beneath the hood of her jacket.

She should have been shocked that Landry hadn't asked more questions about why she was heading into the woods, but based on her hours in his unadulterated presence, she wasn't surprised at all. He was phoning it in these days, for whatever reason. She doubted he'd last at the agency much longer with that attitude. But she didn't have the time or the inclination to dig deeper into what drove him to such epic levels of ennui.

She had an abduction to solve, and based on what she'd learned from her supervisory agent just a few minutes earlier, chasing a ghost into the woods just might be the best use of her time.

"Don't know if it means anything," SAC Chang had told her when he'd called, "but her name pinged in our records because of her familial connection to a terrorist."

At that point, she'd known who the terrorist would be. Hadn't she?

She certainly hadn't been surprised to hear him add, "Her maiden name is Solano."

Sinclair Solano's sister had gone missing the same day Ava had looked up into the crowd at the crime scene and seen the ghost of her brother. And since she didn't believe in ghosts, there was only one explanation.

Sinclair Solano was alive after all.

"Come on, Sin," she muttered, blinking away a film of rain blurring her vision even as it darkened the day. "Where the hell did you go?"

The man she'd met years earlier, before his descent into murder and mayhem, had been a real charmer. Handsome, beautifully tanned, in love with beauty and music and passionate about the world of people around him, he'd been as exotic to her as a Mariposan native, even though he was an American, born and raised in San Francisco. His parents were college professors, he'd told her. His sister was a brainiac who'd skipped grades and was already on the verge of graduating from college at the age of twenty.

He'd liked her accent, argued passionately with some of her politics without making her feel evil or stupid and when he'd kissed her, she would have sworn she heard music.

How he'd gone from that man to the scourge of Sanselmo was a mystery that had nagged her for a long time, until word of his death had reached the news shortly after the terrorist bomb blast he'd set, one intended to take out the new president and his family, went terribly wrong for him and some of his comrades instead.

She was glad, she'd told herself. Poetic justice and all that.

But there was a part of her that had always felt cheated. That curious part of her, the one that had driven her into her current job, that wanted to know why.

Why had he blown her off that last day in Mariposa, knowing her flight would leave the next morning? Why had he grown so cold and distant after talking to his father on the phone?

Why had he left Mariposa for Sanselmo, armed himself on the side of brutal, ruthless rebels and channeled his passion for justice into a murderous assault on a nascent democratic republic?

After word of his death, she'd resigned herself to never knowing the answers to those nagging questions.

Now maybe she'd get a chance to ask them after all.

The rain fell harder around her, seeping under the collar of her jacket. Her trousers were soaked through and beginning to chafe. Worst of all, she had no damned idea where she was anymore. And if the ghost she was chasing had left any sort of trail from here forward, she saw no sign of it.

Trudging to a stop, she just stood still a moment, listening to the woods, taking in the ambient sounds—the susurration of rainfall, the distant hum of engines from the highway north of her position, the slightly ragged whoosh of her own breathing.

Another sound seeped into her consciousness. Footsteps. Careful. Furtive.

Turning a slow circle, she let her gaze go unfocused. Let the wall of green become a blur against which movement might become more evident. She slowed her breathing deliberately, remembering lessons from the shooting classes she'd taken in pursuit of her career, determined to be the best at any task she took on. Her own weapon, a Glock G30S, sat heavily in the small of her back. She reached behind her slowly and eased it from the holster.

She wasn't dressed for stealth on purpose, but her brown jacket, olive-green blouse and dark trousers didn't make her an easy target. She had ordinary brown hair, not a bright shock of red curls that might draw attention her way. Plain olive-toned skin, unlikely to stand out in the gloom. She was in many ways a nondescript woman, which had served her well on the job.

But right now, she felt utterly exposed as the crackle of underbrush filtered through the patter of rainfall.

Someone was watching her. She felt it.

Edging back in the direction she came, she tried not to panic. Coming out here alone had been reckless, especially when she probably could have convinced Landry to come along with her if she'd made the effort.

She hadn't wanted to tell him what she'd seen. That was the truth of the matter. She hadn't wanted to see his skepticism or, worse, his ridicule. Didn't want to hear that she was imagining things.

She knew what she'd seen. She'd looked at Sinclair's photograph for years, even after his death, wondering how the sweet-natured, passionate man she'd met in the Caribbean could have become a terrorist.

The wind picked up, swirling leaves from the trees to slap her rain-stung cheeks. Blinking away a film of moisture, she quickened her steps.

A dark mass rose out of the gloom to her right, slamming into her with a jarring blow before she could react. She staggered against the impact, trying to keep her feet, but shoes slipped on the rain-slick leaves carpeting the forest floor and she hit the ground. Her pistol went flying in the underbrush, out of reach. Breath whooshed from her lungs, and her vision darkened to a narrow tunnel of blurry light.

Rough hands grabbed at her as she gasped for air. Twisting, she tried to see her captor, certain she would see Sinclair Solano's face staring back at her. But the dark-eyed man who held her in his painful grasp was someone she'd never seen before.

He shoved his pistol into the soft flesh beneath her chin, the front sight digging painfully into her skin. *"¡Silencio!"*

Her pulse rattling in her throat, she had no choice but to comply.

# Chapter Two

It had happened in the span of a couple of seconds. One second, Ava Trent been turning back toward the path that had brought her within sight. The next, a man in the familiar jungle camouflage pattern of an *El Cambio* rebel had risen from behind a thick mountain laurel bush and slammed into her like a linebacker. They'd both gone down, but Ava had taken the brunt of the impact, struggling to breathe as the man grabbed her up and jammed a pistol under her chin.

Sin's heart hammered in terror as he scanned the area for an accomplice. There. Emerging from the trees, a second man glided into view, grabbing Ava by the arm.

Two against one, with Ava as the wild card. She'd been carrying a weapon, and back at the crime scene she'd been moving about like a woman with a purpose. Law enforcement, maybe? She'd been circumspect about what she'd be doing when she returned home from vacation, but some things she'd said had hinted at a police job.

Had she recognized him across the parking lot and come out here to find him?

He was armed because Quinn had told him he'd be stupid to walk around unprotected. But despite his reputation, he wasn't a man comfortable with violence. He never had been.

But he could be, under the right circumstances. He'd learned that much about himself in Sanselmo.

Pulling the pistol from the hidden holster inside his jacket, he wished he had a rifle instead. Better accuracy from a distance. But the Taurus 1911 would do.

Across the woods, the man holding the pistol to Ava's chin drew his hand back, bringing the pistol muzzle away from her face. But as he did so, the second man grabbed her from behind in a bear hug, eliciting a grunt of surprise from her as she started to struggle against his hold.

The man with the gun pressed it to her forehead, and Sin aimed the Taurus in his direction, his finger sliding onto the trigger.

Ava slumped suddenly, her arms sliding up and her body dropping, catching the man holding her by surprise. She slipped from his grasp, down to the forest floor.

Sinclair would never get a better chance.

Aiming down the barrel of the Taurus, he fired. Simultaneously, another shot rang out, the crack echoing in the trees, almost drowning out the report of his own weapon. The man reaching for Ava fell backward into the underbrush. The man in front of her pitched forward, firing off a shot of his own as he fell.

Ava's body jerked, even as she rolled away from the falling man, scrambled to her feet and started running. She made it about ten yards before she started to stagger, her legs wobbling beneath her as if they'd gone boneless. She fell forward into the thickening underbrush, disappearing from his view.

Keeping an eye on the two fallen men, Sinclair dashed after her, his heart racing faster than his churning legs. She lay crumpled, facedown, but he could see by the rise and fall of her body that she was still breathing. He stopped next to the two fallen men. The one who'd grabbed Ava first lay facedown, unmoving. The back of his camouflage jacket had a bloody hole in it, somewhere in the vicinity of his left shoulder blade. He didn't appear to be breathing. Nudging with his foot, Sin rolled the man over and took a long look at his face.

*Emilio Fuentes,* he thought, staring into the glassy brown eyes of a man he'd once called friend. His heart contracted.

He picked up the pistol Fuentes had dropped and shoved it into his pocket. He checked the second man, the one at whom he'd aimed his own pistol. Carlito Escalante. A bloody hole in the side of the man's neck was the only obvious injury. Sin checked for a pulse and found none.

A queasy sensation filled his gut, and he swallowed the urge to be sick.

He searched Carlito's body, found a hunting knife besides the pistol the man had dropped, and added both to his pocket, trying not to let his rapid respirations escalate to hyperventilation. He needed his wits about him. His life had just gotten a thousand times more dangerous.

By the time he found the pistol Ava had dropped when she was attacked and turned back to her, she was on her hands and knees, trying to crawl away. He hurried to her side, crouching beside her.

She whirled at his touch, swinging her arm up in a shaky arc before he could react. Suddenly, he was staring down the muzzle of a Glock aimed right between his eyes. Now he knew where the second shot had come from.

She'd had another weapon.

"Ava," he said.

"You're supposed to be dead." Her voice had a raw, uneven tone, the shaking in her hand growing to an alarming wobble.

He reached out and moved her hand away from his

face. She struggled but didn't pull the trigger before he took the gun away and wrapped his arm around her as she started to fall backward. "Whoa, there." Dropping the Glock to one side, he gave her a quick appraisal, looking for her injury.

There. Under the hem of her jacket. Blood spread across the right side of her charcoal trousers and seeped upward onto her olive-green blouse. As she tried to slap his hands away, he tugged the blouse up and away, revealing a ripped furrow in the waistband of her pants. Beneath it, the bullet's path had carved a bloody gouge in the soft flesh just above her hip bone.

"Ow," she groaned as he plucked a piece of scorched fabric from the wound.

He needed to get her back to the motel. And he needed not to get caught. Irreconcilable goals.

"You didn't blow yourself up," she muttered. He looked up from the bullet wound to find her hazel eyes focused on his face.

"Says who?" he asked, reaching in his back pocket for his multibladed knife. There was a set of tweezers tucked into the handle, if he wasn't mistaken. Given the messy condition of her wound, he was probably going to need them.

"You're wanted by the FBI."

"I'm not on the list anymore," he disagreed, sliding the tweezers out. "Dead, you see."

Her mouth twisted with frustration. "You're not dead. And you're under arrest."

He couldn't hold back a grin at her serious expression. "Can I finish cleaning this wound before you take me in?"

"This isn't funny." Moving more quickly than he thought she could, she grabbed the Glock he'd taken from her and swung it back in front of her. This time, her hands didn't shake nearly as hard.

Fear battled with grudging admiration. She was tougher than she looked. "What are you going to do, shoot me?"

"If I have to."

"Getting back to the motel on your own isn't going to be pleasant," he warned, sitting back on his heels.

"I'll deal." Keeping her pistol aimed at his chest, she pushed to her feet, struggling not to sway. "Sinclair Solano, you're under arrest for the murder of three American oil company employees. For starters."

"I didn't kill those men."

"We'll let the courts sort that out." She twitched the Glock's muzzle at him. "Move."

He wasn't going to let her take him in. He'd had his chance to face justice years ago and had traded it for a chance to make things right. But Alexander Quinn had warned him there were no easy outs. Once he went back to *El Cambio* and pretended nothing had changed, he might never be able to clear his name.

He'd taken the chance. Now, it seemed he might have to pay.

"Do you know who those men were?" He nodded toward the two bodies lying several yards away.

Her gaze slanted toward them briefly before locking with Sin's again. "No. Do you?"

"The one who grabbed you was Emilio Fuentes. Major player in *El Cambio*'s military wing. He was Alberto Cabrera's top commander." He watched her expression for any signs of recognition. Her eyes narrowed; she knew something about *El Cambio*, he thought. "The other was Carlito Escalante."

"The Spider," she murmured, recognition dawning.

She wasn't just playing at whatever job she was working, clearly, if she knew Escalante's nom de guerre. He tried not to stare into the muzzle of her Glock. "Why do you suppose two of *El Cambio*'s top enforcers were wandering around the Smoky Mountains?"

"They're looking for you."

He gave a brief nod. "They're looking for me."

"Why?"

"Because I'm not one of them. Because I betrayed them a long time ago, and somehow, they figured out I'm not dead."

Her eyes narrowed in her pain-creased face. "Betrayed them how?"

"Long story, *carida*. Remind me to tell you about it sometime."

"Are there others out here?"

He suspected there were. If Cabrera had sent two enforcers, he'd probably sent a dozen. The arrogant son of a bitch had never economized on anything. "The motel is about a mile in that direction," he said, nodding toward the northwest. "But I can't promise you won't run into more like those two."

Her nostrils flared, the only sign of reaction to his words. "Or maybe you're just telling me that so I'll let you go."

He shrugged. "Your call."

She pushed painfully to her feet, keeping the pistol barrel pointed at his chest. "Walk."

"I'm not going back to the motel with you, so you might as well shoot me now."

A muscle in her jaw twitched dangerously. "Why did you even come back here? You had to know you'd be arrested if anyone ever found you."

"There's a man named Alexander Quinn." Her forehead creased slightly with recognition, so he proceeded without further explanation. "He recruited me years ago. Not long after I joined up with *El Cambio*."

"Recruited you for what?"

A flash in the gloom behind her distracted him. It was quick, but his instincts were honed for action after all these years living on the edge of the razor. He threw himself at her, praying she wouldn't shoot before he knocked her to the ground.

A sharp report shattered the air around them. It took a moment for him to realize it had come from the woods, not from her pistol.

He held her down, lifting his head just enough to peer through the underbrush for more signs of movement. Beneath his body, she wriggled, her breath coming in short, pained gasps.

"Shh," he whispered, dropping his head back below the underbrush.

"Was that—?" Her words came out in a raspy wheeze.

"Someone shooting at us?" he whispered, shifting to give her room to breathe. "Yes. Yes, it was."

RAIN NEEDLED HER FACE, soft prickles she could barely feel. All of her senses seemed gathered on the burning ache of her torn flesh and the dizzying sensation of Sinclair Solano's very warm, very alive body covering hers. She expected more gunfire, but it didn't come.

"They didn't just leave," she whispered, hating that she was on her back, blind to the angle of attack. But moving more than an inch or two might make them easier targets. Sometimes, waiting for a more advantageous situation was the only reasonable option.

Not that she had to like it.

"I know." Sin edged slowly to one side. As the weight of his body eased from hers, she sucked in a deeper breath.

Almost immediately, she wished she hadn't, as the rise and fall of her diaphragm tugged the skin around her wound.

Biting her lip, she carefully rolled to her side. The movement brought her close to Sin again, but she had a better view of the woods in front of them. "There could be people coming from all directions."

"I know."

She had held on to the spare Glock, she realized with a twinge of surprise. For a few moments there, when he'd slammed her to the ground, all she'd been aware of was gutting pain. She eased the pistol forward, trying not to rustle the tangle of undergrowth that hid their position.

"If we can get back to the motel, we'll have backup," she added, slanting a look at him. "Want to rethink the whole resisting arrest thing?"

"I'm not guilty of murder."

She couldn't tell if he was lying or not. It sounded like the truth, but his gaze slanted away from hers as he said it.

"And you're willing to die to avoid defending yourself?"

"Where's your cell phone?" he asked.

She almost banged her head on the ground in frustration. What the hell? Why hadn't she already pulled out her phone and called in the cavalry?

As she dropped her hand to her right pocket, her palm grazed the wound over her hip, and she sucked in a hiss of breath. Biting her lip, she reached into her pocket and pulled out the phone.

It was in pieces. The bullet had apparently hit the metal phone case and deflected into her hip. But not before it smashed into the phone itself, cracking it in two.

She looked at Sin. "Don't suppose you'd lend me yours?"

He shook his head. "I'm not letting you take me in."

"Then I guess we both die out here." Grinding her teeth in anger, she lifted her head briefly, long enough to see above the underbrush. Movement to the south caught her attention, and she ducked again. "They're circling around to the south."

"Maybe checking on Fuentes and Escalante."

She turned her head toward him, her heart freezing for a long, dizzying moment as she realized he gripped a large Taurus 1911, a shiny silver monster of a pistol with a walnut grip.

His gaze met hers. "I'm not going to shoot you." He nodded toward the south. "Might shoot him, though."

She followed his gaze and saw a man dressed in dark green camouflage moving quietly through the underbrush. The same man who'd already shot at them? Or someone new? She wasn't sure.

"How do we get out of here?" she whispered, trying to ignore the burning pain in her hip. If she crouched here much longer in one position, she wasn't sure she'd be able to move when the time came.

"We need a distraction," he murmured.

"Got any ideas?"

"Yeah, one, but I should have pulled the trigger on that option about thirty minutes ago," he answered, his gaze still on the man creeping through the gloom in front of them. "Too late now."

A streak of lightning lit the sky overhead, and the man in camouflage jerked in reaction, especially when a booming crash of thunder followed only a second later.

"Just great," Ava muttered. As if the rain wasn't enough.

"Just might be," Sin said quietly.

She glanced at him. He was still watching the other man, his eyes narrowed in thought.

"What are you thinking?" she asked, uneasy at how

quickly they'd gone from opponents to allies with the addition of the new intruder. She'd do well to remember that, no matter what help Sinclair Solano might be offering at the moment, he was still a wanted man. He was suspected in over a dozen terrorist bombings in Sanselmo, many of which had killed innocent civilians—men, women and even children.

But Sin wasn't the one hunting her now, so she had to be pragmatic about the situation. He seemed to know where he was and what he was doing. And she was bleeding and growing stiffer by the minute.

Another flash of lightning cracked open the sky. This time, the thunder sounded right on its heels, stopping the man hunting them in his tracks. Ava took the opportunity for a quick look around for more men in camouflage. She didn't see anyone else out there, but Sin was probably right. If Cabrera had bothered to send two of his top lieutenants to look for Sin, he'd have sent more than just three people. There might be a whole squad of killers roaming these woods.

Getting out of here wasn't going to be easy.

"Next flash of lightning, I want you to run east, as fast as you can. Due east. About two hundred yards in that direction, you'll find a tent covered with a Ghillie net. Get inside and be ready to shoot anyone who sticks his head inside."

She shot him a look. "Even you?"

"I'll say, 'Alicia is missing,' and you'll know it's me."

"Alicia is missing?" she repeated, not sure if it was smart to admit she knew the connection between her kidnapping victim and the man beside her.

"She is, isn't she?" His throat bobbed as he turned his gaze toward the man still creeping through the trees.

"Cabrera's people almost certainly have her. They took her as a way to put pressure on me."

"Why would they think it would?" she asked, wondering if he'd tell her the truth.

"Because Alicia Cooper's maiden name is Solano."

"Your sister?"

He looked at her oddly. "You already knew that."

She didn't deny it.

He sighed. "I have to find her before they do something that can't be reversed."

"She's with her husband. He'll help protect her."

Sinclair nodded. "If they don't kill him first."

Lightning streaked across the sky, one jagged crack after another. Thunder rolled in a continuous roar, and Sin gave her a nudge. "Now!"

She reversed position, clamping her teeth together as pain raced through her side to settle in a raw burn at the point of her hip. Staying low, she raced east. Or, at least, what she hoped was east. She heard a commotion behind her, gunshots stuttering through the drumbeat of rain.

Head down, she ran faster, deeper into the woods. Pain squeezed tears from her eyes, but she couldn't slow down. Footsteps crashed through the underbrush behind her, but she didn't look back.

The Ghillie shelter rose up in the gloom so quickly, she almost ran headfirst into the tent. Spotting the opening, she wriggled into the small tent and turned until she sat facing front, her knees pulled up to her chest despite the howl of pain from her torn hip. She held her Glock steady by using her knees as a shooting rest, willing her heartbeat to slow and her ragged respiration to even out.

*Alicia is missing,* she thought, trying to piece together the disparate shards of information she'd gleaned over the past half hour. Alicia Cooper was originally Alicia Solano.

Sinclair's sister. Chang had told her that much. But did Alicia know her brother was alive? Did she know why Cabrera's men had taken her and her husband?

Was Gabe Cooper even alive?

"Alicia is missing." Even without the code words, she recognized Sinclair Solano's voice. "I'm coming in."

The flap of the tent opened. She tightened her grip on the Glock, her trigger finger sliding down from where she'd held it flattened against the side of the pistol. She tried not to hold her breath, but air wouldn't seem to move in or out of her lungs while she waited for him to appear.

Then, in the space of a blink, he was there, crawling inside the tent, little more than a dark shadow within the darker confines of the shelter.

"Are you okay?" he asked, his voice barely a whisper.

"I think so."

"I shot a third man when he shot at me. He's dead. But there are others out there. I heard them calling to one another."

She pressed one hand to her mouth, feeling sick. "And we're sitting ducks in this tent."

"We're under shelter. There are alarms outside to let us know if intruders are getting close." He reached for a blanket that lay beside her on the tent floor. She hadn't even noticed it, hadn't realized how hard she was shivering until he draped it over her shoulders. Warmth rolled over her like a wave, driving out some of the chills.

"Better?" he asked.

She nodded. "I didn't notice any alarms outside."

"You wouldn't have," he said with a quirk of a smile. He hunkered down next to her, sticking close enough that the searing heat of his body was as good as a blazing fire. The only thing missing was the comfort of light. The tent remained dark and would only get darker as night continued to fall.

"So what now?" she whispered.

He blew out a long, slow breath. "We wait out the storm and hope those fellows don't find us."

Chapter Three

As plans went, waiting and hoping weren't high on Sinclair's list of great ones. But his burner phone had no juice left. He'd have to get to civilization to charge the phone, and even then, he wasn't sure what, if anything, Alexander Quinn could do to help him find Alicia and her husband.

"I need to go back to the motel," Ava said after a few moments of tense silence. "I have work to do."

"You're a cop?"

She gave him a strange look, then released a soft huff of breath that was almost a laugh. "Oh, right. I left the other jacket in the car."

"What other jacket?"

He could barely make out the curve of her pained smile. "The blue jacket with the big yellow *FBI* on the back."

"FBI." Great. Of all the old acquaintances he could have run into in the middle of the woods, he had to run into the one who worked for the federal agency that had once had his face tacked prominently to every wall of every field office and resident agency in the country.

"We think you're dead, you know. Well, everyone *else* does."

"I'd love for it to stay that way."

"Too bad. I'm not your friend, Solano. I can't look the other way. So if you're going to kill me to stop me from ratting on you, go for it now so one or the other of us can get on with trying to stay alive."

"I'm not what you think I am." He sighed as she gave him a look so skeptical he couldn't miss it even in the near darkness. "I know you've probably heard that before."

"You reckon?"

"There's a lot you don't know."

"Let me guess. You were really a double agent working for the CIA to bring down *El Cambio* from the inside." Her sarcasm had a sharp bite.

*Well,* he thought. *There goes the truth as a viable explanation.*

Awkward silence descended between them again. Strange, Sin thought, how hard it was to talk to her now, when back in Mariposa, all those years ago, talking to Ava Trent had seemed as easy as breathing.

She'd been nothing like any girl he'd ever known, growing up in San Francisco, and he supposed maybe the sheer novelty of her had been the initial attraction. That and her curvy little figure, displayed not in a skin-baring bikini, but a trim racer-back one-piece, standing out on the Mariposan beach amid all those skimpy thongs and barely-there tops. She'd swum the ocean as if it were a sport, tackling waves with ferocity of purpose, all flexing muscles and determination.

Somehow, her lack of self-consciousness about her appearance had only made her more attractive in Sinclair's eyes. And when she'd opened her mouth and that Kentucky drawl had meandered out, he'd been leveled completely. There had been no other word for the way she'd made him feel, as if the earth beneath his feet had liquefied and he couldn't hold a solid thought in his head.

She'd declared he'd like Kentucky, if he was looking

for somewhere new to visit. And he'd almost talked himself into going back there with her.

"How sure are you that it's Cabrera who has your sister?" Ava's whisper broke the tense silence filling the tent.

"Pretty sure," he answered. "Do you have evidence to the contrary?"

She was silent for a moment. "I just got here this afternoon. I didn't have a lot of time to investigate before I went on a ghost hunt."

Feeling her gaze on him in the gloom, he turned his head to find her watching him, eyes glittering. "I didn't think anyone would see me."

"How'd you find out about the kidnapping?"

"I heard the sirens." Reliving that heart-sinking moment when he'd realized all those lights and sirens had been headed for the motel where his sister was staying, he struggled to breathe. "I'd seen a write-up in the local paper about a visit from a previous bass tournament champion. Her husband, Gabe. There was a picture of the two of them, right on the front page of the sports section."

Alicia had looked so beautiful in that photo, he thought. So happy. The guy she'd married seemed solid, too. Quinn had told him a few things about the Coopers, whom Quinn knew through prior dealings with the family. Gabe Cooper had been among the family members who'd done battle with a South American drug lord seeking vengeance against one of the Coopers. Sinclair prayed he'd be just as strong in protecting Alicia.

Of course, Cabrera's men might have executed him the first chance they got. They were nothing if not ruthless.

"They're keeping her alive," Ava murmured. "There's no point in killing her if they want to use her to smoke you out."

"I may have done the job for them."

"Three dead and we're still at large. That's not nothing." Her voice had grown progressively more strained. That wound she'd suffered was probably hurting like hell by now.

"I need to take a look at your wound."

"It's okay."

"It needs to be cleaned out and disinfected. The longer we wait to do that, the more likely infection will set in." It might not be possible to avoid infection even now, but it wouldn't hurt to clean her up. "I have first aid supplies."

"We can't risk a light."

"The Ghillie cover will block most of it, and the woods should take care of the rest, unless they stumble right on us. And if that happens, the light will be the least of our worries."

She released a gusty sigh. "Okay. But be quick."

He grabbed his bag from the back of the tent and pulled out the compact first-aid kit. Fortunately, he'd stocked up a few days ago when he'd made a run to Bentwood to charge his burner phone. Using a penlight to see what he was doing, he pulled out disinfectant, gauze, tape and a couple of ibuprofen tablets to help her with the pain. The kit also offered a bigger pair of tweezers. One look at the messy furrow ripped into the fleshy part of her hip suggested he was going to have to do some careful work to get all the singed fabric out of the wound.

"I'd offer you a bullet to bite," he said, keeping his voice light, "but we may need to conserve them."

"Just get it done." She pushed down her trousers, wincing as the fabric stuck to the drying blood at the edges of her wound.

He handed her the penlight. "Can you hold this for me?"

She positioned the light over her hip, turning her head away and burying it in the elbow crook of her other arm.

He worked quickly, wincing at her soft grunts of pain. The wound was about five inches long and at least a half-inch deep, grooving a path right through the flesh of her hip. It had missed the bone, fortunately, and she had enough curves for the bullet to have also missed most of the muscle. "Looks like it mostly injured fatty tissue," he commented as he dabbed antiseptic along the margins of the wound.

"I'm suddenly feeling less guilty about that chocolate-covered doughnut I had for breakfast," she mumbled.

"We need to get you somewhere cleaner than these woods," he said as he bandaged up the wound.

"I'm counting on that," she answered. "You'll be coming, too."

"I can't do that."

"You don't get a vote."

He looked down at her bared hip, the utter vulnerability of her current pose. "You're in no position to make demands at the moment."

She moved as quickly as a cat, the grimace on her face as she whipped up to face him betraying the pain the move caused her. Still, she had her Glock in his face before he could put down the first aid kit. "Want to bet?"

He couldn't stop a smile, even though he knew it would only make her angry. "You'll have to shoot me, then."

Her lips pressed to a thin line. "Why aren't you dead, Solano?"

"Because I never walked into that warehouse in Tesoro with the rest of the crew." He tamped down the memories—the thunderous bomb blast, the sickening knowledge that people he knew, people he'd lived with and sometimes even liked, were gone, martyrs to a cause he'd once embraced and now despised.

"The authorities in Sanselmo accounted for your body."

"There were ten bodies. Mine just wasn't one of them."

"You killed someone to fake your own death?"

"He was already dead. John Doe from the local morgue."

"You knew those men would die when they went in there. Why would you betray your own comrades that way? I never thought you were amoral. Wrong? Absolutely. Following a fool's path? Certainly. But to kill nine men to fake your own death?"

"It wasn't my doing," he said, not sure how much he should reveal to her about what he'd done all those years ago. Some of it was probably still classified. He and Quinn had never discussed what he would have to tell the world if he were ever caught.

"Don't get caught" had been Quinn's oh-so-helpful advice.

Besides, she had already dismissed the truth as a possible explanation. What good would it do to tell her at this point?

"If it wasn't your doing, whose was it?"

He took a deep breath. "I can't say. There are other people involved. Some of them might still be in dangerous situations."

Her eyes narrowed. "So you're going with the 'secret CIA double agent' story after all? Really?"

He looked away from those sharp eyes, his gaze falling to her midsection, where her unbuttoned trousers were riding down perilously, revealing black panties, the luscious curve of her hips and the sleek plane of her flat belly. His body responded fiercely, a white-hot ache settling low in his groin. It had been a damned long time since he'd been this close to a woman. And this woman, in particular, had gotten under his skin in record time once before.

Clearly, in the eight years since, he hadn't developed an immunity.

He cleared his throat and waved his hand toward her open fly. "You're about to lose your britches."

As she glanced down, he grabbed her wrist, moving the muzzle of her Glock away from his face. Her gaze flew up to meet his, her expression shifting between mortification and anger. But not fear, he noticed. For whatever reason, she didn't seem to fear him.

Lust flared like fire in his belly.

He let go of her wrist. "I told you, I'm not going to hurt you. But I don't like having a gun in my face."

She jerked back from him, but she didn't aim her gun his way again, he noticed with relief. When she spoke, her voice was soft and raspy. "How did you get out of Sanselmo without being caught? How did you make it back here to the States, for that matter?"

"Same answer to both questions. I had help."

"From whom?"

"The good guys."

"Good guys in whose eyes?" Her tone was acerbic.

"Interesting question, that."

"CIA, I suppose?" She looked disappointed that he wasn't coming up with a different story.

*Too bad,* he thought. *You may not like it. Hell, I didn't like it much myself. But the truth is what it is.*

"I'm going to take a look outside. I think it's dark enough to risk it." He turned in the narrow confines of the tent and started crawling toward the exit. As he neared the flap, he felt the heat of her body scrambling up behind him. She nudged her way to his side, her body soft and sizzling hot against his. Another flare of desire bolted through him, making his arms and legs tremble.

He turned to look at her. Her small, heart-shaped face

turned toward his, her eyes large and dark in the faint ambient light coming from outside. "This doesn't require us both," he murmured.

"I'm not letting you out of my sight."

She was going to make his quest to find his sister a little more difficult, he realized. Because if there was one thing he'd learned about Ava Trent during that week they'd spent together in Mariposa, it was the depth of her sheer, dogged determination. She attacked every task she took on with the same pedal-to-the-floorboard pluck.

She wouldn't be easy to shake. And he wasn't going to hurt her.

So how did he plan to proceed?

The easy answer would be to somehow make her an ally rather than an enemy. But short of spilling a boatload of long-held state secrets, how was he supposed to do that? And would she believe him even if he told her every little piece of the truth?

He needed to talk to Quinn, which meant heading for the closest town to charge his burner phone. And the closest town was Poe Creek, about a mile through the *El Cambio*-infested woods. Poe Creek, where cops still swarmed about the motel crime scene. Where Ava probably had fellow agents beginning to wonder where the hell she'd disappeared to and whether it was time to call for reinforcements to go looking for her.

"How many people are with you?" he asked.

She frowned. "I'm not going to tell you that."

"They'll be looking for you. Don't want to shoot the wrong people."

"You won't be shooting anyone," she said firmly.

"We've already shot three people trying to kill us. I'm not going to stop trying to defend myself—or you—just because you've decided to make your name as an FBI agent on my bounty."

She made a low, growling sound thick with frustration. "I don't want to shoot you."

"Good to know."

"But you're a fugitive from justice, and bringing you in is my job."

"Why don't we concentrate on getting out of these woods alive first?" he suggested, trying to sound reasonable. The grumble that escaped her throat at his words suggested he hadn't entirely succeeded.

But she gave a short nod toward the tent flap in response. "Think they're still out there, then?"

"Somewhere," he affirmed. "But now that we know they're looking for me, we can be more careful moving through the woods. I think we can stay a step ahead of them until we get back to civilization."

At least, he hoped they could. Because one way or another, he needed to get word to Alexander Quinn. The spymaster had warned him something like this might happen.

Every man's sin sooner or later came back to haunt him.

HER HIP WAS burning like fire, the pain as effective as a cup of strong coffee to keep her heart pounding and her adrenaline pumping. Without the pain, she might have been tempted to hunker down and wait for daylight, because sneaking through the woods at night was harder than she remembered.

She had grown up in a rural area, traipsed through her share of woods and mountains, but rarely at night, and never with five inches of bullet-grazed flesh playing a symphony of agony with each careful step. But, as she reminded herself in a silent litany as she followed Sinclair Solano through a tangle of underbrush, each step took them closer to civilization. Closer to a clean bandage, prescription antibiotics and painkillers.

Closer to the safety of numbers.

She had come to the conclusion that Sin was being honest about one thing—he didn't intend to kill her, even if she tried to take him into actual custody instead of this parody of custody they were playing out at the moment. But that didn't mean he wouldn't try to stop her.

He'd been at this fugitive thing a long time. Clearly, he was good at it.

So the ball was in her court, she supposed. He might not be willing to kill her to maintain his freedom, but was she willing to kill him if he resisted her attempt to keep him in her custody? Was she willing to let Cade Landry shoot him? Or one of the local cops?

*This shouldn't even be a question, Trent. You're an FBI agent. Taking criminals into custody is part of what you do.*

But Sinclair Solano had saved her life. Put his own life at risk to do it. And when he swore he wasn't the man she thought he was, he seemed to believe what he was saying.

Her boot tangled with a thick root somewhere beneath the mass of vines, scrub and decaying leaves underfoot, tipping her off balance. She stumbled forward, grabbing for something, anything to break her fall.

She slammed into the hard, solid heat of Sin's chest as he moved quickly to catch her. His arms roped around her body, holding her close, lifting her back to her feet.

He didn't let go immediately, his breath hot against her cheek. Despite the pain in her side, despite the adrenaline still flooding her body, she felt an answering rush of heat racing through her veins to settle, heavy and liquid, in the juncture of her thighs.

She wasn't twenty and carefree, enjoying her last taste

of freedom before law school and the FBI career she'd chosen for herself. These woods weren't the cool, lush rainforest surrounding the soaring peak of Mt. Stanley.

And Sinclair Solano had long since ceased to be just some sexy, brooding fellow tourist who'd made her pulse race and her toes tingle with a few hot kisses under the Mariposa moon.

He let her go slowly, his hands sliding down her arms, his fingers brushing hers lightly as he released her. "You okay?" he whispered.

Her voice felt trapped in her throat. She nodded without attempting to free it.

For a long, electric moment, he continued gazing at her. Apparently, Poe Creek had not yet folded up its streets for the night, for faint light glowed in the west, edging his features with a hint of gold. He had tawny skin and dark, dark eyes, and eight years past their brief entanglement, his compelling magnetism still tugged at her unwilling heart.

"What am I going to do with you?" he asked, and she realized with a shiver those exact words were echoing in her own troubled mind.

"Tell me the truth." She couldn't stop herself from taking a step closer, as if he'd tugged an invisible cord between them. "If you tell the truth, I'll know it. And I'll know what to do. Why did you join *El Cambio?* And why did you leave?"

For a tense moment, he stared at her, his expression unreadable. Then, as he opened his mouth to answer, a loud crack sounded from close by.

She dropped, grabbing his arm and dragging him down with her. Adrenaline spiked, sending her heart into a wild gallop as she tried to find cover in the underbrush, her gaze darting around the darkened woods in search of the intruder.

"That wasn't a gunshot," Sin whispered, his face close enough that his breath tickled the tendrils of hair curling on her forehead.

"What was it?"

Before he could answer, a flurry of sound and movement broke the tense quiet of the woods. Thirty yards to the north, two men burst into view out of the underbrush, scrambling and stumbling as they went, throwing fearful looks behind them.

A few yards behind them, a large black bear loped after them, moving with surprising speed.

"I thought black bears didn't attack unprovoked," she whispered, watching the animal crash through the forest after the two fleeing men.

"She may have a cub around here somewhere."

One of the men seemed to finally remember he was armed. He swung his gun hand toward the bear and fired a shot. It missed the bear, the bullet whipping through a thicket only ten yards away from where Ava and Sin crouched.

Sin grabbed her around the waist and hauled her with him behind a nearby tree trunk. The sudden movement pulled at her injury, and she hissed with pain.

"Sorry!" he whispered in her ear, sliding his hand up to her rib cage.

But he didn't let her go.

Another gunshot rang in the woods. Another bullet missed the bear and whizzed harmlessly past their hiding place by a dozen yards. The next time Ava peeked around the tree trunk, the bear was circling back around, heading away from where they crouched. The men were two diminishing shadows in the woods, still on the run.

Ava released a long breath. "That was close. Let's get out of here."

"Wait," Sin murmured, catching her arm as she started to move.

She looked up at him, jerking her arm free of his grip. "What?"

He met her gaze, his eyes burning with fierce intent. "We have to follow those men."

## *Chapter Four*

Clearly, she thought he was crazy. Hell, maybe he was—those men were probably better armed and equipped than either of them, and he had no idea how many of them might be roaming the woods at the moment.

"We need to go back to the motel and report those guys," she said firmly, starting westward.

He caught up with her, taking care not to touch her this time. "The bear scared the hell out of those guys. I'd bet they're heading back to wherever Cabrera has set up camp in these hills. This could be our best chance to find out where that is." His voice went raspy as emotion tightened his throat. "They might lead us to my sister."

Her gaze softened. "They're already out of sight."

"I can track them. I've had a lot of experience in the past few years."

Pinching her lower lip between her teeth, she gazed toward the darkness where the two men had disappeared. She released a huff of breath. "Okay, you're right. We can't let this trail go cold. But we don't do anything but observe when we get there, understand? We find the place, then memorize the trail back for when I have reinforcements."

He wasn't sure he could agree to her stipulation, not with his sister's life at risk. But if he didn't agree, she would dig in her heels and make it next to impossible for him to tail those men. "Understood."

She looked bone-tired briefly before her spine straightened and her chin came up to jut forward like the point of a spear. "You can track them? Then you lead."

He suspected she wanted him in front as much to keep an eye on him as to let him lead the way. He didn't care. He wasn't going to run from her.

Not yet, anyway.

"Let's pack up the tent. We may need to set up camp later." He accomplished the task quickly, and they were underway in minutes. The men hadn't covered their tracks while they were running, but about a mile from where they'd encountered the bear, they stopped blazing an obvious trail through the woods. In the dark, trying to figure out what was evidence of human passage and what was normal woodland wear and tear became a hell of a lot harder, especially with clouds scudding overhead, blocking out most of the moonlight. At least the rain had finally stopped, leaving the ground wet enough for footprints to show up in the softened soil underfoot.

"There." Three miles out, Ava spotted the faint tracks of their human prey. "Aren't those footprints?"

He studied the tracks. "Good eye," he murmured with approval.

"You're not the only tracker around here," she answered bluntly. But she sounded pleased. He spared her a quick look, struck by how pretty she was, even rain-drenched and weary. What makeup she'd been wearing back at the motel had washed away completely, leaving her looking more like the dewy-faced girl from Kentucky he'd found so fascinating when they'd met on the beach in Mariposa eight years earlier.

But looks could be deceiving. No matter how much he

might wish those intervening eight years had never happened, he couldn't deny they had. He'd changed. She'd surely changed as well.

And she was right. They weren't friends. They couldn't be.

"We need to be careful. Now that they're covering tracks, we risk running right up on them. We have to watch for an ambush."

She nodded, her expression grave. "It's not too late to go back. We can come back in daylight. Track them when the light is better."

His instincts rebelled against the idea, but he didn't trust his decision-making skills at the moment. Right now his gut was too full of fear for his sister to provide any objectivity. Tracking two well-armed men in the dark woods was clearly risky.

But was the risk worth taking?

He looked at her. "What do you think?"

She nibbled her lip again. "We keep going. By now they may realize they're missing three of their men. When those guys get back to camp, they could decide to bug out to somewhere else. If we wait until morning, we could follow this trail straight to a dead end."

He loosed a sigh of relief. "I was hoping you'd say that."

They followed the trail another hour, moving with extreme caution as the trail rose upward into the mist-veiled mountains. The climb became steeper and more treacherous, and as they neared a particularly vertical rise, Sin stopped and offered Ava a drink from a water bottle in his backpack.

She drank the water gratefully. "Don't suppose there's any way to go around that hill?"

"Not without losing at least a half hour."

She wiped her mouth with the back of her hand. "Then up we go."

"You go in front," he suggested. "You've got the bum hip. I'll be able to catch you if you lose traction."

She eyed him with caution, clearly weighing her options. No snap judgments from the Kentucky belle, he thought with a hidden smile. He'd always rather liked that about her, if he was remembering correctly.

"Okay." Turning, she reached for a handhold in the steep incline, closing her fingers around a rocky outcropping.

Sinclair stayed close behind her, distracting himself from the gnawing anxiety eating a hole in his gut by enjoying the sway of her curvy backside as she climbed the trail in front of him. She'd filled out a bit in the eight years since he'd last seen her, her once lithe, girlish body developing delightful curves in all the right places. She had the kind of hips that made a man want to sink into her and stay there forever. His hands, gripping a rough-edged rock jutting out of the hillside, itched to close around her round, firm breasts instead....

*Don't get too distracted,* he warned himself sternly.

The hillside started to level out, the climb less of a strain. Ava stumbled as they reached flatter ground, going down on her hands and knees. She stayed there for a moment, breathing hard.

Sinclair knelt beside her, laying his hand on her back. Her back rose and fell quickly as she caught her breath. "Sorry," she rasped.

He rubbed her back lightly. "We can take a break. How's your hip?"

She pushed herself up to a kneeling position and slid down the waistband of her pants to check the bandage. "I think it's okay."

"May I look?"

Her eyes met his, wide and wary in a shaft of pale moonlight peeking through the clouds. But she shifted, giving him better access to her injury.

Gently easing the trousers away from the bandage, he checked more thoroughly. There was a little blood seeping through the gauze, but not enough to worry. She wasn't in danger of bleeding to death.

Infection was still a major risk, however, and the longer she stayed out here in these woods without professional medical treatment, the greater the likelihood of sepsis.

He should have insisted they go back to the motel instead of chasing these men, he realized with a sinking heart. He'd been selfish and, if he was honest with himself, a little bit afraid of facing justice after so long on the run. "We should go back to the motel."

She looked at him as if he'd lost his mind. "Go back down that hill after we just climbed it? Are you kidding me?"

"The longer you and that bullet wound stay out here in these woods, the more likely you'll get an infection. That's nothing to play around with."

"I think I'm good for a few more hours." She pushed to her feet. "Let's go. We're wasting moonlight."

His heart still stuck in his throat, he rose and followed her lead.

Ten minutes later, Sin heard voices. He grabbed Ava's wrist as she continued forward, dragging her back against his chest.

She started to struggle, but he tightened his hold and whispered in her ear, "Voices."

She froze, her head coming up as if to listen.

The voices seemed to be floating toward them on the

wind, coming from somewhere dead ahead. But all Sin could see in front of them were trees, trees and more trees.

Where were the voices coming from?

"Rest a second," he whispered, letting Ava go. "I'll scout ahead. If I run into trouble, you can go for help."

Her lips pressed to a thin line. "I told you I'm not letting you out of my sight."

"Damn it, Ava—"

"I'm not letting you out of my sight," she repeated firmly. "Besides, I'm not sure I could make it back to the motel alone at this point," she added, her voice softening. "So for better or worse, we stick together."

"Stay as quiet as you can," he warned, leading the way forward. He took care with each step, moving heel to toe with deliberation, eyeing the ground ahead of them for any potential pitfalls. The voices ahead grew steadily louder, and he could make out the high, excited pitch of the conversation. Spanish, of course, but he was fluent, so he had no trouble making out the words flying about in agitation.

"How's your Spanish?" he whispered to Ava, who crept up beside him when he paused to listen.

"A little rusty," she admitted. "Haven't had a lot of chances to use it working in the Johnson City resident agency."

"It'll come back to you," he assured her. But he interpreted anyway. "Someone's taking hell for running from a bear."

"Do you recognize who's speaking?"

"Might be Cabrera," he said, uncertain. "There's a little echo. Can't be sure yet."

Suddenly, a woman's voice rang in the night, her Spanish rapid-fire but American-accented. Sin's heart clenched into a hot, hard fist.

Alicia.

*"¿Dónde está mi esposo?"* Fear battled with rage in her voice.

"She wants to know where her husband is," he translated for Ava.

"Yeah, I got that," she whispered grimly. "They probably killed him right off. Got rid of the extra baggage. One less captive to worry about."

Sin had never met his brother-in-law, but he hoped like hell Ava was wrong. He'd found a lot of comfort in the idea of Alicia happily married to a man she loved, a man who was good to her, who loved her and protected her when Sin couldn't.

He'd broken his sister's heart when he'd gone to Sanselmo and joined the rebels. Knowing he was a wanted man, doing things she didn't approve of for reasons she'd never understood—that kind of notoriety must have been hard for her to live with.

The last time he'd talked to her, he'd tried to explain himself, but even if he'd been able to find words to justify his actions, he couldn't tell her the whole truth, not over the phone. Maintaining his cover with *El Cambio* had been crucial to staying alive.

She'd stopped listening anyway. "I hope the next time you set a bomb, you blow yourself up," she'd told him, her voice raw with anger and pain.

Funny, he supposed, that he'd gone out and done exactly that, as far as she and the rest of the world were concerned.

As he strained to discern more of the verbal exchange between his sister and her captors, the cracking sound of a hand hitting flesh jolted through him, and Alicia's angry questions ended in a sharp cry. An answering growl rose in Sin's throat, and he rushed toward the sound of his sister's cry without thinking, stealth forgotten.

Ava's hands circled his arm and she dug her heels in, pulling him backward as he rushed forward. He tried to shake off her grip, but her fingers dug in harder, preventing him from dashing through the underbrush.

"Don't be an idiot!" she growled. "Do you want to get her killed?"

He struggled to control himself, to ease his ragged breathing and hurl cold water on his sudden rage. Ava was right. He knew she was right.

But even as he regained control of his emotions, a white-hot ball of fury festered in the center of his chest, biding its time.

Sinclair would make Cabrera and his men pay for what they'd done to his sister. He was going to find great pleasure in making sure of it.

"They're not going to do permanent damage to her, not while she's leverage," Ava whispered. He wished she sounded more confident.

"She's right there! We can get her away from them."

"Not without knowing how many people we have to take out to do it." Her voice was firmer now, her quiet competence taking some of the edge off his desperation. He grounded himself in her calm gaze, taking a few slow, deep breaths.

"Okay. Okay." He scanned the dark woods, listening to the sound of murmured conversation, trying to figure out from which direction it came. He pointed north, finally. "I think they're ahead that way. We need to get close enough to see what's what, but stay hidden."

"You were *El Cambio*. You know more about how they work than I do. How many men would Cabrera bring with him on a mission like this?"

He could only guess. Cabrera had been ruthless, unwilling to risk any sort of mutiny among his underlings.

He'd trusted few people. Sin had worked damned hard at being one of those people, and if Cabrera was here, looking for him, it was because he knew just how completely Sin had betrayed that trust.

Cabrera might be keeping Alicia alive now as leverage to get to Sin. But he didn't kid himself. Cabrera's only policy was scorched earth. There'd be no witnesses left when he was done.

"It doesn't matter how many. We have to get her away from him." The urgency of his fear forced the words from his tight throat.

"We need to get our eyes on that camp first. Know what we're up against. We need to be smart about it."

He caught her arm, tugging her around to look at him. Her eyes widened, her lips trembling apart.

The urge to kiss her, untimely and entirely out of the question, surged through him as powerfully as fear had done just a moment before. He had the ridiculous sense that if he could just kiss her, if he could feel her warm, soft body pressed to his, feel her fingers on his skin and breathe her breath into his lungs, everything would be okay.

He tore his gaze away, reminding himself that no matter what happened in the next few hours, everything would never be okay.

Ever.

He let her arm go. "Be very quiet and very careful. We'll have only one chance to get this right."

Out of the corner of his eye, he saw her check the magazine of her Glock. He reached into his pocket, pulled out one of the pistols he'd scavenged from Fuentes and Escalante and checked the magazine to see if there were any rounds left. The pistol, an FNS 9, held seventeen rounds. Fourteen remained.

He kept that one for himself and checked the other pistol. It was also an FN Herstel firearm, a twenty-round FN Five-seveN MK2. Eighteen rounds in that magazine. He offered the MK2 to Ava.

"Eighteen rounds. Use it first."

She looked up at him, her eyes suddenly widening and her lips curling inward as she nervously licked her lips.

*This is her first big challenge,* he realized, suddenly feeling deeply sorry for her. Despite her training, despite the FBI credentials in her pocket and the *Special Agent* in front of her name, she'd probably never been in a situation as dangerous as what they were about to face.

"If you don't want to do this, go," he said quietly. "The motel should be due west. Be careful, stay out of sight and you'll probably be there in a couple of hours. But I have to do this."

Her nostrils flared. She took the MK2 from his hands, checked the ammo herself, sighted down the barrel to familiarize herself with it and gave a short nod. "Then let's do this."

Sin felt a cracking sensation in his chest, as if something had broken open and spilled out courage and fear in equal parts. Swallowing the fear and marshaling the courage, he followed Ava forward through the woods.

CABRERA AND HIS men had set up camp in a small, sheltered cove just over the edge of a shallow escarpment. Ava had nearly stumbled over the edge of the bluff, as the trees beyond the valley camouflaged the narrow dip between ridges. She pulled up short, grabbing the trunk of a nearby pine to keep from tumbling over the edge.

Ignoring the pain in her hip and the increasing tremble of her aching thigh muscles, she dropped to her belly, seeking and finding a clearer view of the small valley that lay about twenty yards below the ridgeline.

Sin nudged his way next to her, his body warm against hers. She drew strength and determination from the solid heat of him. *Crazy,* she thought, *that I'm colluding with a terrorist to take down his buddies.*

But since she'd looked up in the parking lot of the Mountain View Lodge and seen a ghost, insanity had become the least of her problems.

From her vantage point, she could see most of the cove. There were four tents set up below. Sheltered by the low bluffs rising on either side of the encampment, Cabrera and his men showed no concern for stealth. All four of the tents were brightly lit from within, conveniently for Ava; shadows within gave her a decent head count of all the people in the camp. One in one tent, two in another, two in the third. Three men, plus Cabrera, standing in a huddle near a small campfire.

But she didn't see a woman. Had they taken her into one of the tents?

The four men moved apart, and then she saw the woman. Sinclair's sister. Small but unbowed, her spine ramrod-straight and her chin lifted, light from the campfire dancing over her delicate features. Next to Ava, Sinclair sucked in a sharp breath.

"Nine men total," she whispered. "And we dispatched three back in the woods."

"There's probably at least one more out there," he whispered back. "Cabrera has a thing about even numbers. An even dozen, plus himself. He'd like that."

"We know your sister's husband isn't down there, and she doesn't seem to know where he went. Maybe Cabrera sent one of his men off with the husband?" She didn't finish her thought—that he'd sent the henchman off to kill Gabe Cooper out of Alicia's sight.

She supposed it was merciful, at least, that they hadn't made her watch his murder. Though from what she'd heard of Cabrera's crimes, kindness and consideration weren't exactly his calling cards.

One of the men below detached from the other group, taking Alicia by the arm. Sinclair stiffened next to Ava, a low growl humming in his throat. She closed her hand over his wrist, afraid he'd launch himself over the bluff to go after his sister's captors.

"We need to go back for help. We can find this place again, can't we?" She knew the general direction they'd gone from where he'd last pitched the tent, and he surely knew how to get to the tent from the motel, since he'd found his way there and back earlier that day.

"I can't leave her there with them."

She tightened her grip on his arm, making him look at her. The look in his eyes set off a low, painful vibration somewhere in the center of her chest. "There's nothing you can do by yourself. We have to get backup, don't you see that?"

"I've seen how backup works," he said in a low, strained voice. "Backup is a damned good way to get a hostage killed."

"I can't leave you here."

"I'm getting her out of there."

She shook her head in frustration. "She thinks you're dead. Let's say you can fight your way through nine well-armed men and get to her. How easy will it be to convince her to come with you? You lied about your death. Before your death, she wished you dead. You said it yourself."

The stricken look in his eyes made her regret her words.

"I don't think she really wanted you dead," she added softly.

He took a deep, slow breath. "Okay. I'll go back with you. But I don't want the FBI involved in trying to rescue her. I remember Waco."

Not the FBI's finest moment, she had to concede. "What would you have me do, then?"

"Does Gabe Cooper's family know about the kidnapping?"

She nodded. "I'm sure they've heard by now. My partner said we'd probably be knee-deep in Coopers before we knew it."

For the first time in a while, Sinclair Solano's lips curved in a broad smile. Overhead, clouds swallowed the moon, plunging the night back into near-total darkness, but not before Ava caught a glitter of satisfaction in his midnight eyes.

"Good," he said softly, gazing down toward the cove again. "I have a feeling we'll need all the Coopers we can get."

# Chapter Five

By midnight, the camp below the bluff had settled down for the night. Two men remained awake, circling the camp with AR-15 rifles strapped over their shoulders. Now and then, the burning ends of their cigarettes flared red in the darkness, narrow ribbons of smoke rising into the air overhead. Except for the occasional murmur of exchanged words between the two guards, all was silent.

Beside him, Ava carefully stretched her legs, grimacing. A whispery groan escaped her throat, barely audible. He slanted a look her way, taking in the faint sheen of perspiration on her forehead and the darkened circles under her eyes.

She was in pain, and he knew it would get worse before it got better.

Nothing was likely to happen here before morning. Even with most of the camp asleep, he and Ava were outnumbered and outgunned. The AR-15 rifles Cabrera's men carried were fitted with magazines that would hold at least thirty .223 rounds each. Almost certainly they had spare magazines in their jacket pockets. He couldn't risk thinking they didn't.

"We should find a sheltered place and set up the tent," he whispered.

Her eyes glittered at him in the dark. "And what? Get some sleep?" She shook her head.

"I need to take another look at that wound."

She dropped her hand to her hip, covering the torn fabric. "I'm okay."

He touched the back of his fingers to her forehead. Her skin was damp but hot. "You may have a fever."

"So give me an aspirin."

Pressing his lips to a thin line, he pulled a bottle of water from his pack and handed it to her. Flipping open another small pocket, he withdrew a packet of acetaminophen tablets. "Here."

She downed the pills with a couple of gulps of water. "Thanks."

"Let me deliver you back to the motel. You need medical attention."

"Deliver *me?*" She narrowed her eyes. "*You're* the prisoner."

He almost laughed but thought better of it. "At least get some sleep."

He could see in her eyes how tempting she found the idea of sleep. It would make her feel considerably better, he knew. The lack of it might hasten the deterioration of her strength.

But she thrust a belligerent chin forward. "I'm good."

Frustrated, he crept away from the edge of the bluff on all fours, rising only when he was sure he couldn't be seen from the cove below. Ava turned, propping herself on her elbows and watching him go, a look of disbelief on her face. Belatedly, she rolled over and scooted backward, mimicking his earlier movements, and finally pushed herself to her feet to face him.

"What are you doing?"

"I'm going to find a place to set up the tent and get

some sleep. Those guys down there aren't going to stay up all night to make things fair. They're getting sleep and they'll be in fighting form in the morning. Will we?"

She looked inclined to argue, but after a tense moment, she lowered her head, her shoulders slumping. He resisted the urge to brush aside the dark curls spilling over her face like a curtain, though his fingers almost ached to do so. She was tired, dirty and downright hostile, but at this moment, in the middle of his churning fear for his sister's safety, he still felt the languid tug of the sexual attraction that had sent him reeling into her path back in the sun-drenched streets of Sebastian, Mariposa.

Why? he thought. Why did it have to be Ava Trent who'd stumbled into the woods in search of him? Anyone else, he'd have ditched by now without a second thought.

Of course, anyone else might have already shot him.

He led the way back through the woods, swallowing an expletive when the heavens opened again overhead and rain started hammering through the canopy of trees. "This looks like a good spot," he muttered, unzipping his backpack. Within a couple of minutes, he'd withdrawn the tightly packed tent and Ghillie cover and set it up between a couple of sheltering mountain laurel bushes. Coaxing Ava inside, he took one last look at the tent, decided it was camouflaged enough for the dark, rainy night and crawled inside.

She had already stretched out on the tent floor, her injured side up. Her breath came in soft, labored pants, but she tried to smile as he settled down beside her. "I don't remember what it feels like to be dry."

"Get out of those wet clothes," he suggested, turning on the dim battery-powered camp lantern he'd pulled from his pack.

She arched an eyebrow in response.

"You'll warm up faster if you're not marinating in rain-soaked clothes." He waved a hand at her rain-drenched jacket and blouse.

With a sigh, she sat up and shrugged off the jacket and blouse. Beneath, her bra was black lace and satin, militantly feminine, as if her inner woman had set up a quiet rebellion against her conservative, businesslike exterior.

And under the black lace, she was all creamy curves and tempting shadows. Her stomach was flat and toned, as if she took care to keep herself in shape, but there was a voluptuous roundness to her, over the layers of muscle, that set fire to Sin's blood.

He dragged his gaze up to hers and found her staring back at him, her eyes fathomless.

"Eight years," she said as if offering an explanation.

"They've been good to you," he answered, trying to regain his equilibrium. He'd thought it impossible to think of anything but his sister's plight now that he'd seen her in captivity. Indeed, the fact that he could feel his body quickening in response to Ava's nakedness made him angry with his own weakness.

She wrapped her arms across her chest and pulled her knees up. "Do you have any extra clothes?"

He hadn't had a chance to wash anything in days, but he supposed soiled was better than wet. He found a T-shirt that didn't smell like days-old sweat and handed it to her. "I don't have any pants that will fit you."

She shrugged on the T-shirt. It was about two sizes too large for her, but her curves helped take up the extra room. Stretching gingerly, she unzipped her trousers and tried to slide them off her hips. Her face went white in the faint glow of the lantern.

He edged closer. "Let me help you."

She looked up with a soft groan. "Easy, okay?"

He took care as he helped her pull the fabric of her trousers away from the wound, willing himself to ignore the feel of her warm, firm thighs beneath his palms or the faint, sweet scent of her bath gel still clinging to her skin. He concentrated instead on her injury, noting that blood seeped through the gauze, aided, no doubt, by the rain-soaked fabric of her pants.

He hoped her clothes were wash-and-wear, because anything prone to shrinking would never survive what they'd just gone through.

"Better?" he asked once he'd pulled her legs free of the pants.

With a nod, she bit her lip and tugged the hem of the borrowed T-shirt over her hips.

"Let's change that bandage," he suggested.

She nodded again, though her brow furrowed with dread. She rolled onto her side, pulling up the hem of the T-shirt to give him a better look at the bullet graze.

It still looked terrible, all ragged, torn skin. But the wound seemed clean enough, and while the skin around the margins was a reddish-purple color, the redness hadn't yet spread much beyond the immediate area.

He talked her through the bandage change, warning her before he swabbed on stinging antiseptic and slathered the area with an antibiotic ointment. He finished off the cleaning with a fresh bandage and a new application of tape. "All done."

She tugged her knees up to her chest, keeping her eyes closed.

"You okay?" he asked.

Her head bobbed in a slight nod.

Turning away, he dug in his supplies for a change of clothes, giving her time to recover. His traveling pack was designed to be able to carry a lot of supplies in a small space, but the tent and Ghillie net took up a lot of room, even folded to their most compact states. He had little more than the clothes on his back, a second pair of jeans and three spare T-shirts, one of which Ava was currently wearing. Other things were stashed in an abandoned building in the town of Purgatory, near Quinn's new investigation agency, but it might be a long time before he'd get the chance to retrieve any of those things. If ever.

He peeled off his wet clothes and pulled out the dry jeans and one of the tees. As he was tugging on the jeans, he heard Ava suck in a sharp breath.

He turned to look at her. Her gaze was fixed on his rib cage.

On the scar.

Most days, he never gave any thought to the triptych of healed gashes that marred his rib cage. Shrapnel wounds from the explosion that had allegedly killed him. He'd cut things too close.

"Who did that to you?" Ava asked softly.

"I did it to myself," he answered just as quietly.

"Blowing something up?"

"Yes."

"You were integral to *El Cambio* for years. What changed? Why does Cabrera hate you so much now?"

He pulled the T-shirt over his head, hiding the scars. Giving himself time to figure out how much, if anything, to tell her about what he'd done to earn Cabrera's thirst for revenge. "Allegiances change."

*Or they're rediscovered,* he added silently.

SHE MUST HAVE SLEPT, for when she opened her eyes, it was with a start, with the jangling nerves of a person roused from slumber to an alien darkness that set her heart racing and her limbs trembling. She sat up quickly, hissing with pain as the movement sent fire racing down one side of her leg.

The ground was hard beneath her, though something with a little padding lay under her legs. Stretching her arm out to one side, she felt a flexible canvas wall. A tent, she remembered. She was in a tent.

With a dead man.

She could hear his breathing, slow and even. Damn it. She'd taken the first watch and promptly fallen asleep.

*Way to go, Special Agent Trent.*

Gritting her teeth against the ache in her hip, she tugged on her boots, crawled forward to the tent opening and dared a peek outside. The view through the Ghillie net was worthless, so she went a little farther, out from beneath the netting, and emerged into the cool, damp woods.

The rain had finally stopped for the night, she saw, leaving a clearing sky overhead, full of endless stars and a waxing moon dipping toward the western horizon. According to her watch, it was a little after 3:00 a.m.

She scanned the woods for any sign of movement, seeing nothing but shadows and gloom. All she heard were the normal sounds of nocturnal creatures going about their nightly activities.

It was so quiet here in the mountains. Peaceful and still. The sky above seemed endless, the stars so thick they looked like streamers of mist streaking across the midnight backdrop. The sight reminded her of a night she'd spent in Mariposa with Sinclair, lying on their backs on the roof of his rented villa watching a meteor show. A smile teased her lips, but the pleasure faded quickly as the reality of her current dilemma forced its way past the memory.

What was she going to do about Sinclair Solano? The world believed him dead, so he wasn't on anyone's radar anymore. No one's but Cabrera's, at least. Legally speaking, there was no longer a warrant out for his arrest. His face no longer graced any Wanted posters.

If she didn't tell a soul about seeing him, who would know? Or care, for that matter? For the past three years, Solano hadn't been involved in any terrorist attacks, had he?

Or had he?

A shiver wriggled down her spine, raising goose bumps on her arms and bare legs. The night was mild, typical for August in the mountains, but despite the hem of the borrowed T-shirt dipping to midthigh, she felt suddenly naked and vulnerable.

She slipped back inside the tent and ran headlong into Sinclair's chest.

His hands caught her upper arms, keeping her from toppling over. "Shh," he whispered when she opened her mouth and drew in a sharp breath.

She swallowed her cry of surprise, her body rattled by another shiver. But this reaction wasn't about the cold night air or her lingering fears.

This was all about the raspy sensation of his callused palms sliding over her bare arms, the heat of his body pressed intimately close to hers. His breath danced over her cheek, making her feel reckless and needy.

"Everything okay?" he whispered.

"Seems to be," she managed to push between her trembling lips.

He wasn't letting her go, she realized. And worse, she wasn't making any move to get away from his gentle caresses.

"You should get some sleep." His face brushed close enough to hers that she felt the light bristle of his beard against her jawline. She clenched her hands into fists, fighting the dizzying urge to rub her cheek to his, to feel the full friction of his stubble against her flesh.

He'd just said something to her, she thought numbly, trying to breathe. What had he said?

He slid his hands up her arms, over her shoulders. They came to rest on either side of her face, cradling her jaw. "Do you remember that night in Mariposa? On the roof of the villa?"

It was too dark in the tent to see much besides the inky impression of his lean, masculine features. She closed her eyes, unable to process anything more than the sensations jittering along her flesh where he touched her. "I remember."

His voice softened to a flutter of breath against her skin. "I was going to meet you the next day. I meant to, right up to the last moment."

Ice spread through her at his soft confession, and she pulled away, remembering what had happened not long after their last meeting. "But you went to Sanselmo instead." She crawled deeper into the tent, curling into a ball with her back to him.

He didn't move for a long moment, his continuing silence posing a temptation to roll over and look at him again. But she fought the urge, burying herself under eight years of anger and disappointment.

She hadn't been naive, even at the age of twenty. She'd known a man like Sinclair Solano, the idealistic son of radicals, might find freedom-fighting in a totalitarian country too tempting to resist. But even while they were soaking up the Caribbean sun, Sanselmo had been holding democratic elections for the first time in decades. They'd voted in a reformer the very day Sin had stood her up to catch a flight out of Sebastian for South America.

Why had he gone there, when what he'd claimed to be

fighting for was already starting to happen? Why had he joined a band of terrorists who, even now, continued to fight against a burgeoning civil society that had already rejected their radical aims?

Maybe he'd just been looking for a noble reason to justify his urge to kill people and blow things up. For too many people in the world, wielding destruction was motive enough for any choice they made.

His clothes rustled as he moved deeper into the tent, settling close to her. At least he didn't touch her. Her body's humiliating inability to resist his touch was something she was going to have to work through sooner or later, hopefully in the privacy of her own little apartment back in Johnson City.

"There was a man in Sebastian," he said. "My father arranged an introduction."

"Grijalva," she said quietly.

He went silent a moment, as if the word surprised him. When the silence continued, she rolled over to look at him. He sat cross-legged, his face turned toward her. In the darkness, his eyes were hidden in the shadows of his craggy forehead and aquiline nose. She could tell he was waiting for her to say more, so she added, "Luis Grijalva, the great reformer. I understand he was martyred a few months later."

Sin's lips flattened. "He was murdered. By Cabrera."

"Terrorists do have a tendency to eat their own." She knew that U.S. authorities had long suspected Grijalva's death had been staged by *El Cambio* as an attempt to discredit the new reformist government. But she was surprised to hear Sinclair admit it.

"Cabrera was the one who reported Grijalva's martyrdom. He accused Mendoza's forces of murdering Grijalva during a peaceful demonstration."

"When did you figure out he was the killer?" she asked.

"I saw it happen."

She stared at him, shocked. "You saw it?"

"It was the anniversary of the San Martín massacre. I guess you'd call it a high holy day for *El Cambio*." His brow furrowed. "Are you familiar with the San Martín massacre?"

She searched her memory. "It had something to do with Cardoso's rise to power, didn't it? A big protest that turned bloody?"

Sinclair nodded. "In the beginning, *El Cambio* was actually made up of democratic reformers trying to stop Cardoso's crackdown on free speech. Instead of the thugs who fill its ranks today, *El Cambio* started as a student movement in Sanselmo's universities. Cardoso was making even the most innocuous political speech illegal in order to maintain and expand his powers as president. The protests grew and expanded in response."

She nodded. She'd done a lot of research into the origins of *El Cambio* after learning Sinclair had joined the movement. By the time he'd signed on, the face of the rebellion had darkened considerably from its pro-democracy origins, though he hadn't seemed to realize it until too late.

"The students decided to hold a rally in San Martín, a little town in the mountains outside Tesoro. The opposition leader, Diego Montero, came to speak. They blocked the main road into the town with their protest, but the people of San Martín didn't care. It was the most excitement that had come to their little village in forever. They turned it into a festival. Until the soldiers came."

The bleak tone of Sinclair's voice set off an echo of dread in Ava's chest. She knew the gist of what had happened next.

"It was a bloodbath. Men, women, children mowed

down by Cardoso's special forces as if they were targets in a shooting gallery." Sinclair closed his eyes, horror twisting his features. "The road into town was twisty, as mountain roads are, and they had set up on a hairpin curve because the mountains made such a picturesque backdrop for the press cameras."

His words sparked a dark memory of something she'd read about the massacre. *"La Curva de los Muertos,"* she whispered, her stomach flipping.

"Dead Man's Curve," he said with a grimace. "There was nowhere to run for so many of the protestors trying to escape the gunfire. The road behind them had been blocked by the booths, and beyond the curve in the road was nothing but a rocky fifty-foot drop-off...." His voice faltered.

"And some people jumped off the cliff rather than be ripped apart by gunfire," she finished for him.

"I should have known, when Cabrera asked Grijalva to meet him there, that he had something more than talk in mind." Sinclair rubbed the furrow between his brows. "Cabrera is fond of symbolism and symmetry."

"He shot Grijalva at Dead Man's Curve?"

"He didn't shoot him. He hacked him to death with a machete."

She shuddered. "You saw it happen?"

He nodded.

"But you kept quiet?" Her voice hardened at the thought. "Your conscience its own martyr to the cause?"

There was only the tiniest of change in his expression, a flicker of movement in his lean jaw, before he answered. "*I* was the martyr."

SINCLAIR HADN'T MEANT to tell her so much of the truth. He supposed he could leave it lie, go back outside and apply himself to the job of keeping watch for what was left of the night. Let her come up with whatever explanation she wanted for his choices.

He could tell, from the horror in her expression, that whatever explanation she settled on was unlikely to be kind to him.

Maybe it would be best for both of them if she continued to see him as a murderer, a terrorist and a coward.

But when he started to move toward the front of the tent, her hand snaked out and caught his wrist. She had small, feminine hands, soft to the touch, but her grip was surprisingly strong.

"How were you a martyr?" she asked.

He thought about that day in Mariposa, when his father's urging had sent him to the beach shack where Luis Grijalva lived in exile from the nation of his birth. He had been a vigorous, fit man in his mid-fifties, old enough to present a wise face to a young man's crusade but still young enough to sway the imagination and engender passion and allegiance.

He'd spoken with passion of Sanselmo's civilized roots and the ravages two decades of totalitarian leadership had left on the land and her people. He'd talked about fairness, freedom, community and revolution, in terms so gentle it could take a while to realize he'd meant the overthrow of Sanselmo's government.

Sinclair had been young. Aimless. Trying to figure out how to stand out in a family of brilliant, passionate overachievers. Even his little sister was starting to outpace him, breezing through her studies as if they were child's play.

He'd wanted to matter.

"I went to Sanselmo because I wanted to make a difference."

"I'd say you managed that," she murmured, her voice as dry as dust.

## Chapter Six

"You can imagine what life was like as the son of Martin and Lorraine Solano." Sinclair's gaze lowered to the ground in front of him. He didn't want to look at her, she realized.

Was he ashamed? She hadn't thought him capable.

"I don't think I can imagine what it's like to have famous parents." Her own parents were farmers, hardworking people who scrabbled for every extra nickel or dime to give their kids a better life. They toiled in anonymity, unknown beyond their small circle of family and friends.

But it had been a good life, even if a hard one. As far as she knew, they had no complaints, even now.

"My parents were celebrities in some political circles." Sinclair's fingers twisted around each other as they spoke. "They had expectations of the kind of lives their children would lead. I was never going to be a brilliant scholar the way Alicia was. I wasn't cut out for academia. But I wanted my life to mean something, the way theirs had."

"You thought joining a South American terrorist group would give your life meaning?" She tried not to sound so harsh, but she had trouble understanding how he could have been so shortsighted. Even at twenty, she'd been able to figure out that a group of heavily-armed rebels wanting to thwart a reform movement already underway couldn't be up to any good.

Why hadn't he seen it?

"I thought *El Cambio* wanted a democratic revolution."

"So did a lot of people. But the Mendoza government was making changes already—"

He shot her a sharp look. "*El Cambio* believed Mendoza was just a puppet for the old Cardoso regime."

"Guess we'll never know, since *El Cambio* killed Mendoza before he could institute all his proposed reforms."

He held her gaze for a long moment, then looked back at his hands again. "Wouldn't have mattered. *El Cambio* wanted the power for themselves. And they were willing to break any rule, all rules, to get it."

"Took you eight months to figure that out?"

"I saw what I wanted to believe and ignored the rest. Chalked it up to the brutality of the regime, goading people into acting in ways they wouldn't otherwise."

"The regime had already changed by the time you went to Sanselmo," she pointed out gently. "Mendoza was cleaning up the government, purging the brutes out of the military. Civil society was forming on its own, without the help of the rebels."

"We wanted everything immediately."

"Because that ever happens."

He shot her an angry look. "People are always promised change when it's time to mark the ballot. But it so rarely happens when the counting is over. The people of Sanselmo had lived with their necks under the boot for too many years."

"I know."

"How?" he asked, sounding curious. "You seem to know a hell of a lot about a South American country most Americans probably couldn't point out on a map."

"I made it my business to find out all about what was going on in Sanselmo," she admitted. "Once I figured out that was where you were headed."

"How *did* you know that was where I was headed?"

"I was already thinking about becoming an investigator by the time we met. I had…instincts for it." And, if she could admit it to herself, at least, she wanted to know just what her holiday fling was about to get himself into.

"Did you follow me?"

"Not exactly." She stretched her legs out in front of her before realizing there wasn't really much room for stretching inside the small tent. She tugged her knees back up to her body. "I followed your trail. Learned you'd talked to a man the locals called *El Pavón*. The peacock."

"*El Pavón?* Hmm." He seemed to give the name some thought. "I suppose, in retrospect, it fit."

From what little she'd been able to see of Luis Grijalva, she concurred. She'd glimpsed him, briefly, in one of the open-market cafés in the Mariposa capital. A trim, compact man with a well-groomed mane of graying hair and a neat mustache and goatee, he'd been a striking figure in his bright island colors and regal bearing.

Even with her inbred skepticism of people who claimed to be revolutionaries, she'd found him charismatic and appealing.

How much more would Sinclair, fed the mother's milk of revolutionary idealism at his parents' feet, have been susceptible to Grijalva's sway? He'd already admitted he'd been looking for meaning in his life.

Grijalva must have seen an easy mark in Sinclair Solano.

"What did you do when you found out I'd talked to Luis Grijalva?" he asked.

Her lips quirked again. "Threw up my hands, called you a fool and hopped the next plane back to the States."

No need to tell him that she'd cried the whole plane trip home.

He shifted restlessly. "You haven't asked the obvious question yet."

She released a long, slow breath. "What question is that?"

He lifted his gaze to meet hers. "Why, if I had figured out what *El Cambio* was all about eight months into my association with them, did I stick around the group for another four years?"

It was an excellent question, but she wasn't sure she wanted to know the answer. Life had been much neater when she'd been able to tuck her memories of Sinclair Solano in a little box she could shove into the back of her mental closet, never to be reexamined. Easier to say, "He was some guy I met on vacation. I hardly even remember him."

Much harder to sit in front of him, his body close enough to send undulating waves of heat washing over her. Close enough to notice, once again, how ridiculously long and dark his eyelashes were, or how his lean features made him almost as beautiful as he was handsome.

"Okay," she said quietly, "I'll bite. Why did you stay with *El Cambio* after you knew what they were?"

His dark eyes held hers, full of secrets and mysteries. But as he opened his mouth, drew in a long slow breath in preparation to speak, something snapped outside the tent.

He whirled to face the entrance, the muscles of his back bunched in anticipation of whatever happened next. He was lean but strong, his body thicker and more toned than it had been when she'd known him before. Life since their interlude in Mariposa had hardened him. Given what he'd been doing for many of those years, she supposed it was no surprise.

He'd trained with terrorists. Hiked through unforgiving jungles and climbed volcanic peaks in the rainforest lair of *El Cambio*. And there was no telling what he'd been doing in the past few years, when the world had thought him dead and gone.

"Stay here," he whispered.

"No," she whispered back, crawling behind him to the tent door.

The Ghillie net extended about five feet past the front of the tent. Sinclair paused under the Ghillie net, peering out into the darkness of the woods beyond. Rain had started falling again, but lightly now, barely seeping through the netting to drip down the back of Ava's neck as she hunched closer to Sinclair. He edged over, making room for her, and peered through the netting, trying to see what may have made the loud cracking noise outside the tent.

Mist rose around them, turning the woods into an ethereal realm of dark shadows and ghostly tendrils of moisture. Staying very still, she peered into the gloom, trying to soften the focus of her gaze so that she'd be better able to spot any sign of movement outside.

But there was nothing. No movement. No sounds.

Sin's hand closed around her elbow, nudging her back toward the tent. She slipped inside, watching as he crawled through behind her.

"Could have been an animal," he said quietly.

She nodded, clenching her jaws against a sudden tremor that rolled through her like an ocean wave.

"We're probably not going to get many better chances to get some sleep," he whispered.

"I don't think I can sleep."

"I don't think you can afford not to."

She knew he was right, but the thought of closing her eyes and relaxing her guard went against all her instincts. Especially when she'd be trusting her life to a man whom, twenty-four hours ago, she'd have called a traitor without a second thought.

"Why did you stay with *El Cambio?*" she asked after a few moments of tense silence.

He didn't answer. She peered through the dark, trying to see his face, but he had settled with his back to her. If he'd heard her question, he clearly didn't intend to answer.

She curled up in a tight knot, wishing she were back at the Mountain View Motor Lodge, tucked into a warm, dry bed. She wished she'd never looked across the parking lot and seen the face of a ghost. She wished someone else had been in the office when the missing-persons call came in from the Poe Creek locals.

In short, she wished she were anywhere but stuck here in a damp tent with Sinclair Solano, the only man she'd never been able to forget—or forgive.

SIN WASN'T SURE why he hadn't answered her whispered question. Only a few minutes before, he'd been on the verge of telling her everything, after all. If they hadn't heard the twig snap, he might have already spilled all the details. So why hadn't he answered when she asked him again?

"Nobody will ever believe your story," Alexander Quinn had warned him when he'd finally come in from the cold. "They'll think you're making excuses for your actions. And the CIA won't be able to back you up. We don't discuss undercover missions that way, especially when we still have ongoing operations in the arena."

Sinclair had accepted the fact that he'd still be living a lie. He'd thought, at the time, it was worth it. It wasn't like he could go back home to his family. His parents had been as blind about *El Cambio* as he had been, and they'd hardly be proud of knowing how he'd worked for the CIA to bring the terrorist group to its knees.

His sister hated him. She'd wished him dead shortly before he'd faked his own demise, and he didn't suppose she'd changed her mind since. Even now, putting his life on the line to rescue her, he doubted she'd be happy to see him. But he'd figured separation from his family was part of the price he'd paid for his mistakes.

Besides, the truth was such a cliché. Disillusioned radical agrees to turn double agent for the CIA.

Who would buy a story like that?

ALEXANDER QUINN TIGHTENED the straps of his backpack and plodded, head down, toward the motel parking lot a quarter mile down the road. He'd dressed for the weather—heavy rain slicker over sturdy jeans and a long-sleeved T-shirt—and his hiking boots were weatherproof by design. To anyone who bothered to notice him, he looked like any of the thousands of hikers who followed the Appalachian Trail during the hiking season, though he was miles west of the trail itself.

A large blue SUV moved past him, headlights slicing through the rainy gloom, and turned into the parking lot of the Mountain View Motor Lodge. The plates, he noted, were local, but a large sticker from a rental car agency covered part of the bumper.

He slowed his pace as he neared the parking lot, keeping an eye on the SUV. He'd been expecting Coopers to converge on the motel ever since he'd seen the first report of the missing tourists. He had a feeling they'd finally arrived.

Six people emerged from the SUV, dark silhouettes in

the pools of golden light spilling from the tall lamps illuminating the motel's parking lot. Four men, two women. As he edged closer, another SUV passed him and pulled into the parking lot, lining up next to the other vehicle. Four more people emerged from the second SUV, three men, one woman.

Quinn paused on the shallow shoulder across the road, watching as the ten new arrivals huddled together in muddy yellow light from the parking lot lamps. He recognized all of them, though he'd had only minimal dealings with most. The occupants of the first SUV were mostly Gabe Cooper's siblings—brothers, J.D., Jake and Luke; sister, Hannah; Hannah's husband, Riley; and J.D.'s wife, Natalie. The second vehicle's occupants were Gabe's cousins, Jesse, Rick and Isabel, plus Isabel's husband, Ben Scanlon.

All experienced trackers, Quinn thought. Good. They'd need all the skills they could muster.

One of the Coopers turned his head suddenly, his gaze locking with Quinn's before he could look away. Jesse Cooper. The other man's eyebrows lifted slightly, but he looked away deliberately, as if ignoring Quinn's presence.

He waited as the Coopers and their various spouses moved around the crime-scene tape and headed for the small motel office located at the far end of the parking lot.

One of them peeled away from the others and started walking toward the edge of the parking lot across from where Quinn stood watching. Not Jesse Cooper, as he might have expected, but Jake Cooper. Gabe's twin.

Jake stood at the edge of the road, staring across the narrow two-lane, as if daring Quinn to make the next move.

He was tempted to turn and walk away. Let the Coopers fend for themselves. They were big boys and girls.

They'd handled tough situations in the past, and Quinn knew they could cope without his help if necessary.

But he had his own reasons for sticking his nose in this missing-persons investigation. He had his own missing person to find.

He crossed the road at a leisurely pace, not making direct eye contact with Jake. He stopped when he reached the parking lot, standing several feet away from the other man. The rain that had been a deluge earlier in the evening had reemerged as a drizzle, generating a ghostly mist that settled across the valley like a gossamer shroud. Though Jake Cooper stood only a few feet away, he looked almost spectral in the swirling fog.

"Do you know who has them?" Jake asked in a conversational tone.

"I have a theory," Quinn answered in a similar tone.

"Care to share it?"

"I don't think it's about your brother. I think it's about Alicia."

Jake's eyes narrowed. "Is it Cooper Security related, then?"

Quinn shook his head no. "It goes back further than that."

"Is it related to Hamilton Gray?"

Quinn hadn't even thought about Gray, the serial killer Alicia had helped capture and convict. "As far as I know, he's still in prison, exhausting all his appeals."

"Then what?" Jake's voice tightened with impatience. "Do you even remember how to hold a straightforward conversation?"

"Alicia had a brother."

Jake stared across the misty void between them. "Her brother's dead."

"Is he?" Quinn started walking away.

"You're a cryptic son of a bitch!" Jake called after him.

Quinn kept walking, unable to argue.

THE BOMB WAS unsophisticated but powerful. ANFO— Ammonium nitrate and fuel oil—easy to procure, easy to use. Some of the *El Cambio* crew had wanted to emulate their counterparts on the other side of the world and use more technologically sophisticated improvised explosive devices, but for sheer destructive force, ANFO worked nicely.

Despite his reputation with the FBI and other American law-enforcement agencies, Sinclair wasn't a bomb maker. There were really only a handful of *El Cambio* operatives who dealt with explosives on a regular basis, but Cabrera and his lieutenants found value in cultivating the idea that all members of *El Cambio* were equally skilled and lethal.

He also liked to make sure that everyone in the group had blood on their hands. Sinclair had been fortunate, to that point, that his skills as an artist and propagandist had kept him out of the real dirty work.

But that day, his time of reckoning had come.

"It's a simple timer," Cabrera had explained as he'd handed Sin the keys to the panel van. "All you have to do is park the truck in front of the warehouse, set the timer for twenty minutes and walk away."

An easy task. And an impossible one.

He hadn't contacted Alexander Quinn in two months. The spy had seemed surprised to hear from him.

"You're blowing up what?" Quinn had asked.

"I'm not blowing up anything," Sin had answered bluntly. "How do I get out of this?"

"You don't," Quinn said. Then he'd rattled off directions that had made Sinclair's head spin.

But he'd followed them to the letter. And at the end of the day, he'd had blood on his hands. Including his own.

But no innocents had died that day.

In the pale gray light seeping through the narrow tent opening, Sinclair looked at the tight white burn scar on the inside of his forearm. It disappeared under the sleeve of his T-shirt, but the puckered flesh extended all the way up his arm. He'd cut things too close that day in Tesoro. Waffled over his choices a little too long.

Nine men had died in the explosion, all *El Cambio* rebels.

Sinclair Solano should have been victim ten, as far as the rest of the world had known. The explosion had blown several of the bodies out into the harbor, including the borrowed body from the morgue. Most of the bodies had been recovered, or at least parts of them had. Enough for a body count. Sinclair himself had gone into the harbor, his shrapnel wounds shrieking with agony as he swam through the burning debris to the rendezvous point he and Quinn had agreed upon.

Quinn had almost given up on him by the time he dragged himself onto the rocks and into his spy handler's strong grasp. The next few hours had been a blur, alternating waves of agony and painkillers. Quinn, meanwhile, had made sure the Sanselmo authorities had a copy of his DNA to make the identification on the unidentified body they pulled from the harbor. Nobody had to know that the DNA actually belonged to the homeless dead man Quinn had procured from the local morgue.

As far as the world was concerned, Sinclair Solano had died that day in Tesoro Harbor. And he'd stayed dead for three and a half long, lonely years.

So how had Cabrera figured out he was still alive?

"What time is it?" Ava Trent's sleepy voice seeped

through his skin into his bones, setting them humming. He looked up to find her propped on her elbows, watching him through a mass of brown, humidity-frizzed hair. She looked tired and a little pale, but he found her tempting anyway. And as much as he'd like to pretend it was situational—three years without sex could make any man crazy—deep down he knew there was something fundamentally different about the way Ava Trent made him feel.

It had been that way eight years ago as well. On an island full of exotic beauties, it had been the fresh-faced, no-nonsense Kentucky farm girl who'd managed to turn him inside out.

He realized she was waiting for an answer, and it took a second to remember what she'd asked. He checked his watch. "Just before six."

"Don't suppose you have any food stashed away in that bag of yours?"

He had a couple of protein bars, but he'd meant to replenish his supplies days ago. He should have gone into town sooner. But he'd thought he had time. What was the rush? He had nowhere to go.

Until he'd heard the news about his sister and her husband going missing.

He opened his pack and tossed her one of the protein bars. "Make it last. There's only one more."

She ripped open the packaging and took a bite, a low moan escaping her throat. He dragged his gaze away, tamping down the arousal throbbing in his veins. He concentrated on the contents of his backpack, noting with alarm that his supplies were rapidly dwindling.

"You ever going to tell me why you stayed with *El Cambio* so long after you knew what they were up to?"

He looked at her, once more tempted to spill everything. But her jaw was set, her eyes sharp with skepticism, and he just wasn't in the mood for her to shoot down the truth again. "Not much point, since you won't believe me."

She shrugged as if it didn't matter, but he could tell she wasn't quite as nonchalant as she wanted to appear. Maybe, sooner or later, she'd be willing to listen.

And maybe he'd be willing to talk. "How soon do you think we can get going?" she asked around another bite of the protein bar.

"As soon as possible," he answered resolutely, zipping his bag. "We need to get back to civilization."

She handed him the remaining half of the protein bar and stretched her limbs, wincing as the motion pulled against her healing wound. Muscles bunched and twitched her jaws, but she managed not to groan, even though Sin could tell she was in pain.

"Maybe you should stay here and rest," he suggested, finishing off the protein bar in a couple of bites. The little bit of food took the edge off his hunger but didn't banish it. He needed real food. A real bath. A real bed.

But not until he got his sister back.

"You're my prisoner, remember?" she asked, grimacing as she pushed herself to a crouch. "You go nowhere without me."

"Right." He exited through the tent and peered through the Ghillie net, surveying the mist-shrouded woods around them. Everything looked quiet at the moment.

But he knew that situation could change in a heartbeat.

# Chapter Seven

The morning was cool, the air misty, as Ava trudged through the woods behind Sinclair. They were still in the middle of sunrise, the sky peeking through the dense trees overhead a rosy pink starting to give way at the edges to a clear, pale blue. The sun remained behind the crest of the mountains to the east, but there was enough light to make them vulnerable if anyone was out there in the woods looking for them, so they moved ahead at a slow, steady pace.

At least, Ava told herself that was why Sinclair was moving so slowly. Because the alternative was admitting that her wounded hip and the previous day's exertions had left her hobbled like an arthritic woman three times her age. She was not ready to face such an embarrassing notion.

They were moving steadily west toward Poe Creek, though the path they took was anything but straight. They stayed close to the trees, moving with as much stealth as they could manage. So far, they'd spotted no sign of Cabrera's men in the woods.

But Ava could feel them nearby, like a poisonous miasma hovering just over the horizon, gathering strength and malignance.

"Need to stop and catch your breath?" Sin paused

behind the trunk of a large fir tree and pulled a water bottle from his backpack. He took a long drink and handed the open bottle to her.

She took a drink. The water was tepid but felt cool and satisfying going down. She handed the bottle back and peered around for any sign of movement. "Do you think they've given up looking for us?"

He shook his head. "I'm not sure they've ever been looking for us, exactly."

"Surely one of those men we've taken out had time to radio back to camp."

"I didn't find any radios on them."

"Then they used cell phones. Or satellite phones. We didn't stop and search them carefully." She grimaced at the flash of pain that shot through her wounded hip. "Maybe we should have."

"We were running for our lives," he said bluntly, stashing the water in his pack. "You need a little longer?"

She squared her shoulders. "No, let's keep moving."

They couldn't have been more than a mile or so from the highway that wound past the Mountain View Motor Lodge, but they were still trudging a winding path through the woods, a long way from anything approaching civilization, nearly an hour later.

The sun was over the mountains by then, angling through the trees in lambent beams that reflected off the low-lying mist. The effect was ethereal, like walking through a golden fog, and if Ava hadn't been so tense and tired, she might have enjoyed the experience.

But all she wanted right now was to reach civilization, where she had options. Last night, she and Sinclair had agreed that setting the FBI on Cabrera's gang might not be the smartest way to go, but daylight had a sobering effect, reminding her that for all the well-documented weaknesses in the organization she called home, the FBI was still well-equipped to deal with ruthless terrorists.

"So are the Coopers," Sinclair said flatly a few minutes later when she voiced her change of heart. "And they have a vested interest in getting Alicia out of there alive, unlike the FBI."

"The FBI isn't in the habit of sacrificing civilians, you know."

He shot a hard, skeptical look her way. "Their track record might suggest otherwise."

"You can't hold a couple of high-profile failures against them. They have a long record of good work."

"You have an institutional loyalty to the Bureau that I don't have."

She wasn't going to win this argument, so she changed tacks. "How do you know the Coopers have even arrived yet?"

"Because that's what the Coopers do." He pulled up short, forcing Ava to stutter-step to a halt to keep from slamming into his back. His shoulders went tense, his head lifting.

"What?" she whispered as he remained utterly still.

"I thought I heard something in the woods ahead." He turned to glance back at her. "Could have been an animal."

*Could have been a terrorist,* she countered silently. She saw a similar unspoken thought glittering behind his dark eyes.

She pulled the MK2 pistol he'd given her the night before from its hiding place in her waistband. "Charge or retreat?"

He took a second to think about it. "Retreat. We could be outnumbered."

And would continue to be outnumbered, she thought

grimly, until they reached civilization and could call in reinforcements.

"What will your partner do when you don't show up for breakfast?" Sin asked a moment later, as they started back-tracking toward another westward trail out of the woods.

She wasn't sure he'd even notice. But she supposed protocol would demand that Landry call in her disappear-ance, even if he thought she might have a good reason for being away from the motel.

"He'll call it in, I guess."

"How soon?"

She glanced at his watch. Almost eight. "I figure we have at least an hour. He's not going to start looking for me before nine."

"It would be better if we could prevent the FBI from swooping in here and causing havoc," he said quietly, as if they hadn't had almost this very argument a few min-utes earlier.

"How are we supposed to find the Coopers?" she asked.

"They'll be at the motel. They've probably already rousted your partner out of bed, as a matter of fact," Sin said with a grimace. "Which might mean that extra hour is as good as gone."

"I thought they liked to do things their own way, with-out official interference," she said.

Sinclair considered the thought. "Maybe. Maybe they'll try to go around your partner. Is he the sort who can be played that way?"

She didn't like to admit it, but Landry's apathy prob-ably made him the perfect FBI agent for the Coopers to deal with. He wouldn't ask too many complicated ques-tions, and he wasn't going to go the extra mile to find out what was really going on behind the scenes of this kid-napping, or even her own disappearance.

She wondered what had happened to Landry to make him such a dead-ender. When he'd first been assigned to the Johnson City office, she'd made a point of looking at his jacket to see what kind of FBI agent he'd been in his last few assignments.

On paper, he'd looked good. Commendations, a good solve rate, plenty of kind words from superiors and peers alike. But at some point between his last big case in the Richmond field office and his reassignment to the Johnson City resident agency, things had changed for Cade Landry.

Maybe, if she and Sinclair got out of this mess alive, she'd make the effort to find out what had happened to Landry. But her case partner's history was so far down her list of things to worry about at the moment, she shoved all thoughts of him aside.

"They'll be able to go around him if that's their intention," she answered Sinclair's earlier question. "Which brings up the next question—if the Coopers are here in Tennessee and are caught up on what's going on, what's their next move?"

Sinclair seemed to give the question some thought as he pushed ahead through the dense underbrush. He moved with fluid grace, she noted as she struggled to emulate his easy gait. He'd had some experience moving silently and maintaining a low profile, obviously.

He'd managed to stay off everyone's radar for three years, after all. The official government assessment had been that he'd died in the harbor explosion three years ago, and nothing had come across her desk to suggest the official assessment was wrong.

Yet, here he was, very much not dead.

She was relieved when he stopped for another rest about twenty minutes later, hunkering down beside her on a fallen tree trunk sheltered from the rest of the woods by a dense stand of young Fraser firs. He offered her a drink of water first, and she took a couple of swigs gratefully, wondering why they weren't any closer to the road after so much trekking through the woods.

"Are we going in circles?" she asked as she handed back the water bottle.

"We did for a bit," he answered, taking one quick drink of water before returning the half-empty bottle to his backpack. "I thought we should take precautions, in case someone is tracking us."

The hair on the back of her neck prickled. "You think that's happening?"

"I think we shouldn't take a lot of chances," he answered after a brief pause. "If any of those men in the woods had a chance to tell Cabrera what was going on before we stopped them, then he knows his plan to kidnap Alicia to smoke me out is working."

"How does he know you're alive? As far as I know, nobody else has a clue you're not fish food in the middle of Tesoro Harbor."

He grimaced at her description. "I don't know."

"Does anyone else know you're alive?"

She could see his thoughts swirling behind his dark eyes. After a moment, he nodded. "At least two people. One I trust completely. One I think I can probably trust, but—"

"But you can't be sure?"

"It would take only a word to the wrong person. A slip of the tongue." He looked as if he wanted to say more, but he stopped, pressing his mouth to a thin line.

"Who's the one you trust?"

She thought for a moment he wasn't going to answer her question. Then he released a quiet sigh and said, "He's a former CIA agent."

She tried not to look skeptical, but the expression in his eyes made it clear she'd failed.

"I know it sounds like a bad movie," he said with another quiet huff of breath. "But it's true. When I lost faith in what *El Cambio* was doing, I turned myself in at the American consulate in Tesoro. The CIA agent was the first person I talked to."

"And he, what? Offered you a chance to go back inside *El Cambio* as a double agent?" she said with a soft laugh.

His lips flattened further. "I told you it sounded like a bad movie."

She stared at him, realizing her outlandish guess was the story he was apparently going with. "Come on."

"It's the truth."

She didn't know what to say. He seemed earnest enough, but she was in no position to believe everything he had to say.

"Forget it," he said after a few seconds. "It's not that important. All you need to know is that this guy I know can help us if I can reach him."

"How do you know he's not the one who betrayed you to Cabrera?"

"Because he put his neck on the line to get me out of Sanselmo safely and set me up with a new identity."

"What new identity?"

"Christopher Peralta. Although I suppose it doesn't really matter anymore. Chris Peralta's been compromised, too." He nodded toward the west. "We need to be on the move."

Her legs were beginning to ache in concert with her bullet wound in protest of so much trudging around through underbrush, but she gritted her teeth and did her best to keep pace with Sinclair.

Somewhere around midmorning, they reached the section of the woods where Ava had run into the ambush the day before. She didn't recognize it, and the bodies of the dead terrorists no longer lay where they'd left them, but Sinclair assured her they'd arrived back in the same place. "I've spent the past year wandering these woods and mountains," he told her as he crouched next to a mountain laurel bush that looked as if it had been shorn in half, several branches now lying broken and flat on the ground. "This is where Escalante's body fell."

"So their compadres retrieved the bodies?"

"They don't want to risk announcing their presence here until they're ready to strike,"

She looked around, trying to picture the place as she remembered it. But everything had happened so fast, including Sinclair's hauling her off to the safety of his tent. She could barely remember the details of the ambush itself, much less where it had happened.

"They're out here looking for us. You know that, right?"

She nodded, trying to ignore the gooseflesh that scattered down her arms in response to his warning. "I know that."

"Then we shouldn't linger." He started walking again.

She trudged behind him, the skin on the back of her neck still crawling.

By NOON, THE temperature had risen to the mid-eighties, and the lingering moisture from the previous night's storms made the woods feel like a sauna. If he'd been alone, Sinclair might have skipped lunch and kept going, but Ava was running on sheer, dogged determination and not much else. "We stop here," he announced, pulling the Ghillie net from his backpack.

She stared at the camouflage net. "We're not going to set up the tent, are we?"

He wondered if she knew how much longing he could hear in her voice when she asked that question. "No, but I figured we'd take a longer rest and eat the other protein bar. Rehydrate. Might as well camouflage ourselves while we're doing it."

While he draped the Ghillie net across several shrubs, giving them a small shelter for their midday rest, she dug in his backpack and pulled out the last protein bar and a bottle of water. "Are there any creeks around here clean enough to risk refilling our water bottles?"

"Yeah, though I'd still rather boil it first. And we're fresh out of fires." He sat down next to a patch of mossy ground and patted the spot beside him. "Sit. Take a nap if you want. It's too hot out there for hiking right now, but if you wait around, we're bound to get an afternoon shower or two. Cool things right off."

"Oh, goody. More rain." But she settled on the patch of moss beside him and tore the paper off the protein bar.

"You'll be glad for the drop in temperature."

"I know." She straightened the grimace from her face and managed a half smile as she broke the protein bar in half and gave him his portion. She ate her half slowly, though she had to be hungry by now. He pressed the water on her as well, not liking her pallor or the rapid rate of her breathing. It would be very easy to fall victim to dehydration and heat exhaustion, especially for a woman who was already injured.

He managed to get half the bottle of water down her before her eyelids began to droop. Edging closer, he let her lean against him, her head wobbling before it finally dropped against his shoulder.

A fluttery feeling settled in the center of his chest, reminding him of a time that seemed a lifetime distant, a time when he'd been a young man on the cusp of his wide-open future. A time when a hazel-eyed girl from Nowhere, Kentucky, had stolen his breath and shown him a whole world of possibilities he'd never considered before.

What if he'd met her that night in Mariposa rather than tracking down Luis Grijalva? Where would he be right now?

*Not here,* he thought. Not hiding in the woods from Alberto Cabrera. Not wondering how much longer Ava Trent could keep walking before her weariness and injury overcame her gritty willpower.

But would *El Cambio* be on the run the way it was now? Would Sanselmo be so close to stability and economic promise if he hadn't taken up Alexander Quinn's offer to turn double agent? So much of the information he'd fed to the CIA had helped defang *El Cambio.* He'd helped put some of the more brutal drug cartels on the run, as well.

Would he really be willing to turn his back on the good things he'd done, no matter how mistaken his choices in the beginning?

God, he needed to talk to Quinn. The man might be as slippery as an eel in slime, but he had a way of getting to the bottom line of any question.

He'd know what to do next.

ALEXANDER QUINN WASN'T a man who liked to sit around and wait for things to happen, even though, technically, his job with the CIA had been all about waiting for things to happen, things he'd set into motion himself. He'd done what he could to put the Cooper family into motion the night before, but so far, they were still holed up in the motel across the road, waiting for God only knew what.

More Coopers to arrive? Not a bad idea, given what Quinn suspected was going on out in those woods.

He was pretty sure Sinclair Solano was still somewhere

in this general area. That fact, combined with the abduction of his sister, could be no coincidence. Someone was clearly trying to use Alicia Cooper to draw her brother into the open.

But who? Who knew Solano was still alive?

Kidnapping a security agent and her tough, physically fit husband from their motel room had been a brazen act. It hadn't been accomplished easily. It had taken planning, and certainly required more than a single perpetrator. Quinn had put out some feelers to his former colleagues at the company, but he'd heard nothing of any interest so far.

He wasn't surprised, exactly, by the lack of response. His recent decision to leave the CIA for private work had caught everyone by surprise. He supposed everyone in the agency had expected him to die somewhere in the bowels of Langley and be entombed there without ceremony, just another gold star on the anonymous wall of honor.

Himself included.

His cell phone hummed lightly against his hip. He reached into his pocket, studied the unlisted number and considered not answering.

But curiosity overcame caution. "Yeah?"

"Did you know the Mountain View Motor Lodge rooms have back exits?" The voice on the other end of the phone belonged to Jake Cooper.

The hair on the back of Quinn's neck prickled. "Where are you?"

"In the woods about a quarter mile from where you're standing."

"How'd you get this phone number?"

"We have friends in your agency."

Probably Sutton Calhoun, Quinn thought. Calhoun had worked for Cooper Security before taking the job

with Quinn. Could have been Adam Brand, too, he supposed—Brand had been close with Isabel Cooper and her
husband, Ben Scanlon.

Conflicting loyalties could be very messy indeed.

"Who's with you?" he asked Jake.

"Luke, Hannah, Riley, Jesse and Rick. Everybody else
has set up a clearinghouse for information at the motel.
We have agents following a lot of potential leads."

"What are the six of you planning to do?"

"Local law enforcement officers had reports of gunshots heard in the woods just east of here yesterday afternoon. It's not hunting season."

Quinn bit back a curse. He hadn't even thought to check
in with the local LEOs. One of the downsides of playing
the lone wolf, he supposed.

"Why are you calling me?" he asked.

There was a brief pause on the other end of the call.
Then Jake said quietly, "We need some information. Did
you know that one of the FBI agents who came to town
yesterday to help the locals investigate has gone missing?"

A ripple of surprise raced down Quinn's back. "For
how long?"

"She disappeared soon after she and her associate arrived. Isabel worked a case with the partner, Cade Landry,
a couple of years ago. She ran into him this morning. Apparently the missing agent never came to pick up the room
key he got for her, wasn't in her room when he tried to
check in with her this morning, and there's no sign she
stayed there at all last night."

Disturbing, Quinn thought. "What do we know about
the missing agent?"

"Ava Trent. Female. Twenty-eight. Brown hair, hazel
eyes. Works out of the Johnson City resident agency.
About six years with the Bureau."

"Any sign of foul play?"

"No. Landry said she wandered toward the woods yesterday afternoon after telling him to get them a couple of rooms. Last he saw of her."

*Wandered toward the woods,* Quinn thought, his eyes narrowing as he turned and looked at the deepening woods behind him.

"We're going to see if we can find any sign of her." Jake's voice broke into Quinn's queasy thoughts. "Want to come along?"

Another downside of getting in the habit of going it alone, Quinn thought. It had never occurred to him to join forces with the Coopers.

It should have.

"What's your exact location?" he asked.

Jake rattled off longitude and latitude numbers. "I assume you have a GPS locator at your disposal?"

"Of course."

"We'll wait fifteen minutes for you to find us. Be here or we leave without you."

Quinn had already started heading in the general direction of the coordinates Jake had given him. "And then what?"

"And then, we go find my brother and Alicia."

"You don't know what you're up against."

"Do you? Does this have something to do with Alicia's brother's activities in South America?"

Quinn couldn't answer. But apparently his silence was enough.

"If he's still alive, there are people who would want their hands on him," Jake murmured, his voice barely audible over the phone. "And they'd have no problem using Alicia as a pawn, would they?"

"If he were still alive, and they thought they could use

her to smoke him out of hiding, no. No, they'd have no problem with that at all."

Jake Cooper muttered a profanity. "Twelve minutes now. Get a move on." He hung up the phone.

Quinn shoved his phone in his pocket and quickened his pace. It might go against his long-ingrained habits to be a team player, but maybe it was time to form some new habits.

Right now, he had a feeling he could use all the help he could get.

# *Chapter Eight*

Ava opened her eyes to a gloomy half twilight. It took a second to gather her wits enough to realize she was napping against a warm, solid body underneath the ruffled camouflage of a Ghillie net.

She sat upright and rubbed her gritty eyes. "How long did I sleep?" she whispered.

"About two hours." Sinclair's quiet voice rumbled through her from the point where their bodies touched, flooding her with instant heat.

She looked at Sinclair, dismayed by how long she'd delayed their escape. "That's too long."

"You needed it." He brushed a tousled hank of hair away from her eyes. His fingertips lingered against the curve of her cheek, setting her skin on fire. "You look better for it."

She tried to drag her gaze away from his, but the light caress of his fingertips on her face seemed to trap her in place. "Sinclair—"

"I never thought I'd see you again. But I thought of you so many times over the years." He spoke as if reluctant, as if begrudging each word that slipped between his lips. But his dark eyes blazed with a pulsating hunger that set off an answering throb low in her belly. "I didn't want to. I wanted to put everything in my former life behind me.

I knew what I was committing to, and I knew I couldn't go back once I made the choice."

"Why?" she whispered. "Why did you choose *El Cambio?* Sanselmo was already beginning to reform the government. If you'd just given them a little more time—"

His thumb brushed over her lower lip. "I was young and impatient. And I had a head full of foolish ideas about the way the world should be."

"Everybody does." She tried to ignore the way his gaze dropped to her lips, but she was powerless against the surge of longing that rose in her chest to strangle her. "You think I didn't have things I wanted to change?"

"You were smart enough to take things slowly." A mournful note darkened his voice. "I had my mother's ideas in my head and my father's passion in my breast. And Luis Grijalva's revolutionary words in my ears. I thought there was no other choice to be made. I wanted to make a difference, and joining the revolution was the only way I could do it."

She could see in his pain-filled gaze how much he regretted his choices. "How many people did you kill for your passion?" she asked, because she needed to remind herself of the monster he'd become, not the foolish boy he'd once been.

"I killed nine people in that last bomb blast," he answered. "I didn't mean to, but they rushed the warehouse early. I tried to time it so that my hands would remain clean, but—" He dropped his hand away from her face.

"You mean the only people you killed that whole time you were with *El Cambio* were your fellow terrorists?"

"I was never a bomber," he said flatly, his fists clenching at his sides.

"But the indictments against you—"

"The government got me mixed up with another rebel,"

he said quietly, his gaze dropping to the ground between them. "My CIA handlers let the mistake remain. It gave me more cachet with *El Cambio,* being one of the FBI's most wanted."

Could he be telling the truth? Or were these more convenient lies meant to manipulate her feelings?

"How can I believe you?" she asked softly, her heart pounding with a different sort of fear.

"I don't suppose you can." He moved, putting distance between them. Despite the warmth of the afternoon, she felt cooler air pour into the widening gap between their bodies.

Sinclair crept to the edge of the Ghillie net and looked out toward the woods. "Rain's about to start again."

"Lovely."

He eased the edge of the netting up, turning to look at her. "The temperature's cooled down considerably, at least. We'll probably make better time now."

Given the way every muscle in her body screeched in protest at her slightest movement, Ava had her doubts about what sort of time they'd be able to make. But she slipped under the net at Sinclair's gesture and waited for him to fold up the camouflage and store it in his backpack again. She took advantage of the brief pause to look around the woods, trying to regain her bearings. The rain clouds overhead obscured the sun, but there was enough variation in the light to figure out which way the sun was headed.

"Ready?" Sinclair asked, his back to her as he strapped on the pack.

She started to nod when she felt something hard and cool press against the side of her neck. She froze in place, her voice stuck in her throat.

As Sinclair started to turn toward her, a gravelly voice

spoke in her ear. "Do not move an inch. Not an inch." The speaker was male, and his drawl was pure American South, without a hint of a Spanish accent.

Sinclair went still, his eyes slanting toward Ava. They widened slightly as they took in whoever stood behind her. "I really thought you were dead," he said, a quizzical tone to his voice.

There was a hint of shock in the Southern drawl when the man behind her spoke again. "Back at ya, son."

Suddenly, Ava understood the cryptic interchange. "If that's a gun you have pressed to my neck," she said quietly, "please put it down. My name is Ava Trent and I'm an FBI agent looking for you and your wife. You're Gabe Cooper, right?"

There was a brief pause as the man considered her words. After a beat, the gun barrel pressed to her neck fell away. "You're FBI?"

She turned slowly to look at him, biting back a quick gasp of surprise. Gabe Cooper looked, quite simply, as if he'd had the hell beaten out of him. Bruises and abrasions seemed to cover every exposed area of his skin. His nose was swollen and probably broken, bruises already forming under his bloodshot blue eyes. Both lips were split and a little bloody, and bloodstains also marred the torn T-shirt he wore over a grimy pair of jeans. His dark hair was damp with sweat and probably more blood, given the large scrape that extended up his forehead into his hairline.

"Out of the Johnson City R.A.," she answered, looking him over for any hidden injuries. Not that the ones she could see weren't enough to qualify him for a trip to the nearest E.R. "How did you get away?"

"A little luck, a little mulish determination." Gabe's split lips twisted in a wretched-looking attempt at a smile. "I had to kill a man, so I'm a little on edge." He looked past her to Sinclair, who was still standing, stiff-backed, in the same position in which he'd stopped at Gabe's command. "You're Sinclair Solano, aren't you?"

Sinclair's dark eyes slanted toward Gabe. Slowly, he turned to face his brother-in-law. "I am."

Gabe shook his head, grimacing a little at the movement. "She kept telling them you were dead. That they'd taken us for nothing."

Sinclair's eyes closed briefly before he looked away from Gabe and locked gazes with Ava. She felt a ripple of pity for the look of sheer misery on his lean, handsome face.

"This never should have happened," he said bleakly.

"No, it shouldn't have." Gabe looked away from Sinclair, his expression darkening. "Now we have to fix that."

"I'll make a trade," Sinclair said. "Me for her. It's what they want."

"They'll just kill both of you," Ava warned, her gut tightening. "Don't do something drastic and foolish."

"Do you know where they've taken her?" Gabe's voice sounded more slurred than before, drawing Ava's gaze quickly to his face. He'd gone pale beneath his tan, and one hand snapped out to grab the slender trunk of a birch sapling.

Ava and Sinclair moved in tandem to catch him before he sagged to the ground. Gabe tried to push them away, but his movements lacked any strength. While Ava eased Gabe to a sitting position, Sinclair unpacked the Ghillie net and the tent, piecing them together with speed and expert precision. He helped her pull Gabe through the tent flap just as the sky overhead opened up, spilling a hard, cold rain that rattled relentlessly against the top of the tent.

"I'm okay," Gabe protested, but Ava didn't believe it for a moment. A quick check beneath his T-shirt revealed large bruises on his stomach and rib cage. She suspected he had matching marks on his back, as well. He might be bleeding internally for all they knew.

"We need to get him emergency treatment," she murmured to Sinclair.

He closed his fingers around Gabe's wrist, checking the man's pulse. A moment later, he checked Gabe's eyes, frowning. "I don't think he's going to bleed to death in the next little bit."

"Didn't you see the bruises?"

"Yes, but he's not showing signs of blood loss or shock."

"And you're a doctor now?"

Sinclair's gaze snapped up to meet hers. "Believe me, I want nothing more than to deliver him to my sister alive and healthy. But if he's killed one of Cabrera's men like he said, you know there'll be *El Cambio* soldiers out there scouring the woods for him as well as us."

"You know I'm still conscious, don't you?" Gabe asked faintly.

"Go to sleep," Ava said shortly.

Gabe arched an eyebrow in her direction.

"Sorry," she added. "But you really do need to rest. I'm not as convinced as the two of you are that you're not bleeding internally. So do me a favor and take advantage of having someone to watch your back. You need to rest."

Gabe Cooper's eyes darkened as he looked at her, but after a few seconds, he closed his eyes and rolled onto his side with a groan, turning his back to them.

Sinclair nodded for Ava to follow him out of the tent. She crawled out behind him, hunkering down beside him near the edge of the Ghillie net. "When the man who took him out to the woods to kill him doesn't come back, Cabrera is going to send out a search party."

"What makes you think they haven't already? We killed a couple of their scouts, too."

"Yes, but they don't know who we are. They can't know for sure that I'm out here taking out their men. For all they know, we could be local law enforcement, and they'd be careful not to tangle with us if they can avoid it."

"But Gabe Cooper is truly dangerous to them if he makes it back to civilization," she said, understanding his point. "Or if he comes after them directly."

"Everybody in Sanselmo's underworld has heard about the Coopers," Sinclair said quietly. "What they did to Eladio Cordero and his band of drug thugs—"

*"Los Tiburones,"* she murmured. Like anyone involved in law enforcement on the East Coast, she'd heard the story about the Cooper family's skirmishes with one of Sanselmo's most vicious and notorious drug lords. Eladio Cordero had sent his thugs, *Los Tiburones,* after Coopers not once but twice over the course of a couple of years. The Coopers had killed or captured all comers, including Cordero himself, accomplishing what Sanselmo's own national army and police force hadn't been able to do.

"Cabrera knows how dangerous the Coopers are," Sinclair said flatly.

"Then why did he take Gabe and your sister in the first place?" she asked. "Why did he risk it?"

"Because *El Cambio* is on a devastating downswing in Sanselmo," he answered, meeting her curious gaze. "Their popularity has dropped like a stone since the current president's new reforms have started yielding positive changes. All the dire predictions and threats from the rebels have been exposed as desperation from a dying opposition."

"And their tactics have grown more brutal than ever."

Sinclair nodded. "They need a victory."

"How does kidnapping your sister and her husband give them a victory?"

"It doesn't. But using them to smoke me out and take me down?"

"Right." She met his dark gaze, her stomach knotting. "*El Cambio* made you into a scapegoat for half their crimes, didn't they?"

He nodded. "They went through a period after my 'death' where they tried to become a political entity rather than a rebel group."

"It didn't take."

"They weren't patient enough to build a platform. Cabrera wanted power and he wanted it fast."

"So he fell back on violence."

"It's what he knows." Sinclair looked up at the sky through the Ghillie net, releasing a soft sigh. The light drizzle had started to pick up force, becoming a steady shower. Water seeped through the Ghillie net, sprinkling them both with warm rain. "Back in the tent. You don't need to get drenched again."

She followed him back into the now-crowded shelter. Gabe remained on his side, his chest rising and falling in a steady cadence.

"I guess he needed rest more than he realized," she whispered.

"You better get some sleep, too," Sinclair answered quietly. "I have a feeling whatever's waiting for us out there is going to be twice as dangerous as before."

THE DRUMBEAT OF rain on the tent put Ava right to sleep, and Sinclair didn't have the heart to wake her. He knew she'd be angry that he let her drift off again, but she needed the rest as much as Gabe Cooper did.

And he needed to think about what he should do next.

Almost a full day had passed since they'd left Cabrera's camp behind, and while Sinclair wanted to believe the terrorist was going to stay put while he and Ava brought in reinforcements, he couldn't shake the niggling feeling that time was running out for them.

They should have reached civilization by now, if they hadn't been forced to go in circles for a while to be sure they hadn't picked up a tail. Running into Gabe Cooper had only slowed them further, and considering the man's physical condition, he wasn't exactly going to help them pick up any speed.

Meanwhile, Cabrera could be moving Alicia to God only knew where, and Sinclair might never pick up his trail again.

He eased out of the tent, taking care not to wake Ava and Gabe. The heavy rain that had begun falling earlier had eased off to a drizzle again, tempting him from beneath the Ghillie net.

Thanks to the rain, the temperature had dropped several degrees. The air had a clean, earthy smell that reminded him of the mountains of Sanselmo after the afternoon rains. He walked farther from the tent, skirting trees to provide himself some cover, in case someone was out there in the woods watching him.

But he saw no sign of movement. No sounds beyond the steady cadence of rain in the trees overhead. He raised the hood of his camouflage jacket to cover his head and hiked deeper into the woods, away from the tent.

He should have left a note, he realized belatedly. Let Ava know what he was planning. But maybe it was better that he hadn't. She'd just try to follow him. After all, he thought with a quirk of a smile, he was her prisoner.

Alone, taking a chance on a less convoluted path through the woods, he made much better time than he and Ava had made that morning, though he took care to mark his trail with notches in the trees he passed. The last thing he wanted to do was lose the trail back to Ava and Gabe Cooper.

Within an hour, he had reached the bluff overlooking the hidden cove where he and Ava had spotted Cabrera's camp below. He eased to the edge and sneaked a peek over the side. The camp was still there, hunkered silently in the rain. There were two men standing guard outside the tents, their postures tense.

They must have already realized several of their men had gone missing. They would be on high alert now.

He edged away from the bluff and rolled into a sitting position, preparing to rise to his feet now that he was far enough from the edge that no one below could see him.

But as he put his hand down to push to his feet, a flash of movement in the woods to his right froze him in place.

Moving only his eyes, he slowly turned his gaze toward the patch of woods where he'd seen something moving. All was still at the moment, but as he held his gaze steady, a dark figure detached itself from the tree where it had been standing a moment earlier and glided toward the bluff.

One of Cabrera's men, Sinclair decided after studying the camouflage pattern the man wore. It was old-school jungle camouflage, nothing an American hunter would wear here in the Smoky Mountains, especially out of season. And if he were law enforcement, the camo pattern might be even more sophisticated.

The man slipped out of sight, and Sinclair allowed himself a long, slow breath. But before he'd had a chance to do more than exhale, another dark figure moved smoothly into view.

Same camouflage pattern. The man was a few yards closer than the previous one had been, close enough for

Sinclair to get a decent look at his face beneath the streaks of camouflage paint. The shape of the man's nose and the craggy brow gave him away—Antonio Cabrera, cousin to Alberto. As ruthless a bastard as *El Cambio* could offer, and *El Cambio*'s enforcers had been notorious for their brutality.

Sinclair froze in place, closing his eyes to slits as Antonio's gaze slid his way. He held his breath and waited.

After a chest-burning interval, Antonio turned away and headed back into the woods, away from the bluff.

Sinclair allowed himself another deep breath, the only movement he dared. So much for hurrying back to the tent before Ava missed him.

He was well and truly trapped.

# Chapter Nine

An early twilight had descended on the woods by the time Ava woke with a start from a dead sleep. She sat up in a rush, her heart pounding in her ears, chased from slumber by a dream she couldn't remember. All that lingered was a sense of imminent danger, as if the fear that had invaded her dreams had retreated only as far as the shadows outside the tent.

"Sinclair," she whispered, trying to calm her breathing, which sounded fast and ragged in the tight confines of the tent.

There was no answer.

She peered around the gloomy interior of the darkened tent. A few feet away, Gabe Cooper was still asleep, his breathing slow and regular. There was no one else inside.

Grimacing as her muscles protested the movement, she crawled to the tent flap and stuck her head outside. The Ghillie net extended another five feet past the door of the tent, but Sinclair wasn't inside the netting.

She rose to a crouch and edged her way to the side of the net, trying to see beyond the camouflage to the rain-darkened woods beyond. She saw no sign of movement other than the steady drumbeat of rain slanting through the canopy of trees.

She had a creeping sense of déjà vu. Here she was,

again, left behind while Sinclair Solano went his own way without telling her what he was planning to do. But this time, there was no plane ticket home, no exciting new career path to take her mind off her woes.

Only dark, perilous woods as far as she could see, full of hidden places where dangerous, well-armed men might be lying in wait.

She slipped back into the tent and edged closer to Gabe, checking the pulse in his wrist. His heartbeat was only slightly faster than it should have been, not fast enough to make her worry that he was losing blood internally.

He stirred at her touch, groaning.

"Sorry, didn't mean to wake you," she whispered.

He rolled onto his back, blinking up at her. "Are we moving?"

"I don't think so."

He pushed himself up on his elbow, grimacing with pain. "Where's Solano?"

"I don't know," she admitted. "I woke up and he wasn't here."

Gabe looked at her a long moment, then muttered a succinct curse.

"Maybe he went out to see if he could find something to eat?" she suggested, wishing she didn't sound quite so pathetically hopeful. She knew damned well that wasn't why he'd left the tent.

He'd decided to go it alone. Just like before. Hell, his mind had already been made up before he'd ever tried to coax her into taking a nap.

Sinclair Solano had a bad habit of doing things his own way, the rest of the world be damned. Clearly, the past eight years had taught him nothing.

"He's not coming back, is he?" Gabe asked quietly.

"I don't think he is," she admitted. His backpack was

gone, although a quick scan of the tent revealed that he'd left two bottles of water with her and Gabe. It might get them back to civilization if they didn't drink too much at a time.

She pushed the thought aside and looked at Gabe. "How're you feeling?"

"Like I ran into a bus."

She rather felt that way herself. "Think you could walk some more before dark?"

He looked around the dim tent. "This isn't dark?"

She checked her watch. "Half past four. We probably have a couple of hours before nightfall."

He stretched carefully, testing his flexibility. From her perspective, he looked as creaky as an old man, but after a moment, he looked up at her and nodded. "I'm game."

Without the backpack, she wasn't sure she would be able to carry the tent and Ghillie net. But Gabe helped her break the tent down and fold it into a compact square. They folded the Ghillie net around the tent and shoved both pieces down the back of Gabe's shirt, holding them in place by tucking in the hem of his T-shirt. He walked hunched over but he reassured her the tent and net were lightweight enough for him to handle.

She put the extra waters in the pockets of her jacket, handed Gabe the MK2 Sinclair had taken off one of the dead Cabrera henchmen, and they started heading west, into a light, damp breeze.

They hadn't gone far, however, before she saw the first sign of a trail through the woods—a nick in the wood of a white birch, clearly a knife mark.

Had Sinclair left a trail for her to follow if they got separated?

She shook her head at first, berating herself for such a hopeless case of wishful thinking. Sinclair didn't want her to follow him. The whole point of leaving while she was asleep was to make sure he got a head start.

Gabe spotted the next notch. "He left a trail," he said quietly.

She paused by the mark on the fir trunk and looked around. What if it hadn't been Sinclair who'd left the trail? What if Cabrera's men were trying to lure them into a trap?

Reaching behind her back, she pulled her Glock from the holster and edged closer to the tree trunk. Gabe Cooper joined her there, the MK2 in hand, his breathing soft but labored.

"You think it might be *El Cambio* instead?" he whispered.

"I don't know."

He looked around, his brow furrowed. "I wish I had a way to reach my family."

"They're probably already out here somewhere, looking for you." She looked at the notch on the tree again. "Could one of them have left this mark?"

He shook his head. "That's not the way we do things."

"Not the way you do things?"

"We learned not to leave any trace of ourselves. No Cooper would leave a trail like this."

So maybe it was Sinclair, she thought, mildly disgusted by how much she wanted to believe it was true. Just how stupid was she, anyway? Was she so susceptible to a pair of chocolate-brown eyes and a lean, cut body that she'd forget eight years of fugitive status?

*Oh, God,* she thought, *don't answer that. Don't depress yourself further.*

"Had my family arrived before you came out here?" Gabe asked.

"Not yet. They had farther to come, and I got here pretty soon after your abduction."

Gabe growled at her words. "*Ambush* is more like it. They caught us when I was in the shower. I came out naked and unarmed to find four men with guns pointed at Alicia's head."

Ava felt a shudder of sympathy at the picture he painted. "I'm surprised they didn't just shoot you," she said bluntly. "Clearly that was always the plan—to get you out of the way."

"They didn't want to chance it right there in the motel. And after they got us out into the woods, I think they realized Alicia would cooperate more easily if I was still in the picture. So they took us to their camp before they dragged me off."

"How did you get away?"

"I overpowered the guy with the gun. He pulled a knife, so I shot him." Gabe's answer was flat and unemotional. "What I did will hit me sooner or later, but right now, I don't feel anything but damned glad to be alive."

"You should be," she answered just as bluntly. She'd killed a man herself the day before, and all she felt right now was relieved to be the one still breathing and walking around.

Well, relieved and completely pissed off that Sinclair had gone off on his own, leaving her behind.

He was her prisoner, damn it. What the hell did he think he was doing?

"There's another one," Gabe said, nodding toward a tree about ten yards to the northeast. She made out the notch in the side of the tree trunk.

So far, the trail Sinclair had left them followed a straight northeasterly path. Toward Cabrera's campsite, she realized. They'd taken a twisty, backtracking path away from the bluff the day before, worried about Cabrera scouts following them in the woods, but apparently, Sinclair hadn't been nearly so cautious alone.

"I think he's heading for Cabrera's camp," she said aloud.

Beside her, Gabe's breath hitched. "You know where the camp is?"

She eyed him cautiously. "We know where it was last night. That doesn't mean it's still there."

"The man who took me away to kill me put a blindfold on me." He leaned his head back against the tree trunk, closing his eyes. "I didn't get it loose until we were at least a half mile away from the camp, so I couldn't get my bearings to find my way back to her." He opened his eyes, meeting her sympathetic gaze. "Tell me you saw her last night. Tell me she's okay."

"We saw her. She was alive and very worried about you."

He closed his eyes again. "We've been through so much together. When we met, she was already in danger, and we survived that case. Then she had to go and join my cousin's security agency."

"More danger?"

"We didn't think it would be so much. She works in a consultant capacity. Profiling and forensic psychology. Very behind-the-scenes. I thought it would be okay. I didn't have to be afraid of that kind of job."

"What happened at the motel had nothing to do with her job."

He pushed away from the tree and gazed into the gloomy woods. "No. It had to do with her damned brother."

Despite his injuries, when he moved, there was a gliding grace to his gait, like a wraith floating through the woods. She tried to mimic his stealth as she followed him from marked tree to marked tree, moving closer and closer to the hidden cove where Cabrera had set up camp.

She was the first to see the camouflaged scout about fifty yards ahead. She caught Gabe's arm, wincing in sympathy as he released a soft hiss of pain between his clenched teeth. Nodding toward the man in camouflage, she pulled Gabe back against the wide trunk of a tall Fraser fir.

The man moved in slow, steady circles amid the thick stand of evergreens to their north. He looked more bored than alert, but the AR-15 rifle he carried would make up for any inattention. In comparison, her Glock, with its large-capacity magazine, was outgunned by a long shot. Even the MK2 couldn't compete.

"Look about fifty yards west," Gabe whispered in her ear.

She followed his gaze and saw nothing but trees. It took a moment to realize the clump of bushes near the edge of the bluff was actually a man in a camouflage coat, hunkered down and utterly still. Only the slow blink of his eyes betrayed his presence at all.

And those dark eyes were looking straight at her.

*Oh, Sinclair,* she thought, her heart contracting with a combination of guilt and empathy. *You came out here to check on your sister.*

His gaze locked with hers for a long moment before his eyes slid half-closed. In that moment, however, a world of communication passed between them. Unspoken words like *Be very, very still. Don't do anything to betray your position.*

"Don't move," Gabe whispered in her ear, his whole body tight with alarm. She froze her position in response, though her eyes slid toward him, trying to figure out what had sparked his sudden tension.

He was no longer looking at Sinclair. Instead, his gaze was locked on to the camouflage-clad scout moving slowly toward their position.

The scout stopped midstep, his head swiveling toward the east. Moving only her eyes, Ava looked where he was looking and saw, with dismay, that Sinclair had moved his position.

He was edging, slowly, stealthily, toward the bluff and the hidden encampment.

Expecting the scout to open fire immediately, she was surprised when he quietly changed directions, heading after Sinclair. If Sinclair realized he was being followed, he showed no sign of it.

"We have to warn him," she whispered to Gabe, already taking a step toward the scout's position.

"No!" Gabe caught her arm, holding her still. "He's leading the guy away from us. He knows what he's doing."

She stared at Gabe, horrified. "He's going to get captured!"

"I think that's his plan."

Stupid man! If Cabrera got his hands on Sinclair, he wouldn't hesitate to kill him where he stood.

"We have to stop this!" she said urgently.

"If we do something now, all three of us will end up dead. We're outgunned and outnumbered."

"So he just sacrifices himself? Do you really think Cabrera will just let your wife go once he's killed Sinclair?"

The bleak look Gabe shot her way answered the question for her.

"We have to stop this," she repeated.

"Are you a good shot with that thing?" He nodded toward the Glock still clutched in her right hand.

"Not from this distance."

"So we have to get closer," he said, already starting to

move, his bruised and bloodied hand tightening around the MK2.

She followed, keeping an eye out for other scouts in the woods. Between her, Gabe and Sinclair, they'd taken out four of Cabrera's contingent of armed soldiers, but there were plenty of henchmen left to worry about. If they weren't careful, they'd all three end up in Cabrera's grasp.

"Solano's heading away from the bluff," Gabe whispered a few minutes later, after their path had wound almost a half mile to the west, away from the encampment. They were about three hundred yards behind Sinclair and the man tracking him, moving more slowly and deliberately to be sure they weren't setting themselves up for an ambush of their own.

"Why hasn't Cabrera's man made a move?" she asked, her tongue thick in her mouth. She hadn't had any water in a while, and she was feeling the effects of thirst.

"I'm not sure," Gabe whispered back. "Maybe they think he's going to lead them to you."

"We're not sure they even know I'm here."

"They know," Gabe assured her. "Just before they dragged me away from camp, Cabrera got a phone call from one of his men, saying he had spotted you in the woods. At least, I assume it was you. Are there any other women roaming these woods packing heat?"

"I shot one of Cabrera's men," she whispered. "Sinclair shot the other, before he could kill me. He also killed a third man."

Gabe turned to look at her, his blue eyes strangely bright in the fading twilight. "They *will* kill us all if they catch us."

"I know."

"So we don't get captured." Gabe turned his head back toward the woods. Ahead, Sinclair's pace had slowed, and the *El Cambio* operative was starting to close the distance between them at an alarming rate.

What was Sin trying to do? Let himself get caught?

Almost as soon as the thought entered her mind, she realized letting himself be captured was exactly what he was counting on. He'd been trying to lure the man away from them the whole time, willing to give himself up to keep them from being found.

Crazy man. For a notorious terrorist, he had an amazingly self-sacrificial code of honor.

"He's going to get caught," Gabe murmured.

"If he does, he's as good as dead."

"Not right away," Gabe disagreed. "Cabrera told his men to bring Solano to him alive."

Her stomach was starting to ache with dread. "He wants to kill Sinclair himself, doesn't he?"

"Yep. Not sure why, but Cabrera really hates Solano."

There was no way they could close the distance between themselves and the *El Cambio* scout before the man reached Sinclair, especially since Sinclair wasn't even trying to stay ahead anymore.

But maybe they could set up an ambush once Cabrera's man had his hands on Sinclair. "We need to split up," she whispered to Gabe.

He looked at the inexorable cat-and-mouse game playing out ahead, then back at her. "Ambush?" he asked quietly.

"We have to try something." She looked away from Gabe, her gaze turning back to the darkening patch of woods ahead where Cabrera's man had closed the distance between himself and Sinclair to less than fifty yards.

Suddenly, seven dark shapes glided out of the trees just behind Cabrera's scout, closing in on him with a mind-shattering combination of speed and stealth. At the last moment, the scout seemed to realize he was surrounded, and the AR-15 came up with a rattle of gunfire.

The sound stopped almost as soon as it started. One sharp bark of gunfire sent the scout sprawling to the ground.

"Well, son of a bitch," Gabe growled under his breath. Ava's gaze whipped up to his face and she saw a slow grin spreading across his face.

"Who are they?" she whispered as he continued smiling.

"Coopers, darling," Gabe drawled, already moving toward the dark figures gliding through the woods ahead. "Who else?"

## *Chapter Ten*

The sight of Alexander Quinn's stony face among his dark-clad rescuers should have been a surprise, but over the past eight years, Sinclair had come to expect the unexpected from his former CIA handler. He'd once joked that he could be stuck at the top of Mount Everest and it wouldn't surprise him to see Quinn in Sherpa gear, climbing to his rescue.

"How'd you find me?" he asked Quinn as the older man left the others to meet him halfway.

"Tagged along with the Coopers." Quinn glanced back at the others who had surrounded the fallen Cabrera soldier. "Want to catch me up?"

As Sinclair started to open his mouth to answer, he caught sight of Ava moving through the woods toward him, her hazel eyes blazing in the fading light. He turned toward her, bracing himself for her fury.

He was not prepared, however, when she launched herself at him, wrapped her arms tightly around his waist and pressed her face to his chest.

He curled his arms around her, his heart pounding as she tightened her grip on his back and rubbed her nose against his collarbone.

"You stupid idiot!" she growled against his shirt, the sound so muffled he wasn't sure he'd understood her.

"Nice to see you, too," he murmured.

She lifted her face away from his shirt, her face glowing with a curious combination of relief and fury. "You were trying to get captured! Have you completely lost your mind? You know Cabrera will kill you on sight."

"He'd kill you and Gabe, too. I wasn't going to let that happen."

"You're lucky that man didn't shoot you the minute he spotted you."

"I didn't figure he would. Cabrera likes to do his own dirty work when it's personal." He smoothed her damp hair away from her pale face. "And what the hell were you doing, following me through the woods like that? If you were in any shape to hike, you should have gone straight back to the motel and called the paramedics for you and Cooper."

"You're my prisoner, remember?" The warmth in her voice was as good as a smile to soften her words. In fact, he thought he heard a hint of exasperated affection in her voice.

"You may need to cuff me," he murmured, deliberately provocative.

Her eyes narrowed slightly before she seemed to realize they weren't exactly alone in the woods anymore. She looked at Quinn, who was watching them with a bemused expression.

"You don't look much like the other Coopers," she said to Quinn.

"That's because he's not one." Sinclair bit back a smile at the way Quinn's eyebrows arched at Ava's acerbic tone. "Ava Trent, this is Alexander Quinn, former spook. Quinn, this is Special Agent Ava Trent with the FBI. I'm her prisoner, it seems."

Quinn's lips quirked slightly before flattening into a neutral expression. "I see."

"Former spook?" Ava asked. "Let me guess. Your CIA handler?"

Even Quinn, with all his years of practice at inscrutability, couldn't hide a flicker of surprise at her words.

Ava's eyes widened as she looked back at Sinclair. "I was kidding."

He shrugged and looked back at Quinn.

"We need to get out of these woods," Quinn said. "Get you all back to civilization and figure out what to do next."

"No," Gabe Cooper said firmly from his position near the other Coopers. "We're not leaving these woods yet. Not until I find my wife."

THE CABRERA SCOUT was dead, taken out by one shot from Rick Cooper's Walther P99. Riley Patterson had been nicked by one of the rounds from the scout's AR-15, but it had caught more jacket than flesh. A large adhesive bandage easily covered the lightly bleeding scratch to his arm, and to her credit, his green-eyed wife, Hannah, seemed to take his injury in stride, as if she was used to seeing her husband under fire.

Hell, Ava thought, maybe gun battles were a daily thing for the Coopers, given the family's reputation for attracting danger.

She was still trying to get all the newcomers sorted out in her head. There were cousins and brothers, including Gabe's twin, Jake, who looked like an unblemished version of Sinclair's battered brother-in-law. He helped his sister Hannah wrap the body of the dead Cabrera henchman in plastic and stash it in the underbrush, while the others spread out, creating a human perimeter around their present position. In the center of that invisible bubble of protection, Quinn quietly debriefed Sinclair and Ava, catching up with all that had happened since Ava walked into an ambush the day before.

She answered his questions, though part of her chafed at being relegated to a grunt in her own investigation. The man was a civilian, for grief's sake. What the hell did he think he was doing, taking over command?

But digging in her heels and trying to assert her command wouldn't really help anything, she realized with frustration. The truth was, she was injured and out of her element. Alexander Quinn and the Coopers had experience dealing with *El Cambio*. Even Sinclair was better prepared to deal with the terrorists than she was.

She was no longer running an FBI investigation. They were running for their lives.

"How many operatives left in camp?" Quinn asked quietly.

"The last time we got a good look, there were nine in the camp. Cabrera and eight others. We've now dispatched five, so eight is probably the most there could be," Sinclair answered.

"It's possible he's sent out other scouts," Ava warned.

Quinn gave her a long, considering look. "Your partner has reported you missing. That probably means we're going to have FBI crawling around these woods sooner or later."

Sinclair groaned deep in his throat.

"Do you have a working phone?" Ava asked.

Quinn's eyes narrowed. "You think calling in is going to put the brakes on the FBI?"

"It might, if I can reach Cade Landry."

Quinn's lips pressed to a tight line, and for a moment, Ava thought he wasn't going to hand over his phone. But finally, he pulled out a slim smartphone and tipped it toward her.

She took the phone and checked the signal. Not great, but at least there were a couple of bars. She dialed Cade Landry's cell number.

He answered on the second ring. "Landry."

"Landry, it's Trent."

Landry muttered a short string of profanity. "Where in God's name are you, Trent?"

"Following a lead," she answered vaguely. "My phone was disabled or I'd have called to let you know."

"There are six agents coming down from Johnson City and Knoxville to look for you."

"Tell them to wait. I've got a peg on where the kidnappers are holed up." That was the truth, at least. "But I don't need an army of suits thrashing their way through here and alerting the perps to our presence."

She thought Landry might argue with her, but to her surprise, he was silent for a moment, then said, "Okay. How much time do you need?"

"A day," she answered after a moment of thought. Surely a day would be enough time for them to figure out how to get Alicia away from Alberto Cabrera. If it took much longer than a day, she had a sinking feeling that Alicia Cooper would no longer be alive.

"I'll try to stall them. Tell them I've heard from you and you're safe." Landry's voice held a surprising hint of concern. "You *are* safe, aren't you?"

"I am," she assured him. "For the time being, anyway."

"Where'd you get a phone?" His earlier concern elided into a flicker of suspicion.

"Long story," she answered.

"You're not alone, are you?"

"No," she admitted. "But I'm not being held captive. I'm with friends."

Landry released another soft curse. "You're with Coopers, aren't you? They're here, you know. Like I warned you."

"I'm with Coopers," she admitted. "And they're good at what they do."

"I won't mention that fact to the suits." Landry sounded resigned.

"Thanks. I'll check back in a few hours to make sure you've been able to keep the suits at bay."

"Your number is blocked. How can I call you back?"

"You can't." She ended the call and handed the phone to Alexander Quinn. "He's going to try to keep the FBI from coming after us."

"Will he succeed?" Quinn asked.

"I don't know," she admitted. "So we'd better figure out what comes next and do it fast."

"What comes next is rest," Sinclair said firmly. "You didn't bring the tent with you, by any chance?"

She looked at Gabe, who was talking to his sister Hannah. "Stashed in the back of Gabe's shirt."

"Smart thinking," Sinclair said with approval as he headed toward Gabe, leaving Quinn and Ava to follow.

"How much has he told you?" Quinn asked quietly.

She glanced at him. "About?"

"His time with *El Cambio.*"

"He says he was a double agent."

Quinn didn't respond.

"Was he?"

"What do you think?"

"I think you have a very adversarial relationship with the truth," she answered gruffly, quickening her pace to walk ahead of him.

He simply lengthened his stride and caught up. "He risked his life for this country's interests. For nearly five years. If you believe anything about Sinclair Solano, believe that."

He said nothing more as they reached the others. Sinclair was helping Gabe pull the tent and Ghillie net from his shirt, while Hannah made soft noises of dismay at the sight of her brother's battered body.

"Those sons of bitches," she growled, holding up the hem of his T-shirt for a better look at the darkening bruise over Gabe's left kidney.

"It's all surface," he assured her.

"We need to get you back to the motel and call a doctor," Hannah disagreed.

"He wouldn't still be walking around if he were badly injured," Quinn told her with an air of careless authority that made Hannah bristle.

"I don't need your opinion," she shot back.

"I'm not leaving these woods without Alicia," Gabe said quietly. "Discussion over."

"We have to assume Cabrera will be expecting to hear back from the man we just took out," Quinn said, ignoring them both. "So he'll send more men out here to see what's going on."

"He might try to move Alicia, too," Ava warned. "If he thinks the camp has been compromised."

"All the more reason to go in there and get her," Gabe said sharply.

Hannah put her hand on her brother's arm. "We're outgunned at the moment. We need to be smart about this."

"She's right," Sinclair said.

Gabe looked at him, a scowl on his dark face. "Oh, good. The dead man chimes in."

"You have every reason to think badly of me," Sinclair

said with a calm dignity Ava wasn't sure she could have pulled off in the same situation. "I'm not asking you to like me. But whether you believe me or not, my only concern is bringing Alicia home safely."

"It's your fault she's in this situation," Gabe growled.

"Keep your voices down," Ava warned quietly. "Sound carries."

"She's right." Hannah's fingers curled more tightly around her brother's arm. "We need to do this the right way."

"And you know what the right way is?" Gabe asked.

Before anyone could answer, Hannah's pocket started vibrating. She pulled out her phone, checked the display and answered. "Yeah?"

After listening a moment, she looked from Gabe to Ava, Sinclair and Quinn. "Okay, I'll tell them." She ended the call and put her phone back in her pocket.

"Tell us what?" Quinn asked.

"Jesse wants a powwow."

"I CAN CALL more Coopers in on this," Jesse Cooper said without preamble after he and Luke had joined the others inside the perimeter, leaving Jake, Hannah's husband, Riley, and Jesse's brother Rick to stand watch.

"We're at a disadvantage," Gabe warned. "They're in a sheltered area. It won't be easy to sneak up on them."

"Understood. But we don't have a lot of options." Jesse worked while he talked, helping Luke and Hannah set up three lightweight tents. Taking a cue from them, Sinclair set up his own tent as well. "We may need to consider negotiating with them."

"Cabrera's not a guy who likes to settle for anything less than what he wants," Sinclair warned.

"And what he wants is to get his hands on you." Gabe gave Sinclair a long, considering look.

"No," Ava said flatly. "That's not going to happen."

"You don't get to make that decision." Sinclair put his hands on her shoulders, turning her to face him.

There was very little moonlight seeping through the occasional breaks in the cloud cover overhead, making it difficult for him to see her expression. But the stubborn jut of her jaw made it clear: she had no intention of supporting his plan to offer himself in a trade for his sister.

She grabbed his arm, her grip strong. "You know it's not that simple. There's no guarantee he'll let her go if he gets his hands on you."

"We can make a straight-out trade part of the deal," he insisted. "They don't get me until she's safe."

"He won't go for that."

"He might. He wants his revenge, and clearly, he's taken a hell of a lot of risks to make it happen. Kidnapping a married couple from a motel and hauling them into the mountains isn't exactly the act of a rational man."

"The dead man had a radio," Jesse interrupted, moving closer to where Sinclair and Ava stood. "Maybe we can contact him that way."

The scudding clouds overhead parted briefly, revealing enough moonlight that Sinclair caught the glare Ava shot Jesse's way. For a woman who'd spent most of the past two days swearing her only interest was bringing him to justice, she seemed pretty invested in keeping him alive.

If only the situation were different....

But it wasn't. Nothing that happened in the next day or so would change the mistakes he'd made. They would never pay for the lives he'd harmed, directly and indirectly. He wasn't going to get a happy ending, and it was time he accepted that fact.

"Why don't we do this?" Jesse said after a long moment of tense silence. "Let's get some shut-eye. Sleep on it. We'll take turns patrolling the perimeter and send out regular scouts to the bluff to make sure Cabrera doesn't bug out on us."

"I'll volunteer," Sinclair said. "I can show you where the camp is."

"We've already located the camp," Luke said quietly. "We went looking for it earlier, while we were sweeping the woods. We have the GPS location set in all our phones now."

Sinclair grimaced. If he'd bothered to keep his phone charged, he might have been able to record the camp location rather than hoping he'd remember how to find it. So much for being his sister's hero. He apparently had trouble finding his backside with his own hands.

"Rest is a good idea." Ava's voice interrupted Sinclair's moment of self-pity. She closed her hand around his biceps and gave a little tug, making him look at her. Her hazel eyes glittered in the filtered moonlight that made her skin look as cool and smooth as porcelain.

"You're going to stay in the tent with me?" he asked.

"You're my prisoner, remember?" A hint of a smile softened her words. "Am I going to have to whip out my handcuffs to make the point?"

"Ooh, would you?" He shot her an exaggerated leer, pleased when she smiled in response.

"Come on." She lifted the flap on the tent and led him inside.

He sat across from her, cross-legged, his knees touching hers. "How's your hip?"

She made a face. "Feels like someone set it on fire and poured alcohol on it, thank you very much."

He didn't like the sound of that. He'd done his best to

clean the wound when it happened, but considering how much they'd been traipsing through the woods over the past couple of days, infection remained a valid threat. "Maybe I should change the bandage. It might be getting infected."

"Not much we can do about it if it is."

"We can get you back to Poe Creek before it gets out of hand."

She shook her head. "You're not benching me on this case."

"Would you rather die of infection?"

"It's not that bad, really." She winced as she shifted position.

"Let me look." Sinclair caught her chin between his fingers, making her meet his gaze. "Some fresh disinfectant and a new bandage may be all it needs, but I have to take a look to know for sure."

She closed her eyes briefly, as if warring with herself, before she unzipped her trousers. Wriggling them down over her hips, she turned on her side, exposing the now grimy bandage he'd taped to her hip the day before.

He removed the bandage as gently as he could, bracing himself for what he'd find beneath it.

"Well?" she asked.

"Not as bad as I feared." The wound, while not appreciably better, was no worse. "A little inflammation, but no obvious infection to worry about. I think we cleaned it up in time. Think you're up for another cleaning?"

She groaned low in her throat. "Oh, why the hell not?"

He grabbed his backpack and pulled out his first aid kit, frowning as he realized he was dangerously low on some supplies. Of course, the hyper-prepared Coopers out there probably had a mini-hospital packed in their supplies if he needed something.

He gathered what he needed and set to work cleaning the edges of the bullet furrow, wincing in sympathy with each of Ava's soft gasps. "Sorry. I know it hurts."

"I'm fine," she gritted. "Just get it done."

He felt almost as relieved as she looked when he patted down the last piece of tape and sat back on his heels. "There you go. How's it feel?"

She shot him a dark look. "How do you think?"

"Terrible?"

She pushed to a sitting position, trying to tug the waistband of her pants back up. But they had become twisted while he was treating her injury, and each tug made her hiss with pain. "It'll be okay by morning."

"Or worse," he warned. "Day two after an injury is almost always worse than day one."

"Thank you, Mary Sunshine," she muttered.

"Here, let me." He tugged her up to a kneeling position. From there, he helped her straighten her trousers so that they slid easily up over her hips.

Her breath burned hot against his cheek, and when he met her gaze, her hazel eyes seemed as dark and deep as midnight. "Thank you," she whispered.

His whole body seemed to contract to one pulsating pinpoint of sensation, his blood coursing like lava in his veins. He felt viscerally conscious of the smallness of the tent they shared, of a turning point not unlike that moment in Mariposa eight years ago, when he'd been forced to make a quick decision about which way his luck would turn.

And despite the myriad reasons why he should leave her again, this time he feared he didn't have the strength to walk away.

# Chapter Eleven

Ava pressed her palm against his sternum. His pulse hammered against her hand, rapid and strong. She felt a vibrant hunger radiating from him, consuming her, swallowing her whole. Somehow, she found enough breath to whisper, "Do you remember that morning when you showed me the canal near the base of Mount Stanley?"

"Yes." His breath stirred her hair, a potent reminder of the way he'd held her that morning on the mist-shrouded canal as they watched the sky turn brilliant colors—mango, salmon, vermillion—as the sun burst over the horizon into the azure sky.

She leaned closer, her cheek brushing his. "Sunrise, remember?"

"I remember." He turned his head until his lips touched her temple. "You told me I was a heathen for knocking on your motel room door so early."

"I was on vacation." She smiled at the memory of her grumpy reaction and his youthful enthusiasm. She'd been angry at him, at first, for dragging her out of bed so early.

And then she'd seen the dark fins break the mirror surface of the canal. One, then two, then a half-dozen, arcing their way through the water in a graceful, soul-stirring dance.

"You were right," she admitted, rubbing her cheek

against his beard bristle again, reveling in the raspy sensation. "It was worth getting up early to see the dolphins run."

He ran his fingers lightly across the skin exposed by her open-necked blouse. "I didn't tell you the whole truth."

Despite the ripple of apprehension his words evoked, she couldn't suppress a shudder of sheer, sensual response to his artful touch. "The whole truth about what?"

"The dolphins didn't run only at sunrise." He brushed his lips against the curve of her cheekbone. His lips were firm, yet soft. She couldn't stop herself from leaning in to his caress. "They ran all the time, morning, during the day, even late at night. I just wanted to see the sunrise with you."

She tipped her head back to look at him. "I've always been such a level-headed person. But you shot that to hell and back, you know? Even after I knew what you'd done, who you'd become, there was a part of me who just couldn't stop wanting to spend another Mariposa sunrise with you."

Sometimes, she'd dreamed of that morning, over and over, as if she could somehow find the right combination of words and touches to keep him with her always.

But she always awakened alone.

He cradled her face between her palms, making her look at him. "Tell me you want me to kiss you. Just like I kissed you that morning. Tell me."

Fear shimmered in her chest, but it was just one of the sensations rocketing through her, and not the strongest. Desire was stronger. Longing was stronger.

Too strong to still the words hammering at the back of her throat. "Kiss me, Sin."

Curling his hand around the back of her neck, he tugged her closer and dipped his head, brushing his lips lightly against hers.

A soft, low sound escaped her throat. Pressing closer, she clutched the sides of his T-shirt in her fists and kissed him back. No hesitation. No reserve. Just a hot, sweet, wet kiss that made her head reel and her heart race.

He dropped one hand to the hem of her shirt and slipped his fingers between her blouse and the flesh beneath, tracing the ridges of her rib cage until he reached her back. "You're so soft," he whispered as he dragged his lips away from hers to press light, teasing kisses down the curve of her jaw. "But you're also strong." He splayed his hand against her spine, his fingers pressing against the muscles of her back. "Fit."

Her seldom-worn skinny jeans might beg to differ, she thought, but she wasn't going to argue with a man whose tone suggested he found her damned near perfect.

"Solano?"

For a moment, she thought she'd said his name herself. But the voice sounded again, a little louder. Just outside the tent. "Solano?"

Sinclair drew away from Ava, his breath coming in staccato rasps. He gazed down at her, his eyes impossibly dark and his expression diamond-hard with desire. "Damn it," he whispered.

"Solano, are you awake?" It was Hannah Patterson. At least, Ava assumed so, since she was the only other woman in their camp.

Ava nodded toward the tent flap. "Better answer your door."

With a groan, he crawled to the tent opening and pushed it open. Hannah stood outside with Alexander Quinn.

"What is it?" Sinclair asked, his eyes narrowed.

"We just got a call from our people at the motel. Someone broke into Agent Trent's motel room and ransacked the place."

Ava groaned. She'd left her things with Cade Landry, including her notebook computer. Had he put those things in her room?

"What that means," Quinn added, his expression grim, "is that Cabrera now almost certainly knows he's dealing with an FBI agent."

Beside her, Sinclair released a soft profanity.

"What am I missing?" Ava asked.

"A lot, apparently," Quinn answered.

"If there's anything Cabrera hates as much as he hates me," Sinclair explained, "it's the FBI."

"Why's that?" Ava asked.

It was Alexander Quinn who answered. "That, Agent Trent, is a long and sordid story."

WHILE HANNAH JOINED her husband and her brother Jake on the perimeter, Jesse and Rick Cooper gathered with their cousin Luke and the others in the center of the small camp, passing around sticks of beef jerky along with a large thermos of hot coffee and several disposable cups. Sinclair poured a half cup for himself and the same for Ava, while she tore into one of the beef jerky sticks.

She looked worried, he thought, and bone-tired. But she was alert enough to ask the obvious question that should have occurred to him. "Is Agent Landry okay?"

Quinn looked surprised by the question. "They didn't bother him. He spotted people in camo leaving your room, but they got away before he could retrieve his gun and go after them."

"And they didn't shoot at him or anything like that?"

"Maybe they didn't want to draw any attention to themselves."

"Did they take anything from the room?"

"Landry wasn't sure what had been in your bags. He

said the computer was still there, but it was out of its bag, plugged in and turned on."

Which answered one question, Sinclair thought. They'd been looking for something specifically about her. "I wonder how they knew she was an FBI agent to begin with?"

"I guess they knew we were in town and did a little snooping around. I didn't even think to check those first two bodies for radios—did you?" she asked Sinclair.

He nodded. "The three we killed definitely didn't have radios on them. But that doesn't mean the others don't."

"How much critical information was on your laptop?" Jesse asked.

"At a glance, not a lot. But it would have information about my relationship with the FBI. They might not easily get into the system, but they could easily enough figure out that I'm FBI connected."

"Maybe that's what they wanted to know," Quinn suggested. "They know someone's out here. I think they're pretty sure Sinclair is one of those people, but they must know he has an accomplice."

"You make it sound like we're the criminals," she grumbled.

Sinclair couldn't stop a smile. "According to you, at least one of us is."

"We can worry about who's guilty of what after we get Alicia out of there." Gabe Cooper's raspy voice came from behind Sinclair's shoulder. He turned to find his brother-in-law standing near the tent where he'd been sleeping, a blanket wrapped around his shoulders. He looked battered and wobbly on his feet, but he shrugged off his brother Luke's offer of help and limped to join their conversational circle.

"Here." Luke unfolded a camp chair and made his

brother sit. "We're trying to figure out the best way to get to Alicia without putting her in more danger."

"He wants to kill me," Sinclair said bluntly, tired of pretending there was any other possible approach to their problem. "He took her to lure me in. So we should use it."

"How? By handing you over like ransom?" Ava shook her head. "That's not an option."

"Why not? She wouldn't be in that camp with Cabrera if it weren't for me. So let's give him what he wants."

"Negotiating with a terrorist never works," Ava argued.

"Sometimes it does."

She was furious with him; he saw the anger blazing in her eyes, turning them as dark as night.

"Agent Trent is right," Quinn said, breaking the tense silence. "Cabrera will just kill you both if you hand yourself over."

"So let's set up an exchange in neutral territory. Open-field exchange, no weapons allowed," Sinclair suggested.

"You're expecting a man like Cabrera to honor that arrangement?" Ava looked at him as if he'd lost his mind.

"He's not going to honor anything like that," Quinn agreed.

"There has to be a way we can make this happen." Tension built in Sinclair's chest until he felt as if his heart was going to implode from the pressure. Alicia had already been with Cabrera for over twenty-four hours. God only knew what he had already done to her. For all they knew, she wasn't even alive anymore, and he was just standing here as if anything mattered besides getting her to safety.

"What if we set up a meeting between you and Cabrera?" Quinn suggested.

Ava wheeled to face the former spy, her shoulders squared. "No way. If Cabrera gets within shooting distance, he'll kill Sinclair and ask questions later. For God's sake, you *know* that!"

"We *don't* know that," Sinclair disagreed. "If there's one predictable thing about Cabrera, it's that he's unpredictable."

"All the more reason we don't risk putting you in the line of fire," she countered, whirling to glare at him. "This isn't a movie. The bad guys don't stand there and give a long speech about their motives before they start shooting. And good guys don't miraculously survive their wounds."

Sinclair leaned closer, touching his fingertips lightly to the curve of her waist just above her injured hip. "Sometimes they do."

"Stop," she growled, although her features softened as he dragged his fingertips around her to settle lightly against her back. "Please."

"I think he might have questions." Sinclair tried to keep his tone reasonable as he dropped his hand back to his side, even though he was chafing against Ava's dogged caution. "He has to wonder if I was the only double agent in his organization. He may think I can finger others."

"Double agent?" Jesse Cooper asked.

Sinclair looked at him, realizing everyone else here, besides Quinn, still thought he was a traitor. Pressing his lips in a thin line, he glanced at the former spymaster, who watched him through narrowed eyes.

"He was working for the CIA for the last five years of his time with *El Cambio,*" Quinn said after a long pause. "It's not widely known, and if you ask the CIA, they'll deny it. But it's true. I handled him during his time undercover."

Sinclair looked at Ava, trying to gauge her reaction. She looked back at him, her expression thoughtful.

"Well, hell." Gabe Cooper was the first to speak, his voice coming out in a raspy grumble. "Does Alicia know?"

"Of course not," Sinclair answered. "I couldn't let anyone know the truth. It could have jeopardized everything."

Gabe shook his head. "She blamed herself for your death, you know."

"What? Why?"

"She says the last time she talked to you, she told you she hoped you blew yourself up in your next bomb."

"Oh." Sinclair rubbed his jaw to hide the flare of old pain that raced through his chest at the memory. "I didn't blame her for that. I blamed myself. As far as she knew, I deserved her disgust."

"She doesn't see it that way." Gabe limped closer, all broad shoulders and belligerent anger. "You have a lot to account for where she's concerned. And don't think your CIA bona fides are going to wipe it all away."

"I don't," Sinclair assured him.

"But they *do* matter," Ava said quietly. "And if it's possible that Cabrera suspects you were a CIA double agent all that time, it's even more insane for you to put yourself out there as a target for him."

"Well, whatever we decide to do, we aren't going to do it before morning." Jesse stepped forward, a commanding presence that even Sinclair, who grew up challenging authority at every turn, couldn't ignore. The elder Cooper had a calm demeanor, an inherent sense of competence, that probably made him one hell of a CEO for a global security company.

He almost gave Alexander Quinn a run for his money.

"Let's sleep on it," the former spy agreed. "We'll take turns manning the perimeter. Four-hour shifts."

"Hannah, Riley, Jake and Rick can cover the next three

hours," Jesse said. "Luke, Quinn and I will spell them at one."

"And at five?" Ava asked.

"You're injured. No guard duty for you. And Sinclair is a target, so no duty for him." Jesse sent Sinclair a look that quelled his argument before he could make it. "At five, we'll regroup and figure out what we plan to do." Jesse gave a brief nod that everyone else seemed to read as a dismissal. They retreated to their tents.

Unfortunately, Sinclair thought as he followed Ava back to the tent, the perimeter guards meant he couldn't easily sneak out of camp to negotiate his own deal with Cabrera.

"You're not thinking of sneaking out, are you?" Ava asked quietly a few moments later as they settled into the cramped confines of the tent.

He couldn't hold back a smile. "What, you read minds now?"

"I read people," she answered, her tone serious. "Part of my job training, you know."

"It's more than your training," he contradicted her, tugging off his hiking boots and wiping them down with a towel from his pack. He picked up her discarded boots, wiping them as well. "One of the first things I noticed about you that first day in Mariposa was how easily you seemed to see past all my outer bluster to the person underneath. It was…disconcerting. And maybe a little exhilarating."

"I didn't read you all that well, in the end." Her quiet tone might have seemed neutral to most people, but maybe he had a little of her people-reading ability as well, for he could sense a layer of pain beneath the words.

"You read me too well," he disagreed, touching her cheek. Making her look at him. "I almost called to tell you I'd go with you on the hike we'd planned that day. I had time before the meeting my father set up with Grijalva. But I knew, deep down, that if I gave you the chance, you'd see what I was up to, that you'd talk me out of meeting Grijalva at all. So I didn't give you the chance."

"I wish you had," she murmured.

He touched her cheek, wishing he'd made a lot of different choices. "So do I."

She closed her hand over his, holding it in place. "So you really were a double agent for the CIA."

"Nah," he said with a smile. "That would be a cliché."

A reluctant smile curved her lips, carving dimples in her cheeks. He'd almost forgotten about those dimples, the way they took ten years off her face and made her look like a mischievous girl instead of a fully grown woman.

Those dimples had disarmed him the first time he'd seen them, years ago on a Mariposa beach. They hadn't lost their power.

He leaned closer, pressing his lips against one of those tiny indentations. "You should get some sleep. Tomorrow's going to be a long day, I think."

She moved her thumb across his chin, her skin making a soft rasping sound against his two-day growth of beard. "I don't think I trust you not to hare off on your own."

He couldn't blame her for that, he supposed, since he'd been thinking of doing that very thing only a few minutes earlier. "I don't suppose I'd be able to sneak past the Coopers anyway," he said with a shrug.

With a soft sigh, her shoulders slumped and she dropped her hand away from his face. "But you'd like to."

It would be easy to back away right now, he thought. Put distance between them, ease the ache of longing that seemed to come with spending time with her. She made him want things he knew, deep down, he couldn't have.

Didn't deserve to have, and certainly not with a woman like her.

But this might be all the time he'd ever get with her. Even if things went perfectly, if he and the Coopers managed to come up with a foolproof plan for getting Alicia back without trading his own life for hers, there was still no chance of a future with Ava Trent. She was an FBI agent and, regardless of the true situation, he was and would always be considered a traitor and a fugitive. Hell, if he just remained a dead terrorist, it would be the best possible outcome.

He put his fingers under her chin, tilting her face up. Willing her downcast eyes up to meet his. After a silent battle of wills, her eyelashes fluttered up to reveal her warm hazel eyes, full of vulnerability and questions.

"I don't intend to go anywhere tonight." He brushed his lips against hers, keeping the touch tender but undemanding. "So let's get some sleep."

She lowered her gaze, turned so that she was lying on her uninjured side and stretched out across the padded bedroll that covered most of the tent floor. Her body rose and fell in a gusty sigh.

He lay next to her, close enough that the heat of her body washed over his own. He edged nearer, until his hips cradled her round backside. Feathering his fingertips down her arm, he whispered, "Is this okay?"

Tension coiled in her body for a long moment before she relaxed, curling herself against him. "This is good," she murmured.

He snuggled closer, wondering with a sinking heart how he was ever going to walk away from her a second time.

# *Chapter Twelve*

The world was dark when Ava woke with a start, chased from slumber by a hazy, ill-remembered nightmare that left her heart pounding and her breath burning like fire in her lungs. For a moment, she couldn't remember where she was or why she was there. A low throb in her hip suggested an injury, and the answering ache in her head suggested a bone-tired weariness.

Then she remembered everything, in a swirling rush, and her pulse ratcheted up another notch as she realized Sinclair was no longer there with her. Which meant—

The tent flap opened, and Sinclair's face appeared in the gap. "The Coopers have coffee going. Want some?"

"God, yes," she muttered, trying to hide her relief at seeing him.

She must not have succeeded, for as he helped her ease her aching body through the narrow tent door, he whispered, "You seem surprised to see me."

She managed a smirk, not willing to let him see just how glad she was to find him still here instead of off in the woods somewhere playing martyr. "Not really. I just figured I'd wake up to find you hog-tied somewhere after the Coopers caught you trying to breach their perimeter."

"Hannah's got a sort of latrine set up behind her tent. Thought you might prefer that to a bush in the woods." He arched his eyebrows at her as he pointed her toward Hannah's tent, making her smile a genuine smile.

When she returned to the campsite, Sinclair had a cup of coffee and a cereal bar waiting for her. There were also more people in the camp, she saw with surprise—more Coopers, by the looks of them. They eyed her with curiosity while Jesse Cooper made the introductions.

"Ava, this is my sister Isabel and her husband, Ben, my cousin J.D. and his wife, Natalie. Izzy and Ben are Cooper Security agents. J.D. flies our company bird, and Natalie is a deputy sheriff." He nodded at Ava. "This is Special Agent Ava Trent with the FBI."

"Don't pretend you'll remember us all." Natalie stepped forward with a quirky grin to shake Ava's hand. She was a tall, muscular woman with friendly green eyes and a mane of wavy auburn hair pulled back in a utilitarian ponytail. "I still get them all mixed up after two years."

"Maybe y'all should wear name tags," Ava answered with a smile as she sat in one of the camp chairs Sinclair had procured for her. They huddled in a semicircle around a small kerosene camp stove that was heating a fresh pot of coffee.

"We'll take that into consideration." Jesse's smile belied the sharp watchfulness in his blue eyes. As she'd noticed the night before, he seemed to carry his role as CEO with him wherever he went, taking charge with the ease of a man used to command. Probably former military, she surmised, taking in his straight spine and broad shoulders. Marine, maybe. Or Special Forces. A man who exuded competence and authority.

Gabe Cooper was looking marginally better that morning after several hours of sleep. Having his siblings around seemed to infuse him with extra energy as well, adding a little spring to his limping gait as he settled in the folding chair next to his twin, Jake. He looked across the small circle at Sinclair for a long moment before speaking.

"I want my wife away from that crazy bastard Cabrera. And it may not be fair of me to say so, Solano, but I'm willing to let you take a risk with your life to get her back."

Ava put her hand on Sinclair's arm and shook her head. "It's not a smart plan."

"With all due respect," Jesse said in a quiet but firm tone, "you haven't actually heard our plan yet."

Biting back a retort, she pinned her gaze on the Cooper Security CEO. "So spill it."

He met her gaze without flinching, his expression hovering between annoyance and amusement. "We set up the exchange with Cabrera. A neutral meeting spot. Armed escort for Solano."

She shook her head. "Not good enough."

"I'm not finished."

Sinclair put his hand on her knee, giving it a light squeeze. "Let him talk. I'd like to know what he's got in mind myself."

"You don't know?" She shot him a look of surprise. She'd assumed Sinclair and the Coopers had discussed everything while she was sleeping and were presenting it to her as a fait accompli.

Jesse walked over to stand in front of Ava and Sinclair. "Solano, you can say no. We'd rather you didn't, but we're not going to shanghai you into playing bait against your will."

"Speak for yourself," Gabe muttered.

Jesse slanted a warning look at his cousin. "We think Cabrera will bring an armed contingent with him, as well. In fact, we'll offer that as a part of the deal—we'll have five armed people escorting Solano. He can bring the same number for himself."

"He has seven men left, if we're right about how many he brought with him," Ava murmured.

"He's fond of even numbers," Quinn said, echoing what Sinclair had told her before. "I'd guess he brought an even dozen. That comports with what Gabe saw before he was dragged out of the camp."

"We figure he'll leave two in camp to guard Alicia," Jesse added.

"Ah," Solano murmured.

"We go in the back door, overpower the two remaining guards and get Alicia out of there," Jesse finished.

Ava nodded, realizing it *was* a pretty good plan. At least, it would be if Cabrera fell for it. And if they were right about how many remaining men Cabrera had with him.

More ifs than she liked.

"Cabrera may not go for it," Sinclair warned, echoing Ava's concerns.

"I think he'll risk it to get his hands on you." It was Luke Cooper who spoke that time, in a low voice that rang with certainty. "I know how people like Cabrera think. Believe me, I've had experience with blood vendettas."

He was *that* Cooper, Ava thought. The one targeted by Eladio Cordero. He'd tangled twice with Cordero and *Los Tiburones* and lived to tell.

"He'll take any chance to get his hands on you," Luke continued. "He won't be able to help himself."

Sinclair shook his head, his dark eyes troubled. "What keeps him and his men from killing the lot of you as soon as they set eyes on you?"

"It's a chance we're willing to take to get Alicia out of there alive," Jesse answered for his cousin. "And we've got better weapons now, too." He nodded toward his cousin J.D., who started handing out rifles and ammunition mag-

azines. AR-15s, mostly, fitted with high-capacity magazines, similar to those some of Cabrera's men carried.
"This should make us at least even. Gabe says they don't
seem to be wearing protective vests, so they're not going
to be invulnerable to our bullets."

"You're talking about a paramilitary assault in the middle of Tennessee," Ava protested.

"Yes. We are." Jesse met her gaze without flinching.
"Can you deal with it?"

As much as she didn't want to admit it, she knew what
he and the others were planning was quite possibly the
only workable solution to their problem. The FBI couldn't
take the same risks to save Alicia that the Coopers would.
And the Coopers were a hell of a lot more motivated than
the government to get Alicia out alive.

"Okay," she said after a long pause. "But I want in on
it."

"You're injured," Sinclair protested, closing his hand
more tightly around her knee.

"I'm fine," she disagreed, ignoring the twinge in her
hip. "And I have no intention of twiddling my thumbs in
the tent while everyone else gets in on the action."

"Actually," Jesse said, "if you're good with a rifle, we
could use another person on the extraction team."

"No," Sinclair said.

"Cabrera won't take women seriously," Luke explained.
"So we're putting all men on the front team. J.D., Jesse,
Rick, Jake and Ben will go with you. Riley took a bul-
let hit last night, so he and Hannah stay here with Gabe."

"Oh, hell, no," Gabe growled. "You're not benching
me."

"Gabe, you're not in any condition to be an asset. You
stay here," J.D. said firmly. "Riley and Hannah stay with

you. You three guard the camp and call for reinforcements if things go belly-up."

"Natalie, Quinn, Luke and I were going to be the extraction team at Cabrera's camp," Jesse's sister Isabel said. She was tall and slim, with deep brown hair pulled back in a ponytail like Natalie's and eyes the color of strong tea. It took a moment for Ava to realize she'd met Isabel before, several years ago.

"You were an FBI agent," she blurted as Isabel's gaze met hers. "We met at a conference six years ago."

Isabel nodded. "I wondered if you'd remember."

Her heart contracted as she remembered something else about the former FBI agent. "Oh, God. Your partner was killed in that explosion in Maryland, wasn't he?"

"Um, actually—" Isabel's husband, Ben, cleared his throat.

"My partner." Isabel waved her hand toward Ben with a quirk of a smile on her face. "Not so dead after all." She slanted a look at Sinclair. "Seems to be a lot of that going around."

Apparently, Ava thought. "So, if I join the extraction team, that's five against hopefully two."

"The more the better," Jesse said. "In case we're wrong about how many men Cabrera has with him."

"Ava is injured," Sinclair said sharply. "She took a bullet to the hip."

"It was a scratch," she protested as the Coopers all turned to look at her. "It's already healing."

Luke gave her a considering look. "Will it stop you from being useful in the raid on the camp? Tell me the truth."

"It's painful, but it's not debilitating. I can do the job."

Sinclair caught her arm and pulled her aside. "It's not just your wound you need to think about," he said quietly.

"If you participate in this raid, you could get in serious trouble with the FBI."

"I know," she answered. "But I can't sit here while y'all risk your lives to get Alicia back. I didn't join the FBI to be hamstrung by rules." She'd been thinking about that aspect of her job for a while now, especially on the days when it seemed she spent more time filling out forms than solving crimes. "I'll deal with the fallout when it comes. But for now, I need to be useful. There are lives at stake. And if we can take out Cabrera here and now, that could save a whole lot of lives back in Sanselmo, as well."

He brushed his knuckles against her cheek, his touch light but the expression on his face dark with emotion. "I don't want anything to happen to you."

"I don't want anything to happen to me, either," she said with a lopsided smile that made his lips curve in response. "Trust me that I know what I'm doing. I've been on raids before." She didn't elaborate that most of them had been carefully controlled scenarios during training. The training was still valid, and she knew what to do. "I can do this."

"If we're going to do this, we need to start getting everything set up now," Jesse Cooper warned from a few feet away.

Ava turned to face him. "Then let's do it."

By 9:00 A.M., Jesse Cooper was ready to make the radio call to Cabrera's camp. The others gathered close around him while he thumbed the speaker switch and spoke Spanish into the radio microphone.

After a long pause, the radio crackled, and a voice on the other end asked in guttural Spanish who was contacting them.

"I want to speak to Cabrera," Jesse answered. "Only Cabrera."

There was another pause before a second voice came over the radio. "I am Cabrera," the voice declared. Jesse looked at Sinclair.

Sinclair nodded, his chest tightening at the sound of his old foe's voice.

"This is Jesse Cooper. We have Sinclair Solano. We're willing to trade him for Alicia Cooper, but we must have evidence that she is still alive and well. Put her on the radio."

"You don't make the rules." Cabrera's tone was pure arrogance, fitting the man Sinclair remembered. "How do I know this is not a trick?"

"We have one of your radios, so you know we've dispatched one of your men," Jesse said coolly. "But if you want to speak to Solano, that can be arranged." He looked up at Sinclair, raising one dark eyebrow.

Sinclair nodded and took the radio. "Cabrera. You want me, you can have me, but only if you let Alicia go."

"Your sister is a beautiful woman," Cabrera said in a tone designed to make Sinclair's skin crawl. Across from him, Gabe Cooper lurched out of his camp chair, held back by his brothers Jake and Luke. Jesse shot his cousin a warning look.

"You're a lot of things," Sinclair said in a voice far calmer than the rage boiling inside his chest, "but you're not a deviant. I have your word as a soldier that you haven't touched her in an inappropriate way?"

"As you say," Cabrera said, "I am not a deviant. She is our guest."

"Then let her go. I will come to you willingly if you let her go."

"I cannot afford to believe you, Sinclair. You have not been the most honorable of men in the past, have you?"

He supposed, from Cabrera's point of view, that fact was inarguable. "I have betrayed you and *El Cambio*. But I'm willing to face your justice now if you will let my sister go unharmed."

"In due time," Cabrera said. "I assume you have an offer more reasonable than the one you just gave me?"

Jesse took the radio from Sinclair. "We'll bring Sinclair to a neutral place in the woods. There's a partial clearing we found last night." He rattled off some coordinates; Sinclair guessed one of the perimeter teams had scouted out a place for the exchange the night before and marked down the GPS coordinates. "I have five men with me besides Solano. You may bring five men of your own. We'll meet and make the exchange."

"We will meet," Cabrera agreed after a pause that lasted so long Sinclair feared the terrorist leader had decided to end the conversation abruptly. Releasing his breath, he sought and found Ava's dark-eyed gaze. Her lips curved in a scared smile, and he closed his hands into fists to keep from grabbing her and pulling her into his arms right here in front of the Coopers.

"Eleven-hundred hours?" Jesse asked.

"As you wish," Cabrera answered. "It would not be a good idea to double-cross me."

Jesse exchanged a look with Sinclair, his expression grim. "You'll have Alicia with you?"

"Of course."

Sinclair shook his head. Cabrera was lying. The question was, did Cabrera know they were lying, as well?

"He may have a trap set if he believes we plan to trick him," he warned Jesse after the other man had shut off the radio.

"Entirely possible," Jesse agreed. "It's a risk we have to take. Everyone in the extraction team has been trained for high-risk situations." He looked at Ava. "At least, I assume the FBI took the time to give you some training?"

"Of course," she answered. "In fact, my first SAC came from the FBI's Hostage Rescue Team, and he was convinced all FBI agents should go through similarly rigorous training. He got our unit into an HRT training course as part of a Homeland Security initiative," Ava said. "It was hard, but I learned a lot about thinking and acting under pressure." She looked first at Jesse, then at Sinclair. "I can do this. I'm prepared."

At the moment, all Sinclair wanted to do was wrap her in cotton and stash her somewhere far from here where she couldn't get hurt. But she wouldn't be Ava Trent if she weren't willing to take risks to help people in trouble. Hell, the first time they'd met on the beach in Mariposa, she'd been helping a little girl find the parents she'd wandered away from. Sinclair had helped her track down the frantic parents and reunite them with their adventurous offspring.

He had to let her do what she was trained to do. Trust her to know her limits.

Trust her to come back to him.

*And then what, Solano? What if you get Alicia back and Ava comes back safely? You're still a wanted fugitive. Remember?*

*No happy endings.*

# Chapter Thirteen

An hour later, Ava slipped back into the tent she and Sinclair shared to find him sitting cross-legged in the center of the small space, his head down and his shoulders slumped. Looking up, he scooted over to make room for her. "How was the planning meeting?"

"We think we have most of the bases covered," she answered, reaching across the narrow space between them to take his hand. "How about you? Scared about playing bait?"

"My idea, remember?" He gave her hand a little squeeze. "All that matters is getting Alicia back to her husband safe and sound. And getting you back to the FBI in one piece."

"That's not all that matters." Her fingers twined through his, her grip strong. "I want you safe, too."

A hardness in his eyes made her stomach ache. "Ava, you know this won't end well for me, no matter what happens."

"Do you have some sort of martyr complex? Is that why you joined *El Cambio* in the first place? Because I don't understand why you value your life so little. You did an amazingly brave thing, working for the CIA the way you did. You probably saved countless lives by keeping *El Cambio* in check all those years." She tugged his hand, her chest tight with frustration as she saw how little her words seemed to affect his sullen mood. "Sin, look at me."

His dark eyes slowly rose to meet her gaze. "There's so much you don't know."

"Then tell me."

He looked away, shaking his head. "There are things I can't tell you because they're classified. And other things I don't want to tell you because they're sources of shame."

"Is that why you haven't tried to clear your name? You think you deserve only bad things from here on out because you made a mistake when you were in your twenties? That's crazy! This whole country was built on the notion of second chances. People can be very forgiving if you give them the chance, Sin. Give them the chance."

"You don't know what I did."

"I'm pretty sure I know most of what you did," she said quietly. "I made it my business to know."

His eyes met hers, dark with dismay. "Made it your business?"

"Not many FBI agents have a vacation fling with a terrorist-in-the-making. It was an anomaly I couldn't resist investigating."

He looked down. "You must have been so disgusted with me."

"I was," she admitted. "And a little disappointed in myself, too. I've always prided myself on my good judgment about people, and there I went, falling hard for a radical with violent tendencies."

"If it makes you feel better, it was the violence that opened my eyes."

"You didn't know they were violent when you joined? You had to know at least some of what they'd been doing in Sanselmo."

"Grijalva sold it as civil disobedience. Vigorous protest taken too far now and then by misguided, desperate *campesinos.*"

"And despite everything in the news about *El Cambio's* acts of terror, you bought that?"

"My parents raised me to question everything, including what I hear on the news. The media is eminently manipulable. Meanwhile, Grijalva was a man of ideas and principles."

"Who was co-opted by men with homicidal intentions."

"Yes. He looked the other way a little too willingly. And he paid for his mistakes with his life."

She could tell from the tone of his voice that Grijalva's death had affected him deeply. "You saw Cabrera kill him, you said."

"I couldn't reach them in time." His voice sounded as bleak as a prairie in winter. "I suppose I'm lucky— Cabrera would have shot me on sight if he'd seen me."

"What did you do?"

"I just wanted to get the hell out of there. Go home and face my mistakes, whatever the cost. So I walked three miles to the capital and turned myself in to the U.S. Consulate in Tesoro."

"Where you met Alexander Quinn."

He nodded.

"That explains your conversion," she said after a moment of tense silence. "But a lot happened in the eight months before you saw the light. You were involved in property destruction, according to the FBI records. *Before* you became a double agent." She didn't know why she was pressing him to admit his crimes; they both knew what he'd done, and none of it was really pertinent to their current problems.

But it mattered, she realized, if there was going to be any chance of a relationship between them that lasted past rescuing his sister. Maybe she was crazy to even think of such a thing, but the truth was, she'd never forgotten Sinclair Solano. He'd been part of her life for years, even after his alleged death. She still had her research notes on his life with *El Cambio.* If she'd ever told her superiors about all the background work she'd done on the group, she might even have talked her way onto one of the FBI's antiterrorism task forces.

But she'd kept Sinclair Solano a secret. Hid his memory in her heart, where it had ached like a splinter for years.

"What do you want from me, Ava?" Sinclair pinned her with a dark glare, as if he could see right through her. "Do you want me to tell you that what I did wasn't really so bad? I can't do that. I designed pamphlets full of pretty lies that led people away from hope into destructive envy. I aided and abetted destruction of property that ruined livelihoods, if not lives. I blew up nine men—and as far as I'm concerned, it doesn't really matter that they were terrorists. I killed them." He passed his hand over his face, as if he could rub away the horror that twisted his expression. "And I made a deal with the devil in order to bring my former friends to their knees."

"I'm not sure Quinn would appreciate being called the devil."

"Quinn knows what he was. What he is."

"Is he why you're here in Tennessee?" she asked. "You didn't come here for your sister—you were already here. No way you could've gotten to that crime scene so fast if you weren't already in the area, especially since you appear to be getting around on foot these days."

"Quinn asked me to do some things for him."

"For his private investigation agency?"

"No, it was something he had going on the side before he quit the CIA." Sinclair shrugged, as if he didn't know quite how to describe what he'd been doing for Quinn. "I was keeping an eye on some bad people. Just reporting to Quinn if I saw something out of the norm."

"Are you still doing that? Is that why you're here?"

"The bad guys are dead now. Anyway, I ran into someone who recognized me a few months back. So I went to ground."

"But you stayed here in Tennessee."

"I like the mountains," he said simply. "They remind me of Sanselmo."

The longing in his voice plucked at the sore place in her own heart. "You miss Sanselmo. In spite of everything."

"In spite of everything," he agreed. "It's a beautiful country. With beautiful, generous people. I regret the pain I caused those people with my stupidity, and I know I can never go back there again. But sometimes, I still dream of the mountains of Sanselmo and I wake up feeling as if I've lost a piece of me."

"I'm sorry."

"Don't be sorry for me," he said sharply. "I made my own bed."

She sucked in a deep breath and took the plunge. "What will you do after this?"

His gaze rose to hers slowly, his expression wary. "After this?"

"When we get Alicia back to her husband. What will you do then?"

"I don't know. Head somewhere else, I guess."

"Why not stick around?"

He shook his head. "I can't clear my name, Ava. The CIA isn't going to vouch for me, and while I might be able to dodge any federal charges, with some help from Quinn and others, my name is ruined. I have nothing to offer anyone."

"Quinn could hire you at his agency."

"To do what? Even if I managed to sort out the mess of my life, my face and name would be imprinted in the minds of the public. What kind of detective do you think I'd make?"

"There are other jobs besides undercover work. You could be an analyst, or—"

He caught her arm, gave it a light shake. "Stop it, Ava. You can't fix me. Don't beat your head against a wall trying."

"So I'm just supposed to watch you walk out of my life again without trying to stop you?" She clamped her mouth shut, realizing too late that she'd revealed more about her thoughts and desires than she'd intended.

"Yes." He lowered his head, his shoulders heaving with a long sigh. "That's exactly what you need to do."

"I don't accept that."

His gaze snapped up, blazing with frustration. He caught her by her arms and gave her a gentle but frustrated shake. "Why can't you let this go? Don't you understand how toxic I am to anything I touch?"

"Don't be so damned melodramatic." She jerked away from his grasp, trying to gain control over her own burst of anger. "Do you think you're the first young radical who's done a few things he regretted? Please. Just look at your parents."

He opened his mouth to protest, but she saw the moment the realization hit him.

"They were part of the Journeymen for Change," she elaborated. "A group who set bombs across U.S. cities in protest against the government and for change. And yes, those bombs even killed a couple of people. Maybe your parents didn't set those bombs themselves, but they supported the causes of the people who did and tried to protect them from prosecution."

His eyes narrowed. "You know a lot about my parents."

"I told you. I made you a subject of study."

"And my sister? What do you know about her?" There was a note of hunger behind his question, she realized, as if he was eager to hear what she had to say.

"She was harder to pin down," Ava admitted. "She didn't live as public a life as your parents. I know she was an excellent student. I knew she'd gotten her masters recently, but I didn't know she'd married into the famous Cooper clan." One reason why she hadn't immediately made the connection with Sinclair.

"My parents must hate that she married an Alabama bass fisherman with close ties to law enforcement and the military." A reluctant smile nudged the corners of his lips upward.

"What do you think about it?" she asked curiously.

"I think Gabe Cooper obviously loves her like crazy, and his family is willing to put a lot on the line to protect her. I might wish her life was a little less adventurous, but that was never Ali's style." His expression when he spoke of his sister was warm enough to heat the tiny tent. "If my parents can't appreciate that, it's their loss."

"I think you should give people a chance to see who you are now, not the misguided man you were eight years ago." She risked touching him again, letting her hand slide slowly upward to rest lightly against his hardened jaw. "And maybe you need to give yourself the same chance. Take a good look at who you've become. Who you are *now* matters, you know. Nobody's life should be judged on one foolish mistake."

"Foolish mistake," he murmured, not moving away

from her touch. His lips curved in a humorless smile. "I think that's painting it a bit kindly."

"I'm not sure it is," she disagreed, letting her hand fall away. There were a lot more things she'd like to say to him, but he already had a lot to think about, and very little time left before he had to go out there and put himself in the crosshairs of a vindictive killer's sights.

She'd just have to hope they'd both live long enough for her to tell him everything else she wanted to say.

In the meantime, she needed to get ready for her own coming challenge. If she and the others in the extraction team didn't do their job, the risks Sinclair was about to take would mean nothing at all.

"Thank you."

Sinclair looked up to find Gabe Cooper standing in front of him, looking even more battered than he had the day before, now that his bruises and scrapes had had time to reach full color. His left eye was swollen to a slit, and he apparently had some swelling in his mouth, because the words came out a little thick-tongued. But the clarity in his blue eyes was unmistakable.

"Don't thank me," Sinclair said darkly. "Alicia wouldn't be in this mess if it weren't for me."

"I learned a long time ago that doing the right thing comes with risks," Gabe said. "From what Quinn tells me, you did the right thing in a very bad situation. There are consequences. But I'll tell you this—as much as I hate the fact that Alicia's out there in trouble because of what you did, I know she's going to be damned glad to know you're alive. And that's even before she's had a chance to learn that she was wrong about you all this time."

"She wasn't wrong. Not exactly."

"I think she'd disagree." Gabe extended his hand. "I

haven't been a fan of yours. I guess time will tell if we'll ever really feel like family. But the fact is, you didn't have to put your neck on the chopping block for her this way. If you were the man you seem to think you are, you never would've offered. So, thank you. And good luck."

Sinclair shook his brother-in-law's outstretched hand, feeling a strange sense of his life starting to spiral out of his control. He'd spent the past six months hiding from the world like wounded prey because a man named Adam Brand now knew he was alive. One extra person in on the secret had been enough to send his high-strung fight-or-flight instincts into a tailspin.

Now a whole extended family would know the truth. His sister would know. There was no way he could ask her to keep the secret from his parents, once she knew—it would be unfair to ask her to do so.

Like it or not, Sinclair Solano was alive and kicking once more, and there wasn't a damned thing he could do to change it.

"You worried?"

He closed his eyes at the sound of Ava's soft query coming from behind him. Turning slowly, he opened his eyes and met her concerned gaze. "A little, I guess. Mostly for Alicia."

"I'm going to be the one to get her out of the camp," she told him. "The others are in charge of taking out the camp guards."

He brushed his fingertips against her cheek. "She'll be in good hands."

"I know you don't think there's any sort of future for you—"

"Ava—"

"Just hear me out." She licked her lips and took a deep breath, looking like a nervous student who'd memorized a big speech and was going to get it said, come hell or high water. "I know you think you're in a dead-end situation. I understand why you feel that way. I do. But you have options. There are people who can and will help you if you'll let them."

"Have you ever considered," he asked, "that maybe I don't deserve anything but a dead-end situation?"

She stepped closer, her voice lowering to a whisper. "Do you think I idealized your memory after you left? Do you think I watched the reports of *El Cambio*'s crimes come rolling across the news feeds and thought, 'Oh, Sinclair's different! He must have good intentions. If only I could tell the world the truth!' Not even close. I hated you. I wanted you caught and punished. I was disgusted with myself for being sucked in by you in Mariposa. So believe me, I've more than considered it. I spent years cheering for your capture and punishment."

Her words rang with truth. And with a bleak undercurrent of old resentment that made his stomach twist into a painful knot.

"But I have more information now," she added in a gentler tone, meeting his gaze without flinching. "And I spent a few minutes talking to Alexander Quinn after we finished our final walk-through of the extraction plan. I know the courage it took for you to stay undercover with *El Cambio*." She lifted her hand as he started to speak. "Just don't. Don't try to tell me I have it all wrong. Do you think the CIA was ignorant of what you did even before you turned yourself in? You were a propagandist. And a bloody fool. But you weren't a terrorist."

"I helped terrorists, Ava. It's close enough."

"You were duped by them into providing aid. That is *not* the same thing."

"People died either way," he growled.

"So to honor their memory, you're going to throw yourself on your sword? How does that honor them?" She caught his hand, wouldn't let go even when he tried to tug his fingers out of hers. "Just think about what I'm saying, okay? We're going to get your sister back. And we're going to all get out of here alive. So you're going to have a future to think about, you hear me? And you'd better start deciding now how you plan to live it."

He meant to let go of her hand, but when he moved, it was to grasp her fingers more tightly in his. "You be careful, okay? Don't make me regret agreeing to this plan."

She rose to her tiptoes and pressed her mouth softly against his. As kisses went, it was quick and almost chaste. But the fire blazing in her hazel eyes when she drew back and looked up at him set off dozens of earthquakes along his nervous system.

"Think about what I said," she murmured, squeezing his hand briefly before she released him and walked over to where the others in the extraction team were waiting for her.

He watched her go, his heart swelling with an unexpected flourish of something he hadn't felt in a long, long time.

Hope.

## *Chapter Fourteen*

The eastern side of the hidden cove where Cabrera had made camp was a gently sloping hill rather than a bluff. Accessible by backtracking through the woods and climbing over a rocky incline for a good half mile, the eastern approach was riskier than the bluff that sheltered the cove to the west. But once Ava and the rest of the extraction team saw their chance to make a move, getting into the camp would be a lot easier than trying to scale the side of the bluff without taking fire from the guards.

Communication consisted of cell phones set on vibrate. Less bulky than radios, J.D. Cooper explained, and quieter, as well. Hannah lent her phone to Ava for the extraction. She was to wait until the others engaged with the guards before she went to the central tent, where Cabrera seemed to be keeping Alicia.

First, however, they had to receive confirmation from Jesse that Cabrera was on the move with his entourage.

They spread out along the slope, about twenty yards from the outer perimeter of the camp, and hunkered down to wait for the signal. All five of them were dressed in camouflage well suited to the terrain and the time of year; even though Ava knew where the others were supposed to be, they were nearly impossible to make out against the scrubby mountainside.

Her hip was giving her hell, but she forced herself to remain utterly still. Surprise depended on stealth. She wasn't going to be the one to blow this extraction, especially not with Alicia's life on the line. Sinclair and his sister deserved a chance to make peace and, maybe, forge a new bond.

She damned well intended to give them that chance.

The phone in her hand vibrated. Slowly, she looked down at the dimmed display. There was a text message from Jesse Cooper.

Go.

It was the signal. It meant Jesse had eyes on Cabrera and his men, and that Alicia was not with them, as they'd anticipated. Nobody had expected the ruthless terrorist leader to actually keep his word. It's why they'd planned for an extraction in the first place.

Like wraiths gliding through the woods, J.D., Natalie, Isabel and Ben moved in a semicircle around the camp. Jesse had armed them with high-capacity rifles as well as pistols, since the guards would probably be similarly armed. Ava's role was to get to Alicia and get her out of the camp, so she made do with the MK2 Sinclair had taken off one of the men who'd ambushed them their first day in the woods.

She heard a shout arise from the other side of the tents. The extraction team had been spotted.

The others no longer bothered with stealth, drawing the guards their way, away from the tents. It was Ava's signal to move.

She ran toward the central tent, staying low to avoid detection and to stay as clear as she could from any cross-fire if the guards began to exchange fire with the rest of the team. Though they were pretty sure Alicia was being kept in the middle tent, she checked the other tents as she went, just to be sure.

When she finally came to the center tent, she paused outside for a second, catching her breath. Adrenaline poured through her, setting her nerves ablaze, but a hint of dread crept into the mix, freezing her in place a few seconds longer than she'd intended.

What if Alicia wasn't inside the tent? Or worse, what if Cabrera had killed her already?

Gritting her teeth, she pulled open the flap of the tent.

Someone flew at her, slamming into her injured hip and knocking her to the ground. Pain flared through her like a lightning bolt, and for a second, she couldn't breathe.

Hands and feet pummeled her, then pulled away. As Ava turned toward her attacker, the bundle of fists and boots coalesced into a slim, dark-haired woman sprinting through the open tent flap and disappearing outside.

Ava pushed herself to her feet and took chase.

"HE DOESN'T HAVE Alicia with him," Jesse warned as he returned to where Sinclair stood near the shelter of a tall maple tree that was already beginning to change color, its leaves taking on the first hints of future autumn splendor. "We knew that would probably be the case."

Sinclair nodded, but the knot in his gut tightened another notch. Now he had to face an almost certain fire-fight while his mind and heart were firmly in Cabrera's camp, where his sister and Ava were in mortal danger.

"Your sister isn't alone, you know." Luke Cooper stood

a few feet away, his gaze directed toward the woods. Cabrera and his men hadn't come close enough for a visual yet, but Sinclair could feel them out there. Ruthless. Relentless. Driven by rage at what *El Cambio* saw as a betrayal of the worst kind.

"I know." His voice came out low and strangled.

Luke spared him a quick glance. "What made you change your mind about *El Cambio,* anyway?"

"Seeing them in action," he answered bluntly. "Realizing just what I had signed on for."

"Rebellions always look better on paper," Luke murmured before he once again fell silent and watchful.

"Tangos five o'clock," Jesse murmured.

Even as his gaze swept northwest in search of whatever Jesse had seen, it took a moment for Sinclair to remember that *tango* was military slang for *terrorist*. Half the Coopers had done time in the military, if memory served.

He spotted the first of Cabrera's crew moving slowly through the woods toward them. It was impossible to recognize anyone from such a distance, so he didn't worry himself with who Cabrera might have on his advance team. Cabrera was the one to worry about.

Three other camouflage-clad men came into view before Sinclair spotted the compact, muscular man bringing up the rear. Sinclair's gaze locked on the last man, certain to his bones that he was watching Alberto Cabrera. The man had a cocksure walk, a powerful, charismatic presence that drew the eye to him automatically.

"Cabrera," Luke Cooper murmured.

"There are only four men with him," Jesse said in a hard tone. "There were five earlier."

Sinclair's gaze slid away from Cabrera, counting the other men in sight. Jesse was right. Four men.

"Either he sent someone around to flank us," Luke murmured, "or he sent someone back to the camp."

Jesse pulled out his phone and typed something quickly while dividing his attention between the approaching men and the phone. He slipped the phone back into his pocket. "Sent an alert to the extraction team." He motioned for Rick and Jake to peel off behind them, in case Cabrera was circling someone around to surprise them from the rear.

Sinclair wasn't worried about their rear flank—he had seen enough of the Coopers in action to feel safe that they could handle anything Cabrera threw their way.

It was the unknown, volatile situation back in Cabrera's camp that had his heart climbing into his throat.

ALICIA COOPER WAS faster than Ava would have thought, fleeing through the thick underbrush with remarkable speed and agility. Ava's injured hip shrieked in protest as she kicked her speed up a notch and set out after the woman she was supposed to be saving.

Suddenly, a flurry of movement in the bushes not far from Alicia sent Ava's heart rate spiking. A man in camouflage swung through the tangle of mountain laurel bushes blocking his way, his rifle barrel rising.

She had little time to aim, but Ava brought up the MK2 and fired a shot toward the man with the rifle. The man dived into the underbrush, swinging his rifle toward Ava.

Ava spared a last look at Alicia, who was zigzagging through the woods away from her and the gunman, before she started shooting and running away from camp in a desperate gamble that she could lure the gunman after her rather than Alicia.

The gamble worked. As soon as she put a little distance between her and the man in camouflage, he came crashing through the underbrush after her, Alicia forgotten, at least temporarily.

She kept moving, flitting between trees to keep cover between her and the man with the rifle, but a few shots zinged entirely too close to her for comfort. Worse, the trees were starting to thin out a bit as the ground began to rise upward, healthy evergreens displaced by dead and dying trees suffering from blight.

As she scanned the woods ahead for her best options, she heard a loud buzz right by her ear. Pulling back, she saw the culprit—a honeybee flitting around her head. A moment later, she saw two more, wheeling and circling near a large hive hanging from a low branch of a nearby hardwood tree.

Hunching her head down, she hurried past the beehive and ducked behind the broad trunk of a moribund Fraser fir several yards up the trail. Breathing hard, she dared a glance back toward her pursuer.

He was thirty yards back but moving quickly. She was losing ground, and her brief slowdown when she encountered the bees hadn't helped.

She aimed her MK2 at the *El Cambio* rebel coming up the hill toward her. "Halt and surrender," she called out in Spanish.

Her answer was a quick trio of shots from the man's rifle, kicking up splinters from the tree offering her cover.

She was never going to be able to outgun him, she realized with a sinking heart. And even if he emptied the rifle, he almost certainly had plenty of extra ammunition on him. She, on the other hand, had only what remained in the magazine and chamber of the MK2. She needed backup, but she'd left the others behind in the camp, dealing with the two guards who'd been watching Alicia.

Her gaze darted back to the beehive again, an idea forming. Lifting the MK2, she waited, her heart in her throat, for the man to slip behind the tree where the hive hung. As she'd expected, he kept close to the trees, using them for cover just as she had. But she didn't need to hit the terrorist.

She just needed to hit the beehive.

The distance wasn't optimal, but the hive was large and its bee-covered profile easy to pick out in the woods. The second the terrorist darted behind the tree holding the hive, she fired the MK2. It bucked in her hand, and for a moment she thought she'd missed.

Then the beehive fell from the tree and hit the ground, splitting open and spilling a cloud of angry honeybees into the air.

She heard the man behind her reel off a rapid-fire stream of profanity in Spanish. Peering out from behind the Fraser fir, she saw the man in camouflage running away, beating his arms around his head and shoulders. Squinting, she could just make out dozens of dark spots flitting around his head, hovering and diving.

Within minutes, he was out of sight, retreating back toward the camp, beating bees off him as he ran. Ava stayed where she was a few minutes longer, just in case he thought about doubling back, then started picking her way through the woods, steering clear of the area near the broken beehive as she tried to regain her bearings.

She'd been running east most of the way, so west would take her back to the cove. South would take her in the direction Alicia Cooper had been running. As she started heading that way, a vibration against her hip sent a jolt through her nervous system before she remembered Hannah's phone tucked in her pocket.

She pulled it out and saw a text message from J.D. Cooper.

Location and status?

She punched in an answer and hit Send. A second later, a message popped up, informing of a message send failure.

"Damned mountains." Shoving the phone in her pocket, she kept moving south.

CABRERA STOPPED FIFTY yards away, barking a command to halt to his four companions. "Be a man, Solano!" he called. "Face me alone."

Sinclair looked at Jesse. "Any news from the camp?" he asked softly.

Jesse shook his head. "Not yet."

"When my sister is safe, I'll meet you anytime, anywhere," he called back. "Those are my terms."

The faint crackle of a radio signal carried across the space between them. One of the men pulled out a radio and spoke rapidly into the receiver. A moment later, the man crossed to Cabrera's side and spoke softly into his ear. Sinclair wondered if they were getting word of the attack on the camp.

Was Alicia safe? Had the extraction worked?

Why hadn't anyone called in yet?

"You're a liar," Cabrera called out. "You will pay for your deception."

Before they could move, Cabrera and his four soldiers turned and started running away, toward the camp.

"Son of a bitch!" Sinclair started after them.

Luke Cooper grabbed his arm, stopping him after a few steps. "We just got the signal. Everybody's clear of the camp. J.D. and the others have Alicia. She's safe."

Sinclair's knees trembled beneath him. He held on to Luke's arm to keep from falling. "Are you sure?"

"Just got the confirmation signal from Isabel," Jesse said, crossing to where Luke and Sinclair stood. Jake joined the cluster as well, though Rick, Sinclair noted, remained vigilant, watching the woods where Cabrera and his men had disappeared.

"What about Ava?" Sinclair asked.

"She hasn't signaled in yet, but they definitely said they had Alicia, and it was Ava's job to get her out of there, so—" Jake paused at the sight of Sinclair's scowl. "I'll see if I can reach her on the phone."

"Thanks."

"We need to bring in the FBI now. Let them round up Cabrera and his men," Luke said. "We came for Alicia. No point in putting ourselves at further risk when the Feds can handle it from here."

"Agreed." Jesse frowned at the phone.

"What's wrong?" Sinclair asked, watching Jesse with growing dread.

"She's not answering any texts," he answered. He pushed a few more buttons. Seconds later, his phone vibrated. "J.D. says she didn't check in when they sent a request for a status update."

"Damn it!" Sinclair scraped his fingers through his hair, adrenaline building inside him until he felt as if he were about to explode. "This thing isn't over until we find Ava."

"Cell coverage is spotty in the mountains," Luke said, his reasonable tone doing nothing to quell Sinclair's anxiety.

"I'm going to find her." Sinclair started hiking south, toward the area where the extraction team had made their approach.

"Cabrera will kill you if he finds you," Jesse warned.

Sinclair stopped and looked back at the Cooper Security CEO. "Not if I find him first."

"I'll come with you," Luke said, starting after him.

Sinclair turned and put his hand up. "Rendezvous with the others as planned. Get Alicia out of here safely. I'll find Ava and we'll meet up with you as soon as possible."

Luke held out his cell phone. "At least take this."

Sinclair took the phone. "Thanks."

"Call if you need us." Luke looked as if he wanted to say more, but Sinclair didn't give him the chance. Picking up speed, he headed deeper into the woods, his pulse pounding in his head.

He should never have let Ava be part of this plan. He should have taken her straight back to the motel that first day, his own safety be damned.

He just hoped she wasn't about to pay for his mistakes.

SHE WAS LOST. Utterly, hopelessly lost.

Ava faltered to a stop by a fallen maple tree and sat on the crusty trunk, wiping perspiration out of her eyes and wishing she'd brought a bottle of water with her. But she and the rest of the extraction team had agreed to travel light in order to move with the most speed and stealth.

Great idea, until someone gets lost.

The sun had been approaching its zenith when dark clouds blew in from the west and covered it. Impossible to know for sure, without the position of the sun to guide her, if she was even still heading south.

She rather doubted it, since she'd been hiking for what felt like nearly an hour without coming across the rendezvous site they'd agreed on. Worse, she was getting no cell coverage now, not even a single bar, and the GPS program utterly refused to cooperate in giving her some sense of her bearings.

Maybe she should just stay put. Wasn't that what the experts said to do when you got lost in the woods? Stay put and let people find you.

The Coopers would wonder why she hadn't phoned in. They'd come looking for her. All she had to do was wait.

Except there were more people in these woods than Coopers. What if they hadn't been able to round up Cabrera and his men? What if he was still here somewhere in the woods, looking for his now-missing prisoner and the people who had stolen her from him?

He might consider an FBI agent a pretty good substitute. A hostage, at least, to get him out of these woods and on his way to the safety of Sanselmo's deep, green jungle.

If she kept sitting here, waiting for someone to rescue her, she might end up on the wrong end of an AR-15 with no way to protect herself but a handgun she could barely shoot straight.

She peered up at the overcast sky, trying to discern a lighter spot, an area that might reveal the position of the sun.

After a couple of moments, the clouds thinned out, revealing a faint hint of blue sky and the unmistakable glare of sunlight somewhere to her left. She checked her watch. Ten after noon. At this time of year, the sun would already be dipping toward the west.

Which meant that south was dead ahead.

All she had to do was keep going straight, and sooner or later, she'd find her way back to the Coopers.

WITHIN THIRTY MINUTES, Sinclair was descending the sloping southern approach to the cove where Cabrera had hidden his camp. He moved slowly, kept close to trees and bushes providing cover, well aware he wasn't as camouflaged as the extraction team had been.

The camp was still. According to the plan, J.D., Isabel and the others were supposed to subdue the camp guards and leave them tied up in the camp for the mop-up. Sinclair supposed it was possible that Cabrera had already found his men incapacitated and freed them, but if he had, there was no sign of them there in the cove.

The tents were still there, however, and for a moment, Sinclair wondered if Ava could be tied up inside one of them, a new captive Cabrera could hold over Sinclair's head.

It wasn't possible that Cabrera knew how much Ava had come to mean to him. But if nothing else, Cabrera probably had a pretty good idea just how strong Sinclair's sense of responsibility could be. After all, he'd put his life on the line for five years to make up for a year's worth of youthful stupidity and destruction, hadn't he?

Cabrera might be willing to gamble that Sinclair would trade himself for almost anyone he could take captive.

The central tent had been the one where Cabrera had been keeping Alicia. If he had Ava, that's where he'd be keeping her, as well.

There was only one way to find out, he realized, his pulse quickening with a combination of fear and determination.

He had to go into the camp and look.

# *Chapter Fifteen*

She was definitely not going south anymore, Ava decided as she took one more faltering step and realized, with alarm, that she was fewer than thirty yards from the sheltered cove where Cabrera had set up camp. The tops of the tents were visible from where she stood frozen in place.

And there was someone moving around down there.

Easing behind the closest tree trunk, she bent down, trying to figure out at what point she could no longer see the camp. If she moved in a crouch, she decided, she could get to the next tree down the slope without being spotted from the cove.

Before she moved, she checked her phone. Bars! She punched in a quick answer to J.D. Cooper's earlier status request, then rose just far enough to see what was going on below in the camp.

She'd been right. Someone was definitely moving around down there, gliding from tent to tent. She caught a glimpse of dark hair, a patch of camouflage, the sharp angle of a cheekbone.

Her heart skipped a beat.

It was Sinclair. What on earth was he doing in Cabrera's camp?

She started forward, then went utterly still, her gaze snagged by movement across the camp. A broad-shouldered man of medium height swept his way toward the encampment, showing no sign of stealth or concern, only a singular, relentless intent evident in his dark face. Though she'd seen only a blurry photo once several years earlier, she knew gut-deep that she was watching Alberto Cabrera heading straight for the raided camp.

And Sinclair Solano.

If she called out to warn him, she might alert Cabrera to his presence as well as hers. But if she remained silent, Cabrera might catch Solano by surprise.

The cell phone she'd almost forgotten vibrated in her left hand, giving her a start. Swallowing a gasp, she tucked herself more firmly behind the tree trunk offering her cover and looked at the display.

The text was from Jesse Cooper.

Your GPS display shows you're at Cabrera's camp. Get to cover and do not move. Cabrera and his men are as yet unaccounted for.

*Tell me about it,* she thought, her gaze moving back to the camp. Cabrera had reached the floor of the shallow cove and was moving without hurry to the area where the tents were clustered.

A crackling noise to her left drew her gaze away from Cabrera. A second man stepped into view in the woods west of her, his gaze on the encampment a few dozen yards down the gentle slope. He had a rifle in one hand, ready if needed, and he spoke something low and unintelligible into the radio in his other hand.

Ava heard the crackle of a radio drift up to her position and realized it must have been Cabrera's handset. She could no longer see the terrorist leader, but if she'd heard the sound, then Sinclair surely had. He'd know he was no longer alone in the camp.

But how on earth could he get out of there without being caught?

The henchman had now moved close enough that Ava could hear Cabrera's reply through the radio he held. Enough of her rusty Spanish lingered in her memory to decipher what he was saying. "The camp guards are missing as well as Solano's sister. I've sent the others out to find them. Join Esperanza in the south. Go."

Though in most cases it was hard to make out nuances through the distortion of the radio, there was no way to miss the anger in Cabrera's terse reply. The man in the woods wheeled around and started back from where he came.

One down, Ava thought, eyeing the camp again. One left. Between them, she and Sinclair might be able to overpower Cabrera.

But only if Cabrera didn't shoot first and ask questions later.

"WHAT AREN'T YOU telling me?"

The rising tone of Alicia Cooper's voice drew Quinn's attention away from the woods for a moment. Gabe Cooper's pretty young wife, though pale-faced and grimy from her ordeal, seemed otherwise uninjured. But she could tell Jesse and the others weren't telling her everything they knew.

"Just tell her," he said bluntly, returning his gaze to the tree line in search of intruders.

"Is Gabe badly hurt? Is that what you're keeping from me?" Her voice rose with alarm, to Quinn's dismay. Despite evading Cabrera and his men thus far, they weren't entirely out of danger, not as long as the terrorist and his crew of bandits still roamed the woods.

The Feds were taking their own sweet time getting there for the mop-up. Not that Quinn was surprised; one reason he'd left a job he'd otherwise loved for so many years was how increasingly hidebound the federal bureaucracy had become, making it nearly impossible to carry out the only mission that really counted—protecting American freedom.

But really—how long could it take to get a crew of FBI agents from Knoxville or Johnson City? An hour? They should already be here. But they'd have to set up a staging area and swing their badges around until they got their pecking order straight, and by then, Cabrera and his gang of not-so-merry men could have taken half the county hostage.

"Gabe has bruises and abrasions. Maybe a cracked rib. But he's already starting to heal up," Jake assured her in a quiet tone. "You know how tough he is."

"I wish he didn't have to prove it quite so often." Her voice lowered back to a soft murmur, almost too low for Quinn to catch. A moment later, however, he heard her voice again from just a couple of feet away. "What do you want them to tell me?" she asked.

He glanced down at her, struck by how much she looked like her brother, despite the differences in them. Solano was tall and slim, like his elegant mother, while Alicia had inherited her father's short stature and heavier build. On her, the extra pounds looked good, located in all the right places and kept in check by her boundless energy and self-discipline. But she and Solano shared the same soulful dark eyes, the same olive skin and raven-wing hair. And in those brown eyes, he saw the same sharp intellect that had convinced him to give her brother a second chance all those years ago.

"Quinn," Jesse Cooper warned.

Quinn ignored him. She was tough and she had a right to know the truth. "They're not telling you that your brother, Sinclair, is alive and he's here in Tennessee."

Behind her, Jake Cooper's expression darkened with anger, and somewhere nearby, one of the other men muttered a curse. But Quinn ignored them, his gaze locked on Alicia's face, trying to gauge her reaction.

At first, there was confusion. "What?"

"He didn't die in the explosion in Sanselmo," Quinn explained, trying to soften his normal blunt tone as he watched her emotions flicker across her face in a constant, changing stream. Confusion became disbelief, then anger, then consideration, and finally, shining like jewels in her dark, dark eyes, the first radiant gleam of hope.

"They identified his body. We supplied DNA samples—"

"I arranged for the DNA to match the body of the cadaver we planted in the warehouse," Quinn said.

She shook her head. "That was three years ago. If he's still alive—"

"He's still technically a fugitive from the law," Quinn told her quietly. "We weren't ready to bring the truth out into the open."

Confusion returned to her expression, and her voice hardened. "What truth? Why would the CIA help him after all he did?"

"Most of what he did was spy on *El Cambio* for us."

Next came the shock, tempered only slightly by a hint of guilt and dismay. "He was working for the CIA the whole time?"

"Not the whole time. But after the first eight months? Yes. He was."

One grimy hand fluttered up to cover her trembling lips.

"The bomb in the harbor warehouse was meant to be his way out. Nobody was supposed to die except him, you see. The other casualties weren't planned. Cabrera sent some of his men to the warehouse early to make sure your brother wasn't pulling a fast one. Seems he'd begun to suspect Sinclair of not being a loyal soldier for the cause."

"My God," she murmured, dropping her hand away from her mouth. Her dark eyes widened as all the implications of what Quinn was saying apparently began to sink in. "That's why Cabrera took me? To get to Sin?"

"Cabrera never said?" Jake stepped up, putting a comforting arm around Alicia's shoulders.

She looked up at her husband's twin. "He never said. I thought it had something to do with the Coopers' problems with the Cordero drug cartel or something. You know *El Cambio* and the cartels are all knotted up with each other." She looked back at Quinn. "Where's Sin? Why isn't he here?"

It was Jesse Cooper who answered. "He's gone after the woman you barreled over in Cabrera's camp."

She looked at her boss, frowning. "The FBI agent?"

"At the time he left, she hadn't checked in yet."

"But if he's still a fugitive—"

"Seems they knew each other before," Quinn said.

Alicia's gaze wasn't the only one that swung his way at his statement.

"Before when?" Luke asked.

"Before now," he answered. "Actually, from what I'm told, they met shortly before he joined *El Cambio*."

"And nobody thought to mention that before we let him run off in search of her?" Jesse asked.

"Would it have made a difference?" Quinn asked reasonably.

Jesse frowned but didn't reply.

"He's out there in the woods now?" Alicia asked, her voice edged with a combination of fear and anger. "With Cabrera still on the loose and thinking he's a traitor to *El Cambio*?"

"Technically, he *was* a traitor," Quinn said.

She nearly growled at him. "Why the hell aren't we out there helping him instead of standing around waiting for the damned feds? Or don't in-laws count as Coopers around here anymore?"

The Coopers looked at each other uncomfortably, as if they hadn't yet realized that Alicia's connection to the Cooper family made Solano something close to family as well.

Jake was the first one to speak. "Ah, hell. Which way did he go?"

THERE WAS NO way out. And maybe that was for the best, Sinclair thought, since the showdown between him and Alberto Cabrera was long overdue. They could end the blood feud here. Now. Just the two of them. Nobody else caught in the crossfire.

Too much blood had already been shed because of the two of them.

The FN9 he'd taken off one of Cabrera's men still held seventeen rounds. It might not be a match for the AR-15 strapped over Cabrera's shoulder the last time Sinclair had seen him, but it could do some damage before Cabrera's bullets could take him down.

It would be a fitting final act to his own sorry life, he thought, to make sure Cabrera never got the chance to kill another innocent.

He crouched low in his hiding place between two of the tents, keeping his ears open for sounds of Cabrera's movement. So far, the terrorist leader seemed to have no fear, no sense that he might not be alone in the encampment. But Sinclair didn't let himself believe there was a chance to take Cabrera out without risk to his own life. Whatever else he might have been, might still be, Sinclair knew he wasn't the sort of man who could fire on someone who didn't fire on him first. Not without another life at stake.

He'd already searched the whole camp. No sign of Ava. Alicia was safely in the protection of the Coopers. And Cabrera had sent all his men into the woods to look for their missing comrades and their escaped captive.

He and Cabrera were alone.

Time to end it.

But as he settled himself to wait, he realized he no longer heard Cabrera moving around. Frowning, he tamped down the urge to move from his hunkered position to see where Cabrera had gone and listened harder for any sound of movement outside the tents.

When it came, it was loud and impossibly close. The harsh, metallic click of a revolver cocking inches from his ear.

"Oh, this is delicious." Instead of Spanish, Cabrera spoke in perfect, lightly accented English. He'd gone to college in the U.S., Sinclair knew, though by the time they'd met in the jungles of Sanselmo, Cabrera had eschewed English almost completely in favor of his native language. But he'd been quick to tell Sinclair about his time at UC Berkeley, where both of Sinclair's parents were professors. Cabrera had taken classes from both of his parents. Sinclair had never figured out whether Cabrera considered Sinclair's connection to Martin and Lorraine Solano to be a plus or a minus.

"Took you long enough," Sinclair answered in English as well. "I've been waiting for you here a long time."

"You have your sister," Cabrera murmured, his voice laced with suspicion. "So why would you come back here?"

Sinclair wasn't about to tell him about Ava. If she wasn't here, that meant she was still somewhere out there in the woods, possibly attempting to avoid the *El Cambio* search party. He wasn't about to put Cabrera and his men on her scent.

"No answer?" Cabrera prodded.

"Just wanted to catch up with old acquaintances," Sinclair answered, starting to turn toward Cabrera.

The hard edges of Cabrera's gun barrel pressed firmly into the flesh at the side of Sinclair's head. "Put down your weapon. Or," he added after a beat, "perhaps I should say Carlito Escalante's weapon?"

Sinclair lowered the FN9 to the ground. Cabrera kicked it, letting the steel toe of his boot thud solidly into Sinclair's thigh.

Sinclair gritted his teeth against a sharp explosion of pain in his leg.

"Any other weapons?"

He wasn't about to let Cabrera strip him of his Taurus. He'd go down fighting first. The revolver gleaming in his peripheral vision would be easier to deal with than the AR-15 that was no doubt still strapped over Cabrera's shoulder, but it would be lethal enough if he lost his last weapon.

Cabrera jabbed the barrel of the revolver against his head hard enough to send pain skating through his scalp and down the back of his neck. He felt a trickle of wetness sliding down his temple and realized the edge of the gun barrel had drawn blood that time.

"Weapons?"

"You're just going to kill me anyway," Sinclair growled, wondering how quickly he could get the Taurus out of the holster attached to his ankle. Quickly enough that Cabrera couldn't blow a hole in his head as he moved?

Not likely.

"What are you waiting for?" he asked when Cabrera didn't respond. "Why don't you just go ahead and shoot me?"

"You tempt me beyond words," Cabrera said sharply.

"If you really wanted me dead, you'd have shot me. But you don't, do you?" Sinclair moved his head slowly to the side to look up at Cabrera. As he did so, his gaze snagged on a flicker of movement in the wooded slope rising behind the camp. Whatever moved went still before he could identify what he'd seen, but he let his gaze linger a moment longer.

"Oh, I want you dead," Cabrera assured him. "I will kill you today. But first, I must know why."

"Why what?" Sinclair asked, softening his focus on the woods in an attempt to spot any further movement among the trees.

"Why you betrayed me."

*Betrayed me,* Sinclair silently echoed Cabrera's words. Not *El Cambio.* Not the cause. But Cabrera himself.

He'd known Cabrera's vendetta must be personal. But he hadn't realized just how personal.

"We were comrades. Compadres." Resentment suffused the terrorist's soft words. "I entrusted my plans to you, and you betrayed me."

"You murdered Luis Grijalva. You stood on the most sacred site of Sanselmo history and took him down like a rabid dog."

Cabrera spat out an obscenity in Spanish before he regained his composure. "He was no rabid dog," he resumed in English. "He was a mouse. A gutless, scared little mouse who lacked the machismo to do what the revolution required."

"There was no revolution left." Just as Sinclair had concluded he'd imagined the movement in the woods, he saw another flicker of motion. A head peeking out from behind the trunk of a tree. Tangled brown hair, barely visible above a camouflage-painted face.

Ava. His heart contracted painfully with a jolt of terror.

She was out there, watching. And if there was one thing he'd learned about Ava Trent over the past three days, it was that she had the heart of a lion and the soul of a warrior.

She was out there in the woods right now, intent on finding a way to come to his rescue. He knew it as surely as he knew the sound of his own voice.

And her lion's heart and warrior soul would get her killed if he didn't find a way to stop her.

He struggled not to let his fear show as he turned his gaze to meet Cabrera's, scrambling mentally for the dangling thread of their conversation. "The revolution was over before I ever set foot in Sanselmo," he continued, hoping the trembling in his legs didn't make it to his voice. To his own ears he sounded impossibly calm.

He hoped he wasn't fooling himself.

"That is a lie," Cabrera spat. "The revolution continues, even today."

"You want power and money. You want carte blanche to punish the world for your shortcomings, to hide your animalistic rage behind a cloak of revolutionary zeal. You killed Grijalva because he reminds you of your own failures. Your own lack of machismo."

Cabrera swung the butt of the revolver toward Sinclair's head, his movement impulsive and made jerky by his rage. Sinclair had just enough warning to duck, the hard edge of the gun butt scraping against the side of his head rather than landing a direct blow.

On his hands and knees, he spared a desperate glance toward the woods, hoping Ava would stay put.

Of course, she didn't. She was already on the move, her pistol gripped in her right hand while she used her free hand to balance as she scrambled in a crouch down the shallow slope.

*Don't do it, Ava!*

He ducked belatedly at a flurry of motion in his peripheral vision. The butt of Cabrera's revolver caught him squarely in the cheek, sending a blinding cascade of sparkling stars across his field of vision as pain exploded through his brain.

The stars twinkled out, but the pain kept pounding a brutal cadence through the side of his face, rolling in syncopated waves of agony.

"I *am* the revolution," Cabrera declared. *"Soy La Curva de la Muerte."*

Ava was getting close now, Sinclair saw as he let his gaze slide her way. Too close. Soon, Cabrera would see her. He would fire on her, and there would be nothing Sinclair could do to stop him.

There was nothing he wouldn't risk to stop that nightmare from happening.

Grabbing Cabrera's arm, he jerked the man around to face him until the terrorist's back was turned to Ava. "You are nothing, Alberto. You are the garbage real men wipe from their shoes."

Cabrera responded by pressing the barrel of the revolver against the center of Sinclair's forehead.

"And you," Cabrera answered in a rush of cold fury, "are a dead man."

# Chapter Sixteen

Ava froze in place, shuddering as her sudden stop sent pebbles tumbling down the hill in front of her. Once Sinclair grabbed Cabrera, turning him so that his back was to Ava, she knew Sinclair had spotted her.

But all rational thought fled her brain in a heartbeat when she saw Cabrera press the revolver to Sinclair's head. His voice rose to a crescendo of rage, ringing through the woods.

"And you are a dead man."

*No, no, no.* She was still too far away, her skill with the unfamiliar MK2 too unpredictable to make the shot.

"Kill me now and you'll never know which of your trusted men is a traitor," Sinclair replied. He sounded unnaturally calm, she thought. As if he didn't fear anything. Not even his own death.

That idea scared her nearly as much as the sight of Cabrera's finger trembling on the trigger.

She made her fear-paralyzed limbs move, took a careful step down the hill. If Sinclair could just stall Cabrera until she was close enough to take a decent shot—

"There is no other traitor," Cabrera declared, harsh laughter tinting his voice. "My men worship me."

"Your men fear and loathe you," Sinclair replied with contempt.

*Stop it,* Ava thought as she pushed her way downhill more quickly, afraid that Cabrera had already neared his snapping point. *Stop antagonizing him. Stall him, don't push him into pulling the trigger!*

"You think you're brave? You think you show courage speaking to me this way?" Cabrera asked. "You are a fool."

She was close. So close. Just a few more yards…

Her foot slipped on a loose rock, sliding out from under her. She tried to catch herself without falling, but her scramble for footing dislodged more rocks, and there was nothing quiet about their tumbling cascade down the slope. They clacked like castanets against each other as she ended up hitting hard on her backside, the jolt jarring up her spine until her teeth crashed together, making her see stars.

When her sight flooded back a second later, she was staring down the barrel of Alberto Cabrera's revolver.

CABRERA WHIRLED AT the sound of rocks falling behind him, his revolver already whipping up toward Ava. She'd dropped her gun hand to stop her fall, leaving her utterly defenseless.

With no time to go for his own weapon, Sinclair threw himself on Cabrera's back and went for the revolver.

The gun fired with a deafening crack, and Ava cried out.

Sinclair tried raise his head to relocate her position but Cabrera had wrapped his arm around his neck and was pulling him down to the ground with him, grinding his forehead into the dirt. Sinclair tightened his grip on Cabrera's gun arm and locked his legs around the man's thighs to hold him immobile while they struggled for control over the weapon. His fingers dug into Cabrera's chest.

No, he thought. Not his chest—

Cabrera slammed his elbow into Sinclair's chin, knocking his head back with a jarring crash of bone on bone. Sinclair's grip on Cabrera's wrist slipped, and he felt himself falling away, his head spinning from the impact. He grabbed at the man's legs just as Cabrera brought the pistol up again.

A crack of gunfire split the air. But it hadn't come from Cabrera's pistol, Sinclair realized as Cabrera reeled backwards, staggering to keep his footing. Sinclair reached for the Taurus 1911 tucked into his leg holster, his suddenly sluggish brain trying to catch up, to tell him something important.

Something life-or-death.

Cabrera didn't fall. He threw away the pistol and grabbed the AR-15 rifle that had fallen to the ground during his struggle, swinging the rifle barrel toward Ava just as she fired another shot.

The bullet hit Cabrera in the chest. Sinclair saw him take the body blow and reel backward again.

But he still didn't fall.

Vest, he thought. He's wearing a protective vest.

And Ava wasn't.

He could go for a headshot, but if he missed, it would be too late. There was no time to aim.

Once again, he threw himself at Cabrera. The AR-15 barked three times in rapid succession as they tumbled to the ground. Sinclair prayed Ava hadn't been in the line of fire.

Then, suddenly, she was there, flinging herself on top of Cabrera's head and shoulders. She trapped the rifle under one knee and clamped his head between her knees, shoving the barrel of the MK2 against the base of Cabrera's skull.

"Move again," she growled, her breath coming in harsh gasps, "and I will fire two bullets into your brain stem. ¿*Comprende?*"

Cabrera went utterly still.

Sinclair wiped a film of blood from his head wound out of his eyes and met Ava's wild-eyed gaze across Cabrera's prone body. "You hit?"

"No," she breathed. "You?"

"Not with a bullet," he answered, poking at the swollen lump on his cheekbone. His jaw didn't feel too great, either.

But he'd live. At least, he would if they could avoid the rest of Cabrera's men.

"His men are out looking for you and the others," he warned.

"I know. I almost ran into one of them." Between her knees, Cabrera hissed something Sinclair couldn't quite make out. But Ava seemed to understand what he said, if the rough jab of her pistol barrel against his neck was anything to go by. "I told you to stay still," she rasped.

Sinclair grabbed the butt of the AR-15 and nodded to Ava. "Move your knee."

She let up pressure on the rifle and he jerked it from Cabrera's grasp. He considered tossing it aside before he remembered they weren't out of danger yet. He slipped the strap over his own shoulder instead.

"Can you grab the phone out of my pocket and contact Jesse?" she suggested, both of her hands still occupied with keeping Cabrera in place.

As Sinclair started to reach for the phone, he saw a half-dozen camouflage-clad figures glide into view, coming at them from what seemed like every direction.

He already had the AR-15 in his hands before the nearest man held up his hand and he recognized the sharp blue eyes of Jesse Cooper.

He let loose a flurry of profanities as his whole body turned into a trembling mass of nerves. "You damned near became a casualty, Cooper."

"That Cabrera?" Jesse asked, nodding at their captive.

"Yes, but his men are still out there."

"Yeah, well, so are the Feds, finally." Alexander Quinn stepped forward, stopping to look down at Cabrera. "You'd have saved us all a lot of time and money if you'd just shot him."

Sinclair glanced at Ava, letting himself drown a little in her mountain-pool eyes. "She did."

"It didn't take," she murmured, her lips curving in the faintest hint of a smile.

"Sin?"

The voice, soft but so familiar it made his chest ache, came from behind him. He closed his eyes against the sudden flourish of pain, almost hoping he'd imagined her voice.

"Oh, my God, Sin."

He opened his eyes and she was there, almost a decade older and even more beautiful than he remembered, despite her ragged appearance, pale face and shadow-smudged eyes. Tears burned like acid in his eyes and he blinked them away, not wanting anything to mar his first look at his sister in over eight years.

"I'm so sorry, Ali," he whispered. The words seemed to scrape his throat raw. "I'm so sorry."

Quinn bent next to him, grabbing Cabrera's legs. He nodded for Sinclair to move away from the captive. "I've got him."

Sinclair rose on unsteady legs, barely able to hold his

sister's wide-eyed gaze. Love and shame battled inside him, two sides of the same emotion, each vying for supremacy.

"Why didn't you let us know?" Alicia asked, tears sliding over her cheeks.

Answering despair roped around his chest and squeezed as he searched for an answer that wouldn't break her heart and his.

"He couldn't," Ava said in a flat tone when he didn't answer. She'd come to stand near him, he saw. J.D. Cooper had taken over restraining Cabrera. "He knew you couldn't keep that secret from your parents."

A hard jolt of pain zigzagged through him at her words. Not because of the implied insult to his parents but because she understood, instinctively, what had kept him silent.

He loved his parents, but he didn't trust them to choose his word over that of people they considered their ideological allies. They'd never seemed to move past their own youth, when radicalism was romantic, exciting and, in some cases, worthwhile.

They'd never apologized for their association with killers, preferring to pretend that the deadly incidents were tangential to the work of the Journeymen for Change and that the widespread destruction of businesses and property their bombs had wrought had been entirely defensible.

Would they choose the side of the son who'd sold his soul to the CIA?

"Of course," Alicia murmured. "You'd been working for the CIA. Martin and Lorraine Solano's son." Her lips curled in a bleak smile. "They'd have been appalled."

"I knew you hated me anyway. I thought maybe it would be best for us all if we just left it that way," he admitted, loathing how cowardly the explanation sounded.

"I never hated you. I was angry and hurt by the things I

thought you'd done, but I could never hate you." She took a step away from her brother-in-law, a step toward Sinclair. "For the record, if you'd told me the truth, I would have kept it from our parents. I'm not blind to the way they are."

"You were so young when I left. I wasn't sure—"

"I never romanticized what our parents did, like you did."

He nodded slowly. "So that just leaves cowardice, I guess. I didn't want you to see what a fool I'd been."

"You weren't a fool." She took another step toward him, moving with care, as if she saw him as a wild animal on the brink of flight. He almost smiled at the thought, because in so many ways, that was exactly who he'd been for the past few years. "You were young and conscientious. Looking for something in this world worth believing in. You just chose the wrong thing. But if anything Quinn's been telling me is true, you paid for that mistake beyond what anyone could have asked of you."

"Don't." His voice came out rough and hard, even though he hadn't intended it. "Don't turn me into a hero."

"Too late for that, bud." Ava slapped his shoulder from behind, making his nerves jangle. "You're already a hero."

He glanced at her, saw the emotion blazing in her hazel eyes, and felt like a fraud. He wanted to yell at her, at Alicia, at all of the Coopers standing there looking at him with admiration and sympathy.

They didn't know. They didn't understand what he'd done.

But he didn't get the chance to respond. The sound of dozens of feet crashing through the woods around them put everyone on alert. The Coopers whipped around to face the newcomers, weapons raised and ready.

"Put down the weapons!" The command filtered through a bullhorn, ringing through the woods.

Dozens of black-clad men and a couple of women circled the encampment, a variety of pistols and rifles aimed
their way.

The Feds had finally arrived.

AVA HAD NEVER been the most patient of women, but her
years in the FBI had taught her that justice had its own
timetable, and it was almost always slower than she liked.
Always before, she'd managed to tamp down her irritation
with the slow grind of bureaucracy and let the situation
play out to its natural end.

But Sinclair Solano was a hero, not a terrorist. And so
far, not a single FBI agent, not even her SAC, Pete Chang,
would listen to her.

"He's not dead, so the warrant for his arrest stands,"
Chang told her in a voice that suggested he suspected
her of having lost her mind during her days with Sinclair Solano.

"Stop looking at me as if I have Stockholm syndrome,"
she growled. "I wasn't his captive. He was mine. And if
you don't believe me, go find Alexander Quinn and he'll
tell you."

"Mr. Quinn seems to be hard to find at the moment,"
Chang told her with a grimace. "And from what I've heard,
he's hardly what you'd call a reliable witness. The man
spent two decades lying for a living."

"Then talk to the Coopers."

"Solano's in-laws, you mean?"

If there had been anything in the interview room to
wrap her hand around, she'd have thrown it at Chang, her
career be damned. "If you put him in prison, he will be
at Cabrera's mercy. You think *El Cambio* doesn't have a
prison network?"

"I know they do." Chang's placating tone scraped

every nerve she had. "I'm sure the courts will make sure Solano's put in solitary."

"He doesn't belong in jail at all!" Ava gripped the edge of the table in front of her, frustration boiling inside her. "He put his life on the line for this country for five years."

"He blew up nine people in Tesoro."

"Nine terrorists who showed up before they were supposed to. The bomb was meant to go off with no one in the warehouse."

"So your buddy Solano says."

"So Alexander Quinn said."

"Quinn again."

Ava clamped her mouth shut. "I want to see Solano."

"I don't think that's a good idea."

"With all due respect, sir, I don't care what you think about the idea."

Chang's eyes narrowed. "You're treading a very dangerous line, Agent Trent."

"Then let me stomp all over it," she said, her patience gone. She pushed to her feet and glared down at the SAC. "I quit."

Chang's dark eyebrows rose. "I beg your pardon?"

"I no longer work for the Federal Bureau of Investigation, effective immediately." She pulled her credentials wallet from her pocket and shoved it across the table to him, then turned to go.

Chang grabbed her arm, jerking her back to face him. "Nobody said you could leave."

"Are you charging me with anything?"

Chang looked as if he'd like to say yes, but finally he shook his head and let go of her arm. "No."

Only because the fallout would be a PR nightmare, she thought with an inward grimace.

"It was nice working with you, Pete. Well, up to today."

She spared him a final, regretful look, and walked to the interview room door.

It was locked, but when she hammered on the door, the guard outside opened it and didn't try to stop her when she walked into the hall.

A half-dozen of her fellow agents and several Poe Creek police officers watched her with curious expressions as she silently walked the short gauntlet of onlookers toward the front exit of the Poe Creek police station. As she stepped outside, a blustery wind blew needles of rain into her face and she remembered with dismay that her car was back in Johnson City. She and Landry had come to Poe Creek in a bureau-issue sedan.

With a groan of exhaustion, she dropped to the top step of the police station's shallow front stoop and fought the urge to cry.

"Need a ride?"

She looked up to see Hannah Cooper looking down at her with sympathetic eyes. "How'd you know?"

"Tiny police station. Voices carry." She offered her hand to Ava, helping her to her feet.

"Don't suppose you know where they've taken Sinclair, do you?" she asked Hannah as they reached a rental sedan parked near the edge of the visitor's parking area.

"No. Alicia sent me in search of answers, but nobody's talking." Hannah adjusted the steering wheel and buckled her belt before looking across the seat at Ava. "I guess you didn't get any answers, either."

"No. Apparently I'm an unindicted co-conspirator to Sinclair, as far as the FBI is concerned." She found the strength to strap the seat belt around her and slumped against the seat. "He's a terrorism suspect. You know as well as I do he could be halfway to some secret CIA interrogation facility by now."

"The CIA knows who he is and what he really did," Hannah reminded her. "I'd be more worried that someone in Homeland Security wanted to make a name for himself off Sinclair's reputation."

Ava groaned. "Thanks. That makes me feel so much better."

"Quinn's gone back to Purgatory. He said he has better resources back at The Gates and thinks he can at least find out where Sinclair is." Hannah was heading back toward the motel, Ava realized. She supposed the rest of the Coopers had decided to rendezvous there once the FBI finished debriefing them.

"Are any of you in trouble?" she asked.

"Our Alabama concealed-carry licenses are good here in Tennessee, our weapons all comport with state and local laws, and the only shots we took were in self-defense." She shot Ava a weary grin. "Plus, our legal team is formidable enough to give even the FBI nightmares. I think we're good."

"How's Gabe?"

"A lot better now that Alicia's back."

"Did Alicia and Sinclair get any more time together before the Feds took him away?" Ava had been whisked into protective custody so quickly that she'd missed most of what had happened at the camp. During her two-hour debriefing at the police station, she'd managed to learn that the rest of Cabrera's men had been rounded up.

A local doctor had also examined her right there at the station, cleaned and re-bandaged her gunshot wound, given her an antibiotic shot and ordered her with kindly sternness to see her personal physician as soon as possible to get a prescription for more antibiotics.

She'd expected a little more pushback about the four *El Cambio* thugs she, Sinclair and the Coopers had killed, but apparently neither the FBI nor local law enforcement was eager to arrest American citizens for shooting foreign terrorists in self-defense. She might yet have to lawyer up, but for now, she knew better than to ask any questions when they were letting her walk out a free woman.

If only Sinclair had received the same treatment.

"No. They grabbed him up pretty fast."

"And whisked him away to God knows where."

"We're going to find him," Hannah said with quiet fervor as she slowed the car to turn into the motel parking lot.

Ava nodded, but she couldn't quite muster up the same confidence. She knew how Byzantine a system they were dealing with.

By turning in her badge, she'd just locked herself on the outside. And thrown away the key.

# Chapter Seventeen

As incarceration on a charge of terrorism went, Sinclair supposed his stay in the federal custody could have been worse. He'd been stuck in the federal prison in McCreary, Kentucky, undergoing intensive interrogation for three days, but nobody had waterboarded him, and any sleep deprivation he was dealing with came from his own copious store of old, familiar regrets.

They had kept him in solitary so far. One hour of physical activity, alone, outside his cell. The other twenty-three hours were spent in his cell, also alone, or across the table from a steady stream of less-than-friendly representatives of a veritable alphabet soup of federal law enforcement agencies.

It came as no surprise when the guard rapped on the bars of his cell around ten on the morning of his fourth day of custody and told him he had another visitor.

The visitor, however, came as a surprise indeed.

"You're looking better than I expected," Jesse Cooper said, his expression neutral but a hint of sympathy warming his blue eyes. "How're they treating you?"

"Like a terrorism suspect." Sinclair took a seat at the table across from the Cooper Security CEO, rattling his shackles to underscore his point. "How'd you talk your way in here?"

"Some people high in the government owe me a favor or two."

"Don't suppose you could call in a chip to get me out of here?"

"I can do better than that. I convinced Gerald Blackledge to give Alexander Quinn twenty minutes of his time."

"Senator Gerald Blackledge?" Sinclair asked. "The same Senator Blackledge who called me vermin in a *60 Minutes* interview?"

Jesse's lips twitched at the corners. "Yes, that Gerald Blackledge."

"God help me."

"That's up to God, but Gerald Blackledge knows a hero when he hears about one. He's all over the Department of Justice to cut you loose and give you a damned medal while they're at it."

Sinclair frowned. "I'm no hero."

Jesse shrugged. "Not sure you're going to convince many people of that when they hear the risks you took in Sanselmo working for the CIA."

"The CIA's never going to let that information go public."

"You're probably right." Jesse folded his hands on the table in front of him, the skin over his knuckles tightening as he leaned forward a few inches and pinned Sinclair with his cool blue gaze. "So let's get to the next part of this interview. Why did you tell the warden you wouldn't see Alicia if she showed up for a visit?"

He hadn't thought she or anyone else he knew would be able to find him this quickly. The Feds had worked hard to keep the news of his arrest from reaching the newspapers until they'd made sure all of the *El Cambio* elements who'd sneaked across the border with Cabrera had been rounded up. But just in case the Coopers were as good as he'd heard—and apparently they were—he'd made sure his sister was on the "do not admit" list.

"I don't want her to see me here," he said.

"She spent years thinking you were a dead terrorist. I doubt seeing you here is going to make her think worse of you."

"She needs to forget she ever saw me again. Go on with her life like it was. She's happy, isn't she? With her work and her marriage?"

"She is." Jesse's eyes narrowed. "She'd be happier if you were part of her life again."

"How'd you find me so fast?"

"Blackledge, again. In some ways, he's more powerful than the president."

Sinclair supposed so. The wily old Alabama senator had been in congress for over two decades, and he had the clout and powerful committee assignments that came with that sort of longevity. "My parents would have a stroke if they knew Blackledge, of all people, had made himself my benefactor."

Jesse Cooper grinned at the comment. "That's what Alicia said."

Sinclair had assumed his sister had informed their parents he was still alive, but if either of them wanted to see him, he hadn't heard any word that they'd tried to make contact. "Do my parents know I'm alive?"

Jesse's grin faded. "Yeah. They're still processing the information."

A kind way of saying they weren't yet decided on whether to forgive him for working with the CIA against a group for which they'd had a lot of sympathy. Of course, they probably still saw *El Cambio* through the rose-colored lenses of their romantic radicalism.

Eight months with *El Cambio* had crushed his own illusions into dust.

"Alicia says to tell you they'll come around. Eventually."

He suspected his sister was overly optimistic. He'd known when he'd taken up Alexander Quinn's offer of an undercover assignment that his parents would probably never understand his choice.

But Martin and Lorraine Solano hadn't stood in the shadows on *La Curva del Muertos* and witnessed Alberto Cabrera slice an old, deluded man damned near in two for daring to question *El Cambio's* actions and motives.

"Ava Trent resigned from the FBI."

Sinclair's gaze snapped up to meet Jesse's. "Resigned? Or was pushed out?"

"Resigned. Although she seems to think they'd have pushed her out sooner or later, since she wasn't going to toe the Bureau line about you."

"She shouldn't have let me screw up her career," he muttered, swamped with regret.

"She said you'd say that."

"Does she know I'm here?" He hadn't put her on the "do not admit" list, he realized. He supposed he hadn't thought she'd try to find him, considering the hell he'd brought into her life over the past week.

Or, maybe, he'd secretly wanted to leave open the possibility that she'd show up one day, flash those pretty hazel eyes at him and declare her undying devotion?

Fool.

"She does," Jesse said. "She's here, as a matter of fact."

Despite his best efforts, he couldn't quell a rush of excitement. "Here in McCreary?"

"Here, waiting in the warden's office."

A flood of adrenaline jolted through him, doubling his

heart rate in seconds. Ava was here. She was here. If he asked, someone would bring her to see him.

He could almost picture her, those mountain-pool eyes, that wicked smile. Those delicious curves he could still feel under his palms as if his hands had perfect memories.

Jesse's eyes narrowed again. "Are you going to let her see you?"

He clenched his fists around the chains of his shackles. "Not like this."

Jesse gave him a long, considering look. "Blackledge won't stop until you're out of here. You realize that, right? You won't be here forever."

"It doesn't matter," Sinclair answered, refusing to let himself hope. "There's nothing for me out there anyway."

"Quinn wants you to go back to Purgatory and work for him at The Gates."

"Sure he does."

"You think I'd make something like that up?" Jesse flexed his hands. "Alicia made me promise to offer you a job at Cooper Security instead."

Sinclair laughed. "Don't strain yourself complying."

Jesse smiled. "You're not really right for the kind of work we do at Cooper Security, to be honest. From what little Quinn has told me, your skill set is better suited to investigation. Our company is security-oriented. We have only a small corps of investigators and no current openings."

"I'm not getting out of here anytime soon anyway."

"Clearly, you've never met Senator Blackledge."

Two hard raps sounded on the interview room door. It opened a second later, revealing Dunn, the guard who'd brought Sinclair in shackles from his cell. "Time's up."

"You won't see Ava, will you?" Jesse asked as he stood.

Sinclair almost said yes. But he caught himself before

he made the mistake. "No. Tell her to go home and for-get about me."

"Yeah. I'll do that." Sarcasm tinted Jesse's reply.

Once Jesse had gone, Dunn escorted Sinclair back to his cell and relieved him of his shackles with another guard looking on.

"Thanks," Sinclair said.

Dunn's gaze whipped up as if suspecting him of being sarcastic. Only after a long, considering moment did his expression clear. He gave a slight nod as he locked the cell door. "Keep your head down."

Sinclair planned on taking that advice to heart. If he wanted to survive life in prison, he had a feeling he'd need to keep as low a profile as possible.

"WHY THE GATES?" Ava asked a few seconds into her slow circuit of Alexander Quinn's corner office. It was a remarkably Spartan space for a man who'd lived such an exotic life for nearly two decades. A plain walnut desk, a built-in book case only a quarter full. No photographs on the desk, only a blotter and a pen holder.

Quinn leaned back in his leather desk chair, his hands steepled over his flat belly. "Adam Brand suggested it. You know Brand from your time with the FBI, don't you?"

"By name and reputation, mostly." She stopped at the window, her attention snared by the striking view of the mist-shrouded Smoky Mountains to the east. "Why'd he suggest The Gates as the name for your agency?"

"Purgatory. The gate thereof." As she turned to look at him, Quinn's lips curved in what passed, for him, as a smile. "It's a bit fanciful for my tastes, but I'll admit it's evocative. A few good men and women, standing in the breach between heaven and hell."

"Think a lot of yourselves, do you?"

His smile broadened a twitch. "Do you want the job or not?"

She turned back to the window, her pulse pounding a nervous cadence in her ears. Decision time. The offer was better than anything else that had come her way in the month since she'd turned in her creds to Pete Chang and resigned from the FBI. The pay was good, the surroundings gorgeous, and Purgatory was actually a shorter drive from her parents' farm in southeastern Kentucky than Johnson City had been.

But if she was serious about putting her feelings for Sinclair Solano behind her, was it really wise to take a job with the man who'd been his CIA handler for five years?

"I want the job," she said.

Quinn nodded as if he'd never had a doubt what her answer would be. "How soon can you start?"

"Tomorrow." The sooner she got her mind off her regrets, the better. Work would give her something else to think about, at least.

And if the mountains cradling the investigation agency's quaint Victorian mansion-turned-office reminded her a little too keenly of her brief reunion with Sinclair Solano, she'd just have to deal.

"Have a seat while I get the paperwork started." He waved at the pair of sturdy leather chairs in front of his desk as he rose and headed for the door.

She did as he asked, though the minute the door clicked shut behind him, she got to her feet again and returned to the window. The sky visible over the mountain peaks was a tumultuous gunmetal-gray, darker clouds scudding across the sky with a threat of rain.

It reminded her of standing in the parking lot of the

Mountain View Motor Lodge in Poe Creek, locking gazes with a dead man.

She closed her eyes as the door opened behind her, not willing to let Quinn see her regrets.

"Oh, sorry, I thought this was Quinn's office—"

She thought for a second that she'd conjured up the deep, smooth timbre of Sinclair Solano's voice. She turned slowly, expecting to find the room empty, the door still closed.

But a pair of dark eyes stared back at her, widening with surprise. Lean features, even more starkly angular than before, softened around the edges as he spoke. "Ava."

"I thought you'd gone back to California. Family reunion." He'd been released from prison over a week ago. The news reports had gone rabid for the story of the terrorist turned CIA double agent, especially when it became clear that there might be a Solano family feud brewing between the new American hero and his parents.

Interest had finally begun to wane when formal statements from the elder Solanos indicated a reconciliation had occurred during a family get-together at the family's Napa Valley vacation home.

"Yeah, well. It got a little frosty among the grapes, so I thought it was time for a change of scenery." His gaze softened as it wandered over her. "You look good. How's your hip?"

"Mostly healed. Looks like there'll be a scar." There was something surreal about hearing the casual tone of her reply when every nerve ending in her body had sparked alive at the sight of him. She felt herself straining helplessly toward him, iron to a magnet.

"What are you doing here?"

"Taking a job."

He stared at her silently, tension building second by second.

"Is something wrong?" she asked finally when he didn't say anything more.

"Quinn hired me this morning. Officially this time." His brow furrowed. "He didn't mention he'd offered you a job, as well."

"Oh." She tried not to feel the sharp arrow of pain that arced through her chest at the wary look in his eyes. "I haven't signed a contract. I can still decline the job."

"Do you want to decline?"

She wasn't sure what he was asking. Or what the brief flare of animation behind his expression meant. "No. I don't. I need a job, and this one seems right up my alley."

"I wouldn't blame you if you'd rather not run into me every day. Considering what helping me out did to your previous career."

Did he really blame himself for her losing her FBI job? "I quit the FBI. They didn't fire me."

"After what you did for me, you didn't have any hope of advancement."

Probably not, considering how annoyed the U.S. Attorney General had seemed about having a senator turn the prospect of a high-profile terrorism conviction into a forced *mea culpa* for arresting an America hero. But Ava didn't care. It was worth everything she'd given up to give Sinclair a chance at living a halfway normal life again.

Even if he didn't want to live it with her.

"I don't think my prospects were all that good anyway." She wished she could read his mind, see what he was thinking behind those cautious brown eyes. "Have you gotten to spend any more time with your sister?"

He smiled for the first time, genuine emotion peeking

through his wall of reserve. "Yeah, I have. She's surprisingly forgiving, considering."

"You have time to make things up to her now."

"I wish—" He stopped midsentence, his lips pressing together.

"You wish what?" She wanted to believe the flicker of feeling darkening his eyes was for her. But she'd already spent two weeks of her life trying to see him when he was in the federal prison in McCreary, only to have him refuse her attempts at contact.

How much clearer did he have to make his intentions before she'd stop wishing for things she couldn't have?

"Never mind." She turned back toward the window, the mist softening the mountains coming from her eyes rather than the lowering gray sky.

"I wanted to see you." The admission came out hoarse. Raw.

She blinked, tears spilling over her lower lashes. She brushed them away with her fingertips. "Who was stopping you?"

"I stopped myself. I thought it would be better."

"For whom?"

There was a long silence, so long she was tempted to turn to look at him. She managed to stay still, to keep looking at the mountains. No more tears fell. She wouldn't let them.

"For you." His voice was closer when he finally spoke. Inches away, not feet.

She closed her eyes, wondering how close she would find him if she turned around. Once again, she willed herself to remain still. She'd made her intentions clear during her two-week vigil at the prison. If he regretted turning her away, if he wanted to change his decision, he had to do the work.

She was done.

"I didn't have that right, did I?" His voice softened until it felt like a caress. "You have a right to make your own choice. It's not like my track record of decisions is anything to emulate."

"I liked the decision you made to take a stand against *El Cambio,*" she admitted. "Would have been nice to know about it a lot sooner, but you can't have everything."

"The danger for me isn't over. Probably won't be as long as *El Cambio* exists. They took a hit losing Cabrera and his men, but there are others like him. There will always be others like him."

"I know. I knew that when I hung around the prison for two weeks hoping you'd be brave enough to talk to me."

"I'm sorry."

"Are you?" She almost gripped the window sill in order to keep from turning to look at him. "You didn't come here looking for me. If you hadn't walked in to find me here, would you be saying any of this?"

"Not this soon, I guess." He touched her, a light brush of fingertips along the curve of her shoulder. It felt like fire, even through her clothing. She tried not to tremble, but her control over her body went only so far.

His hand closed over her shoulder, the grip almost tight enough to hurt. His voice came out in a raspy half whisper. "I missed you. I thought I wouldn't, not after a few days. I went so many years without seeing you that I'd almost convinced myself I forgot you. But I never did." His breath burned against her cheek as he bent to speak in her ear. "I never will. This is probably a terrible idea, and I should probably tell you to run away from me as fast and as far as you can, but I just can't do it anymore. I don't want you to go. I want you with me. I missed you so much when I was at McCreary that I thought I'd shatter."

A shudder of raw need snaked through her, and her resolve crumbled. Whirling to face him, she wrapped her arms around his waist and pressed her face into the curve of his neck, basking in his heat and his strength as he crushed her closer to him. "I missed you, too."

He kissed her temple, her forehead, and finally her lips. What started as a tender caress caught fire and blazed to an inferno that left her gasping for breath and trembling on the verge of complete surrender.

He tore his mouth from hers, cradling her face between his palms. "This is crazy, isn't it?"

She nodded. "Probably."

His lips curved. "I find I don't care."

She grinned back at him. "I find I don't, either."

He kissed her again. She felt his body vibrating with the strain of maintaining control. She wished she had half his self-control, because her helpless response to his touch was embarrassing.

"Did Quinn mention anything about the company policy toward office relationships?" he murmured against her mouth.

She struggled to think. Had Quinn even mentioned any rules? Hell, right now, she wasn't sure she even remembered who Quinn was. That was how completely rattled she was by Sinclair's kisses. "I don't know."

"Doesn't matter. I can quit if he gives us any trouble." Sinclair kissed her again, tugging her closer.

"My only relationship policy is, don't bring your dirty laundry to work, no sex on company furniture and don't let it affect your work." Quinn's voice sent a quiver of shock through Ava's already rattled nerves.

She jerked away from Sinclair and looked at the man standing in the doorway, one shoulder leaning against the door frame. He held a few sheets of paper stapled together in one hand.

Pushing away from the door, he crossed to his desk and set the papers in front of the chair she'd vacated earlier. "Your contract, Ms. Trent. If you still intend to sign it." Without another word, he left the office, closing the door behind him.

"Do you intend to sign it?" Sinclair reached for her again, brushing a lock of hair away from her cheek.

She looked at the papers on the desk, then back at him. "No sex on the company furniture?"

A slow smile curved Sinclair's beautiful lips. "Does the floor count as furniture?"

She smiled at him, her heart galloping like a thoroughbred in her chest. Brushing her lips against his as she eased herself from his grasp, she crossed to the desk and picked up the papers. Plucking a pen from the holder on Quinn's desk, she slanted a look at Sinclair over her shoulder. "Eight years ago, about three hours into our acquaintance, I called my mother and told her I thought I'd met the man I was going to love for the rest of my life."

His dark eyes shined back at her, full of emotion that only underscored the growing certainty that she was making the right decision, not just about the job but the rest of her life. "What did she say to that?"

"She said I should take my time before I jumped into anything." She clicked the button of the pen and signed the papers, happiness bubbling up in her chest until it erupted in a helpless smile. "I think eight years is enough time, don't you?"

He crossed the space between them and tugged her into his arms, pressing his forehead to hers. "I do," he agreed, his mouth brushing hers. "I really do."

\* \* \* \* \*

*Award-winning author Paula Graves's new miniseries,*
THE GATES, *is just getting started.*
*Look for CRYBABY FALLS, on sale next month!*

**"I believe you. Again, I believe you saw a man and heard an engine."**

When she turned her head, her face was only inches away from his. She wished with all her heart that she could be someone he trusted.

"You're the only one."

"When I saw that you weren't in the car, I was scared." His voice dropped to a whisper. "If anything bad had happened to you, I'd never forgive myself."

She wanted to lean a little closer and brush her lips across his. A kiss—even a quick kiss— wasn't acceptable behavior, but she couldn't help the yearning that was building inside her.

"Do you want me to go back to the car?"

"I want you where I can see you. Stay with me."

# SNOW BLIND

## BY
## CASSIE MILES

MILLS & BOON

Published in Great Britain 2014
by Mills & Boon, an imprint of Harlequin (UK) Limited,
Eton House, 18-24 Paradise Road, Richmond, Surrey, TW9 1SR

© 2014 Kay Bergstrom

ISBN: 978-0-263-91371-2

46-0914

Printed and bound in Spain
by Blackprint CPI, Barcelona

Though born in Chicago and raised in L.A., *USA TODAY* bestselling author **Cassie Miles** has lived in Colorado long enough to be considered a semi-native. The first home she owned was a log cabin in the mountains overlooking Elk Creek, with a thirty-mile commute to her work at the *Denver Post*.

After raising two daughters and cooking tons of macaroni and cheese for her family, Cassie is trying to be more adventurous in her culinary efforts. Ceviche, anyone? She's discovered that almost anything tastes better with wine. When she's not plotting Mills & Boon® Intrigue books, Cassie likes to hang out at the Denver Botanical Gardens near her high-rise home.

To the brilliant RMFW romance critique group
and, as always, to Rick.

# *Chapter One*

If ninety-two-year-old mogul and client Virgil P. Westfield
hadn't died last night under suspicious circumstances, legal
assistant Sasha Campbell would never have been entrusted
with this important assignment in the up-and-coming resort town of Arcadia, Colorado. She draped her garment
bag over a chair and strolled across the thick carpet in the
posh, spacious, brand-new corporate condo owned by her
employer, the law firm of Samuels, Sorenson and Smith,
often referred to as the Three *S*s, or the Three Asses, depending upon one's perspective. Currently, she was in their
good graces, especially with her boss, Damien Loughlin,
Westfield's lawyer-slash-confidant back in Denver, and
she meant to keep it that way. With this assignment, she
could prove herself to be professional and worthy of pro-
motion. Someday, she wanted to get more training and
become a mediator.

"Where do you want the suitcase?" Her brother Alex
was a junior member of the legal team at the Three *S*s and
had driven her here from Denver. He hauled her luggage
through the condo's entrance.

"Just leave it by the door. I'll figure that out later."

Before the mysterious death of Mr. Westfield, she and
Damien had been scheduled to stay at the five-bedroom
condo while attending a week-long series of meetings with

the four investors who had financed Arcadia Ski Resort—Colorado's newest luxury destination for winter sports.

That plan had changed. Damien would stay in Denver, dealing with problems surrounding the Westfield estate, and Sasha was on her own at Arcadia. Nobody expected her to replace a senior partner, of course. She was a legal assistant, not a lawyer. But she'd been sitting in on the Arcadia meetings for months. They knew and trusted her. And Damien would be in constant contact via internet conferencing. Frankly, she was glad she wouldn't have to put up with Damien's posturing; the meetings went more smoothly when he wasn't there.

Drawn to the view through the windows, she crossed the room, unlocked the door and stepped onto the balcony to watch the glorious sunset over the ski slopes. Though the resort wouldn't be officially open until the gala event on Saturday, the chairlifts and gondolas were already in operation. She saw faraway skiers and snowboarders racing over moguls on their last runs of the day. Streaks of crimson, pink and gold lit the skies and reflected in the windows of the nine-story Gateway Hotel opposite the condo. In spite of the cold and the snow, she felt warmed from within.

Life was good. Her bills were paid. She liked her job. And she'd knocked off those pesky five pounds and fit into her skinny jeans with an inch to spare. Even the new highlights and lowlights in her long blond hair had turned out great. She was gradually trying to go a few shades darker. At the law office, it was bad enough to be only twenty-three years old. But being blonde on top of that? She wanted to go for a more serious look so she'd be considered for more of these serious assignments. Alex tromped onto the balcony. "I can't believe you get to stay here for five days for free."

"Jealous?"

"It's not fair. You don't even ski."

He gestured with his hands inside his pockets, causing his black overcoat to flap like a raven's wings. There hadn't been time for him to change from his suit and tie before they'd left Denver. Throughout the two-and-a-half-hour drive, he'd complained about her good luck in being chosen for this assignment. Among her four older brothers and sisters, Alex was the grumpy one, the sorest of sore losers and a vicious tease.

She wouldn't have asked him to drive her, but she'd been expecting to ride up with Damien since her car was in the shop. "This isn't really a vacation. I have to record the meetings and take notes every morning."

"Big whoop," he muttered. "You should send the late Virgil P. a thank-you card for taking a header down the grand staircase in his mansion."

"That's a horrible thing to say." Mr. Westfield was a nice old gentleman who had bequeathed a chunk of his fortune to a cat-rescue organization. His heirs didn't appreciate that generosity.

"Speaking of thank-you notes," he said, "I deserve something for getting you a job with the Three Assses."

The remarkable sunset was beginning to fade, along with her feeling that life was a great big bowl of cheerfulness. "Number one, you didn't get me the job. You told me about the opening, but I got hired on my own merits."

"It didn't hurt to have me in your corner."

Alex was a second-year associate attorney, not one of the top dogs at the firm. His opinion about hiring wouldn't have influenced the final decision. "Number two, if you want to stay here at the condo, I'm sure it can be arranged. You could teach me to ski."

He gave her an evil grin. "Like when we were kids and I taught you how to ride a bike."

"I remember." She groaned. "I zoomed downhill like a rocket and crashed into a tree."

"You were such a klutz."

"I was five. My feet barely reached the pedals."

"You begged me for lessons."

That was true. She'd been dying to learn how to ride. "You were thirteen. You should have known better."

His dark blue eyes—the same color as hers—narrowed. "I got in so much trouble. Mom grounded me for a week."

And Sasha still had a jagged scar on her knee. "Way to hold a grudge, Alex."

"What makes you think you have the authority to invite me to stay here?"

"I don't," she said quickly, "but I'm sure Damien wouldn't mind."

"So now you speak for him? Exactly how close are you two?"

Not as close as everybody seemed to think. Sure, Damien Loughlin was a great-looking high-powered attorney and eligible bachelor. And, yes, he'd chosen her to work with him on Arcadia. But there was nothing between them. "I'd have to call him and ask for an okay, but I don't see why he'd say no."

"You've got him wrapped around your little finger."

Alex made a quick pivot and stalked back into the condo. Reluctantly, she followed, hoping that he wouldn't take her up on her invite. Spending five days with Alex would be like suffocating under an avalanche of negativity.

Muttering to himself, he prowled through the large space. On the opposite side of the sunken conversation pit was an entire wall devoted to electronics—flat-screens, computers and gaming systems.

"Cool toys," her brother said as he checked out the goodies. "Damien is the one who usually stays here, isn't he?"

"Makes sense," she said with a shrug. "He's handled most of the legal work for Arcadia."

"He's kept everybody else away from the project."

"It's his choice," she said defensively. The four Arcadia investors were rich, powerful and—in their own way—as eccentric as Mr. Westfield had been about his cats. They insisted on one lawyer per case. Not a team. The only reason she was in the room was that somebody had to take notes and get the coffee.

"Binoculars." Alex held up a pair of large black binoculars. "I wonder what Damien uses these for."

"He mentioned stargazing."

"Grow up, baby sister. His balcony is directly across from the Gateway Hotel. I'll bet he peeks in the windows."

"Ew. Gross."

Carrying the binoculars, he marched across the room and opened the balcony door. "The guests at that hotel are super rich. I heard there'll be a couple of movie stars and supermodels at the big gala on Saturday."

"Alex, don't." She felt as if she was five years old, poised at the top of the steep hill on a bike that was too big, destined for a crash. By the time she was on the balcony, he was already aiming the binocular lenses. "Please, don't."

"Come on, this is something your darling Damien probably does every night before he goes to bed."

"No way. And he's not my darling Damien."

"I've heard otherwise." He continued to stare through the binoculars. "I'm actually kind of proud. Kudos, Sasha. You're sleeping your way to the top."

She wasn't surprised by gossip from the office staff, but Alex was her brother. He was supposed to be on her side. "I'm not having sex with Damien."

"Don't play innocent with me. I'm your brother. I know better. I remember what happened with Jason Foley."

Jason had been her first love in high school, and she'd broken up with him before they'd gone all the way. But that wasn't the story he'd told. Jason had blabbed to the whole school that she had sex with him. He'd destroyed her reputation and had written a song about it. "How could you—?"

"Trashy Sasha." Her brother recalled the title to the song. "No big deal. You could do a lot worse than Damien Loughlin."

"That's enough. You should go. Now."

He lowered the binoculars and scowled disapprovingly at her. "Even if you weren't having sex with him, what did you think was going to happen this week? You were going to stay here alone with him."

"It's a five-bedroom condo. I have my own bedroom, bathroom and a door that locks." And she didn't have to justify her behavior. "I want you to leave, Alex."

"Fine." He set the binoculars down, stuck his hands into his overcoat pockets and left the balcony.

She followed him across the condo, fighting the urge to kick him in the butt. Why did he always have to be so mean? Alex was the only person in her family who still lived in Denver, and they worked in the same office. Would it kill him to be someone she could turn to?

At the door, Alex pivoted to face her. "I'm sorry. I shouldn't have said anything."

"You got that right."

"You're too damn naive, Sasha. You look around and see rainbows. I see the coming storm. This condo is a first-class bachelor pad, and Damien is a smooth operator. You'd better be careful, sis."

"Goodbye, Alex."

As soon as the door closed behind him, she flipped the

dead bolt, grabbed the handle on her suitcase and wheeled it across the condo into the first bedroom she found in the hallway. Her brother was a weasel for trying to make her feel guilty when she had every reason to be happy about this assignment. The fact that Damien and the other partners trusted her enough to let her take notes at these meetings was a huge vote of confidence. She wasn't going to be a paralegal for the rest of her career, and she'd need the support of the firm to take classes and get the training she needed to become a mediator.

She unpacked quickly. In the closet, she hung the garment bag with the dress she'd be wearing to the gala—a black gown with a deeply plunging neckline. Too plunging? Was she unconsciously flirting? Well, what was she supposed to do? Shuffle around in a burka?

Across the hall from her bedroom, she found a hot tub in a paneled room with tons of windows and leafy green plants. Damien had mentioned the hot tub, and the idea of a long, soothing soak was one of the reasons she'd agreed to this trip. She'd even brought her bathing suit. Following posted instructions, she turned on the heat for the water.

On her way to the kitchen, she paused in the dining area by the back windows. On a bookshelf, under a signed serigraph of a skier by LeRoy Neiman, was a remote control. She punched the top button and smooth, sultry jazz came on. Another remote button dimmed the lights. Another turned on the electric fireplace in the conversation pit. Though she didn't want to think of this condo as a bachelor pad, the lighting and sexy music set a classic mood for seduction.

In the kitchen, she checked out the fridge. The lower shelf held four bottles of pricey champagne. Not a good sign. It was beginning to look as if Alex the grump had been right, and Damien had more than business on his mind.

She should have seen it coming. This was Jason Foley all over again, strumming his twelve-string and singing about Trashy Sasha. If she wanted to squash rumors before they started, she'd get a room at the hotel. As if she could afford to stay there. And why should she run off with her tail between her legs? She hadn't done anything to be ashamed of.

Her fingers wrapped around the neck of a champagne bottle. She was here and might as well enjoy it. She popped the cork and poured the bubbly liquid into a handy crystal flute that Damien had probably used a million times to seduce hapless ladies. And why not? He was single, and they were consenting adults.

"Here's to you." She raised her glass in toast to her absent boss and took a sip. "This is one consenting adult you're not going to bed with."

Taking the champagne with her, she changed into her bathing suit and went to the hot tub, where she soaked and drank. All she had to do was just say no. If people wanted to think the worst, that was their problem.

The windows above the hot tub looked out on a pristine night sky. As she gazed at the moon and stars, her vision blurred. Was she getting drunk? *Oh, good. Real professional.* Clearly, three glasses of champagne were enough.

Leaving the tub, she slipped into a white terry-cloth bathrobe that had been hanging on a peg. Though she wasn't really hungry, she ought to eat. But first she needed to retrieve the binoculars Alex had left on the balcony.

After a detour to the bedroom, where she stuck her feet into her cozy faux-fur boots, she crossed the room and opened the balcony door. The bracing cold smacked her in the face, but she was still warm from the hot tub and the champagne. She picked up the binoculars. Even if Damien was a womanizer, it was ridiculous to think that he might be a Peeping Tom. He probably couldn't see into the hotel at all.

Holding the binoculars to her eyes, she adjusted the knobs and focused on the nine-story building that was a couple of hundred yards away. Only half the windows were lit. The hotel guests might be out for a late dinner. Or maybe the rooms were vacant. The resort wouldn't officially be open until after the Saturday-night gala.

Her sight line into one of the floor-to-ceiling windows was incredibly clear. She saw a couple of beautiful people sitting at a table, eating and drinking. The woman had long black hair and was wearing a white jumpsuit, an elaborate gold necklace draped across her cleavage. She was stunning. The man appeared to be an average guy with dark hair and a black turtleneck. Sasha's view of him was obscured by a ficus tree.

Spying on them ranked high on the creepiness scale, but the peek into someone else's life was kind of fascinating. Sasha noticed they weren't talking much, and she wondered if they'd been together for a long time and were so comfortable with each other that words were unnecessary. Someday she hoped to have a sophisticated relationship like that. Or maybe not. Silence was boring.

Despite telling herself to stop spying, she switched to a different window on another floor, where two men were watching television. In another room, a woman was doing yoga, moving into Downward-Facing Dog pose. Apparently, the floor-to-ceiling windows were in only the front room, which was fine with Sasha. She had no intention of peering into bedrooms.

A shiver went through her. It was cold. She should go back inside. But she wanted one last peek at the dark-haired woman and her male companion. They were standing on opposite sides of the small table. The woman threw her hands in the air. Even at this distance, Sasha could tell she was angry.

Her companion turned his back on her as if to walk away. The woman chased after him and shoved his shoulder. When he turned, Sasha caught a clear glimpse of his face. It lasted only a second but she could see his fury as he grabbed the woman's wrist.

Sasha couldn't see exactly what happened, but when the woman staggered backward, the front of her white jumpsuit was red with blood. Before she fell to the floor, he picked her up in his arms and carried her out of Sasha's sight.

She'd witnessed an assault, possibly a murder. That woman needed her help. She dashed into the condo and called 911.

The phone rang only four times but it seemed like an eternity. When Sasha glanced over her shoulder to the balcony, she noticed the lights had gone out in the would-be murder room. Had she been looking at the fifth floor or the sixth?

When the dispatcher finally picked up, Sasha babbled, "I saw a woman get attacked. She's bleeding."

"What is your location?"

Sasha rattled off the address and added, "The woman, the victim, isn't here. She's at the Gateway Hotel."

"Room number?"

"I don't know." There was no way to explain without mentioning the binoculars. "It's complicated. This woman, she has on a white jumpsuit. You've got to send an ambulance."

"To what location?"

"The hotel."

"What room number?"

"I already told you. I don't know."

"Ma'am, have you been drinking?"

The emergency operator didn't believe her, and Sasha didn't blame her. But she couldn't ignore what she'd witnessed. If she had to knock on every door to every room in that hotel, she'd find that woman.

## Chapter Two

Responding to a 911 call, Deputy Brady Ellis drove fast through the Apollo condo complex. His blue-and-red lights flashed against the snow-covered three-story buildings, and his siren blared. From what the dispatcher had told him, the caller had allegedly witnessed an assault at the Gateway Hotel, which seemed unlikely because the hotel was a distance away from the condos. The dispatcher had also mentioned that the caller sounded intoxicated. This 911 call might be somebody's idea of a joke. It didn't matter. Until he knew otherwise, Brady would treat the situation as a bona fide emergency.

He parked his SUV with the Summit County Sheriff logo emblazoned on the door in the parking lot and jogged up the shoveled sidewalk to the entryway. Five years ago, when he first started working for the sheriff's department, this land had been nothing but trees and rocks that belonged to his uncle Dooley. These acres hadn't been much use to Dooley; they were across the road from his primary cattle ranch and too close to the small town of Arcadia for grazing. When Dooley had gotten a chance to sell for a big profit, he'd jumped on it.

Some folks in the area hated the fancy ski resort that had mushroomed across the valley, but Brady wasn't one of them. Without the new development, Arcadia would have turned into a ghost town populated by coyotes and chipmunks. The influx of tourists brought much-needed business and cash flow.

The downside was the 250 percent increase in the crime rate, which was no big surprise. Crime was what happened when people moved in. Coyotes and chipmunks were less inclined to break the law.

Outside the condo entryway was a buzzer. He pressed the button for Samuels, Sorenson and Smith, which was on the third floor. When a woman answered, he identified himself. "Deputy Brady Ellis, sheriff's department."

"You got here fast," she said. "I'll buzz you in."

When the door hummed, he pushed it open. Instead of taking the elevator, Brady climbed the wide staircase. On the third floor, a short blonde woman stood waiting in the open doorway. She wore black furry boots, a white terrycloth bathrobe cinched tight around her waist and not much else. She grabbed his arm and pulled him into the condo. "We've got to hurry."

He closed the door and scanned the interior, noticing the half-empty bottle of champagne. "Is anyone here with you?"

"I'm alone." Her blue eyes were too bright, and her cheeks were flushed. Brady concurred with the dispatcher's opinion that this woman had been drinking. "What's your name?"

"Sasha Campbell." She hadn't released her hold on his arm and was dragging him toward the windows—attempting to drag him was more accurate. He was six feet four inches tall and solidly built. This little lady wasn't physically capable of shoving him from place to place.

"Ms. Campbell," he said in a deep voice to compel her attention. "I need to ask you a few questions."

"Okay, sure." She dropped his arm and stared up at

him. "We need to move fast. This is literally a matter of life and death."

Though he wasn't sure if she was drunk or crazy, he recognized her determination and her fear. Those feelings were real. "Is this your condo?"

"I wish." Her robe gaped and he caught a glimpse of an orange bikini top inside. "I work for a law firm, and the condo belongs to them. I'm staying here while I attend meetings."

"You're a lawyer?"

"Wrong again. I'm a legal assistant right now, but I'm going to school to learn how to become a mediator and…" She stamped her furry boot. "Sorry, when I get nervous I talk too much. And there isn't time. Oh, God, there isn't time."

He responded to her sense of urgency. "Tell me what happened."

"It's easier if I show you. Come out here." She led him onto the balcony and slapped a pair of binoculars into his hand. "I was looking through those at the hotel, and I witnessed an attack. There was a lot of blood. Now do you understand? This woman might be bleeding to death while we stand here."

He held the binoculars to his eyes and adjusted the focus. The view into the hotel rooms was crystal clear. As unlikely as her story sounded, it was possible.

"Exactly what did you see?"

"Let's go back inside. It's freezing out here." She bustled into the condo, rubbing her hands together for warmth. "Okay, there was a black-haired woman in a white jumpsuit sitting at a table opposite a guy I couldn't see as well, because there was a plant in the way. I think he was wearing a turtleneck. And I think he had brown hair. That's right, brown hair. She had a gold necklace. They were eating. Then I looked away. Then I looked back."

As she spoke, her head whipped to the right and then to the left, mimicking her words. Her long blond hair flipped back and forth. "Go on," he said.

"The woman was standing, gesturing. She seemed angry. The guy came at her. I could only see his back. When the woman stepped away, there was blood on the front of her white jumpsuit. A lot of blood." Sasha paused. Her lower lip quivered. "The man caught her before she fell, and that was when I got a clear look at his face."

"Would you recognize him again?"

"I think so."

The details in her account made him think that she actually had seen something. The explanation might turn out to be more innocent than she suspected, but further investigation was necessary. "Do you know which room it was?"

She shook her head. "They turned out the lights. I'm not even sure it was the fifth floor or the sixth. Not the corner room but one or two down from it."

"I want you to remember everything you told me. Later I'll need for you to write out your statement. But right now I want you to come with me to the hotel."

For the first time since he'd come into the condo, she grinned. Her whole face lit up, and he felt a wave of pure sunshine washing toward him. He stared at her soft pink mouth as she spoke. "You believe me."

"Why wouldn't I?" Immediately, he reined in his attraction toward her. She was a witness, nothing more.

"I don't know. It just seems... I don't know."

"Are you telling me the truth?"

"Yes."

"Get dressed."

She turned on her heel and dashed across the condo to

the hallway. He heard the sound of a door closing. As he moved toward the exit, he checked out the high-end furnishings and electronics. Bubbly little Sasha seemed too lively, energetic and youthful to be comfortable with these polished surroundings. She lacked the sophistication that he associated with high-priced attorneys.

It bothered him that she'd expected he wouldn't believe her statement. Even though she'd related her account of the assault with clear details, she seemed unsure of herself. That hesitant attitude didn't work for him. He was about to go to the hotel and ask questions that would inconvenience the staff and guests. Brady needed for Sasha to be a credible witness.

When she bounded down the hallway in red jeans and a black parka with fake fur around the collar, she looked presentable, especially since she'd ditched the fuzzy boots for a sensible pair of hiking shoes. Then she put on a white knit cap with a goofy pom-pom on top and gave him one of those huge smiles. Damn, she was cute with her rosy cheeks and button nose. As he looked at her, something inside him melted.

If they'd been going on a sleigh ride or a hike, he would have been happy to have her as his companion. But Sasha wasn't his first choice as a witness. At the hotel, he'd try to avoid mentioning that she'd been peeping at the hotel through binoculars.

Sasha climbed into the passenger side of the SUV and fastened her seat belt. A combination of excitement and dread churned through her veins. She was scared about what she'd seen and fearful about what might have happened to the woman in white. At the same time, she was glad to be able to help. Because of the circumstance— a strange, unlikely moment when she'd peeked through those binoculars at precisely the right time—she might save that woman's life.

She glanced toward Deputy Brady. "Is this what it feels like to be a cop?"

"I don't know what you mean."

"My pulse is racing. That's the adrenaline, right? And I'm tingling all over."

"Could be the champagne," he said drily.

She'd all but forgotten the three glasses of champagne she'd had in the hot tub. "I've been drunk before, and it doesn't feel anything like this."

When Brady turned on the flashing lights and the wailing siren, her excitement ratcheted up higher. This was serious business, police business. They were about to make a difference in someone's life, pursuing a would-be killer, rescuing a victim.

Her emotions popped like fireworks in contrast to Brady's absolute calm. He was a big man—solid and capable. His jawline and cleft chin seemed to be set in granite in spite of a dimple at the left corner of his mouth. His hazel eyes were steady and cool. In spite of the sheriff's department logo on the sleeve of his dark blue jacket and the gun holster on his belt next to his badge, he didn't look much like a cop. He wore dark brown boots and jeans and a black cowboy hat. The hat made her think he might be a local.

She raised her voice so he could hear her over the siren. "Have you lived in Arcadia long?"

"Born and raised," he said. "My uncle Dooley owned the land where your condo, the hotel and the ski lodge are built."

"You're related to Matthew Dooley?"

"I am."

That wily old rancher was one of the four investors in

the Arcadia development. Dooley was big and rangy, much like Brady, and he always wore a cowboy hat and bolo tie. During most of the meetings in the conference room at the Three *S*s, he appeared to be sleeping but managed to come alive when there was an issue that concerned him.

"I like your uncle," she said. "He's a character."

"He plays by his own rules."

And he could afford to. Even before the investment in his land Dooley was a multimillionaire from all the mountain property he had owned and sold over the years. Brady's relationship to him explained the cowboy hat and the boots. But why was he working as a deputy? "Your family is rich."

"I'm not keeping score."

"Easy to say when you're on the winning team." Her family hadn't been poor, but with five kids they'd struggled to get by. If it hadn't been for scholarships and student loans, she never would have finished college. Paying for her continuing education was going to be a strain. "What made you decide to be a deputy?"

"You ask a lot of questions."

She sensed his resistance and wondered if he had a deep reason for choosing a career in law enforcement. "You can tell me."

He gave her a sidelong look, assessing her. Then he turned his gaze back toward the road. They were approaching the hotel. "When we go inside, let me do the talking."

"I might be able to help," she said. "I'm a pretty good negotiator."

"This is a police matter. I'm in charge. Do you understand?"

"Okay."

Though she was capable of standing up for herself, she didn't mind letting him do the talking. Not only was he a local who probably knew half the people who worked here, but Brady had the authority of the badge.

After they left the SUV in the valet parking area outside the entrance, she dutifully followed him into the front lobby. In the course of resort negotiations, she'd seen dozens of photographs of the interior of the Gateway Hotel. The reality was spectacular. The front windows climbed three stories high in the lobby-slash-atrium, showcasing several chandeliers decorated with small crystal snowflakes. A water feature near the check-in desk rippled over a tiered black marble waterfall. The decor and artwork were sleek and modern, except for a life-size marble statue of a toga-clad woman aiming a bow and arrow. Sasha guessed she was supposed to be Artemis, goddess of the hunt.

Occasional Grecian touches paid homage to the name Arcadia, which was an area in Greece ruled in ancient times by Pan the forest god. Sasha was glad the investors hadn't gone overboard with the gods-and-goddesses theme in the decorating. She stood behind Brady as he talked to a uniformed man behind the check-in counter. They were quickly shown into a back room to meet with the hotel manager, Mark Chandler.

He came out from behind his desk to shake hands with both of them. His gaze fixed on her face. "Why does your name sound familiar?"

"I'm a legal assistant working with Damien Loughlin. I'll be attending the investors' meetings this week."

"Of course." His professional smile gave the impression of warmth and concern. "I've worked with Damien. His help was invaluable when we were setting up our wine lists."

"Mr. Chandler," Brady said, "I'd like to talk with your hotel security."

"Sorry, the man in charge has gone home for the day. We're still in the process of hiring our full security team."

"His name?"

"Grant Jacobson. He's from one of our sister hotels, and he comes highly recommended."

"Call him," Brady said. "In the meantime, I need access to all video surveillance as well as to several of the guest rooms on the fifth and sixth floors. There's reason to believe a violent assault was committed in one of these rooms."

"First problem," Chandler said, "most of our video surveillance isn't operational."

"We'll make do with what have."

"And I'd be happy to show you the vacant rooms," he said. "But I can't allow our guests to be disturbed."

"This is a police investigation."

"I'm sorry, but I can't—"

"Suit yourself." When Brady drew himself up to his full height, he made an impressive figure of authority. "If you refuse to help, I'll knock on the doors myself and announce that I'm from the sheriff's department."

Chandler's smile crumpled. "That would be disruptive."

Brady pivoted and went toward the office door. "We're wasting time."

She followed him to the elevator. His long-legged stride forced her to jog to keep up. Chandler came behind her.

On the fifth floor, Brady turned to her. "It wasn't the corner room, right?"

She nodded. "Not the corner."

He went to the next door. His hand rested on the butt of his gun.

Hurriedly, Chandler stepped in front of him and used the master card to unlock the door. "This room is vacant. Can you at least tell me what we're looking for?"

Without responding, Brady entered the room and switched on the light. The decor was an attractive mix of rust and sky-blue, but the layout of the furniture wasn't what Sasha had seen through the binoculars. "It wasn't this room," she said. "There was a small table near the window. And a ficus tree."

"You're describing one of our suites," Chandler said. "Those units have more living space and two separate bedrooms."

"I don't see signs of a disturbance," Brady said. "Let's move on."

"The room next door is a suite," Chandler said. "It's occupied, and I would appreciate your discretion."

"Sure thing."

Brady's eyes were cold and hard. It was obvious that he'd do whatever necessary to find what he was looking for, and she liked his determination.

The door to the next room was opened by a teenage girl with pink-and-purple-striped leggings. The rest of the family lounged in front of the TV. Though this didn't appear to be the place, Brady verified with the family that they'd been here for the past two hours.

"No one is booked in the next suite," Chandler said.

"Could someone unauthorized have used it?" Brady asked.

"I suppose so."

"Open up."

Though the layout was similar to the one she'd seen, Sasha noticed that instead of a ficus there was a small Norfolk pine. Brady made a full search anyway, going from room to room. In the kitchenette, he looked for dishes that had been used. And he paid special attention to the bedrooms, checking to see if the beds were mussed and looking under the duvet at the sheets.

"Why are the beds important?" she asked.

"If he carried a body from the room, he might need to wrap it in something, like a sheet."

A shudder went through her. She didn't want to think of that attractive, vivacious woman as a dead body, much less as a dead body that needed to be disposed of. The excitement of acting like a cop took on a sinister edge.

On the sixth floor, they continued their search. As soon as she entered room 621, Sasha knew she was in the right place. There was a table by the window, and she recognized the leafy green ficus that had obscured her view of the man in the turtleneck. The room was empty.

"As you can plainly see," Chandler said, "there are no plates on the table. According to my records, this room is vacant until Friday night."

Brady's in-depth search came up empty. No dishes were missing, the beds appeared untouched, and there wasn't a smear of blood on the sand-colored carpet. But she was certain this had been the view she'd seen. "This is the right room. I know what I saw."

"What were they eating?" Brady asked.

She frowned. "I don't know."

"Think, Sasha."

She closed her eyes and concentrated. In her mind's eye, she saw the dark-haired woman gazing across the table as she set down her glass on the table. She poked at her food and lifted her chopsticks. "Chinese," she said. "They were eating Chinese food."

"I believe you," Brady said. "I can smell it."

She inhaled a deep breath. He was right. The aroma of stir-fried veggies and ginger lingered in the air.

"That's ridiculous," Chandler said. "None of our hotel restaurants serve Chinese food. And I don't smell anything."

"It's faint," Brady agreed.

"Even if someone was in this room," the hotel manager said, "they're gone now. And I see no evidence of wrongdoing. I appreciate your thoroughness, Deputy. But enough is enough."

"I'm just getting started," Brady said. "I need to talk to your staff, starting with the front desk."

Though Chandler sputtered and made excuses, he followed Brady's instructions. In the lobby, he gathered the three front-desk employees, four bellmen and three valets. Several of them gave Brady a friendly nod as though they knew him. He introduced her.

"Ms. Campbell is going to give you a description. I need to know if this woman is staying here."

Sasha cleared her throat and concentrated, choosing her words carefully. "She's attractive, probably in her late twenties or early thirties. Her hair is black and long, past her shoulders. When I saw her, she was wearing a white jumpsuit and a gold bib necklace, very fancy. It looked like flower petals."

One of the bellmen raised his hand. "I carried her suitcases. She's on the concierge level, room 917."

"Wait a minute," said a valet. "I've seen a couple of women with long black hair."

"But you don't know their room numbers," the bellman said.

"Maybe not, but one of them drives a silver Porsche."

"Get me the license plate number for the Porsche." Brady nodded to the rest of the group. "If any of you remember anything about this woman, let me know."

The employees returned to their positions, leaving them with Chandler. His eyebrows furrowed. "I suppose you'll want to visit room 917."

"You guessed it," Brady said.

"I strongly advise against it. That suite is occupied by Lloyd Reinhardt."

The name hit Sasha with an ominous thud. Reinhardt was the most influential of the investors in the Arcadia development. He was the contractor who supervised the building of the hotel and several of the surrounding condos. Knocking on his door and accusing him of murder wasn't going to win her any Brownie points.

## Chapter Three

Frustrated by the lack of evidence, Brady wished he had other officers he could deploy to search, but he knew that calling for backup would be an exercise in futility. For one thing, the sheriff's department was understaffed, with barely enough deputies to cover the basics. For another, the sheriff himself was a practical man who wouldn't be inclined to launch a widespread manhunt based on nothing more than Sasha's allegations. Brady hadn't even called in to report the possible crime. Until he had something solid, he was better off on his own.

But there was no way he could search this whole complex. The hotel was huge—practically a city unto itself. There were restaurants and coffee shops, a ballroom, boutiques, a swimming pool and meeting areas for conferences, not to mention the stairwells, the laundry and the kitchens—a lot of places to hide a body.

Sasha tugged on his arm. "I need to talk to you. Alone."

He guided her away from Chandler. "Give us a minute."

In a low voice, she said, "There's really no point in going to the ninth floor. The man I saw wasn't Mr. Reinhardt. He was taller and his hair was darker."

"How do you know Reinhardt?"

"From the same meetings where I met your uncle." She shook her head, and her blond hair bounced across her forehead. "There are four investors in Arcadia—Uncle Dooley, Mr. Reinhardt, Katie Cook the ice skater and Sam Moreno, the self-help expert."

He nodded. "Okay."

"Mr. Reinhardt isn't what you'd call a patient man. He's going to hate having us knocking on his door."

Brady didn't much care what Reinhardt thought. "What are you saying?"

"It might be smart for me to step aside. I don't want to get fired."

He tamped down a surge of disappointment at the thought of her backing out. During the very brief time he'd known Sasha, he'd come to admire her gutsiness. Many people who witnessed a crime turned away; they didn't want to get involved. "Have you changed your mind about what you saw?"

"No," she said quickly.

"Then I want you to come to room 917, meet this woman and make sure she isn't the person you saw being attacked."

"And if I don't?"

"I think you know the answer."

"Without my eyewitness account, the investigation is over."

"That's right." He had no blood, no murder weapon and no body. His only evidence that a crime had been committed was the lingering aroma of Chinese food in an otherwise spotless room.

"A few hours ago," she said, "everything in my life seemed perfect and happy. That's all I really want. To be happy. Is that asking too much?"

He didn't answer. He didn't need to. She understood what was at stake. As she considered the options, her eyes took on a depth that seemed incongruous with a face that was designed for smiling and laughter.

"It's your decision," he said.

"I've always believed that life isn't random. I don't know why, but there was some reason why I was looking into that room at that particular moment." She lifted her chin and met his gaze. "I have to see this through. I'll come with you."

She was tougher than she looked. Behind the fluffy hair and the big blue eyes that could melt a man's heart was a core of strength. He liked what he saw inside her. After this was over, he wanted to get to know her better and find out what made her tick. Not the most professional behavior but he hadn't been so drawn to a woman in a long time.

Chandler rushed toward them. Accompanying him was a solidly built man with a military haircut. He wore heavy boots, a sweater and a brown leather bomber jacket. Though he had a pronounced limp, his approach lacked the nervousness that fluttered around the hotel manager like a rabble of hyperactive butterflies.

"I'm Grant Jacobson." The head of Gateway security held out his hand. "Chandler says there was some kind of assault here."

When Brady shook Jacobson's hand, he felt strength and steadiness. No tremors from this guy. He was cool. His steel-gray eyes reflected the confidence of a trained professional with a take-charge attitude. Brady did *not* want to butt heads with Grant Jacobson.

"Glad to meet you," Brady said. "I have some questions."

"Shoot."

"What can you tell me about your surveillance system?"

"It's going to be state-of-the-art. Unfortunately, the only area that's currently operational is the front entrance." A muscle in his jaw twitched. "By Friday everything will be up and running with cameras in the hallways, the meeting rooms and every exit."

If the hotel security had been in place, they'd have had a visual record of anyone who might have entered or exited room 621. "Was there a security guard on duty tonight?"

"There should be two." Jacobson swiveled his head to glare at the hotel manager. "When law enforcement arrived on the scene, those men should have been notified."

Chandler exhaled a ragged sigh. "I contacted you instead."

"Apparently, we have some glitches in our communications." Jacobson looked toward Sasha. "And you are?"

"A witness," she said. "Sasha Campbell."

"It's a pleasure to meet you, Sasha." When he returned her friendly grin, it was clear that he liked what he saw. "And what did you witness?"

Wanting to stay in control of the conversation, Brady stepped in. "We have reason to believe that a woman was attacked in her room. Right now we're on our way to see someone fitting her description."

"Where?"

"Room 917."

"Reinhardt's suite," Jacobson said. "I'll come with you."

With a terse nod, Brady agreed. He could feel the reins slipping from his grasp as Grant Jacobson asserted his authority. The head of security was accustomed to giving orders, probably got his security training in the military, where he had climbed the ranks. But this was the real world, and Brady was the one wearing the badge.

Jacobson dismissed the hotel manager, who was all too happy to step aside as they boarded the elevator. The doors closed, and Jacobson asked, "Where did the assault take place?"

"One of the suites on the sixth floor," Brady said.

"I assume you've already been to that suite."

"We have, and we didn't find anything."

"What about the Chinese?" Sasha piped up.

He shot her a look that he hoped would say *Please don't try to help me.*

"Chinese?" Jacobson raised an eyebrow.

Brady jumped in with another question. "What can you tell me about the key-card system?"

"Why do you ask?"

"No one was registered to stay in that room."

"And you're wondering how they could get access," Jacobson said. "The hotel has only been open a week on a limited basis, which means the new employees are being trained on all the systems. In the confusion, someone could have run an extra key card for a room."

"You're suggesting that one of the employees was in that suite."

"It's possible." Jacobson shifted his weight, subtly moving closer to Sasha. He looked down at her. "Are you staying at the hotel?"

"I'm in a corporate condo," she said. "I work for the Denver law firm that's handling the Arcadia ski-resort business."

"Interesting." His thin lips pursed. "How did you happen to witness something on the sixth floor?"

Before Brady could stop her, Sasha blurted, "Binoculars."

"Even more interesting." He hit a button on the elevator control panel, and they stopped their upward ascent. The three of them were suspended in a square box of chrome and polished mirrors. They were trapped.

Jacobson growled, "Do you want to tell me what the hell is going on?"

"Police business," Brady asserted. "I don't owe you an explanation."

For a long five seconds, they stood and stared at each other. Their showdown could have gone on for much longer, but Brady wasn't all that interested in proving he was top dog. He had a job to do. And his number-one concern was finding a victim who might be bleeding to death. Though his instinct was to play his cards close to the vest, he needed help. He'd be a fool not to take advantage of Jacobson's experience in hotel security.

"Here's what happened," Brady said. "Ms. Campbell happened to be looking into the suite. She saw a man and woman having dinner—"

"With chopsticks," Sasha said.

Brady continued, "There was an argument. Ms. Campbell didn't see the actual attack, but there was blood on the woman's chest. She collapsed. The man caught her before she hit the floor."

"A possible murder," Jacobson said. When he straightened his posture, he favored his left leg. "How can I help, Deputy?"

Ever since they got to the hotel, Brady had been moving fast and not paying a lot of attention to standard procedures. At the very least, he should have taped off the room as a crime scene. There was enough to think about without Sasha distracting him. "You mentioned that you had two men on site. I'd appreciate if you could post one of them outside room 621 until we have a chance to process the scene for fingerprints and other forensic evidence."

"Consider it done." Jacobson pulled a cell phone from the pocket of his leather jacket and punched in a number. While it was ringing, he asked, "What else?"

"I want to check the surveillance tapes from the front entrance," Brady said.

"No problem." Jacobson held up his hand as he spoke into the phone and issued an order to one of his security men. As soon as he disconnected the call, he turned to Brady again. "Anything else?"

"Where's the closest place to get Chinese food?"

"Don't know, but that's a good question for the concierge on the ninth floor." He pushed a button on the elevator panel, and they started moving again. "Now I have a request for you. I'd like to do most of the talking with Reinhardt."

"Why's that?"

Jacobson's brow furrowed. "Because this is his fault."

WHEN THE ELEVATOR doors opened, an attractive woman with her white-blond hair slicked back in a tight bun stood waiting. Sasha's friendly smile was met with a flaring of the nostrils that suggested the woman had just poked her nose into a carton of sour milk.

"This is Anita," Jacobson said as he guided them off the elevator. "A top-notch concierge. She's been in Arcadia for less than a week, and I'll bet she knows more about the area than you do, Deputy."

His compliment caused Anita to thaw, but only slightly. Her voice dripped with disdain. "Mr. Chandler said you want to see Mr. Reinhardt, but I'm afraid that will not be possible. Mr. Reinhardt asked not to be disturbed."

"You're the best," Jacobson said, "always protecting the guest, always operating with discretion. But this is a police matter."

"Can't it wait until tomorrow?"

"I'm afraid not," Jacobson said.

Brady showed his badge. "We'll see him now."

Anita stared at one man and then the other as though she was actually considering further resistance. Changing her mind, she pivoted, led the way to the door of room 917 and tapped. "Mr. Reinhardt, there's someone to see you."

She tapped again, and the door flung open.

Sasha found herself staring directly at a red-faced Lloyd Reinhardt. She assumed his cherry complexion was the result of sunburn from skiing without enough sunscreen. The circles around his eyes where his goggles had been were white, like his buzz-cut hair. The effect would have been comical if his dark eyes hadn't been so angry. His face resembled a devil mask, and he was glaring directly at her.

Through his clenched jaw, Reinhardt rasped, "What?"

Sasha gasped. She had no ready response.

Jacobson stepped in front of her. "We had a conversation last week, and I warned you that the hotel shouldn't open for business until I had all security measures in place."

"I remember. You wanted a ridiculous amount of money to keep the computer and electronics guys working around the clock on the surveillance cameras."

"And you turned me down," Jacobson said. "Now we have a serious situation."

"I hope you aren't interrupting my evening to talk business," he said. "How serious?"

"Murder," Jacobson said.

Reinhardt narrowed his eyes to slits. With his right hand resting on the edge of the door and his left holding the opposite door frame, his body formed a barrier across the entrance to his room. The white snowflake pattern on his black sweater stood out like a barbed-wire fence. "I want an explanation."

"May we come in?" Jacobson asked.

Reinhardt glanced over his shoulder. It seemed to Sasha that he was hiding something—or someone—inside the room. He wasn't having an affair, because—as far as she knew—he wasn't married. But what if the dark-haired lady was somebody else's wife? Or what if she was the victim, lying on the carpet bleeding to death? Sasha cringed inside. Nothing good could come of this.

Reinhardt stepped aside, and they entered. The luxury suite on the concierge level had more square footage than her apartment in Denver. The sofas and chairs were upholstered in blue silk and beige suede. There was a marble-top dining table with seating for eight. In the kitchen area, a tall woman with long black hair stepped out from behind the counter. She wore white slacks and a white cashmere sweater that contrasted with her healthy tan.

Though she wasn't the woman Sasha had seen through the binoculars, this lady could have been a more athletic sister to the other. After she introduced herself as Andrea Tate, Sasha glanced at Brady and whispered, "It's not her."

The conversation between Reinhardt and Jacobson grew more heated by the moment. Jacobson had advised against opening until all the security measures were in place and his staff was adequately trained. He blamed Reinhardt for everything. For his part, Reinhardt was furious that someone dared to be murdered in his hotel.

Reinhardt turned away from Jacobson and focused on her. "I need to speak with Damien as soon as possible. There are liability problems to consider."

"Yes, sir." She hadn't even considered the legal issues.

"Who was killed?"

Sasha froze. Her lips parted but nothing came out. She couldn't exactly say that a murder had been committed. Nor did she have a name. And she was reluctant to point to the sleek black-haired woman and say the victim looked a lot like her.

Brady spoke for her. "I can't give you a name."

Reinhardt whipped around to face him. "My publicity people need to get on top of this situation right away. The grand opening is Saturday. Who the hell got killed?"

"We don't know," Brady said, "because we haven't found the body."

Though it didn't seem possible, Reinhardt's face turned a deeper shade of red. He punched the air with a fist. "A murder without a body? That's no murder at all. What kind of sick game are you people playing?"

Panic coiled around Sasha's throat like a hangman's noose. She wanted to speak up and defend herself, but how? What could she say?

Jacobson sat in one of the tastefully upholstered chairs and took an orange from the welcome basket. He gestured toward the sofa. "Have a seat, Reinhardt. I'll explain everything."

While Reinhardt circled the glass coffee table and lowered himself onto the sofa, Brady took her arm. "We'll be going."

"Wait for me outside," Jacobson said.

They made a hasty retreat. As soon as the door to Reinhardt's suite closed behind her, Sasha inhaled a huge gulp of air. It felt as if she'd been holding her breath the whole time she'd been in the suite. She shook her head and groaned.

"You look pale," Brady said. "Are you okay?"

"I'm in so much trouble."

"You did the right thing," he reassured her.

That wasn't much consolation if she ended up getting fired. Reinhardt had said that she needed to contact Damien, and she knew that was true. But she wanted to be able to tell him something positive. "Is there anything else we can do?"

"I've got an idea."

He crossed the lounge to the concierge desk where

Anita sat with her arms folded below her breasts and a smug expression on her face. "I warned you," she said. "Mr. Reinhardt doesn't like to be interrupted."

"Jacobson said you know this area better than anyone."

"It's my job," she said coolly.

"If I wanted Chinese food, where would I go?"

"There's a sushi bar scheduled to open next month. Right now none of the hotel restaurants serve Asian cuisine. And I'm sure you know that the local diners specialize in burgers, pizza and all things fried."

Sasha walked up beside him. Her legs were wobbly, but she'd recovered enough to understand what was going on. Anita was acting like a brat as payback for them not listening to her earlier. The concierge would be in no mood to help. The best way to get through to her was to be even snottier than she was.

"She doesn't know," Sasha said, not looking at Anita. "She's not as good at her job as she thinks she is."

"I beg your pardon."

"Well, it's true." Sasha flipped her hair like a mean girl. "If one of the people up here on the concierge level requested *moo shu* pork, you'd just have to tell them to suck an egg."

"For your information, missy, I've been providing gluten-free Asian food fried in coconut oil for a guest and his entourage since last Saturday. One of the chefs in the Golden Lyre Restaurant on the first floor of the hotel cooks up a special batch. I had it tonight myself."

"Who's the guest?" Brady asked.

"Sam Moreno, the famous self-help guru. He has a special diet."

Sasha should have guessed. One of the main investors of the Arcadia resort, Mr. Moreno was always requesting special foods and drinks. "He's picky, all right."

Anita leaned across the desk and whispered, "And he's staying right down the hall."

Of course he was. Sasha groaned. She just couldn't catch a break.

# Chapter Four

Three hours later Brady drove Sasha back to the corporate condo. His shift was over, and there didn't seem to be anything more he could do at the hotel. He'd tracked the evidence to a dead end, leaving the matter of the assault-slash-murder unsolved and the hotel staff irritated.

The logical thing would have been for him to drive home to his cabin behind the horse barn on Dooley's ranch, yank off his boots and go to bed. But he was reluctant to leave Sasha. Halfway through his investigation, it had occurred to him that she might be in danger. If she had, in fact, witnessed a murder, the killer might come after her next.

When he parked his SUV in front of her building, she turned to him with the grin that came so naturally to her. "Thanks for the ride."

"Hold on, I'll walk you in."

"That's not necessary."

He hoped she was right and he was overreacting to the possibility of a threat. "Not a problem."

A porch light shone outside the door to the condo entrance, and a glass panel beside the door gave a view inside. Nothing appeared to be out of the ordinary. When she unlocked the outer door, he followed her inside. She hit the button on the elevator and the doors swooshed open.

The interior of the elevator was extra large to accommodate skis and other winter sports equipment.

As she boarded, Sasha said, "I should apologize. I think I got you in trouble."

The sheriff had been none too pleased when Brady had asked for a couple of men to fingerprint and process the suite on the sixth floor. It hadn't helped that the room was clean. They'd found nothing to corroborate Sasha's story.

"Not everybody was ticked off," he said. "Grant Jacobson was real pleased with the way things turned out."

Jacobson had used the incident as a learning tool to train his newly hired staff. Investigating a possible homicide also gave him an edge in talking to Reinhardt about the importance of security at a top-rated hotel. His budget had been tripled.

"Jacobson is intense," she said as she got off the elevator at the third floor. "What's his story?"

"He's former military, Marine Corps." He was a man to be respected. "Did you notice his limp? He lost his left leg above the knee in Afghanistan."

Her blue eyes opened wider. "I didn't know."

"According to his staff, he snowboards and skis. One of the reasons he took this job at Gateway was the availability of winter sports."

"I'm just glad he's on our team."

When she reached toward the lock on the condo door, he took the key from her. "I'll open it. I should go first."

"Why?"

"In case there's someone inside."

She took a step back, allowing his words to sink in. "You think someone might have broken into the condo and might be waiting for me."

"I don't want to alarm you." He kept his voice low and calm. "But you're a witness to a possible murder."

"And he might want me out of the way."

She was a loose end. An efficient killer would come back for her. Brady drew his weapon before opening the door. "Wait here until I check the place out."

As soon as he entered, he hit the light switch. At first glance, the condo appeared to be empty, but he wasn't taking any chances. This possible killer had already out-smarted him once tonight.

Quickly, he went from room to room, taking a look in the corners and the bathrooms and the closets. The only bedroom that was occupied was the first one on the right, where Sasha had unpacked her suitcase. It smelled like ripe peaches, a sweet fresh fragrance that reminded him of her and got under his skin. The only other room that had been used was the hot tub, where a damp towel hung from a rack by the door.

"All clear," he said as returned to where she was stand-ing.

"Good. I've had more than enough excitement for one night." She peeled off her parka and hung it on a peg by the door. In her white sweater and red jeans, she reminded him of a pretty Christmas package waiting to be unwrapped. "Are you hungry?" she asked.

"I had some Chinese."

"Me, too. I felt guilty eating it and thinking that this might have been the last meal for the black-haired woman."

In the restaurant kitchen at the hotel, it hadn't taken long for them to locate the off-the-menu Chinese food. A cooking station had been set up near the rear exit with fried rice, gluten-free noodles and organic stir-fry veggies available to anyone who came by and scooped a serving into a carryout box.

"That was our best clue," he said.

"How do you figure? None of the kitchen staff remembered who had stopped by and loaded up on free food."

"And that's the clue. The killer was nobody remarkable. He was somebody the staff had seen before."

"And what does that prove?"

"It's likely this is an inside job."

"Somebody who works at the hotel?" she asked.

"Or somebody who has been around this week. A workman. A consultant."

"It's a long list of possible suspects."

He'd gathered a lot of information tonight but hadn't had a chance to put things together or draw conclusions. Tomorrow when he wrote his report, there'd be time enough to figure things out. He followed her to the kitchen, where she opened the door to the fridge and peeked inside.

She looked up at him. "There's nothing in there but condiments and champagne."

"Try the freezer," he said. "Some of these condos stock up on gourmet frozen deliveries when they're expecting guests."

"I'm not hungry enough for a full meal." She moved to the cabinets above the countertops. "Maybe just a cup of tea. Would you like some?"

His boots were pointed toward the exit. He should go home. He'd delivered her safely and done all that could be expected. "I ought to call it a day."

She held up a little box of herbal tea bags. "I can make you a cup in just a minute."

"Good night, Sasha."

"Wait." With the tea box clutched in both hands like a precious artifact, she took a step toward him. "Please don't go."

The pleading tone in her voice stopped him in his tracks. He saw tension reflected in her baby-blue eyes, and the upturned corners of her mouth pulled tight. Until now she'd managed to hold her emotions in check. Not that she lacked passion. Her moods flitted across her face with all the subtlety of a neon billboard. This was different, darker. "What is it?"

Her brave attempt at a smile failed. "I don't want to be alone. Tea?"

"Sure." How could he refuse? He shucked off his dark blue uniform jacket and sat on a stool at the kitchen counter. "I hope I didn't scare you when I did a room-to-room search in here."

"I'm glad you did." Looking away from him, she continued as though talking to herself. "I'd told myself that I didn't have anything to worry about, but I couldn't help thinking about what it meant to be a witness. That guy could come after me. But I know I'm safe here. All the doors and windows are locked. This is a secure building."

"It's okay to be scared."

Still holding the tea, she rested her elbows on the opposite side of the counter and leaned toward him. "When I'm worried, it helps to talk about it. Do you mind?"

"Starting from the beginning?"

"We don't have to go that far back," she said. "I've already decided that I'll never drink champagne again."

He remembered her flushed cheeks and bright eyes when he first came to the condo. "Were you drunk earlier?"

"No, but I was silly and unprofessional. If I hadn't had a glass or two—" she winced "—or maybe three, I might not have picked up the binoculars and looked into the hotel. I wouldn't have seen anything."

"Is that what you'd want?"

"Not knowing would be easier. If I hadn't seen the attack, I could have watched TV and gone to bed and had pleasant dreams." When she looked down at the tea box in her hand, her blond hair fell forward, hiding her expression. "I have no regrets. I'm glad I saw. That man can't get away with murder."

He reached across the counter to comfort her. He clasped her hand in his, rubbing the delicate skin of her palm with his thumb. In a casual way, they'd been in physical contact all night as he guided her through the hotel and bumped against her in the elevator. But this touch felt significant.

Her gaze lifted to meet his eyes, and he felt an instant, deep connection to her. At that moment, she became more than a witness. His instinct was to pull her into his arms and cradle her against his chest until her fears went away.

No way could that happen.

She'd blamed the champagne for making her behave in a less-than-professional manner. What was his excuse? He knew better than to get personal with a witness, especially someone who was only passing through Arcadia. Reining in his instincts, he released her hand and sat back on his stool. "What did you want to talk about?"

"I'm not sure when it started," she said, "but I've been having that weird feeling you get when someone is watching. You know how it is? The hairs on the back of your neck stand up and you see things in your peripheral vision."

"When did the feeling start?"

"Not when we first arrived at the hotel. Not when we were going through the rooms. It was after we saw Reinhardt and I swallowed my tongue." Her voice broke. "Talk about being in trouble. I'm up to my armpits. I don't know how I'm going to find the nerve to show up for that meeting tomorrow."

"You didn't do anything wrong."

"Oh, but I did. It's my job to facilitate the discussion and make things easier for the investors. Instead, I created a big fat problem." A tear slipped over her lower lashes and slid down her cheek. "I'm going to get fired for sure."

He wanted to wipe away her tears and tell her that everything was going to be all right, but he wasn't a liar. He was a cop, and the proper procedure for answering a 911 call didn't include cozying up to the witness.

Circling the counter, he rifled loudly through the cabinets until he located a stainless-steel teakettle, which he filled with water and placed on the burner. When he faced her again, she had regained her composure.

"Okay," he said, "skip ahead to the time when you felt like you were being watched."

She thought for a moment. "When we were at the front desk, finding out how the key cards for the hotel rooms worked, I started to take my parka off. I shivered. Then I felt the prickling up and down my arms. It was like a warning. I looked around, but I didn't notice anybody watching me."

The front desk was located in the wide-open atrium area where dozens of people came and went. Plus there was a balcony overlooking the marble pond and the statue of the huntress. They could have easily been spotted. "Why didn't you tell me?"

"I didn't want to interrupt. It seemed like we were making some progress. The key cards were a pretty good clue."

Using the computerized system, they'd learned that key cards had been made for the suite on the sixth floor. The key had been activated prior to the time when she saw the couple having dinner, indicating that someone could have been in the room. "If the security cameras in the hallway had been operational, we'd have this all wrapped up."

"Do you think he was planning to kill her from the start?" She bit her lower lip. "That the murder was premeditated?"

"I don't know."

"I think it was," she said. "It took some planning for him to get her alone in that room without anybody knowing."

Premeditation made sense to Brady. The slick way the body had been whisked away without leaving a trace seemed to indicate foresight. For the sake of argument, he took a different view. "He might have just wanted a free night at a classy hotel, eating free food and enjoying the view."

"When I was first watching them, I thought they were a couple. They weren't talking much, and I thought it was one of those comfortable silences between people who have been together for a long time."

"Like a husband and wife?"

"Not really." She shook her head. "The woman was all dolled up, and that made me think they were on a date. Her fancy gold necklace isn't the kind of thing a wife would wear."

"Why not?"

"It's too formal. I think she wanted to impress him with her outfit, and he was doing the same by taking her to the expensive suite." As she chatted, she began to relax. "If he was trying to impress her, he wasn't planning to hurt her."

"And his attack wasn't premeditated." He found a couple of striped mugs in the cabinet above the sink, and she popped a tea bag in each. "Is that your theory?"

"That's one theory," she said. "But it leaves a lot of details unexplained. I saw him pick her up in his arms. He must have gotten blood on his clothes. How could he risk walking through the hall like that?"

The teakettle whistled, and Brady poured the boiling

water over the tea bags. He had a couple of theories of his own. "When the forensic guys went over the room, they didn't find a single drop of blood. Not even when they used luminol and blue light. He was tidy. He could have covered the blood with a jacket and slipped on a pair of gloves."

She nodded. "And he could get rid of those clothes when he left the hotel."

Brady didn't often handle complicated investigations, and he appreciated the chance to discuss the possible scenarios. He probably shouldn't be having this talk with her, but there wasn't anybody else. Due to the lack of evidence, the sheriff was going to tell him to forget about this investigation. Jacobson might be inclined to throw around a few ideas, but his plate was full with getting the hotel security up and running.

Brady sweetened his tea with sugar and took a sip. The orange-scented brew tickled his nostrils. "His real problem was disposing of the body. If he carried her any distance, there would have been a trail of blood drops."

When she lifted the mug to her lips, her hand was trembling so much that she set it down again.

"Sasha, are you all right?"

"It's okay." She lifted her chin. "Keep talking."

Her struggle to control her fear was obvious. He didn't want to make this any harder for her. "Maybe we should go and sit by the fireplace."

"I said I was fine." Her voice was stronger. "You were talking about a blood trail."

"If he'd planned the murder," he said, "he could have arranged to have one of those carts that housekeeping uses to haul the dirty sheets."

"That doesn't seem likely. How could he explain having a maid's cart standing by?"

"It's hard to imagine that he wrapped her up in a sheet

or a comforter and didn't leave a single drop of blood. What if he ran into someone in the hallway?"

"But he didn't have to go far," she said, "only down the hall to the elevator. That goes all the way down to the underground parking."

Brady preferred the idea of the maid's cart. "He could have been working with someone else."

A shudder went through her, and she turned away from him, trying to hide the fear that she'd denied feeling a moment ago. "Would there be a lot of blood?"

He didn't want to feed her imagination. "There's no way of knowing. This is all speculation."

"The red blood stood out against her white clothing. It happened so fast. One minute she was fine. And the next…"

Witnessing the attack had been hard on Sasha, more traumatic than he'd realized. And he was probably making it worse by talking about it. He set down his tea and lightly touched her back above the shoulder blade. "I shouldn't have said anything."

She spun around and buried her face against his chest. Her arms wrapped around him, and she held on tight, anchoring herself. Tremors shook her slender body. Though she wasn't sobbing, her breath came in tortured gasps.

"I'm sorry, Brady, really sorry. I don't want to fall apart."

"It's okay."

"I can't forget, can't get that image out of my head."

Her soft, warm body molded against him as he continued to hold her gently. He wished he could reach into her mind and pluck out the painful images she'd witnessed, but there was no chance of wiping out those memories. All he could do was protect her.

## *Chapter Five*

The next morning, Sasha put on a black pinstriped pantsuit,
ankle-length chunky-heel boots and a brave face. After her
breakdown last night, she felt ready to face the day. Being
with Brady had helped.

Not that he had treated her like a helpless little thing,
which she would have hated. Nor had he been inappropriate in any way, which was kind of disappointing. He was
sexy without meaning to be. She wouldn't have objected to
a kiss or two. Usually, she wasn't the kind of woman who
threw herself into the arms of the nearest willing male, in
spite of what her obnoxious brother thought. But Brady
brought out the Trashy Sasha in her.

In the condo bathroom, she applied mascara to her pale
lashes and told herself that she was glad that he hadn't
taken advantage. He was different. Brady believed her,
and that made all the difference.

She checked the time on her cell phone. In fifteen minutes, Brady would stop by to pick her up. He still had
concerns about her safety and wanted to drive her to her
meeting with the four investors, and she was excited to
see him. As for the meeting? Not so much.

It'd be great if the partners treated her the way they
usually did, barely noticing her existence. But she feared
they'd be critical about her behavior last night, accusing

her of not acting in the best interests of the resort. Applying a smooth coat of lipstick, she stared at her reflection in the bathroom mirror and said, "I can handle this."

Her cell phone on the bathroom counter buzzed. She read a text message from Damien that instructed her to conference with him. In the kitchen, she opened her laptop and prepared for the worst.

Damien Loughlin's handsome face filled the screen. His raven-black hair was combed back from his forehead. He was clean-shaven and ready for work in a white shirt with a crisp collar and a silk necktie.

"What the hell were you thinking?" he growled. It was so not what she wanted to hear.

"I'm not sure what you're referring to."

"Spying on the hotel through binoculars." Unfortunately, he had it right. "Why would you do that?"

She didn't even try to explain. "I witnessed an assault, a possible murder."

"And then you traipsed over to the hotel and got everybody worked up."

"By *everybody,* I'm guessing you mean Mr. Reinhardt."

"Damn right, I mean Reinhardt. He's one of my most important clients, and you brought a cop to his doorstep."

Damien hadn't asked if she was all right or if she needed anything at the corporate condo, but then again, that really wasn't his problem. She was his assistant, and her job was to fulfill his needs in the investors' meeting.

"Last night," she said, "I was working with the police, following a lead."

"You're not a cop, Sasha." His dark eyes glared at her with such intensity that she thought his anger might melt the computer screen. "I expect more from you."

"You won't be disappointed," she said. "I'm prepared for the meeting today."

"If anyone asks about last night, I want you to tell them that it's being handled by local law enforcement. You're not to be involved in any way. Is that clear?"

"I understand." But she couldn't promise not to be part of the investigation. Witnessing a crime meant she had an obligation to help in identifying the killer or, in this case, the victim.

Hoping to avoid more instructions, she changed the topic. "How is Mr. Westfield's family?"

Damien leaned away from the computer screen and adjusted the Windsor knot on his necktie, a move that she'd come to recognize as a stalling technique. When he played with his tie, it meant he wasn't telling the whole story. "The family is, of course, devastated by his unfortunate death. Virgil P. Westfield was in his nineties but relatively healthy. He had several good years left."

Sasha tried to guess what Damien wasn't saying. "Are the police investigating his fall down the staircase?"

"They are," he admitted, "and you're not to share that information with anyone, especially not the Arcadia investors."

She hadn't been aware of a connection between Westfield and the people who founded the ski resort, but there were frequent crossovers among the wealthy clients of Samuels, Sorenson and Smith. Damien also represented Virgil's primary heir, a nephew. "Are there any suspects?"

"Let's just say that we're looking at the potential for many, many billable hours."

That was a juicy tidbit. Was the heir a suspect? For a minute, she wished she was back in Denver working on this case with Damien. If the nephew was charged with murder, the trial would turn into a three-ring circus, given that Westfield was a well-known eccentric and philanthropist who had left a substantial bequest to a feral-cat shelter.

Criminal cases were much more interesting than property disputes and corporate law.

"I'll stay in touch today," she said.

"No more drama," he said before he closed his window and disappeared from the screen.

*No more drama.* The last thing she wanted was more trouble.

TUCKED INTO THE passenger seat of Brady's SUV, she fastened her seat belt and watched as he took off his cowboy hat and placed it on the center console. He combed his fingers through his unruly dark brown hair. He looked good in the morning. Not all sleek and polished like Damien but healthy, with an outdoorsy tan and interesting crinkles at the corners of his greenish-brown eyes. She wondered how old he was. Maybe thirty? Maybe the perfect age for her.

He gave her a warm grin. "You look very—"

"Professional?" She turned up the furry collar on her parka. "That's what I was going for."

"I was going to say pretty. I like the way you've got your hair pulled back in a bun."

"A chignon," she corrected, "which is just like a bun, only French."

"And I especially like this." When he reached over and tucked an escaped tendril behind her ear, his fingers grazed her cheek. "Your hair is a little out of control."

"Like me." His unexpected touch sent a spark of electricity through her. She pushed that sensation out of her mind. They weren't on a date. She continued, "I'm a little out of control but very professional."

"If you say so."

He drove through the condo parking lot and turned onto the main road. Today his features were more relaxed, and his smile appeared more frequently. The optimism she'd felt when she first came to Arcadia returned full force. Who could be glum on a blue-sky day with sunlight glistening on the snow?

"Anything new on the investigation?" she asked, even though Damien had specifically told her not to get involved.

"The sheriff doesn't want anything to do with it. He says looking into a murder without a body is a fool's errand. Then he said it was my assignment. I guess that makes me the fool."

"Ouch."

"It's not so painful," he said. "I'd rather be hanging out at the hotel than writing up speeding tickets. If I plan it right, I might even find a reason to investigate on the ski slope."

"Are you a skier or snowboarder?"

"Both," he said. "You?"

"Neither."

"Are you a Colorado transplant?"

"I'm a native, born in Denver, the youngest of five kids. Our family moved around a bit when my dad changed jobs, but I came back here for college. I just never got into skiing. Lift tickets are too expensive."

"So you're a city girl."

"But I'm in pretty good shape." Thanks to a corporate membership in a downtown Denver gym, she took regular yoga classes and weight training. Neither of those indoors exercises would impress Brady. "I do a little figure skating."

"You can show me. That's where we're headed, right? The brand-new Arcadia ice rink?"

"As if I'd get on ice skates in front of Katie Cook." Sasha scoffed at the thought. "Ms. Cook has won tons of championships. She was with the Ice Capades."

Katie Cook was one of the four investors. Her agenda for the Arcadia development had been crystal clear from the start. She wanted a world-class ice-skating rink capable of hosting international events and rivaling the facilities in Colorado Springs, where many athletes trained.

The first meeting was scheduled to be held in the owners' box overlooking the ice. Construction costs on the rink with stadium seating had gone over budget, and Sasha suspected that Ms. Cook intended to placate the other three business investors by showing how well her ideas had turned out.

The drive took them past the ski lodge and hotel into the town. At eight thirty-five several vehicles were parked at a slant on the wide main street that split the town of Arcadia. Unlike the gleaming new facilities for the lodge and hotel, the town was plain and somewhat shabby, with storefronts on either side of the street and snow piled up to the curbs. Brady pointed out the Kettle Diner. "They have really good banana pancakes."

"I'm not really a fruit person, but I love bananas."

"Why's that?"

"I like something I can peel."

"Me, too."

She'd like to peel him, starting with his hat and working her way all the way to his boots. Before she got completely sidetracked with that fantasy, she looked over at the small grocery store on the corner.

"I should stop there," she said. "I need some basic food supplies for the condo."

"We'll do that after your meeting. I'll be back at the rink at noon to pick you up."

Having him chauffeur her around seemed like a huge inconvenience to him, especially on a gorgeous day when she couldn't imagine anything bad happening. "Maybe I should arrange for a rental car."

He pulled up at a four-way stop and turned toward her. "Until we know what's going on, I'm your bodyguard. You don't leave your condo without me."

"Do you really think that's necessary?"

"I'm not taking any chances with your safety."

She didn't bother arguing. His stern tone convinced her that he wasn't joking. She remembered how she'd felt last night in his arms—safe, secure and protected. "I've never had a bodyguard before."

"Then we're even. I've never needed to protect anyone 24/7."

"Really?"

"Arcadia isn't like the big city. The last time we had an unsolved murder up here was over ten years ago. That was before I became a deputy."

"You were a cowboy." She picked up his hat and would have put it on but didn't want to mess up her chignon.

"I never stopped being a cowboy."

"What does that mean?"

He combed through his wavy hair again. "Once a cowboy, always a cowboy. It's who I am. Growing up on a ranch is different than the city. The pace is slow but there's always plenty to do. You learn to watch the sky and read the clouds to know when it's going to rain or snow. As soon as I could walk, I was on a horse."

"What about friends?"

"I mentioned the horse."

"It sounds lonesome," she said.

"I spent plenty of time alone. I like the quiet."

On the outskirts of town, she spotted the Arcadia Ice Arena—a domed white building with a waffle pattern and arched supports across the front. A marquee in front welcomed new guests to the grand opening this weekend, featuring a special show by Katie Cook.

The large parking lot in front had been snowplowed. Only a few other vehicles—including an extralong Hummer—were parked at the sidewalk leading to the entrance. As Brady drove closer, she felt a nervous prickling at the nape of her neck under her chignon. A shiver trickled down her spine.

She glanced to the left and to the right. She saw a maintenance man with a shovel and the driver for the Hummer, who leaned against the bumper. Keeping her nerves to herself might have been prudent, but she didn't want to take any chances.

"I've got that feeling again," she said. "It's like somebody is watching me."

Brady leaned forward and looked across the front. "I'll find an entrance that's closer."

He drove parallel to the sidewalk until they were beside the young man wearing a parka with an arm patch indicating he was maintenance. "Is there a back entrance to the arena?" Brady asked through the open window of his SUV.

"Yeah, but it's locked. I'll have to open it with my key."

"Hop in."

With the maintenance man in the backseat, Brady circled the parking lot to the less impressive rear of the arena. The vehicles parked in this area were trucks and unwashed cars.

Brady turned to her. "I'll escort you inside. Stay in the car until I open your door."

Though her feeling of apprehension lingered, she needed to be on time for the meeting. She clutched the briefcase holding her laptop and note-taking equipment against her chest. "We have to hurry. I need to find the owners' box."

The maintenance man said, "I can show you where it is."

"You go first," Brady told him. "We'll follow."

After the maintenance man unlocked the rear door, Brady rushed her into a huge kitchen with gleaming appliances and stainless-steel prep tables. She recognized the chef from the hotel who made the Chinese food for Sam Moreno. He was arguing with a tall woman dressed in a black chef's jacket.

Sasha checked her wristwatch. Six minutes until the meeting was supposed to start. She nudged the maintenance man and said, "Which way do we go?"

"Out that door." He pointed.

They dashed through the swinging door from the kitchen into another room and then into a concrete corridor that curved, following the outer edge of the arena. At the far end of the curve, she glimpsed a figure dressed all in black. He had something in his hand. A gun?

Brady stepped in front of her. His weapon was in his hand.

"Don't move," he shouted. "Sheriff's department."

The figure disappeared.

# Chapter Six

Brady took off in pursuit. The curved corridor had narrow windows on the outer wall, admitting slashes of sunlight across the concrete floor. The opposite side was lined with spaces for vendors and entrances into the arena. He glanced over his shoulder and saw Sasha and the maintenance guy running behind him. As a bodyguard, he should have dropped back and made sure she was protected. But he was also a cop, and he sure as hell didn't want this guy to escape.

The only way the man in black could have vanished so quickly was by diving through an entrance to the arena. Brady made a sharp left and charged through the open double doors nearest where he'd seen the man standing. Inside, the tiers of stadium seating were in darkness, but the massive ice arena was spotlighted. A Zamboni swept around the edges of the ice. In the center, a delicate woman in a sparkling green costume spun on her skates.

Sasha, followed by the maintenance man, ran up behind him. "Did you find him?"

"Not yet." He scanned the dark rows of seats. The man in black had to be hiding in here; there was nowhere else he could have gone.

"I beg your pardon," said a tenor voice with a light British accent. "I believe there's been a misunderstanding."

Brady pivoted on his boot heel and looked up to see a man in black standing on the tier of seats above the entryway. When Brady started to raise his weapon, Sasha held out the arm holding her briefcase to block his move.

With her free hand, she waved at the suspicious figure. "Good morning, Mr. Moreno. I'd like to introduce Deputy Brady Ellis."

So this was Sam Moreno, the self-help guru who preached a philosophy about turning one's goals into reality with positive thinking and regular attendance of his seminars. Brady wasn't familiar with Moreno's program, but he suspected a scam. In his experience, the best way to reach a goal was hard work. And he really didn't like the way Moreno demanded special treatment, ranging from the food he ate to the hours of sleep he required. Last night Brady had wanted to question the guru about his menu of organic Chinese food but had been convinced by Sasha not to disturb the supposed genius.

Brady holstered his gun and climbed the stairs to shake hands. Up close he noticed Moreno's fine, smooth olive complexion. His features were as symmetrical as an artist's drawing of a face and he sported neat black bangs across his forehead. He stood nearly as tall as Brady, and his body was trim, almost too thin.

"Pleased to meet you," Brady said. "Why did you run?"

"I make it a point to be punctual. Our meeting was scheduled to start."

"For future reference, when a law enforcement officer tells you to stop, you should obey. I thought that cell phone in your hand was a weapon."

"Rather a large mistake on your part." Moreno's smile stopped just short of a smirk. "Deputy, I'm sensing some anxiety on your part."

"No, sir." Brady wasn't anxious; he was irritated by this

self-important jerk and his phony accent. Given the slight-est provocation, Brady would be happy to arrest the self-help celebrity. "I have some questions for you."

"Regarding what?"

"Murder," Brady said.

Citing a violent crime usually got someone's attention, but Moreno didn't react. "I have nothing to hide."

"Where were you last night?"

"In my suite at the Gateway Hotel. I had dinner at six, meditated until seven-thirty and worked on my next book with my secretary until nine when I went to bed."

"Did you leave the suite?"

"I don't believe I did." He gave a thin smile. "You can check with the concierge."

"Okay," Sasha said. "Which way to the owner's box?"

Moreno gestured over his shoulder toward a long glass-enclosed room at the top of the lower seating area. Lights shone from the inside. Standing in the center was Lloyd Reinhardt and his black-haired female companion, who was, according to introductions last night, an assistant.

The public address system crackled to life, and a wom-an's voice boomed through the speakers. "Good morning, everyone. It's me, Katie Cook, and I'd like for you all to come down to the edge of the rink."

After her announcement, she stood in the middle of the ice, preening like the champion she was, waiting for the others to do her bidding. Brady didn't know how Sasha could work with all these egomaniacs. Each one seemed worse than the last.

Uncle Dooley was the next voice he heard. The old cowboy came out of the box, cleared his throat and called out, "Hey there, Katie. I ain't going nowhere until some-body turns on the lights. I can't see a damn thing in here."

As the Zamboni drove off the ice, Katie gestured to

a high booth at the end of the ice. The arena lights came to life, and Brady had a chance to see the interior seating that rose all the way up to the rafters. This vast area could represent a threat to Sasha. There were a lot of places for an attacker to hide. "How big is this place?"

"Six thousand seats," Sasha said.

"Do you still feel like you're being watched?"

"I'm nervous." Her slender shoulders twitched. "I know it's cool in here but I'm sweating like I'm in the Bahamas."

"Maybe we should get you away from this place."

"No," she said with a shake of her head. "My nerves aren't because I feel like I'm being watched. I'm scared because this meeting isn't going the way I expected. How am I supposed to keep track of what people say if we're hanging out by the skating rink? I wonder if I should check in with my boss."

"He probably doesn't expect you to record every word."

"You're right. That's logical." Unexpectedly, she grasped his hand and gave a quick squeeze. "Thanks, Brady."

He doubted she was in danger. The killer wouldn't risk an attack with all these witnesses. "Go get 'em, tiger."

"I can do this," she said as she drifted toward the rink.

His uncle tromped down the concrete stairs and stood beside him. "Hey, Brady, I understand you raised a ruckus at the hotel last night."

"Just doing my job."

"Did you come here to cause more trouble?"

"Maybe," Brady said.

"I suggest you start by harassing Simple Sam Moreno. He's as slippery as a river otter but not as cute."

Brady watched as the three other investors gathered beside the ice. Katie Cook was joined by two male skaters in black trousers and tight-fitting long-sleeved shirts with matching sequin patterns. Reinhardt brought his attractive assistant with him. And Moreno had an entourage of five, all of whom were dressed in simple but expensive black-and-gray clothing.

It occurred to Brady that he might get the inside scoop on these people by observing them in action. Not that he had much reason to suspect they were involved in the random assault of the woman with black hair. He asked Dooley, "Mind if I tag along with you?"

"I'd be glad for your company. This bunch drives me crazy." He descended the stairs and spoke to the group. "Brady is going to join us."

"Why?" Reinhardt demanded. "We don't need a cop."

"He's not just a deputy. He's my nephew," Dooley said, "and I want him here."

"It's all right with me," Katie said. "I have skates here for all of you, and I want you to put them on and join me on the ice so you can get the full experience of the Arcadia Ice Rink."

"Not necessary," Reinhardt grumbled. "I can get the experience just fine from where I'm standing."

"Be a good sport," she cajoled. "This is my one day to talk about my special contribution, and it's important for you to understand my perspective."

Moreno and his crew were already putting on their skates. He glanced at Reinhardt. "I suggest you cooperate. I'd like to deal with our business here as quickly as possible, and Katie seems to have a plan."

Still muttering to himself, Reinhardt sat on a rink-side bench to put on the skates.

Uncle Dooley wasn't going to play. He stepped up to the edge of the rink and leaned across the railing. "Sorry, Katie, but I can't skate, and I'm not going to risk a broken hip."

She patted his cheek. "I understand, Dooley."

The old man took a seat, and Brady sat beside him. He nudged Dooley with his elbow. "You don't seem to mind being around Katie Cook."

"She ain't bad to look at. As a pro athlete in her forties, she's past her prime, but she's got a nice shape."

Brady seconded that opinion. With her trademark short haircut and long legs, Katie had a pixie thing going on. She'd piled on too much makeup for his taste, but she was cute.

He watched as the others stepped onto the ice. In a display of showmanship, Katie and her two companions glided and twirled across the glistening white surface, seemingly immune to gravity as they leaped through the air. Others were more hesitant. A couple of people fell and shrieked as their butts smacked the ice. His focus went naturally to Sasha.

Her neat pinstriped business suit wasn't meant to be an ice-skating costume, but she looked good as she set off skating down to the far end of the rink and back. Moving more like a hockey player than an ice dancer, she picked up speed as she went. Her forward momentum started a breeze that tousled her tidy chignon. Her cheeks flushed pink with exertion, and she was beaming. Her smile touched something deep inside him.

"That one's real pretty," Dooley said. "How'd you get hooked up with our little Sasha?"

"She's a witness to a possible murder. And I'm not hooked up with her."

"Don't lie to me, boy. The only other time I've seen that goofy look on your face was when you were twelve years old and your daddy bought you that roan filly named Harriet."

The fond memory made him grin. "Harriet was a beauty."

"It's about time you started looking at women that way. How old are you? Thirty?"

"Thirty-one," Brady said, "old enough that I don't need advice on women."

"Yeah? Then how come you're still living alone in that cabin of yours?"

"Maybe I like it that way."

"Your aunt says you're the next one in line to get married and start popping out babies for her to play with. She'd be over the moon if I told her you had a serious girlfriend."

Brady couldn't imagine Sasha living with him in his isolated cabin. She was a city girl. Her work at the Denver law firm was important to her, and she wanted to be a professional. Living on a ranch would bore her to tears.

That was what had happened with his mom. Though she'd tried her best to adjust to country life, she needed the stimulation of the city, and she'd divorced his dad when Brady was ten years old. Mom had stayed in touch, even after she started a new family in Denver, where she had a little flower shop. He'd wanted to stay angry at her, even to hate her. But he couldn't. She was different from Brady and his dad, but she wasn't a bad person.

"You know, Dooley, not everybody is meant to get married."

"Not according to your aunt. She wants everybody matched up two by two."

It hadn't worked that way for his parents. Divorce was probably the best thing that happened for them.

Eight years ago, when his dad passed away, his mom had come to Arcadia and stayed with him. Though he was a grown man who didn't need his mommy, he'd appreciated her support through that rough time. She'd encouraged him to follow his heart and find work that was meaningful. That was when he became a deputy.

Though born and raised a cowboy, Brady had always wanted a job that allowed him to help other people. Joining the sheriff's department was one of the best moves he'd ever made.

He looked down at the ice where Sasha was swirling along. She was bright, energetic and pretty. Not meant for ranch life. He turned to Dooley and shook his head. "She's not my girlfriend."

FOR A COUPLE of minutes, Sasha allowed herself to enjoy the pure, athletic sensation of liquid speed as she flew across the ice in the cool air of the arena. Looking up into the stands, she spotted Brady sitting by his uncle. Both men seemed to be watching her, and she liked their attention. Maybe she wasn't as graceful as Katie Cook but she was coordinated. Earlier she'd mentioned to Brady that she knew how to skate, and she was tempted to try a fancy leap. Or not. Showing off usually got her into trouble.

Reinhardt's companion, Andrea Tate, zoomed up beside her and asked, "Do you have any idea what's going on here?"

"Not a clue." And Sasha was a little bit worried about her responsibilities for the meeting. Her boss wasn't going to be pleased with this impromptu skating event. "It seems like we should be sitting around a conference table talking."

"Boring," Andrea said with a toss of her head that set her long black ponytail swinging.

Though Sasha agreed, she couldn't say as much. "But necessary. How did you meet Mr. Reinhardt?"

"I sell real estate. He's a developer." She lowered her voice. "For an old guy, he's got a lot of energy."

Sasha looked across the ice to where Reinhardt was

standing, bracing himself against the waist-high wall at
the edge. His stance seemed uncertain. "Bad ankles?"

"Guess so," Andrea said. "Race you to the other end."

"You're on."

Together they took off. Sasha's thigh muscles flexed,
and she used her arms to ratchet up her speed as she
charged down the ice, nearly mowing down one of Moreno's minions. She and Andrea hit the far end of the rink
in a tie. Laughing, she shook hands with the other woman.
Her excitement dimmed as she realized how much Andrea resembled the victim. It didn't seem right to forget
about her.

She spotted Katie Cook nearby and swooped toward
her, hoping she could get the actual meeting started. After
a fairly smooth stop, she clung to the edge of the rink. "Ms.
Cook, this is a beautiful arena."

"Please call me Katie, dear. You're not a bad skater."

"It means a lot to hear you say that. I saw you once in
an Ice Capades show, and you were magical."

Katie's pale green eyes sparkled inside a ring of extralong black lashes. "Was that the ballroom-dancing
show?"

"Forest creatures," Sasha said. She'd been only ten at
the time and didn't remember it well but had looked up the
show online to make sure she could talk to Katie about it.
"You were a butterfly and were lowered from the ceiling."

"Such fun." Katie combed her fingers through her pixie-
cut hair and rested her hand on her hip. Her pose seemed
studied, as though she were arranging her body to show
off her curves.

"Could you tell me what you're planning for the meeting?" Sasha asked. "I want to make sure I can record everything for Mr. Loughlin."

"What a shame that Damien couldn't be here," she said. "I was looking forward to seeing him on skates."

"He sends his deepest regrets."

"Poor old Virgil P. Westfield." Her head swiveled, and her pale green eyes focused sharply. "I've heard rumors that the police are investigating his death."

This topic was exactly what Damien had told her *not* to talk about. Sasha clenched her jaw. "I really can't say."

"But Damien is the Westfields' attorney, isn't he?"

"Yes."

Sasha felt herself being drawn into a trap and was grateful when Sam Moreno joined them. He skated as well as he did everything else; she'd seen him pull off a single axel leap without a wobble.

He asked, "What are you ladies talking about?"

"Westfield," Katie said.

"So tragic." He shook his head and frowned. "The police think he was murdered."

Sasha silently repeated her mantra: *say nothing, say nothing, say nothing.*

"I knew it," Katie said. "My husband consulted with his cardiologist last year. I know for a fact that Virgil P. had the heart of a man half his age."

Apparently, the ice-skater didn't have a problem with sharing confidential medical information. Sasha pinched her lips together, refusing to be drawn into the conversation.

"Westfield's mind wasn't sharp," Moreno said. "I heard he wanted to leave his fortune to his cat. Is that right, Sasha?"

It wasn't. She wanted to speak up and defend Mr. Westfield, who hadn't been senile in any way. *Say nothing, say nothing.* She tried to change the subject. "I wasn't aware that you all knew each other."

"My relationship with Westfield was long-standing and true," Moreno explained. "Like many people who have spent their lives accumulating property, he neglected the inner growth that would make his life truly meaningful."

"And profitable," Katie said cynically. "I'm sure you told him how to invest."

"I advised," Moreno said. "He listened."

Sasha had been involved with the investors long enough to understand the subtext. All of them made their money with real estate. Dooley got his land the old-fashioned way: he had inherited thousands of acres in the mountains. Reinhardt was a developer. Katie Cook and her surgeon husband owned commercial buildings in downtown Denver. And Sam Moreno reaped commissions for turning land into cash on a house-by-house basis.

The Arcadia project was supposed to be a nest egg for all of them. Their plan was for the resort to continue to turn a profit without much in the way of further investment. Sasha wasn't sure how Westfield fit into this picture.

She heard Brady calling her name and turned toward the far end of the ice, where he was waving to her. Happily, she grabbed the excuse and skated away from Katie and Mr. Moreno.

When she reached the edge, she leaned toward Brady. "Thanks for giving me an excuse to get away from them."

"You're welcome, but that wasn't my intention."

"What is it?" she asked.

"Your briefcase is ringing." He held it up.

She scrambled off the ice and sat on a bench before opening it. The last thing she needed was to spill the documents inside or to break her laptop.

This call had to be from Damien. She didn't expect good news.

# *Chapter Seven*

"The reason I wanted you all to skate," Katie Cook said, "was so you could experience the very impressive potential of the Arcadia Ice Rink for yourselves. Not only is this an outstanding facility for skating and training, but the six thousand–seat venue can be used as a stadium for special events."

Sasha adjusted the screen on her laptop, where the face of her boss stared out at the investors and their entourages. Damien hadn't wanted to conduct the first part of the meeting here, but Katie hadn't offered him an alternative.

Still wearing her skates, Katie pushed away from the edge of the rink toward the center. This must have been a signal because the man who had been operating the PA system started playing the opening to Ravel's *Boléro*. After an impressive two-minute version of her famous routine, Katie skated back toward them. Her message was clear: *I've still got the moves.*

"My connections in the skating world are excellent," she said. "I intend to host a national championship at the Arcadia Ice Rink this year, with television coverage, but I will need other revenue streams to make this a profitable endeavor."

"I'm in," Sam Moreno said. "I'll host a minimum of two

seminars at this location. If the partners agree to finance my ashram, I will do more."

"Your what?" Reinhardt demanded. "Ashram?"

"It's a retreat devoted to meditation and study with live-in residents."

"Here we go," Reinhardt growled. "I've been waiting to hear some half-baked scheme from you that was going to cost me money."

"Your investment will be minimal," Moreno assured him, "and far outweighed by the benefits."

"Gentlemen," Damien said from the computer. "May I have your attention?"

His computerized voice was less than commanding, and Reinhardt ignored him. "I'm not putting one penny into financing some hippie-dippie ashram."

On Damien's behalf, Sasha spoke up, "Excuse me."

"What?" Reinhardt said.

She held up the computer. "Mr. Loughlin has something to say."

On the screen, her boss straightened his necktie in his classic stalling move. Then he said, "Today the stage belongs to Katie Cook. We need to stay on topic. I suggest that we adjourn to the owners' box. Immediately."

As they lumbered off the ice and changed into street shoes, Sasha turned the computer screen toward herself. "Any suggestions, boss?"

"I need to go. Try to keep the talks on track. Only contact me if it's absolutely necessary."

The screen went blank. She was glad that he trusted her enough to leave her on her own. At the same time, she was completely freaked out. These people were all strong personalities who could trample her like a herd of wild rhinos. Somehow she had to maintain control.

On the way to the owners' box, she stopped where Brady was standing and looked up at him. If he came with her to the meeting, she'd feel as if she had at least one person on her side. "Are you going to stay?"

He fired a quick glance around the ice rink. "I think you'll be safe here with all these witnesses."

"I'm not worried about being physically attacked." His presence gave her confidence. He was strong and solid and trustworthy—the opposite of most of the partners. "I don't know how I'll keep this meeting on track."

"You'll manage." He gave her a wink. "You're a professional."

Though she straightened her spine, she didn't feel in control. She'd already made the mistake of allowing Katie Cook to lure them onto the ice. Damien wouldn't be pleased if she didn't cover all the items on the agenda. "Tell me again."

He held her upper arms and looked directly into her eyes. "You're a pro. You'll handle these people and be done by noon. Then I'll take you out for a cheeseburger and fries."

"Nice incentive," she said with a nod. "I love cheeseburgers."

"I had a call from Jacobson and need to head back over to the hotel."

"A clue?"

"Maybe." He stepped away from her. "I'll be back to pick you up. Don't go anywhere alone. Don't leave without me."

She was sad to see him go. Her feet were itching to run after him and pursue the investigation. In some ways, tracking down a mysterious killer felt far less dangerous than being locked in a boardroom with the business leaders.

AT THE HOTEL, Brady didn't have to look hard to find Grant Jacobson. The head of Gateway Hotel security was striding toward him before Brady reached the front desk. Jacobson greeted him with a nod and jumped directly to what he wanted to say; he wasn't the kind of guy who wasted time with "hello" or "goodbye."

"I've apprised the staff on the day shift about the black-haired victim. A couple of them identified Andrea, the woman who was with Reinhardt."

"How do you know it was Andrea?" Brady asked.

"They saw her with Reinhardt. He's the big boss, so people notice what's going on with him."

In his casual but expensive leather jacket, Jacobson fit in well with the hotel guests who were on their way to a late breakfast or early lunch in one of the hotel's cafés. He continued, "Since last night, we've searched this place from top to bottom looking for evidence, like a blood trail or a piece of jewelry or a purse."

Brady caught a hint of self-satisfaction in Jacobson's attitude. "You found something."

"Come with me."

They exited onto the street, where the valets turned toward them and backed off when Jacobson indicated with a quick gesture that he didn't need their assistance. The former military man had already trained the staff to understand his needs and to know how to respond. A born leader, Jacobson could have been running a battalion rather than security for a hotel. This job might be a kind of retirement for him with the beautiful surroundings and lack of problems.

"Speaking of Reinhardt," Brady said, "has he given the go-ahead on getting your electronic surveillance operational?"

"You bet he has." Jacobson's expression was grim. "There's nothing like a tragedy to focus attention. Reinhardt agreed to several upgrades, and I have a full contingent of electricians and computer techs on the case. By tonight I'll have the hallways, elevators and underground parking area wired."

LEAVING THE ENTRYWAY, Jacobson led the way around to the sidewalk on the right side of the building. It was sunny and warm today. The artificial snow–making machines would be working overtime on the slopes tonight. Half-way down the block, on the other side of the ramps leading to underground parking, Jacobson stopped at the curb beside a dark green SUV.

"This vehicle was here overnight," he said.

As far as Brady could tell, the parking spot was legal. The SUV didn't have a ticket tucked under the windshield wiper. "How do you know it was here?"

He nodded toward the entrance to underground parking. "My parking space is down here, and I saw that SUV when I came in last night. When I left, it was the only vehicle parked on the block. It was still there this morning."

A car parked on the street hardly counted as evidence, but Brady was grasping at straws. Until now he'd had nothing but Sasha's testimony to go on. "I'll run the plates."

"I already did." Jacobson shrugged. "I don't want you to think I'm stealing your thunder, but I have a couple of connections, and I thought I could check it out and save you the time if it wasn't relevant."

Brady squared off to face him. Jacobson had seriously overstepped his authority. "This isn't your job. You're not a cop."

"I understand."

"And I don't have to tell you proper procedure."

"Yeah, yeah, I should have notified you first."

"Damn right you should have."

When Jacobson locked gazes with him, Brady knew

better than to back down. Maybe he wasn't getting much help from the sheriff. And maybe he was a newbie when it came to homicide investigations. But he was still in charge. If this killer got away, Brady would take the blame.

Jacobson gave a nod. "I like you, kid. If you ever decide to leave the sheriff's department, you've got a job with me."

"I'm glad you're on my side," Brady said, echoing the statement Sasha had made earlier. "Show me what you found."

Jacobson pulled a computer notepad from his inner jacket pocket and punched a few buttons. "The plates belong to Lauren Robbins of Denver. This is her driver's license."

The photo showed an unsmiling thirty-seven-year-old woman with brown eyes and long black hair. She fit the description Sasha had given.

IN THE LUXURIOUS owners' box at the Arcadia Ice Rink, Sasha helped the catering staff clean up the coffee mugs, plates and leftovers as the meeting wrapped up. No surprise decisions had been made. The discussion among the business partners had been relatively calm and rational. It seemed that the three men were more than happy to leave control of this operation to Katie Cook as long as she didn't exceed her stated budget.

Sasha's main contribution had been to make sure everything was recorded for future reference. She also kept the coffee fresh and the juice flowing, made sure the fruit was organic and sorted the gluten-free pastries for Moreno and his minions.

Her boss had joined them for the last couple of minutes via computer. "To summarize," Damien had said from his computer screen, "existing contracts are still in order. And

I will prepare a new agreement that will allow Moreno to use the arena facilities for two recruitment sessions."

"At a sixty-five percent discount," Moreno said.

Katie Cook rolled her heavily made-up eyes. "Fine."

"Tomorrow," Damien said, "we meet at Dooley's ranch. For those of you who don't want to drive, a van will be waiting outside the hotel at eight-thirty."

"Are you joining us?" Katie Cook asked.

"I'm sure as heck going to try," Damien said.

"Is there anything we can do for Virgil P. Westfield's family?" she asked. "When is the funeral?"

"Your condolences are appreciated. The funeral won't be until next week."

Katie smirked as though she'd discovered a clever secret. "No funeral is scheduled because there's going to be an autopsy. Am I right?"

"Yes," Damien said hesitantly.

"I knew it," she crowed. "The police suspect murder."

"Cause of death was a blow to the head caused by falling down the grand staircase in his home. The coroner will perform an autopsy to determine if he fell because of medications he was taking."

"Or if he was pushed," Katie said.

"At present," Damien said, "the police consider Westfield's death to be an accident. That's all I can say for now. If you have concerns or questions, don't hesitate to ask Sasha and she'll be in touch with me."

As Damien had requested, Sasha turned off the computer screen and officially closed the meeting. She gave the group a reassuring smile and said, "I'll see you all tomorrow. Have a great day."

She noticed that Brady had entered the room and was talking with his uncle as the others exited. Reinhardt and Andrea approached the two cowboys. In his usual gruff manner, Reinhardt demanded information about the supposed hotel murder. Brady told him he was following up on several leads.

"But you still don't have a body," Reinhardt said.

"Not yet."

"Waste of time," Reinhardt muttered.

In short order, the room was empty except for her and Brady. The tension in the air dissipated, and it was quiet. Sasha exhaled a sigh of relief, rotated her shoulders and stretched her arms over her head. Since most of her hair had already escaped the chignon, she pulled out the last few clips and tossed her head.

Being done with the meeting reminded her of the feeling she'd had as a kid when the final bell rang and school was over for the day. She wanted to skip or run or twirl in a circle. *I'm free!* Even better, she was in the company of somebody she liked. Better still, they were going to get cheeseburgers.

Her natural impulse was to give Brady a big hug, but she stopped herself before grabbing him. "Thanks for coming."

"I wasn't going to leave you here unprotected." The dimple at the left corner of his mouth deepened when he grinned. She'd like to kiss that dimple. "Good meeting?"

"No yelling. No huge arguments. Katie had a chance to name-drop every superstar in the ice-skating world. Reinhardt was satisfied with the numbers, especially since Katie's rich hubby has agreed to take up any slack. Moreno hinted about this ashram he wants to build. And then there's your uncle Dooley."

"Who slept through it," Brady said.

"Good guess."

"He's never really sleeping. He hears everything."

"I know," she said.

"That's kind of like you," he said. "You pretend to be

busy filling coffee mugs but you're really keeping track. I came in early enough to hear you give the summary for your boss. Very complete and concise."

"Thank you."

His compliment made her feel good. In her position as a paralegal, few people even acknowledged her presence. Brady listened to everyone, including her. That was a useful attribute for a cop.

He sat at the table and patted the seat of the chair next to him. "Are you ready for some bad news?"

"Not really." But she sat beside him anyway.

As he scrolled through several entries on his cell phone screen, he said, "Jacobson noticed a car on the street that hadn't moved since last night. He checked out the license plate and found the owner."

He held the screen so she could see the driver's license. The photograph showed an attractive black-haired woman. Though Sasha was somewhat relieved to know that she hadn't imagined the attack, she hated to think of what had happened to her.

He asked, "Is this the woman you saw?"

"I think so. It's hard to say for sure from this little picture. Who is she?"

"Her name is Lauren Robbins. One of the other deputies has been doing research on her but hasn't found much. She lives alone in the Cherry Creek area in Denver."

"Those are pricey houses," Sasha said.

"She's a self-employed real-estate agent who works out of her home office, so we can't talk to her employer to get more information. We also know she doesn't have a police record."

"I could check with my office," she offered. "We do a lot of real-estate work, and she looks like somebody who handles high-end properties."

"That's not your job."

That was exactly what Damien would have told her. "I want to help."

"I promise to keep you updated. For now, let's get lunch."

She really wished there was a valid reason to spend more time with him. She liked watching him in action and especially liked the way she felt when she was with him. For now, she'd just have to settle for a juicy cheeseburger.

## *Chapter Eight*

At the Kettle Diner on Arcadia's main street, Sasha dunked a golden crispy onion ring into a glob of ketchup and took a bite. There was probably enough gluten and trans fat in this one morsel to put Sam Moreno into a coma, but she wasn't hypervigilant about her diet. Moreno and his minions considered their bodies to be their temples. Hers was more like a carnival fun house.

Across the booth from her, Brady watched as she mounted a two-handed assault on her cheeseburger. "Hungry?" he asked.

"Starved." She glanced down at the onion rings. "Want one?"

"I've got fries of my own," he said. "When was the last time you ate?"

"I grabbed some munchies during the meeting." But she hadn't had a decent meal all day. "As you know, there's not much food in the condo."

"We'll stop at the grocery before I take you home. Is your boss going to be joining you this afternoon?"

"He hasn't told me." She hesitated and set her amazing cheeseburger down on her plate. Though there was no need for further explanation, she wanted Brady to understand the arrangement at the condo. "When Damien gets here, he'll stay in his bedroom and I'll stay in mine. There's nothing going on between us."

"I didn't think there was."

She was a little bit surprised. Everybody else seemed quick to assume that she was sleeping with the boss. "Well, you're right. How did you come to that conclusion?"

"You're easy to read." He washed down a bite of burger with a sip of cola. "When you look at your boss on the computer screen, your expression is guarded and tense. There's no passion. It's not like the way you look at those onion rings."

Or the way she looked at him. "So, bodyguard, will you be staying with me for the rest of the day?"

"I'd like that."

"Me, too."

"But I'd better take you back to the condo. It's got a security system. You'll be safe there."

He was right. The smart thing would be to go back to the condo and review the files for tomorrow's meeting. Hanging out with Brady wouldn't be professional, and Damien had specifically told her not to get involved with the police. But she wanted to get involved—in a more personal way—with Brady.

"After lunch," she said, "what are we going to do?"

"We'll get you some groceries, then I want to take you by the hotel. Jacobson put together some surveillance footage of the front-desk area during the time when you felt like someone was watching you."

"And you think I might see the killer on the tapes."

"Does that scare you?"

"I don't think so." When she was with him, she felt safe. "If there's anything else I can do, I'm up for it. It's such a gorgeous day. I want to be outside. Even though I'm working, this trip to Arcadia is kind of a vacation for me."

"Is that so?" He swallowed a bite of burger. "I've never thought of my job as a vacation."

"If I come with you, I promise not to get in the way."

"We'll see."

His gaze met hers and, for a moment, he dropped his identity as a cop. He looked at her the way a man looked at a woman, with unguarded warmth and interest. She could tell that he wanted to spend time with her, too.

By bringing her to the local diner in Arcadia rather than going back to the hotel or the condo, he was sharing what his life was like in this small community. Half the people who came through the door of the Kettle Diner greeted him with a smile or a friendly nod. These were the locals—the ranchers and the skiers and the mountain folk. The laid-back atmosphere fit her like an old moccasin and was a hundred times more comfortable than the thigh-high designer boots worn by the guests at the Gateway Hotel.

"I'm looking forward to seeing Dooley's ranch tomorrow," she said.

"I don't know what he's got up his sleeve, but it'll be nothing like Katie Cook's presentation at the ice rink."

"No *Boléro?* No cowboys in matching sequin shirts?"

"All he wants is for his fellow investors to understand the needs of the community."

Dooley's viewpoint had been consistent throughout the planning and negotiations. Of course, he'd jumped into the development for the money, but he also wanted to protect the environment and to make sure the locals weren't misused. "I don't think he likes Moreno's idea of building an ashram where his followers could live."

"Dooley won't mind. We've got a long tradition of weird groups seeking shelter in the mountains."

"Like what?" she asked.

"Back-to-nature communes, artist groups, witch covens." He shrugged. "You never know what you're going to find when you go off the beaten path. There's room in these mountains for a lot of different opinions, as long as everybody respects each other."

Brady's cell phone rang, and he picked up. After a few seconds of conversation, his easygoing attitude changed. Tension invaded his body. His hazel eyes darkened. She could tell that something had happened, something important.

Sasha finished off the last onion ring and watched him expectantly as he ended the call.

"We have to go," he said.

"What is it?"

"They've found a body."

BRADY SHOULD HAVE taken her back to her condo, but it was the opposite direction from the canyon where they were headed. Also, he couldn't drop Sasha off without entering the condo and making sure the space was secure. This would take time they didn't have, and he wanted to be among the first at the crime scene.

Beside him in the passenger seat, Sasha cleared her throat and asked, "Are you sure this is our victim?"

"The 911 dispatcher seemed to think so." The report had mentioned a woman with black hair. "We don't get a lot of murders up here."

"What happens next? Are you still in charge?"

"I'm not sure."

The sheriff had been happy to send him on a fool's errand, but finding a body meant that this was a legitimate murder investigation. No doubt the state police would be involved. The body had to be sent to Denver or Grand Junction for autopsy since the local coroner was an elected official who didn't have the training or facilities for that type of work. Brady had the feeling that everything was about to go straight to hell.

"I wonder," Sasha said, "if there's anything I can do to minimize the negative publicity for the resort."

As he guided the SUV onto a two-lane mountain road, he glanced over at her. "You're doing some corporate thinking."

"I know." Her grin contradicted the image of a cool professional. She held up her pink cell phone. "Is it okay if I call my boss and tell him that a body has been found?"

"You'd better wait until we have confirmation on her identity."

She dropped the phone. "Just tell me when."

He drove his SUV onto a wide shoulder on the dirt road and parked behind a state patrolman's vehicle. On the passenger side, a steep drop-off led into a forest where nearly half the trees had been destroyed by pine beetles and stood as dry, gray ghosts watching over the new growth. There wasn't much room on the narrow road. When more law enforcement showed up, it was going to get crowded.

He turned to Sasha. "You have to stay in the car."

"Let me come with you. I won't get in the way."

He'd seen how deeply traumatized she'd been by witnessing the attack, and he didn't want to give her cause for future nightmares. "This isn't something you should have to see."

"I'll look away."

"A curious person like you?" He didn't believe that for a minute. "This is my first murder investigation, but I've seen the bodies of people who died a violent death. It's not like on TV or in the movies, where the corpse has a neat round hole in their forehead and otherwise looks fine. Death isn't pretty."

"Are you trying to protect me?"

"I guess I am." He added, "And I don't want to be distracted by worrying about what's happening to you."

"Aha! That's the real reason. You think I'll get into trouble."

She did have a talent for being in the wrong place at the wrong time. "This is a crime scene. Just stay in the car."

Reluctantly, she nodded. "Okay."

"With the doors locked," he said.

"Can I crack a window?" she muttered. "If I was a golden retriever, you'd let me crack a window."

"I'll be back soon."

He exited his vehicle and strode through the accumulated snow at the edge of the road to where two uniformed patrolmen were talking to an older couple dressed in parkas, waterproof snow pants and matching knit wool caps with earflaps. Their faces were as darkly tanned as walnuts.

After a quick introduction, the woman explained, "We only live a couple of miles from here and we cross-country ski along that path almost every day."

She pointed down the slope to a path that ran roughly parallel to the road. Though this single-file route through the forest wasn't part of an organized system of trails, the path showed signs of being used by other skiers.

Just down the hill from the path, he saw a gray steamer trunk with silver trim leaning against a pine tree. The subdued colors blended neatly with the surroundings. If these cross-country skiers hadn't been close, they might not have noticed the trunk.

"That's a nice piece of luggage," the woman said. "It looks brand-new."

"So you went to take a closer look," Brady prompted.

"That's right," her partner said. He was almost the same height as she was. Though they had introduced themselves as husband and wife, they could have been siblings. "We figured the steamer trunk had fallen off the back of a truck. You can see the marks in the snow where it skidded down the hill."

His observation was accurate, but Brady added his own interpretation. He imagined that the killer had pulled off the road, removed the luggage from the trunk of his vehicle and shoved it over the edge. This wasn't a heavily populated area, and there was very little traffic. If it hadn't been for the cross-country trail, the trunk could have gone undiscovered for a very long time.

"Did you open it?" he asked.

"We did," the man said. "The only way we could hope to find the owners was to see what was inside. I used my Swiss Army knife to pop the locks."

His wife clasped his hand. "I wish I hadn't seen what was in there. That poor woman."

"Can we go?" the man asked. "We did our civic duty and called 911. Now I want to get back to our cabin, chop some firewood and try to forget this ever happened."

One of the patrolmen stepped forward. "Come with me, folks. I'd like for you to sit in the back of my vehicle and write out a statement for us. Then I can drive you home."

Brady appreciated the willingness of the state patrol to help out. He knew both of these guys, had worked with them before and didn't expect any kind of jurisdictional problems. Truth be told, he doubted that any of the local law enforcement people would be anxious to take on a murder investigation.

His cell phone rang, and he checked the caller ID. Sasha was calling, probably bored from sitting alone. Ignoring the call, he turned to the patrolman who was still standing at the side of the road beside him. "How'd you get here so fast?"

"Me and Perkins happened to be in the area when the alert went out. You're the deputy who searched the Gateway Hotel for a missing dead body. Brady Ellis, right?"

Brady nodded and scraped through his memory for the patrolman's name. "And you're Tad Whitestone. Weren't you about to get married?"

"We did the deed two months ago, and she's already pregnant."

"Congrats," Brady said.

"Yeah, lucky me."

"Have you climbed down to take a look inside the trunk?"

"Not yet."

"What's stopping you?"

Officer Whitestone pursed his lips. "We were kind of waiting for you, Brady. I've done a training session on homicide investigation, but I don't know all the procedures and didn't want to get in trouble for doing it wrong."

Brady didn't make the mistake of thinking that the state patrol guys respected his expertise. When it came to homicide procedure, he was as clueless as they were. But he wasn't afraid to take action. A cold-blooded murder had been committed, and he intended to find the killer.

"Let's get moving. Do you have any kind of special camera for taking crime-scene photos?"

Whitestone shook his head. "All I've got is my cell phone."

"We'll use that." Brady grabbed the phone from his fellow officer.

As they descended the slope, he took a photo of the skid marks from the road and another of the track made by the cross-country people. Halfway down the hill, they were even with the steamer trunk. It was large, probably three feet long and two feet deep. The lid was closed but both of the silver latches on the front showed signs of being pried open.

Brady snapped another photo. Using his gloved hand, he lifted the lid. A woman dressed in white was curled inside with her legs pulled up to her chin. Her wrist turned at an unnatural angle. Her fingers were like talons. Dried blood smeared the front of her pantsuit, streaked across her arm and splattered on the gold necklace encircling her throat. Her black hair was matted and dull. Her blood-smeared face was a grotesque mask. Her lips were ashy gray. Her eyes were vacant and milky above her sunken cheeks.

There were broken plates thrown in with her, and also a fork and globs of Chinese food and wineglasses with broken stems. The killer had cleaned up the hotel room and dumped everything in here. He was disposing of the trash, treating a human life like garbage.

"Damn," Whitestone said, "that's a lot of blood."

"She must have bled out while she was in the trunk." For some reason, he recalled that the average woman had six to seven pints of blood in her body. He couldn't help but shudder.

"Do you think she was still alive when he locked her in there?"

"I hope not."

If the murder had happened the way Brady imagined, the killer had stabbed her and stuffed her in this trunk immediately afterward so he wouldn't leave any bloodstains behind. The steamer trunk must have been standing by, ready to use, which meant the crime was premeditated.

He looked away from the dead woman and up at the road. Two more police vehicles had arrived. This situation was about to get even more complicated. After Brady snapped several photos from several different angles, he closed the lid.

"I'm going back to the road," he said. "I'll wait until the sheriff gets here before I do anything else."

"No need to call an ambulance," the state patrolman said.

But there was a need, a serious need, to get this investigation moving forward. This killer was brutal, callous. The sooner they caught him, the sooner Sasha would be out of danger.

When he reached the road, he went directly to his SUV to check on her. He yanked open the driver's-side door.

Sasha was gone.

# *Chapter Nine*

Cradling her cell phone against her breast, Sasha crept along the twisting two-lane road. If she took two giant steps to the right and looked over her shoulder, she could see Brady's SUV and the police vehicles. Standing where she was, beside a stand of pine trees, they couldn't see her and vice versa.

In spite of the noise from that group, she felt as if she was alone, separated, following her own path. Maybe she should turn around and go back. Maybe she'd already gone too far.

A gust of wind rattled the bare branches of a choke-cherry bush at the edge of the forest to her left. The pale afternoon sun melted the snow on the graded gravel road, and the rocks crunched under her boots when she took another step forward.

Was she making a huge mistake?

When Brady had left her in the SUV, she had fully intended to stay inside with the doors locked, but she'd been staring through the windshield and noticed movement in the forest. She'd wriggled around in her seat and craned her neck to see beyond the state patrol vehicle parked in front of them. From that angle, she'd seen what looked like a man dressed in black. He had moved in quick, darting steps as though he was dodging from shadow to shadow in the trees.

And then he had disappeared.

She'd wondered if she was looking at the murderer. Had he come back to the scene of the crime? Who was he? A witness? Had she actually seen anything at all?

After the embarrassing disbelieving response she'd gotten when she witnessed the attack through the hotel window, Sasha hadn't wanted to make a mistake. She didn't want to be the girl who cried wolf when there was nothing there.

That was her reason for opening the door to the SUV and stepping into the snow at the edge of the road. In the back of her mind, she'd heard Brady's voice telling her to keep the doors locked and to stay out of trouble. But it wasn't as though she'd been planning to run off and get lost. As long as she stayed fairly close to the SUV, she ought to be okay.

She'd gone around the front of the state patrol car in the opposite direction from where Brady and the two officers had been talking to two elderly people who resembled garden gnomes. Squinting against the sunlight reflected off the snow, she'd tried to see the shadowy figure again. If she didn't see him, she'd run back to the SUV and hop inside and Brady would never know that she'd disobeyed his instructions.

When she'd spotted him again, the state patrolman had been escorting the gnomes into the back of his vehicle. Instead of addressing the patrolman and possibly spooking the shadow man, she'd darted across the road and hidden behind a granite boulder. At that point, it had occurred to her that if she was looking at the killer, she might be in danger.

Using her cell phone, she'd called Brady. He hadn't

answered, and the shadow man had been moving farther away from where she stood. Sasha had made the decision to follow him and find out where he was going. If she kept a distance between herself and him, she ought to be safe. And if he suddenly turned and came toward her, she could always yell for help.

She'd gone around one twist in the road and then another. Still close enough to see Brady's SUV, she moved cautiously forward, trying to see the man in black. The wind had died, and the forest had gone still. There was no movement, not even the shifting of branches. The shadow man was gone.

There had been a whir as an engine started up. Not a motorcycle in this much snow—it was probably one of those all-terrain vehicles. Should she try to follow him? Would he come back in this direction?

"Sasha!"

She heard Brady call her name and turned toward the sound. Chasing after a shadow made no sense, especially if he'd taken off on an ATV. She jogged back down the road to where Brady stood beside his SUV. He looked worn-out and tired. His mouth pulled into an angry scowl with no sign of dimples.

Immediately, she regretted causing him to worry. "I'm sorry."

"Where were you?"

"I thought I saw someone sneaking around in the forest, and I got out of the SUV to get a better look."

"Why?"

"I was trying to be helpful. I thought maybe this guy was a witness."

"Or the killer," Brady said coldly. "You put yourself in danger."

"No, I didn't." She'd been cautious. "I kept my distance.

If he'd come toward me, I would have had plenty of time to run back to the car."

"What if he'd had a gun? Tell me how you were planning to outrun a bullet."

It hadn't occurred to her that he might be armed. If this was the killer, he'd used a knife to attack the black-haired woman, but that didn't mean he couldn't have a gun. "I thought about the danger," she said. "That's when I called you, and you didn't answer."

"Because I trusted you to stay in the car," he said. "I don't understand. One minute you're scared. The next you're tracking down the killer."

"Yesterday I witnessed an attack and nobody believed me. I didn't want to go through that again. That's why I went after him. I wanted to be sure. Can you understand that?"

"Barely."

She reached toward him. When he didn't respond, she dropped her hand to her side. "For what it's worth, he was headed in that direction and I heard an engine starting up."

"A car engine?"

"More like a motorcycle," she said. "Like an ATV."

A siren blared, and red-and-blue lights flashed as another SUV from the sheriff's department joined them. She counted five vehicles. The road was blocked in both directions.

Sasha had the distinct feeling that she didn't belong here. These law enforcement guys had their jobs to do, and she was in the way. Without another word, she walked past Brady on her way to his SUV, where she would sit inside with the windows rolled up like a good little golden retriever. When she came even with him, he caught her arm and leaned close to talk to her.

"I believe you. Again, I believe you saw a man and heard an engine."

When she turned her head, her face was only inches away from his. She wished with all her heart that she could be someone he trusted. "You're the only one."

"When I saw that you weren't in the car, I was scared." His voice dropped to a whisper. "If anything bad had happened to you, I'd never forgive myself."

She wanted to lean a little closer and brush her lips across his. A kiss—even a quick kiss—wasn't acceptable behavior, but she couldn't help the yearning that was building inside her. "Do you want me to go back to the car?"

"I want you where I can see you. Stay with me."

She positioned herself beside him and put on her best attitude. At the firm, she was accustomed to meeting all kinds of big shots, shaking hands and then quietly fading into the wallpaper.

Brady introduced her to Sheriff Ted McKinley, an average-sized guy with a bit of a paunch, slouchy shoulders and a thin face. He shook her hand and gave her a grin. At least, she thought he was smiling. His bushy mustache made it hard to tell. "You're the little lady who caused all this trouble."

"All I did was call 911," she said.

"Well, you sure got Deputy Ellis all fired up."

He clapped Brady on the shoulder. Though the two men weren't openly hostile, she could tell they didn't like each other. Brady had a cool, easy confidence. In spite of his less-than-official uniform, he was every inch a deputy—the man you'd want to have around in a crisis. By contrast, the sheriff, who wore regulation clothes from head to toe, seemed unsure of himself. He had a nervous habit of smoothing his mustache.

Brady got right down to business. "The body resembles

the woman in the driver's license photo, Lauren Robbins. Is there any more information on her?"

"Not yet."

"Did you assign anybody to do that background research?"

The sheriff pulled on his mustache. "Are you telling me how to do my job?"

"No, sir."

"I wanted more to go on before I started a full-scale investigation. My resources are limited. You know that."

Brady's jaw tensed. She could tell that he was holding back his anger. If she'd been in his position, she would have lashed out. The sheriff's reluctance to act was causing them to waste time.

"How long," Brady asked, "before we have an ID on the dead body?"

"Not long." The sheriff glanced toward the edge of the road where other deputies were climbing down the slope. "We're using that mobile fingerprint scanner so we can confirm her identity real quick."

"Is that equipment working?"

"It's pretty handy." He scowled. "Did you talk to the couple who found the body?"

Brady nodded. "The state patrol took their statement."

Another vehicle pulled up, and the sheriff grumbled, "Look at this mess! And it's only going to get worse. You know what they say about too many cooks."

"They spoil the broth," Sasha said. She understood how the sheriff might be frustrated and would have felt sorry for him, but this wasn't a cooking class; it was a murder. He needed to take charge.

"I knew something like this would happen when the new ski lodge was built," he said. "I told your uncle Dooley."

"I know," Brady said.

"We used to have a nice quiet little county. Crime rate was next to nothing. Now we've got ourselves a damn murder."

She could tell from the annoyed look on Brady's face that he'd heard this story before. He asked, "Sheriff, what do you want me to do?"

"Hold tight for a couple of minutes. We're waiting for the coroner. The state police are going to loan us some expert forensic investigators. And I've already contacted mountain rescue so they can bring the steamer trunk up in a rescue basket. It's a hell of a thing, isn't it? Stuffing a body inside a piece of luggage?"

He looked to Sasha for a response, and she nodded. "It's awful."

"You work for Damien Loughlin, don't you?"

Another nod.

"Well, you can tell him not to worry. We've got everything under control."

*Or not.* In her view, the situation at the crime scene was teetering on the brink of chaos.

Brady stepped forward. "If you don't mind, Sheriff, I'd like to follow up on another lead. I thought I heard an ATV starting up. Maybe I can follow the tracks and find a witness."

"You go right ahead." The sheriff sounded relieved. "There's nothing for you to do here but stand around and watch."

Brady wasted no time before directing her to his SUV. It took some maneuvering to separate his vehicle from the others, but they were on their way in a few minutes, and she was glad to leave the crime scene in their rear-view mirror.

The state patrolmen, the deputies, the sirens and the flashing lights created a wall of confusion between her and the truth. A woman had died in a horrible way. Like it or not, Sasha was part of that death. She needed to make sense of the terrible thing that had happened, to fit that piece into the puzzle of her life.

Alone with Brady, her mind cleared. She relaxed, safe in the belief that he would protect her.

"Sheriff McKinley seems…overwhelmed," she said.

"But he's still coming up with cutesy sayings about too many cooks spoiling the broth."

"How did a man like that get to be sheriff?"

"It's an elected position, and he's a nice guy, so people vote for him. Being sheriff used to be easy. McKinley spent most of his day sitting behind his desk with his feet up. The Arcadia development changed all that."

"Is he capable of investigating a murder?" she asked.

"He's got as much experience as any of us. Which is to say—none."

She found it hard to believe that Brady had never done anything like this before. Last night he had approached people with an unshakable attitude of authority. He'd asked the right questions and looked for evidence.

"What about you?" she asked. "Would you want to be sheriff?"

"I want to keep things safe." He pulled over to the edge of the road. "Is this the area where you heard the engine?"

She pointed to the left side of the road, the opposite side from where the body was found. The snow-covered land rose in a gentle slope with ridges of boulders and scraggly stands of pine trees. In her business suit and boots with chunky heels, she wasn't dressed to go tromping around the mountains. "Do we have to hike up there and look around?"

"If I was a real homicide detective, I'd send six forensic

experts to comb the hill for clues and track down that ATV. I'd have a suspect in custody before the day was over."

"But all you've got is me."

"And it doesn't seem worth the effort to search the whole mountain for a track that may or may not have been left by the guy you saw." He slipped the SUV into gear. "There's a dude ranch not far from here, and they've got several ATVs. Let's start there."

"Good plan," she said gratefully. She didn't want to do too much unnecessary hiking in these boots.

"The old man who owns the dude ranch is buddies with my uncle."

"Is he in favor of the ski resort development or opposed?"

"He's prodevelopment." He glanced toward her. "Seems like you've caught the gist of our local politics."

"It's hard to miss."

"Most people in Arcadia are glad to have the new opportunities and the employment, but there are many—like the sheriff—who think the ski resort is nothing but trouble."

"Change is hard," she said.

"But necessary. Slow waters turn stagnant."

He drove out of the forest into a wide snow-covered valley surrounded by forested hills and rocky cliffs. In the distance, a spiral of smoke rose from the chimneys of a two-story log house with a barn and other outbuildings. Several horses paced along the fence line in a field.

Though she spotted two ATVs racing across the meadow, she forgot about the investigation for a moment. These mountains took her breath away. She was, after all, a city girl. Being here was like visiting another world. "It's beautiful."

"I used to come to the dude ranch all the time when

I was a kid to help out with the horses." He cranked the steering wheel and made a quick right turn onto a single-lane dirt road. "I want to show you something."

When the SUV turned again, she didn't see anything resembling a road. The tires bumped across a stretch of field, and she bounced in the passenger seat. "Where are we going?"

"This area is dotted with hot springs and artesian pools." He parked at the foot of a cliff, flipped open the glove compartment and took out a flashlight. "I'm taking you to a place I used to go as a kid. A cave."

She jumped from the vehicle and chased after him as he hiked up a narrow path. Afternoon sunlight glared against the face of this rocky hillside, and the snow was almost entirely melted. Even in her chunky-heeled boots, she was able to keep up with him.

This little detour was totally unexpected. *A cave?* Until now Brady had been straightforward and purposeful. Though she loved a surprise, she asked, "Why are we going to a cave?"

He turned to face her. "I need to catch my breath."

"I'm not sure what that means."

"There's a lot going on. I need to slow down so I can think." He pointed to a dark shadow against the rock face. "This is the entrance."

When she looked closer, she saw a narrow slit that was only as high as her shoulders. If she hadn't been standing right beside it, she wouldn't have noticed the entrance. She looked up at his broad chest. "How are you going to fit in there?"

"Carefully." He ducked down, took off his hat and turned on the flashlight.

After she wedged herself through the entry, she felt his hand on her arm as he pulled her forward and halted. With the flashlight beam, he swept the walls of a small chamber with a rock floor. The ceiling was just high enough for him to stand upright. The air was thick and moist…and warmer than outside. "Is this a hot spring?"

"Not hardly. The temperature in here is a steady fifty-three degrees, summer and winter." He guided her forward. "Be careful where you step. The footing is uneven."

He led her through the first chamber into a second room that was longer. The flashlight beam played across the wall and landed on a jagged row of stalagmites rising from the floor in weird milky formations. Other stones dripped down from the ceiling.

"It looks like teeth," she said, "like the teeth of a giant prehistoric monster."

"Listen," he said.

She cocked her ears and heard nothing but the beating of her own heart. "Perfect silence."

"Hold on to me." He wrapped his arm around her. "I'm going to turn off the flashlight."

She slipped her hand inside his jacket and pressed against him. Absolute darkness wrapped around them.

*Chapter Ten*

With the impenetrable darkness came a sense of disorientation. Brady held Sasha close to him. Though the interior of the cave was utterly black, he closed his eyes. He'd never practiced meditation, but he suspected it was something like this. An emptiness. A feeling of being suspended in space, not knowing which way was up and which was down.

Breathing slowly, he tried to rid his mind of chaos and confusion. Specifically, he wanted to erase the image of the dead woman stuffed inside the trunk.

"Brady?" Sasha's sweet voice called to him. "Are you all right?"

"I'm fine," he said, not wanting to alarm her.

There had been so much blood. Her pristine white jumpsuit had been soaked with it. Her lips were gray. Her cheeks sunken. Her eyes dull and vacant. The fingernails on one hand were broken. Had she been alive when he forced her into the trunk? Had she struggled?

He held Sasha tighter, absorbing the gentle warmth that radiated from her. Her arms were inside his jacket, embracing him. He leaned down and inhaled the ripe peach fragrance of her shampoo.

"You're so quiet," she said.

"Thinking." He couldn't release the image of death.

Maybe he wasn't meant to forget. Maybe he needed to be reminded, to keep that memory fresh throughout the investigation.

"Would you mind turning on the flashlight while you think?" she asked. "The dark is kind of creeping me out."

He turned on the light. In the glow, he looked down at her delicate features, her wide blue eyes and her rose-petal lips. Before the intention had fully formed in his mind, he was kissing those lips.

Her slender body nestled against him just the way he had imagined it would. Even through layers of clothing, they fit together perfectly. He glided his free hand around her throat to the nape of her neck, where his fingers tangled in her silky hair. He tasted her mouth again. So sweet.

He shouldn't be kissing her but had no regrets. When they separated, his gaze held hers for a long moment. In the damp, mysterious atmosphere of the cave, they shared a silent communication. The attraction that was building between them didn't need words.

His hand clasped hers, and he aimed the flashlight beam toward the end of the long room. "This goes back thirty feet, and then it links with another through a narrow split in the rock."

"Are we going there?" she asked.

"Not today. These caves twist and turn for a long distance. I've never been to the end."

"I'd like to come back and explore," she said.

"Maybe we will."

But now they needed to return to the real world. When he wriggled through the small opening leading from the cave, the late-afternoon sun seemed strangely cold and harsh. Out here they had very little protection from the brutal killer who had taken a woman's life. So far this investigation was reaping more questions than answers.

Brady straightened his shoulders. He had to make the best of a bad situation with a sheriff who couldn't tell his ass from a hole in the ground and a killer who always stayed several steps ahead. No matter how much he wished he'd been better trained for a homicide investigation, Brady had to work with the tools he'd been given.

"After we're done at the dude ranch," he said, "I want to go back to the hotel and look at those surveillance tapes. Our best chance of finding the killer is if you can identify him."

"I hope I can," she said.

"And I wouldn't mind talking through the investigation with Jacobson. He's got good insights."

"I've got insights," she said. "You can talk to me."

"I know. And you're smart."

"Smart and professional."

"But I don't want to drag you any deeper into this." His number-one priority was to protect her. "I don't suppose there's any way I could talk you into going back to Denver."

"And lose my job?" She shook her head. "I'm staying right here until the meetings are over."

In the SUV, he backed up, turned and drove back toward the road leading to Jim Birch's dude ranch. He couldn't help but notice that Sasha was staring at him. She was a chatty person who liked to talk things through, and he really hoped that she didn't feel compelled to discuss the meaning of that kiss in the cave. It had happened. As far as he was concerned, they should leave it right there.

When she cleared her throat, he braced himself. All he could tell her was the truth. He liked her a lot, and that kiss seemed like the right thing to do in the moment.

She said, "What do people do at a dude ranch?"

Relief surged through him. He liked her even more.

"They want the Old West experience. Riding horses and eating beans and burgers from a chuck wagon around a fire. The owner of this place, Jim Birch, plays a guitar and sings."

"Sounds like the Old West in a movie. Do real cowboys do any of those things?"

"I ride," he said. "I've eaten beans. And I even play the guitar a little."

He parked his SUV in a line of other vehicles at the side of a long bunkhouse. There seemed to be a lot of guests at the dude ranch. Together he and Sasha walked toward the main house, where Jim Birch and two other old cowboys were sitting on the front porch drinking from mugs. It was a little too chilly to be outside, and Brady guessed that Jim's wife had shooed the men out of the kitchen while she prepared dinner.

Jim rose to greet him. "I haven't seen you in a while. Is deputy work agreeing with you?"

"Can't complain."

"Sure you can." Jim Birch was big and tall and everything about him was boisterous, from his thick red muttonchop sideburns to his silver rodeo belt buckle the size of a serving platter. "I'd complain if I had to see Sheriff Ted McKinley every day. That man has the vision of a cross-eyed garden slug."

His buddies on the porch chuckled and raised their mugs. Brady figured they were drinking something stronger than coffee.

Jim gave Brady a hug and welcomed Sasha, telling her that she was as pretty as a sunflower in spring. Jim was known for having a way with the ladies. All the women loved him, but Brady knew for a fact that Jim had never betrayed his marriage vows. His wife—an energetic little woman who was as plain as a peahen—was the love of his life.

Brady said, "I saw a couple of your ATVs out in the field. Do you have many guests staying here?"

"Only one family. The rest are visitors." He lowered his voice. "You can tell your uncle Dooley that he's not the only one getting rich off the new development. I'm thinking of selling this place."

"Who's the buyer?"

"I've got a couple of buyers on the hook. One of them is kind of flaky and wants to turn the ranch into a sanctuary for unwanted house pets. The other is serious. I'm not supposed to say who he is until the deal is final, but he's one of the partners in the Arcadia project."

"Sam Moreno," Sasha said. "He wants to develop an ashram where his followers can live."

"How'd you guess that?"

"I work for the law firm handling the resort business."

"You're a lawyer?"

"Legal assistant," she said.

Jim patted her shoulder. "Smart and pretty. Brady should hang on to you."

"How'd you get to know Moreno?" Brady asked.

"I can tell you one thing," Jim said. "It wasn't from taking any of his seminars. That stuff is a truckload of hooey."

Brady agreed. He'd taken an immediate dislike to the smooth, handsome Moreno when he first met the guy, and that hostility deepened when he thought of the dude ranch being turned into a New Age enclave. "Has Moreno been visiting you this afternoon?"

"Him and a bunch of his people. They seem okay for city folks. They wear too much black for my taste, but they took to riding the ATVs like kids on a playground."

THEY FOLLOWED JIM into the house, where his wife provided steaming cups of strong coffee and a plate of sliced zucchini bread. She barely had time to say hello before she rushed back into the kitchen to deal with one of Moreno's people, who was making sure the food met all the organic standards the guru required.

Sitting at the dining room table with Jim Birch, Brady asked, "If you sell this place, what will you do?"

"For one thing, I'll quit worrying about paying my bills. It's been a rough couple of years with the economy slowing down and people cutting back on their vacations." He rested his elbows on the table and shrugged. "What's your uncle going to do?"

"I'm not sure." Brady looked toward Sasha. "I'll bet she can tell you more than I can."

"He won't quit ranching," she said. "He's made that clear from the very start."

"There you go," Jim said. "Maybe I'll go to work for Dooley. Wouldn't that be something? Us two codgers out riding herd."

Sasha excused herself from the table. "I just checked my phone, and I have a couple of messages I should answer."

As soon as she left the room, Jim gave him a grin and wiggled his eyebrows. "You're sweet on her."

"She's a witness."

"And a pretty young woman," he said. "Is there anybody else you're seeing right now?"

Brady glared at the grizzled old man with red sideburns. "Who do you think you are? Dr. Phil of the Wild West?"

"It's about time for you to settle down and start raising a family."

No way was he discussing his personal life with Jim

Birch. "I didn't see a for-sale sign on your property. How did Moreno know to get in touch with you?"

"I've been quietly shopping around. There's a couple of people from Denver who are interested. I talked to my real-estate lady this afternoon, and she thought she might be able to get the buyers into a bidding war."

"What's her name?"

"Andrea Tate."

She was Reinhardt's black-haired companion. An interesting link. "How long have you been working with her?"

"I met her a couple of years ago. She showed up when the Arcadia development was under way, looking for more property that could be used for condos."

The dude ranch and the acres attached to it wouldn't be suitable for skiers, who would want to be closer to the slopes. The drive from here on the road that followed Red Stone Creek was twenty minutes in good weather. And it would be a shame to tear down the big house and the barn, which were kept in good repair.

When Sasha came back into the room, her mouth was tight, and twin worry lines appeared between her eyebrows.

"That was the property manager at the condo," she said. "There's been a break-in."

SASHA WAS GLAD that Brady put her problem first. Though he had intended to wait at the dude ranch until he had a chance to question Moreno, they left immediately to survey the damage at the condo.

The route he took avoided the high road where the body had been found. Instead, the SUV zipped along a snow-plowed asphalt road that followed the winding path of a creek. The late-afternoon sunlight shimmered on the rushing water as it sliced through a landscape of bare cottonwoods and aspens. After two days of good weather, the snow had partially melted away, leaving the rocks bare.

Brady used the police radio on his console to contact the sheriff and tell him about the change in their plans. After a quick discussion, Sheriff McKinley decided to let the security company employed by the property manager investigate the break-in, dusting for fingerprints and picking up forensic clues.

Though Brady didn't look happy about the decision, he had no choice but to accept it. All the deputies working for the sheriff's department were busy at the crime scene or dealing with a three-vehicle accident on the highway. This small county wasn't equipped to handle complicated investigations.

"One more thing," the sheriff said over the radio. "We have an ID on the body. You were right. She's Lauren Robbins, age thirty-seven, from Denver."

"I'll stay in touch," Brady said.

When he ended the call, his jaw was tight. The moment of calm they'd experienced in the cave had been replaced by a new layer of tension. She wished she could do or say something to help him relax, but the situation seemed to become more and more frustrating.

The only bright moment had come when he'd kissed her. Holding her in the darkness, he'd been so amazingly gentle. At the same time, she'd felt the power of their attraction as though they were drawn together, as though they belonged together. She knew better than to expect another kiss. Not while there was so much going on. He glanced over at her. "How are you doing? Are you okay?"

"I've been better." She looked down at the laptop she held on her lap, thinking that she should contact Damien and tell him what had happened. "What if you had dropped me off at the condo instead of taking me with you to the crime scene?"

His brow tightened. "I don't want to think about it."

"Was the intruder after me?"

"The break-in wasn't a coincidence," he said. "I don't care what the sheriff says or how stretched our manpower is. Until this is over, you are my assignment. I'm your bodyguard 24/7. Remember? That's our deal."

Did that mean he was going to stay at the condo tonight? In spite of a logical ration of fear, her heart took a happy little leap. Spending the night with Brady wouldn't be the worst thing that had ever happened to her.

"Tell me about the phone call from the property manager," he said.

"She said that the security company notified her as soon as the alarm went off."

"When was that?"

"She gave me a precise time, but I don't remember what it was. A few minutes before she called me." Sasha liked to have things right. She should have written down the time. "She went directly to the condo. There isn't any damage that she noticed, but she's waiting for me to get there before she files a report."

"How did the intruder get in?"

"They picked the lock on the balcony door." She clutched her laptop to her chest. "I'm glad I had my computer and the Arcadia files with me."

Brady glanced over at her. "To enter through the balcony, the intruder would have had to climb up the side of the building to reach the third floor."

"That's crazy," she said. "Who would do that? A ninja?"

In spite of the tension, he chuckled. "Yeah, that's it. You're being stalked by ninjas."

And she hoped they'd left some kind of clue.

*Chapter Eleven*

At the condo, Sasha spoke to the property manager and took a look at the balcony door. Since the lock had been picked, the door didn't show any damage. If the security firm hadn't received an electronic alert, she might never have known that the place had been broken into.

Brady was talking to the security men, who were shining some kind of blue light on the wall, dusting for fingerprints and inspecting the side of the building where the intruder had climbed from one floor to the next. Now was her chance to take her laptop into the bedroom for a private conversation with Damien. She placed the computer on a small table by the window and sat in a chair facing it. The bed would have been more comfortable, but she needed to look professional.

Every time she talked to Damien, it seemed as if she was telling him about another problem. Her job was to avoid negative situations, not to create disasters. The least she could do was present a neat appearance. She even took a moment to brush her hair and apply a fresh coat of lipstick.

It took a few minutes to pull her boss out of a meeting with the Westfield family. When his face popped up on the screen, he looked angry.

"I'm busy, Sasha. What is it?"

She didn't apologize for interrupting him. He needed to know about damage to corporate property; her call was appropriate. "The condo was broken into."

"What? Why?"

She was painfully aware that the break-in could be blamed on her involvement in the murder investigation, but she didn't want to spin it that way. "Nothing appears to be stolen, but I'm not familiar with everything that's in here. Could they have been looking for something valuable?"

"You mean like a safe? Or documents?" He frowned as he thought. "Not as far as I know. I'll check with the other partners at the firm."

"When I fill out the insurance claim, I'll reserve the right to add more items until after you've had a chance to make an inventory." She'd handled forms like this before. It shouldn't be a problem. "The intruder came through the balcony door, and the lock isn't damaged. Should I have it changed anyway?"

"I want a dead bolt installed," he said. "And I want it done this afternoon."

"I'll inform the property manager." So far, so good. She might be able to end this conversation without mentioning the murder. "I'll take care of it."

"Wait a minute," he said. "Were you there when the break-in occurred?"

"No, sir, I wasn't."

"Where were you?"

The accusing tone in his voice irritated her. Shouldn't he be concerned about her physical safety? She tried not to glare at his image on the computer screen. "I was at a crime scene. The police discovered the body."

"Oh, yes." His upper lip curled in a sneer. "Is this about the apparent murder you witnessed?"

"It's a real murder." She could accept his dismissive

attitude toward her, but she wouldn't allow him to belittle the horrible crime that had been committed. "She was killed in a callous and cold-blooded manner. They found her remains stuffed inside a piece of luggage. Her name was Lauren Robbins."

His eyes widened and he drew back from the screen. "What was that name again?"

"Robbins, Lauren Robbins. She's thirty-seven and lived in Denver."

"She's Lloyd Reinhardt's ex-wife."

Stunned, she felt her jaw drop. "No way."

"Damn it."

"Did you know her?"

"An attractive woman with long black hair, very classy. She looks a lot like her cousin, who is also in real estate. In fact, I think they worked together for a while."

"Andrea Tate." She choked on the name. "Her cousin is Andrea Tate."

"Yes," he said.

"She's here in Arcadia, staying at the hotel. She's dating Mr. Reinhardt."

Damien's face got bigger as he leaned close to the screen. "Listen to me, Sasha. Our firm can't be involved with this investigation. You need to back away from this as quickly as possible."

She wished that she could. "That won't be possible."

"Why the hell not?"

"I have to cooperate with the police."

"That doesn't mean you have to be in their pocket. Stay as far away from the investigation as you can."

What about Brady? What about her need for a bodyguard? She wanted to keep her job, but she wouldn't risk her life to stay employed. Her brain clicked through possibilities. "Do you think Mr. Reinhardt will be a suspect?"

"Cops always go after the ex-husband."

"Then it's important for me to stay on their good side," she said. "I witnessed the murder, and I know Reinhardt didn't do it. I'm his alibi."

WHEN SASHA STUMBLED out of the bedroom, she'd changed out of her business suit, which was much the worse for wear after hiking along the dirt road and climbing into a cave. She'd slipped into comfortable hiking shoes, jeans and a maroon ski sweater with a snowflake pattern on the yoke.

Damien hadn't fired her, but she could feel it coming. Her neck was on the chopping block and the axe was about to fall. Not only would she be losing a job, but she couldn't count on a good recommendation. Somehow she had to get back in her boss's good graces. Finding the murderer would be a good start. Damien couldn't fire her if she proved that Reinhardt was innocent…if he was innocent and hadn't hired someone to kill his ex-wife.

She approached the dining table in front of the balcony window where Brady was talking to a guy wearing a black baseball cap with Arcadia Mountain Security stenciled across the front. If she'd been alone with Brady, she would have jumped into his arms and clung to him while she poured out her fears about losing her job.

But there were other people around, and she needed to behave in an appropriate manner. First she spoke to the property manager and arranged to have a dead bolt installed on the balcony door. Sasha also explained that she'd like to wait before filing an insurance claim, per Damien's request.

The property manager made a note in her pad and asked, "Will you continue to stay at the condo?"

It was a good question, one that she couldn't answer for

sure. The place had already been broken into; it might be targeted again. "Let's assume that I am. Is there any way you could stock the refrigerator? Nothing fancy, just cold cuts and bread and fruit."

"Of course," she said. "Damien has a standard list of food supplies when he comes up here, but he didn't mention anything for this trip."

*Thanks, Damien.* "His standard list will be fine."

While the property manager hurried off to do her duties, Sasha sat at the table beside Brady. Her desire to be close to him was so strong that she actually leaned toward him and bumped her shoulder against his arm. He glanced toward her and flashed a dimpled grin. "I think we finally got lucky."

"How so?"

He introduced the security guy. "This is Max. We went to high school together."

Reaching over, she shook Max's hand. "Nice to meet you."

"Max has already done the fingerprinting and found nothing. Not a big surprise. When we checked out the balcony, we found signs that the intruder climbed from one level to the next, and he used some kind of grappling hook."

"I've never seen anything like it before," Max said. "It's good to know about. We'll make sure all our properties have better locks on the balcony doors."

"If the sheriff had been handling this, it would have taken hours, waiting for one of the two guys who handle our forensics." Brady leaned his elbows on the table. "I don't mean to bad-mouth Sheriff McKinley, but every deputy in the department should be equipped with simple forensic tools and trained on how to use them."

"Things are changing around here," Max said. "A lot

of us think it's time to elect a new sheriff. Maybe somebody like you, Brady."

"Yeah, yeah," he said as he brushed the suggestion aside. "Even better news is that Max's security firm has surveillance video of the balconies. We're waiting for it to be transferred to his digital screen."

"So we can actually see the guy breaking in?"

"That's right."

He laced his fingers together, put his hands behind his head and leaned back in his chair, looking pleased with himself. She hated to burst this bubble of contentment, but she'd already decided to tell him what Damien had said. The victim's relationship to Reinhardt and Andrea wasn't privileged information, and Brady would find out soon enough even if she didn't speak up.

"I mentioned the name of the victim to Damien Loughlin."

"That's okay. It's about to become common knowledge."

A lazy grin lifted the corners of his mouth. The way his gaze lingered on her face made her wonder if he'd been having the same thoughts about touching and being close. She hoped so. She wanted another kiss, just to make sure the first one hadn't been a fluke.

She blurted, "Lauren Robbins was Reinhardt's ex-wife. Her cousin is Andrea Tate."

Brady snapped to attention. In the blink of an eye, he lost the lazy cowboy image as he pushed away from the table and took out his cell phone. "I'd better inform the sheriff."

The thought of paunchy old McKinley wiggling his mustache at the ferocious Lloyd Reinhardt worried her. Reinhardt would eat the sheriff alive. "It might be best if you're the one who breaks the news to Reinhardt."

"I'll bet that news has already been broken. You told Damien, Reinhardt's lawyer."

Obviously, Damien would call his top client to inform him of the investigative storm cloud headed in his direction. She hadn't seen the problem from that perspective. "I shouldn't have said anything."

As Brady walked away to make his phone call, he shrugged. "It's okay. You didn't know."

Once again she'd stumbled into a mess. Balancing between the police and the lawyers was a tricky business. Investigating leads would be even more complicated. She'd seen the killer and could say for certain that it wasn't Lloyd Reinhardt. He hadn't wielded the knife that had killed his ex-wife, but he surely could have hired the man who had.

AFTER BRADY FINISHED his call to the sheriff, he took his seat at the table to watch the surveillance video from Max's security company. The fact that Reinhardt and his companion had been part of the victim's life didn't bother him as much as their connection to Sasha. Less than an hour ago, he'd found Sam Moreno in an area where Sasha thought she'd seen a stalker. Now Reinhardt was a suspect. It felt as if danger was inching closer, reaching out to touch her. The killer knew who she was and what she had seen.

When he glanced at her, he saw the worry in her eyes. Quietly, he said, "Don't let this get to you. I'll keep you safe."

"I feel bad for telling Damien."

"That's not your problem," he said.

"I wasn't planning to say anything to him. The words just kind of spilled out."

Max placed the computer screen in front of them. "Ready?"

"Okay," she said as she sat up straight in her chair and

focused those pretty blue eyes on the screen. "How does this work?"

"On most of the properties we're hired to protect, we set up stationary digital surveillance cameras on several angles. They record continuously, have night vision and store twelve terabytes of data. The feed for this camera was accessed at our office and transferred here to me."

"That's what I'm talking about," Brady said. He loved gadgets. "The sheriff's office could use a bunch of these."

"To do what?" she asked.

"We could put them at banks or high-crime areas." Referring to a "high-crime area" in this quiet little county might be exaggerating a bit. Most of their arrests took place outside the two taverns at the edge of town. "Or on the traffic lights."

"And how many traffic lights are there in Arcadia?"

"Five," he said. "Every one of them could have a camera."

The screen came to life, showing a wide high-resolution picture of the back side of the condo building. The trees bobbed in the wind. There was no one around.

"I'll zoom in," Max said.

The picture tightened on the three balconies in a vertical row. The floor of the lowest was over an attached garage, about ten feet off the snow-covered ground. A tall pine tree partially hid the view.

Brady saw a figure dressed in black wearing a ski mask. "There he is."

With quick, agile movements, the intruder tossed a hook attached to a rope over the banister on the first balcony and climbed up. He used similar moves to get to the third floor. His entire climb took only about ten minutes.

"He's good," Sasha said. "I thought I was kidding about ninjas."

"Could be a rock climber," Max said. "Looks like he's wearing that kind of shoe."

Brady was impressed with both the skill of the intruder's ascent and the speed he showed in picking the lock. "This isn't the first time he's done this. When it comes to break-ins, this guy is a pro."

Almost as quickly as he'd entered, he appeared on the balcony again.

"It doesn't look like he's carrying anything," Max said. "He didn't come here to commit a robbery."

Brady knew why the intruder had made this daring entry into the condo. He was after Sasha. His intention had been to find her and silence her.

On his climb down, the figure in black slipped at the lowest balcony and took a fall. When he rose and moved away from the building, he was limping.

"I hope his leg is broken," Sasha said.

Brady looked toward Max. "Did your cameras pick up his escape? Did you see a vehicle?"

"Sorry, there wasn't anything else."

This footage was enough to convince Brady of one thing. Sasha was in very real danger. There was no way she could stay at this condo by herself.

## Chapter Twelve

Brady had insisted that Sasha pack her suitcase and leave the condo. It hadn't taken much to convince her that she'd be safer somewhere else. That video of the guy in black creeping up the wall like a spider was all the motivation she needed.

The best plan, in his eyes, would be for her to come home with him. Not the most appropriate situation, but the most secure. As they drove to the hotel to look at the security tapes, he mentioned that possibility.

"Maybe you should spend the night with me…at my cabin." A warm flush crawled up his throat, and he was glad that the afternoon sunlight had faded to dusk. He didn't want her to see him turning red. "I have an extra bedroom."

"Wouldn't that be a problem for you? Since I'm involved in the investigation."

"It's not like you're a suspect. I wouldn't be harboring a fugitive." People would talk, but he didn't mind the wagging tongues and finger-pointing. Maybe she did. "Your boss might not approve."

"He's not happy with me." She exhaled a long sigh. "I'll be lucky to get out of this investigation without being fired."

"You haven't done anything wrong."

"Actually, it was a big mistake for me to pick up a pair of binoculars and look through somebody's window."

"If you hadn't witnessed the murder, we wouldn't have learned about it for a long time. The killer cleaned up after himself too well."

"You would have found out today," she said. "The cross-country skiers would still have discovered the body."

"Maybe or maybe not," he said. "Because we were poking around last night, the killer might have been in a hurry to dispose of the body. He might have chosen the most expedient dumping site rather than the best place to hide that steamer trunk."

For a moment, Brady put himself in the killer's shoes. At first the murder had gone according to his plan. He'd stabbed the victim and dumped her into the trunk without spilling a single drop of blood on the floor. After he'd cleaned up the room, throwing everything into the trunk, he'd wheeled the steamer trunk into the hall and down to the parking garage. If anyone had seen him, it wasn't a problem. Nobody would question a man with a suitcase in a hotel.

The killer must have been pleased with himself, thinking he'd gotten away with a nearly perfect crime. And then, less than an hour after the attack, an eyewitness appeared and a deputy started asking questions. The killer's careful planning had failed. He must have been reeling from shock.

"If we ever catch this guy," Brady said, "it will be because you happened to be looking in the right place at the wrong time."

She reached across the console and touched his arm. "That makes me feel better."

Her touch reminded him of the other reason he wanted her to stay at his cabin tonight. He needed another kiss. To be honest, he craved more than kissing. He wanted Sasha in his bed. Every moment he spent with her heightened that longing. He had memorized the shape of her face and the way her eyes crinkled when she smiled. His ears were tuned to the warm cadence of her voice and her light, rippling laughter. He wanted to hold her close and inhale the peachy scent of her shampoo. No matter how inappropriate, he wanted her. It was taking a full-on exertion of willpower to hold himself in check.

He swallowed hard. "What do you say? My cabin?"

"I won't stay at the condo."

He held his breath. "And?"

"I should get a room at the hotel." At least she didn't sound happy about it. "If Jacobson has all the surveillance in place, it ought to be safe."

*Rejected.* He decided not to take it personally. "I'll arrange it."

"I'd rather be with you."

He knew that. A couple of times today, he'd caught her looking at him with a sultry heat in her eyes. "My offer stands."

"I've got to be professional, to concentrate on my job."

"I understand. Don't worry about the cost of the hotel. The sheriff's department can spring for a room to protect a witness."

When he drove toward valet parking outside the Gateway Hotel, he spotted the sheriff's SUV. "McKinley is already here, probably questioning Reinhardt."

She groaned. "That's not going to go well."

"I think we should join them."

"We?" Her voice shot up a couple of octaves. "You mean both of us?"

"Andrea just lost her cousin. She might appreciate having another woman to talk to."

"But there's a confidentiality thing," Sasha said. "I'm not a lawyer, but the firm I work for represents Reinhardt and the other investors. If they say anything to me in private, I should tell Damien first."

"Not a problem. We'll make sure you're not alone when you talk to them." He parked the SUV and turned to her. "That's a good rule. Until we know who hired the ninja, you can't be alone with any of the partners or their people."

"You suspect all of them? Even Katie Cook?"

"She could have hired a killer."

"But why? What's her motive?"

"Something to do with real estate," he said. "Didn't she have two male skaters with her? Two guys wearing black?"

"And sequins," Sasha said. "Not many ninjas wear sequins."

He wouldn't have been surprised by anything. This investigation had taken more twists and turns than the road over Vail Pass.

WHEN SHE AND Brady entered Reinhardt's suite on the concierge level of the Gateway Hotel, she could feel tension shimmering in the air. Sheriff McKinley and another deputy stood in the middle of the room, holding their hats by the brims and looking confused, as though they couldn't decide if they should apologize to Reinhardt or arrest him.

Pacing back and forth, Reinhardt was easier to read. He was outraged with a capital *O*. As soon as he saw Sasha, he came to a stop and jabbed his index finger at her.

"She can straighten this out," he said. "She works for my lawyer, and my lawyer told me not to say a damn thing to the cops until he gets here. Tell them, Sasha."

Heads swiveled, and all eyes turned toward her. Though trained as a paralegal and familiar with these simple legal parameters, Sasha wasn't accustomed to having anyone seek her opinion. It was time for her to rise to the occasion.

She inhaled a breath and spoke clearly. "Mr. Reinhardt is correct. He's not required to talk to the police without having his lawyer present."

"When's the lawyer getting here?" the sheriff asked.

"Tomorrow." She *hoped* Damien would be here tomorrow.

"What about you?" McKinley was almost whining. His mustache drooped dejectedly. "You're present. Doesn't that mean he can talk to me now?"

"I'm not an attorney, just an assistant."

"You're wasting your time," Reinhardt said. "I haven't done anything wrong. Lauren was my ex-wife, but that doesn't mean I didn't care about her. When you came in here and told me that she was murdered, it hurt."

"Shut up, Lloyd." Andrea rose from the chair where she'd been curled up with a wide-bottomed whiskey glass cradled in both hands. "You were over Lauren."

"I didn't hate her."

"Probably not." Andrea wobbled on her feet. "You gave her a good settlement and always sent the alimony checks on time. Lauren was the bad guy in your divorce. I loved my cousin, but she spent money like a wild woman. Wouldn't listen to anybody."

Sasha could see that Andrea was on the verge of a crash. When she got closer to her, she caught a whiff of strong alcohol. "I'm sorry for your loss. Is there anyone I can contact for you?"

"My mom." A tear skidded down her tanned cheek. "Lauren's parents are dead. My mom is the one who handles all the family business. She lives in Texas, but she'll hop a plane and be here quick."

"Come with me into the bedroom," Sasha said, "and we'll make that phone call."

"Oh, God, there's going to be a funeral. Lauren would want an open casket. How did she look? No, don't tell me. I don't want to know." Andrea plunked back into the chair and held up her glass. "I need more of this."

Sasha didn't argue. She took the glass and went across the suite to the wet bar, where a bottle of amber whiskey stood on the counter. All the men were watching her, and she sensed their uneasiness when it came to comforting a nearly hysterical woman. For Sasha this kind of situation wasn't a big emotional stretch. She came from a big family where somebody was always in crisis.

Though she hadn't planned it, she was in charge. "I have an idea about how we can handle the legal situation. I can contact Mr. Loughlin on my computer, and he can take part in the talks with Mr. Reinhardt."

"Do it," Reinhardt said.

After delivering the drink to Andrea, she whipped open her briefcase and set up the communication with Damien. The sheriff, the other deputy and Reinhardt sat around the table with the computerized version of Damien overseeing the conversation.

Sasha returned to Andrea. "Let's make your phone call."

"She didn't deserve to die." The strong, attractive lines of her face seemed to be melting. "Lauren did some real stupid things, but she wasn't a bad person."

Sasha signaled for Brady to join her. "I could use some help here."

Together they guided the black-haired woman across the suite and into the bedroom, where she threw herself facedown on the bed and sobbed. Sitting beside her, Sasha patted her back and murmured gentle reassurances. When

Brady started to leave, she waved at him and mouthed the words *You have to stay.*

He shook his head and silently said, *No.*

She couldn't let him go, not with the confidentiality problem. She mouthed, *Please, please, please.*

Scowling, he leaned his back against the wall and folded his arms across his chest.

When the storm of weeping had subsided, Sasha said, "Brady is going to stay in here with us, okay?"

"Whatever." Andrea levered herself up to a sitting position but was still slouched over so her hair fell forward and covered her face. "Brady's okay. I've heard about him."

"From Jim Birch," Sasha guessed.

"He's a sweet old guy." She inhaled a ragged breath and pushed her hair back. In spite of her tears, she was still attractive. "He always tells me I look like an Apache maiden, wild and beautiful."

The colorful compliment sounded exactly like something Jim Birch would say. "Have you known him long?"

"I've been working with him for a couple of years. I met him when I came up here with Lloyd to check on the development at Arcadia. I had time to explore while Lloyd was fussing around with the construction crews."

"Was he still married to Lauren then?"

"No, they've been divorced for five years. Lauren was actually working with me when I first started talking to Jim Birch about selling his property. She tried to steal his listing away from me, the bitch." Her hand flew up to cover her mouth. "I shouldn't say that now that she's dead."

"I won't tell."

Sasha wrapped her arm around the other woman, encouraging her to lean against her shoulder. She hoped the physical contact would bring some comfort.

Sasha couldn't get over the similarities between Andrea

and the victim. The hair. The sense of style. It wasn't surprising that Reinhardt had gone from one cousin to the other. "Are you and Mr. Reinhardt in a serious relationship?"

"We're just dating. He's a little old for me, but I like powerful men. And I've been attracted to Lloyd for a long time, even when he was still married to Lauren." She swiped at her swollen eyes. "Brady, can you get me an aspirin from the bathroom?"

Though he did as he was asked, he stayed within earshot, and she was glad that he did. She figured that they were going to get more information from Andrea than the sheriff would uncover in his interrogation of Reinhardt.

"Don't get me wrong," Andrea said. "I never made a move on Lloyd when he was married. That's not how I roll."

"Dating married men is never a good idea."

"Not like you and Damien," Andrea said. "Wasn't he voted one of Denver's most eligible bachelors?"

"Not my type." Sasha didn't want to go through this song and dance again. "We aren't dating."

"But you were going to be together at the corporate condo."

"I'm moving to the hotel tonight."

Andrea accepted three aspirin tablets and a glass of water from Brady. She looked from him to Sasha and back again. "Poor Damien. I think you found something more interesting in the local scenery."

Sasha glanced over at Brady. She was anxious to shift the topic back toward the investigation. "Tell me about you and Lloyd."

"We started spending more time together about three months ago. It was just after Lauren tried to pull a fast one and steal Jim Birch. She had a buyer who was perfect for the dude-ranch property, and she took him up for a show-ing without telling me. When I found out, I started a bid-ding war using my contact with Sam Moreno."

"That was three months ago?"

"Give or take." Andrea swallowed the aspirin.

The timing was interesting. At the investors' meetings, Moreno had never spoken of his intention to buy the dude-ranch property. The first mention of his ashram was today. For some reason, he'd kept this plan a secret.

Reinhardt had the most to lose from Sam Moreno break-ing away from the group to set up his own development, as he was the one the business partners had agreed would su-pervise all new construction. Was it pure coincidence that he'd started dating Andrea at that time? Was he using her?

She gave Andrea a smile. "Are you ready to make that call to your mom?"

"Might as well get it over with."

"If you want, I'll stay with you."

She tossed her head, and her long black hair fell back over her shoulders. "I'll do it alone."

"Don't hesitate to give me a call if you want to talk." Sasha rose from the bed. "Again, you have my deepest condolences."

She was at the bedroom door when Andrea called to her. "Here's a little something that you and Brady might be interested in knowing."

"What's that?"

"The person in the bidding war with Moreno was none other than Virgil P. Westfield."

That little tidbit was more than unexpected. It was a bombshell. Sasha knew that several of the investors had ties to Westfield but hadn't suspected that they were ac-tually doing business with him. At ninety-two, how much business did he undertake? "Was he Lauren's client?"

"You bet he was. She had that old man tied up in knots."

And now that old man was dead.

Sasha caught a glint of awareness in Andrea's eye. The supposedly grief-stricken cousin knew exactly how important this information was to the investigation. Apparently, Andrea wasn't above doing a bit of scheming on her own.

# Chapter Thirteen

Returning to the meeting at hand, Sasha felt the need to inform the computerized version of Damien that she needed to view some surveillance tapes in the hotel security office. As usual, he brushed her off, telling her that he still had important matters to discuss with Reinhardt and the sheriff.

*How typical!* His conversation with the others was important. And her role as an eyewitness—the only witness—wasn't.

She held her tongue as she and Brady went past the concierge desk on their way to the elevator. There was no sign of ice-cold Anita, the concierge, and Sasha was glad. The last thing she needed was another condescending comment. When she hit the button to summon the elevator, she couldn't contain her frustration for one more moment. She exploded. "I can't believe this."

"What?"

"Damien didn't tell me that Mr. Westfield was working with Lauren Robbins. Those should have been the first words out of his mouth."

"Are you sure he knew?"

She'd never been more sure of anything in her life. "Westfield was one of his big clients. If he was planning to buy a huge parcel of mountain property, Damien would know everything about it."

"Maybe he didn't think it was important."

"Don't you dare defend him!" She hit the elevator button again. "I've been doing the best I can in a messy situation, and my boss is holding back information, treating me like a lackey. Which, I suppose, is how he sees me. I'm *not* another attorney, not a colleague. I'm just the girl who gets coffee."

"Hey." He held up a hand to stop her rant. "I just watched you take charge with a sheriff, two deputies and a billionaire developer. You're doing a hell of a good job."

Those were exactly the words she needed to hear. Together they entered the elevator. The instant the doors whooshed closed, she went up on her tiptoes, threw her arms around his neck and kissed him hard. With his hands at her waist, he anchored her against his hard, muscled body.

Though she had initiated the kiss, he took charge. His mouth was firm and supple, not at all sloppy. When his tongue penetrated her lips, he set off an electric chain reaction. Her entire body trembled. Her heart raced.

Too soon the elevator doors opened on the first floor. She gave a frantic little gasp as she pulled herself together and stepped away from him.

Standing directly outside the elevator was Grant Jacobson. His stern features were lit with a huge grin.

"Let me guess," Brady said. "The surveillance in the elevators is operational."

"And I can transfer the picture to this portable screen." He held up a flat device slightly larger than a cell phone. "Too bad I'm not in the blackmail business."

"It's nice to see you again," Sasha said. She was trying

her best not to be embarrassed…and failing. The thrills hadn't stopped. Her mouth tingled. If her lipstick hadn't already been worn off, it would have been smeared across her face.

Jacobson chuckled. "Oh, but the pleasure was all mine."

"Did you have some surveillance for me to look at?"

"Right this way."

There were desks, computers, filing cabinets and a large wall safe in the front area of the hotel security area. Through another door was an array of screens and graphics that displayed every inch of Gateway property.

"We're wired," he said. "Every public space, all the hallways and the parking lots are covered. Nothing happens here that I don't notice."

"I'm impressed," she said. "You got this done in a day?"

"It's amazing how fast problems go away when you throw handfuls of money at them."

Brady meandered through the desks with separate consoles, occasionally leaning down to check out various switches and dials. He stood in front of the big screen in the front of the room where several camera feeds were playing simultaneously. "Nice stuff."

"Top-of-the-line."

"Later I want a detailed tour. But right now we're in kind of a hurry."

"Give me the time and the place you want to look at," Jacobson said. "I'll pull up the relevant camera feed on the big screen."

"Front lobby," he said. As he guessed at the time, she realized that all this had happened in a twenty-four-hour time span. She had witnessed a murder, had had her life threatened, was probably going to lose her job and had kissed an incredible man…twice. It hardly seemed possible that her life had changed so radically in one day.

A split-screen picture appeared. Last night there had been two cameras in the lobby, both showing wide views. Right away she spotted herself and Brady standing together behind the check-in counter. If she recalled correctly, the hotel manager had been giving them a lecture on the key-card system and how it worked.

She looked at herself on the screen. The highlights in her hair looked great, but there wasn't a lick of styling, just messy curls, and her clothes looked as if she'd gotten dressed in the dark. Standing beside Brady, she seemed petite and maybe a little timid. On the other hand, he was confident, strong and altogether terrific—a movie star with his big shoulders and his cowboy hat. It was hard to take her eyes off him, but she glanced around at the other people milling in the lobby. None of them seemed particularly suspicious, but she recalled the creepy feeling of apprehension, as though someone was watching her.

"I don't see him," she said.

"Keep watching," Jacobson said. He froze the picture. A laser pointer appeared in his hand and he aimed the red dot at a man who was talking on his cell phone. "How about this guy? He seems to be standing around for no reason."

She shook her head. "He's too tall."

For another ten minutes, she watched people coming and going, stopping beside the statue of Artemis the huntress, meeting and saying goodbye. Nothing stood out. It had been a long shot to think that she'd see the killer strolling through the lobby, but she had hoped for an easy solution.

Behind her back, Brady was telling Jacobson about the break-in at the condo. "Climbed up the wall like a ninja and picked the lock in two minutes flat."

"Sounds like a pro," Jacobson said.

"Exactly what I said."

"You're not going to let her go back there alone, are you?"

"She thought it would be best if she stayed at the hotel."

Sasha wanted to interrupt and tell them that she'd changed her mind. Spending the night with Brady sounded like a wonderful idea. From a logical standpoint, it made sense because the meeting tomorrow morning was at Dooley's place. From an emotional perspective, she wanted to take those kisses to the next level.

Usually, she wasn't so quick to fall into a man's arms and allow herself to be swept away. The days of Trashy Sasha had made her wary, and she hated the way other people were so quick to judge. Even Andrea thought she was sleeping with her boss.

But Brady was different. He was a decent man and would never purposely do anything to hurt her. Frankly, she wouldn't mind if rumors started. He was someone she'd be proud to be with.

Before she could speak up, Jacobson and Brady had arranged for her room at the Gateway. Jacobson guaranteed her safety and promised to have one of his men regularly patrol her floor.

As they made their way back to the concierge level to pick up her computer, she thought she might remind Brady of his duties as a bodyguard and hint that he might want to stay in her hotel room tonight…just to be sure she was safe. But she didn't want to push too hard.

Computer in tow, they entered her appointed room. It wasn't fancy, just a very nice suite with windows facing the ski slope, where the snow machines were now working full blast. She pulled the curtain and turned toward him.

Brady wasn't sidling around the bed. He was much too masculine to be shy, but he seemed to be avoiding the largest piece of furniture in the room as he leaned his hip against the dresser. "I'll be back tomorrow morning to pick you up for the meeting," he said.

"You don't have to. I can ride in the van with the others."

"I want you to stay away from the investors," he said. "I didn't much like these people before, but now they're all suspects."

"It's crazy, isn't it? I mean, what are the odds? I witness a murder and it turns out that the people I'm working with are suspects."

"I would have said the same thing, but I checked with Jacobson. This week, before the grand opening, over half the people staying at the hotel are connected with the resort partners. They're employees or consultants or independent contractors."

"Or minions," she said, thinking of Moreno.

"He's got a mob of followers."

She peeled off her jacket and tossed it over a chair. Sitting on the edge of the bed, she took off her boots. Though they were comfortable shoes, taking them off felt like heaven. She stretched her feet out and wiggled her toes. "Uncle Dooley isn't a suspect."

"Don't be so sure. Virgil P. Westfield has been around for a long time. Dooley might know him." Brady grinned. "But my uncle isn't a subtle man. If he had a beef with Westfield or our victim, he'd come after them with six-guns blazing."

"What about Katie Cook?"

"She knew Westfield, and she was real interested in the status of the police investigation into his death."

A thought occurred to her. "Could these two deaths be related?"

"It's possible." He shrugged. "But we don't know for sure that Westfield was murdered. Did Damien mention anything to you?"

"Not much." Her boss didn't talk things over with her—not even the legal issues related to the partners and their meetings. "As far as he's concerned, I'm a tape recorder with legs. My job is to listen and keep track of what's being said. Not to think for myself."

"I'd like to hear your opinion."

Talking about the murders was draining all the sexiness out of the room, which was probably for the best. Though she hadn't given up on more kissing, she liked the part of their relationship where they talked to each other.

Hopping off the bed, she went to the chair where she'd dropped her jacket and sat. "If both of these people were murdered within a day of each other, it seems like there has to be a connection."

"The only thing we know is that they were working together in a bidding war for the dude-ranch property."

"Lauren might have been involved in other real estate purchases with him," she said. "Mr. Westfield made his fortune buying and selling commercial properties in Denver. He owned much of the land where the Tech Center is now located."

"His work was similar to what Reinhardt does."

"You're right." She hadn't made that connection before because Westfield and Reinhardt had the kind of profession that didn't really fit a category. "Lauren Robbins must have learned all about that buying and selling when she was married to Reinhardt. Being part of Westfield's operation was a natural step for her."

When Brady took off his cowboy hat and raked his fingers through his unruly brown hair, it was all she could do not to reach out and touch him. Talking was interesting and even productive, but she was itching to get closer. The light reflecting from his hazel eyes enticed her. If she gave in to her desires, she'd fly across the hotel room and into his arms.

"Do you remember," Brady asked, "what Andrea said about her cousin having the old man wrapped around her finger?"

She nodded. "That makes me think their relationship wasn't strictly business."

"Was Westfield married?"

"His third wife died four years ago."

If Lauren Robbins was aiming to be the next Mrs. Virgil P. Westfield, that would be a whole other motive for murder. No matter how vigorous Mr. Westfield was, the man was ninety-two years old. His heirs wouldn't be happy if he married again.

"How about kids?" Brady asked. "Did he have children?"

"Never had any of his own. His greatest love was for his cats. He always had five or six running around the mansion, and he built an incredible cat condo that went up two stories. They were all strays." She remembered a pleasant afternoon with the old man while he discussed a property sale with Damien. They drank tea and the cats had cream in matching saucers. "He used to say that the cats were his real family."

"What's going to happen to his inheritance?"

"He has a nephew who works for the family foundation and is his primary heir. But there's a big chunk of change set aside for a cat shelter."

Brady grinned. "That's a man who goes his own way. I like that."

"I liked him, too."

A stillness crept into the room. Her sweater seemed too warm. Her clothing too confining. She couldn't keep her gaze from drifting toward the king-size bed, which seemed even bigger and more dominating. She wished they could lie beside each other, not necessarily to do anything else. Yeah, sure, who was she trying to kid? She wanted the whole experience with Brady.

He moved away from the dresser. "I should be going."

Silently, she begged him to stay. Could she ask that of him? What if he said no? Not knowing what to say, she stammered, "I g-g-guess I'll see you in the morning."

He was at the door. His hand rested on the knob. "As soon as I leave, flip the latch on the door. Don't let anybody else in the room. Promise me."

"I'll be careful."

He opened the door. "Pleasant dreams."

As she watched the door close behind him, the air went out of her body, and she deflated like a leftover balloon at a party. Was it too late for her to run down the hall and tackle him before he got into the elevator? She bounced to her feet but didn't take a step. She wasn't going to chase him down. She'd missed her chance for tonight.

Following his instruction, she flipped the latch on her door, protecting herself from accidental intrusions by maids and purposeful assaults from ninjas. Nobody would come after her in the hotel, would they? Jacobson had surveillance *everywhere*. She was safe.

On the way to the bathroom, she peeled off her sweater. Underneath, she wore a thermal T-shirt, and she got rid of that, too. What she needed was a nice long soak in the tub, and then she'd fall into that giant bed. Stripped down to her underwear, she heard a knock on the door to her room. Her heart leaped. Was it Brady coming back? She could only hope that he'd gotten down to his SUV, realized that he needed to spend the night with her and returned.

She grabbed an oversize terry-cloth robe from a hook in the bathroom and dashed to the door. On her tiptoes, she peeked through the fish-eye.

It was Sam Moreno.

# Chapter Fourteen

Panic bubbled up inside her. Sasha's fingertips rested on the door. Only this thin barrier separated her from a man who might have plotted two murders. And now he was coming for her. When he knocked again, she jumped backward and clutched the front of her bathrobe.

"Sasha, it's me, Sam Moreno. I wanted to talk to you."

"This isn't…" She heard the tremor in her voice and started over. She didn't want him to know she was scared. "This isn't a good time."

"It's important."

The logical side of her brain—the left side—told her that she was overreacting. She didn't *know* that he was the killer. She had no compelling reason to believe that he was guilty. But she'd be a fool to invite him into her room. If they stood in the hallway, Jacobson's surveillance camera would be watching and Moreno wouldn't dare try anything.

She grabbed her cell phone and held it so Moreno would see that she was in constant contact with others. As she opened the door, her heart beat extra fast. She couldn't help thinking of how quickly the man in black had killed Lauren Robbins. One slash of his knife, and she was dead.

Sasha stepped into the hallway. "What's wrong, Mr. Moreno?"

His clothing wasn't all black for a change. He wore a dark rust-colored turtleneck under a black thermal vest. His olive complexion was ruddier than usual, making his dark eyes bright. Though he was a very good-looking man, he wasn't very masculine. His smile was almost too pretty. She reminded herself not to be charmed by that smile. She'd seen Moreno in action at one of his seminars and had been amazed at his charisma. People wanted to believe him, especially when he told them that they were empowered and could have anything they dreamed of.

"May I come into your room?" he asked.

"I'd be more comfortable here," she said. Her left hand had a death grip on the front of her robe, and she held up the cell phone in her right. "You said this was important."

"I came to you as soon as I heard the name of the murder victim," he said. "I knew Lauren Robbins."

His timing surprised her. Since she and Brady had received confirmation on the victim's identity a couple of hours ago, it seemed as if everybody else should know. "How did you hear about this?"

"When we got back to the hotel, one of my assistants told me that the sheriff was questioning Reinhardt. That's when I heard Lauren's name. I came looking for you immediately."

"Why me?" She glanced down the hallway. Though she saw no sign of the surveillance camera, she knew it was there.

"I'll be truthful with you." His lightly accented voice held a practiced ring of sincerity. In the self-help business, everything was based on trust. "Damien Loughlin is the lawyer, but you're the person who really gets things done. Isn't that right?"

His question had a double edge. Of course, she wanted to be respected as a proactive person, but she knew better than to criticize her boss. "Is there something you wanted to tell me about Lauren Robbins?"

"I want you on my side." There was the disarming piece of honesty, accompanied by his smile. "Lauren was handling a real-estate transaction for me at Jim Birch's dude ranch. Earlier today you and Brady were there."

His smile and the persuasive tone of his voice were working their magic. She felt her fear begin to ebb. "If you know anything about the murder, you should talk to the police. And I'm certain that Damien would want to be present when you do."

"Am I a suspect?"

Echoing the words she'd read in every detective novel, she said, "Everybody is a suspect."

"Rest assured that I didn't do anything wrong. I'm here to help the investigation. That's all." He held out both hands with the palms up to indicate he had nothing to hide. "I knew Lauren well. She was a strong woman, tough and perhaps too ambitious. Her dream of wealth clouded her other perceptions and made it difficult for her to find peace."

In his description, she recognized several of his catch-phrases. "I'll pass that along."

"You remind me of her," he said, "in a good way."

She knew that he was dangling a carrot in front of her nose. Thousands of people were his followers and hung on his every word. Why shouldn't she get a free reading? "How so?"

"You have ambitions, Sasha. And you must honor those ambitions. If you conceive it, you can achieve it. And you're also a caretaker. I'd guess you came from a big family with four or five siblings. Are you the youngest?"

"Yes." For half a second, she wondered how he had

known about her family. Then she realized that personal information wasn't hard to come by on the internet.

"You like the balance offered by a legal career," he said, "but you don't like the restrictions of law. You're more suited to a profession like mediation."

He was accurate. She felt herself being drawn in.

Moreno continued, "Don't worry if you lose the job with Damien. You're the type of person who finds opportunities. With your optimism and enthusiasm, you'll be hired again." He paused. "I could help you. I could be your mentor."

He reached toward her and made contact with the bare flesh of her hand holding the phone. His touch was warm and meant to be soothing. He wanted her to trust him. That was what this conversation was about. He wanted her to be on his side.

But she pulled her hand away. She'd seen him in action and knew his routine too well. Sasha wasn't suited for the role of minion. She didn't look good in all black. "I appreciate that you came forth with this information, and I'll pass it on to Damien."

Down the hall, the elevator opened. She saw Grant Jacobson striding toward them and almost cheered.

Jacobson greeted Moreno and turned to her. "Step inside with me, Sasha. We have something to discuss."

Relief swept through her. She bid Moreno good-night, went into her room with Jacobson, closed the door and leaned her back against it. "Thank you."

He glared. "Didn't Brady tell you not to open the door for anyone?"

She nodded. "But I knew you'd be watching. That's why I didn't let him into the room."

"You can't take chances like that. It's not safe."

"I won't do it again."

There was nothing soft or comforting about his presence. Jacobson didn't lead by gently convincing his followers; he demanded respect. And she had no intention of disobeying him. She thanked him again, and he left.

After she showered and changed into a soft cotton nightshirt, she snuggled between the sheets and turned out the light. Lying in the dark, her mind ping-ponged from one thought to another. She remembered the moments of tension and considered the web of complications that stretched from the murder of Lauren Robbins to the suspicious death of Virgil P. Westfield. Were they connected? Or not? Connected? Or not?

And she thought of Brady. Her memory conjured a precise picture of his wide shoulders, narrow hips and long legs. He was totally masculine, from the crown of his cowboy hat to the soles of his boots. The hazel color of his eyes darkened when he was thinking and shimmered when he laughed. And when he kissed her... She sank into the remembrance of his kiss, and she held that moment in her mind. When she slept, she would dream of him.

BRADY WOKE AT the break of dawn. The light was different today; there was more shadow and less sun. A storm was coming.

Farmers and ranchers had the habit of checking the weather before they did anything else. He was no exception to that rule. Looking out his bedroom window, he watched the clouds fill up the sky. Though he was no longer a cowboy responsible for winter chores, the snowy days were vastly different from the brilliant, sunny ones they'd been having. For a deputy, the snow meant more traffic accidents and a greater likelihood of hikers being lost in the backcountry.

He glanced back at his bed, extralong so his feet didn't

hang off the end, and wished she was there. He understood why she'd turned him down when he asked her to come home with him. Spending the night with him wouldn't be appropriate for either one of them. His *only* assignment today would be protecting Sasha. Though he was glad, he had hoped to be more involved in the investigation. Last night Sheriff McKinley had told him that the Colorado Bureau of Investigation was taking over. It made sense. The CBI had the facilities and the trained personnel for autopsy and forensics. With the proper warrants, they could search the financial records of the suspects to find out if they had made payments to hired killers.

Still, Brady hated to give up jurisdiction. Stepping back and letting the big boys take over felt like failure. This was his county, his case. As a lawman, he wanted to see the investigation through to the end.

Usually, he made his own coffee in the morning. But he knew Dooley would be having the investors over for a meeting in a couple of hours. There might be some special tasty baked goods in the kitchen of the big house that was down the hill, about a hundred yards away from his two-bedroom log cabin.

He got dressed and sauntered along the shoveled path leading to the big house. As soon as he opened the back door, he was hit by the aroma of cinnamon and melted butter mingled with the smell of freshly ground coffee.

Clare and Louise, the women who did most of the cooking on the ranch, gave him a quick greeting and shoved him toward the dining room, where the table was filled with plates of cinnamon rolls and muffins, as well as regular breakfast foods—platters of bright yellow scrambled eggs, bacon and hash-brown potatoes. Five or six cowboys sat around the table, eating and drinking from steaming mugs of coffee. Chitchat was at a minimum. This was a working ranch, and they were already on the job.

Brady followed the same protocol. When he sat, the guy on his left nudged his shoulder. "I heard you found a dead body."

"That's right."

"Somebody got murdered at that fancy hotel."

"Yeah."

The cowboy across the table leaned back in his chair. "I bet McKinley is pulling his mustache out."

"Pretty much," Brady said.

"How about you? Are you playing detective?"

Brady sipped his coffee. "The CBI is stepping in to take over."

"That's a damn shame." Dooley appeared in the doorway from the kitchen. "We don't need a bunch of CBI agents in suits to come prancing around and solving our problems."

Brady loved his great-uncle, the patriarch of their family, and he agreed with him. They weren't the sort of people who gave up. "We've got no choice. The state investigators have trained experts and fancy electronic investigation equipment. With our budget, we can barely afford gas for the vehicles. The sheriff's department needs help."

"I think we need a new sheriff," one of the cowboys said. "Somebody like you, Brady."

Why did everyone keep saying that? Running for sheriff was a heavy responsibility and a long-term commitment for someone his age. "You just want a free pass on parking tickets."

"Amen to that."

"It doesn't take a budget to solve a crime." Dooley hitched his thumb in his belt. "You need what we used to call poker sense. If you want to find a liar, look him straight in the eye. If he blinks, he's got something to hide."

"And how does that work in a court of law?"

"You got to trust your gut," Dooley said. "You've met all these suspects, Brady. Now you go with your gut. Ask yourself who did it, and you're going to get a reply. And you'll probably be right."

The name that popped in his head was Lloyd Reinhardt. He didn't know why, didn't have a shred of proof, but somehow his subconscious had picked Reinhardt, the ex-husband, the man with a lot of money invested. "In the meantime, my assignment is to make sure our key witness is safe."

"Sasha Campbell," Dooley said. "Watching her all day shouldn't be too hard."

The cowboy next to him perked up. "Is she that cute little blonde?"

Because Brady knew how hard Sasha worked to be thought of as professional, he said, "She's more than cute. She works for the law firm with the partners at Arcadia, setting up the meetings and recording what goes on."

"Brady's right," Dooley said. "She's ten times smarter than her boss. But she's also nice to look at."

He couldn't argue.

On the drive over to the hotel to pick her up, he tried to reconcile his different images of Sasha. Her warmth and her smiles were natural, and she liked to think the best of people. But she wasn't a pushover. Though she didn't dress in low-cut blouses or wear sultry makeup, she had that girl-next-door kind of sexiness that made a man sit up and take notice. When she was being professional, she was smart and efficient, whipping out her laptop computer and keeping everyone on track.

Thinking about her ever-present briefcase reminded him

of how much she relied on electronics to do her job. Everybody did. It was only the dinosaurs like Dooley who figured you could count on your gut feelings. The rest of the world was plugged in, including Lauren Robbins. She was a businesswoman. Where were her electronics? Her cell phone had been recovered with her body, but where were her computer and her electronic notepad? She wouldn't have left those items at home. Not if she'd been planning to do business in Arcadia.

At the hotel, he circled around to the side where her car was still parked at the curb. He'd told McKinley about the vehicle, but the sheriff apparently hadn't had time to get it towed. And the CBI hadn't taken notice.

Brady parked his SUV in front of her car. Had Lauren left anything inside? He should tell someone else to check it out.

Or maybe he should do a tiny bit of investigating on his own.

In the back of his SUV, stored inside his locked rifle case, were the low-tech tools used to break into a car when somebody had accidentally lost their keys.

He unlocked the gun case and took out a wooden wedge and a metal pole with a hooked end. Over the years, he'd helped lots of folks who had gotten stuck in bad places without their keys, and he was good at breaking in. Many of the newer vehicles were impossible to unlock but this dark green American-made SUV wouldn't be a problem for him.

He used the wedge to pry open a narrow space at the driver's-side window, stuck the pole inside and wiggled it around until he could manipulate the lock. There was a click. He opened the door.

The SUV was a little beat-up on the inside, showing its age, and he wondered if Lauren wasn't as successful as she tried to appear in her gold necklace and classy outfit. She might have parked out here on the street so the valets wouldn't notice her less-than-glamorous car.

Wearing his gloves, he made a quick search of the car, front and back and under the seats. When he opened the glove compartment, he found a black patent leather notebook about the size of a paperback novel. He snapped a couple of photos on his phone of the notebook inside the glove box. Then he removed it. Bulging with Post-its and scribbled notes, the sides were held together with a fat rubber band.

The notebook was the nonelectronic, messy way people used to keep track of their appointments and phone numbers. Lauren Robbins had hung on to these scraps of paper and notes to herself for some reason.

His fingers itched to search through the pages. He should turn this evidence over to the CBI, but it wouldn't hurt to take a look inside first. At least, that was what he told himself.

## Chapter Fifteen

Brady knocked only once on the door to Sasha's hotel room before she flung it open. She grabbed the front of his jacket and pulled him inside—a surprising show of strength for such a tiny little thing.

"I'm staying with you tonight," she announced. "I'm all packed and ready to go. We can drop my suitcase off at your cabin after the meeting at Dooley's."

"Fine with me." Better than fine—this was exactly what he wanted. "What changed your mind?"

"I don't want to be accessible to these people. Last night Moreno showed up at my door. Then I got a call from Andrea, begging me to come up to her room. She really laid on the guilt, talking about how it's so hard to be a woman working in a man's world, and how ambition killed her cousin. Maybe I should have gone to her, but I was too scared."

"You were smart."

"I don't feel safe here." Her shoulders tensed. "I saw a woman get killed in this place. This hotel doesn't exactly whisper 'home, sweet home' to me. I was even too nervous to call room service this morning."

"So you haven't had breakfast?"

"I attacked the minibar and had a couple of granola bars and some orange juice."

"There's plenty to eat at the ranch."

He grabbed the handle on her suitcase. Before they left the hotel room, he inhaled a deep breath. "Peaches, smells like peaches."

"It's my shampoo."

Light glinted off the golden highlights in her hair. For a moment, he pretended that they weren't caught up in a murder, that they were just a couple planning to spend the night together. Too bad that life wasn't that easy.

They left the room and went down the hall to the elevator. In the lobby, Moreno separated from a small group of his followers and came toward them. Trying to read his expression, Brady concentrated on his intense dark brown eyes. Moreno hardly seemed to blink. He circled Sasha like a great white shark.

His mesmerizing gaze fastened on her. "Did you sleep well?"

"Well enough," she said politely. "And you?"

"I required two meditation sessions to relax my mind enough to achieve REM sleep. It's difficult to process a murder. The energy in the hotel needs a psychic adjustment."

"Better not let Reinhardt hear you say that," she said. "Not while he's getting ready for the grand opening."

"I was concerned about you."

Brady's protective senses went on high alert. If Moreno so much as touched Sasha, he'd knock the guru flat on his buttocks.

Moreno continued, "You shouldn't stay here, Sasha. This place is not conducive to your goals and aims. You've made great progress for someone your age, and I'd hate to see you hurt. My people and I will be moving to Jim Birch's dude ranch. I propose that you come with us."

"I've made other arrangements," she said.

"Please reconsider. I have your best interests at heart."

Brady inserted himself between them. "She's made other plans. Back off."

Moreno's eyes flared with anger. The corner of his mouth twisted into a scowl. He wasn't accustomed to being told he couldn't have what he wanted. Turning his shoulder to exclude Brady, he spoke to Sasha. "When you need me, I'll be here for you."

He pivoted and rejoined his people, who waited in a dark cluster like a flock of crows.

In a low voice, Brady said, "I don't trust that guy."

"Same here."

"What was he saying about your ambitions?"

"The usual line. If you conceive it, you can achieve it."

He took her elbow and walked her through the lobby. "Do you believe that?"

"Sure I do. That's the thing about Moreno. Most of his philosophy makes sense, and I like taking a positive approach. But you can't control everything. Sometimes you win, sometimes you lose. And sometimes you look through a window and see a murder being committed."

Across the lobby, he spotted Sheriff McKinley accompanied by two strangers carrying suitcases. Brady guessed they were the agents from CBI. The appointment notebook he'd picked up in Lauren's SUV burned against the inner pocket in his jacket. Police procedure dictated that he turn the evidence over to them, but he wanted a chance to look at it first. He hustled Sasha toward the exit, hoping to avoid the agents.

"Wait a minute," she said. "I'd like to get a cup of coffee before we go."

A reasonable request. He had no logical reason to say no. Still, he tried to divert her. "We could stop at the diner."

"No need to go to extra trouble." She veered in the

direction of an espresso kiosk that was set up near the black marble waterfall. "The aroma is calling to me."

Keeping his back to the check-in desk, he went to the kiosk. With any luck, they could grab a coffee and get the hell out of the lobby before the sheriff saw him. If Brady was introduced to the CBI agents, he'd have no excuse for not handing over Lauren's notebook. He would be purposely obstructing their investigation.

At the kiosk, Sasha stared up at the dozens of possible combinations. "Let's see. What do I want?"

"Coffee, black," he suggested.

She licked her lips. "I'll have an extralarge double-shot caramel macchiato with soy milk."

He groaned. "I almost forgot you were a city girl."

"My neighborhood barista knows me by name." She stared through the glass case at the pastries. "And throw in one of those low-fat blueberry muffins."

Brady felt a tap on his shoulder. Slowly, he turned to face Sheriff McKinley. Standing to his left were two men in conservative jackets and sunglasses.

"I thought that was you," McKinley said. "Deputy Brady Ellis, I'd like to introduce Agent Colton and Agent Zeto from the CBI."

Brady shook their hands and tried to tell himself that he wasn't really lying. Yes, he was withholding evidence. But it was only temporary. Sooner or later he'd hand over the notebook. "Pleased to meet you."

When Sasha was introduced, her beaming smile lightened the mood.

Agent Zeto held her hand a few seconds too long. "We'll need to take a statement from you."

"No prob," she said. "Right now I have to run. But after the meeting with the resort investors, I'm totally available."

"We'll be in touch."

On that less-than-promising note, Brady whisked her through the lobby. They'd be seeing the agents again. He'd have to come up with an excuse for why he'd mishandled evidence. Maybe there wouldn't be anything useful in those pages, and he could ignore the notebook altogether. But that wasn't the way police procedure worked. He had to take responsibility.

Outside, the temperature had dropped and snowflakes dotted the air. He bundled Sasha into the SUV and set out on the familiar route to Dooley's ranch. Though there was less traffic than usual on the streets, more skiers were out. Some were riding a shuttle to the lodge by the gondola and chairlift. Others were walking with their gear in tow.

Sasha sipped her fancy coffee drink. "Anything new with the investigation?" she asked.

"Nothing I'd know about."

"What does that mean?"

His natural inclination was to keep his mouth shut. She didn't need to be bothered by his problems, but she'd find out soon enough when Agent Zeto interviewed her. "I'm off the case."

"Why?"

"The sheriff handed jurisdiction to the CBI. They have better resources."

"What about me? Are you still my bodyguard?"

"You bet I am."

He'd demanded that position. McKinley wanted to assign Brady to traffic duty, but he'd flat out refused. Sasha needed his full-time protection.

Even if he hadn't been attracted to her, he'd have felt the same way about protecting a witness. The main reason he'd gone into law enforcement was to keep people safe. It might be corny, but he still believed that it was his duty to serve and protect.

"It doesn't seem fair," she said. "You've already made a lot of headway."

He wanted to believe that was true. Though he lacked the formal training to conduct a homicide investigation, he had a lawman's instincts and an innate ability to see through alibis and find the truth. Like his uncle had said, poker sense. Brady needed to learn to trust his gut.

"There's only one thing that's important," he said, "finding the killer and making sure no one else gets hurt."

"You're not giving up, are you?"

He glanced over at her. She was as pretty and as sweet as a cupcake with sprinkles, but her big blue eyes were serious. "You ask the hard questions."

"Well, it's important to me. As you keep pointing out, I'm in danger. I could get killed. And you could…" Her voice faded, and her delicate hand fluttered.

"What? What could I do?"

"I haven't known you for a long time, but I believe in you. I believe you're a good detective." She shrugged. "At the risk of sounding like Moreno, you need to believe how good you really are."

"You're saying I shouldn't quit."

"That's what I'm saying."

"I'll try to work with the CBI." Even if giving up jurisdiction made him feel like a second-string player, he had a unique perspective on the crime. Because of his uncle and Sasha, he was intertwined with the suspects. Answering the 911 call meant he'd literally been in at the start.

Even if he wanted to, he couldn't quit his investigation.

WITH EVERYONE GATHERED in the huge front room at the big house on the ranch, Dooley took a position in front of the big moss-rock fireplace where a gas fire radiated heat. Brady stood at the back of the room, watching. Moreno sat on a heavy leather chair that looked like a throne while three of his minions perched in a row on the sofa, drinking herbal tea. Katie Cook and her distinguished white-haired husband shared a love seat. Reinhardt, looking as tense as a clenched fist, sprawled on another sofa, with Andrea Tate sitting as far away from him as she could at the opposite end.

Sasha had set up the computer with Damien Loughlin's face on a table near the fireplace.

Dooley hitched his thumbs in the pockets of his jeans and started talking. "I was planning to saddle up a bunch of horses and get all of you outside where you could appreciate this mountain land and understand the need to preserve our resources. But I'm not going to drag you out in the snow."

"Thank you," Katie said. "I would have been concerned about being injured."

"Wasn't worried about you," Dooley said. "I didn't want any of the horses to take a tumble."

Brady stifled an urge to chuckle. His plan had been to watch the start of the meeting and then go into Dooley's office, where he could study the contents of Lauren's notebook. But he'd changed his mind. His uncle was up to something, and he wanted to know what it was.

"I figure you all know what I want out of this partnership," Dooley said. "I've been consistent. Every time we talk about our needs, I tell you that I want a percent of profits to go into land management."

"And we're on your side," Reinhardt said. "We all agree that we need to hire a qualified person to coordinate with the BLM, the EPA and the Forest Service. It's in everybody's interest to care for the land and the wildlife."

There were murmurs of support that ended with the

computerized version of Damien saying, "Now that we have that wrapped up, I'd like to discuss our current problem."

"Whoa there, counselor." Dooley bent down to talk to the computer screen. "I've got something more to say. We had a murder in Arcadia. And our sheriff's department ain't equipped to handle the investigation. Law enforcement needs to expand, and we need to pay for it."

"I disagree." Reinhardt raised his hand. "That's a problem for the county."

"You're a fine one to talk. If you'd had your hotel security up and running, we'd have arrested the killer."

"I paid for it," Reinhardt grumbled. "My security man, Grant Jacobson, has complete surveillance on the hotel. Hey, that's an idea. Instead of funding the local law enforcement, why not hire Jacobson to handle security for all the ski resort properties."

"Including the condos?" Damien asked.

"Most of them already employ a security company."

"What about the ice rink?" Katie asked.

"And outlying areas," Moreno said.

"Relax." Reinhardt spread his hands in an expansive gesture. "Jacobson is a pro. He could set up a police force that would make this the most secure area in Colorado."

Brady didn't like where this conversation was headed. The very idea of a private police force should be nipped in the bud. If Dooley didn't say something to put them on the right track, he'd have no choice but to step forward.

"How much would this cost?" Moreno asked.

One of his followers piped up, "It'd be worth the price. We have high-profile people who attend our seminars— movie stars and politicians. Their safety is of paramount concern."

"Same here," Katie said. When it came to name-dropping, she would not be outdone. "I'm bringing in famous athletes and champion skaters, many of whom need bodyguards."

From across the room, Dooley met his gaze and gave him a grin. "Let's hear what Deputy Brady Ellis has to say."

Brady stepped away from the wall. "First of all, let me make it clear that I appreciate Grant Jacobson's skills, his leadership ability and his experience. He's a hero."

"Damn right," Reinhardt said.

"But the Arcadia partners can't set up their own private vigilante force. You can't station armed guards on every street corner, and you wouldn't want to."

"He's right," Katie said. "Arcadia should be about recreation and fun. I'm acquainted with many athletes from Russia and China, and their bodyguards are very subtle. We should consult with them."

Ignoring her, Brady continued, "Our sheriff's department usually works just fine. The 911 system is efficient. Our efforts are well coordinated with mountain rescue, helicopter evacuations and ambulance services. Still, Dooley has a point. We could use more personnel, more equipment and more funding."

"If I'm going to pay for it," Reinhardt said, "I want to be in charge."

"That's exactly why a private police force doesn't work," Dooley said in his deceptively soft drawl. "If you run the police, it puts you above the law."

"What are you saying?"

"You're a suspect in this murder."

Reinhardt surged to his feet. "Wrongly accused. I've been wrongly accused."

"I understand why the police are looking at you," Katie

chirped. She almost sounded cheerful. "Lauren Robbins was your ex-wife."

"I didn't kill her. Tell them, Andrea."

Without looking up, she murmured, "He was with me."

"You people have it all wrong. I didn't hate Lauren." He glared like a trapped animal. "I respected her. She was more than a wife. We worked together. She wasn't much of a salesperson, but she was the best bookkeeper I've ever had."

Sasha stood. "Excuse me. Damien has something to add."

"Wait," Moreno said. "I want to hear more from Reinhardt. If he's charged with murder, it tarnishes all our reputations."

"What murder charges?" Reinhardt snapped.

"I heard the police were about to arrest you."

"You heard wrong."

"Excuse me," Sasha said more loudly. "Please take your seats."

Grumbling, they did so. She turned up the volume for Damien's computer image. "Thank you," he said.

They muttered a hostile response.

He continued, "Over the next few days, you're all going to be questioned by the police and the CBI. Do not—I repeat—do not speak to anyone without having me present. Even if you choose to bring in your own attorney, I wish to be included at all of these interviews."

"How are we supposed to do that?" Dooley gave a snort. "You're a hundred and seven miles away."

"I'm leaving Denver within the hour," Damien said. "I'll be in Arcadia this afternoon. In the meantime, may I remind you that there's a law enforcement officer in the room with you? Do not speak of the crime in his presence. Is that clear?"

Their heads swiveled as they turned toward Brady. He put on his hat and gave a nod. "I was just leaving."

He stepped onto the front porch, closed the door behind himself and inhaled a deep breath. The killer was one of them. He knew it and so did they.

# Chapter Sixteen

Sasha took her laptop into Dooley's office—a large space filled with oak file cabinets, a giant desk and half a dozen mounted heads on the walls. Avoiding the marble-eyed gazes of the taxidermy collection, she sat behind the desk and placed the screen on the desktop so she could talk to Damien.

As soon as his computerized face appeared, he asked, "Are we alone?"

She looked up at a snarling bobcat. "Kind of."

"What does that mean?"

She turned the computer so he could see the collection. "Dooley is big on protecting the environment, but I guess he's also a hunter."

"What the hell is that thing?"

She followed his computerized gaze. "Moose. He's got a beard. Did you know mooses had beards? That doesn't sound right, does it? *Mooses?* Should it be *meese?*"

"Sasha, pay attention. Are there any other people in the room?"

"No, sir."

Reinhardt and Andrea were already on their way back to the hotel. Moreno and his entourage were in the dining room sharing tea and special gluten-free coffee cake with

Katie and her husband. Brady had made himself scarce after Damien pointed out that he was the enemy.

Though she understood that attorneys and police sometimes had different agendas when it came to crime, she'd always thought they were after the same thing: justice. Damien would tell her that she was being naive. So would her brother Alex. They'd remind her that the duty of a lawyer was to represent their client, whether they were guilty or not.

But it didn't feel right. If Reinhardt was responsible for the murder of his wife, Sasha wanted to see him in prison. Maybe she was in the wrong profession.

Outside the window, the wind whooshed around the corner of the big house. The snow had begun to fall in a steady white curtain.

She confronted computerized Damien. "If you're coming up here this afternoon, you should get on the road. The weather is starting to get nasty."

"Duly noted."

"I spoke to the property manager at the condo this morning. She stocked the refrigerator with your standard food order."

"And there's champagne for us in the fridge, right?"

*For us?* "Three bottles."

"There were supposed to be four."

"I opened one the first night," she said.

"You naughty girl," he said with a smirk. "Did you try the hot tub?"

"Yes." Hoping to squelch any flirting, she added, "I remembered to bring my bathing suit."

"Clothes aren't really necessary. Not in the privacy of the condo."

She was beginning to feel as if the proper attire for a spin in the hot tub with Damien would be a suit of armor.

"Anyway, the condo is ready for you. The property manager assured me that the dead bolt on the balcony door has been installed."

"Why are you telling me this? Aren't you staying there?"

"After the ninja break-in, I didn't feel safe. I booked a room at the hotel last night."

She was certain that Damien wasn't going to appreciate her plan to spend tonight with Brady, but her mind was made up. When it came to her job, she'd do what was required, but her sleeping arrangements were her own private business.

"I'll be at the condo tonight," he said. "You can move back."

"I have other plans." Hoping to avoid a discussion of where she'd be sleeping, she changed the topic. "What time do you think you'll be arriving? I can set up appointments with the CBI agents."

"What are these plans of yours?"

"Staying with a friend."

"Don't be ridiculous, Sasha. I was looking forward to spending time with you. We could discuss your future with the firm."

Talking about her career goals with a senior partner was a hugely tempting opportunity. She'd been employed at the Three *S*s for only a year. Most legal assistants went forever without being noticed. Damien hadn't actually said anything that would cause her to mistrust him. "I'd like to have that talk. I hope to get started taking classes to learn mediation in the spring."

"I'm sure you do." When he straightened his necktie, playing for time, she knew there was something he wasn't telling her. "Right now we'll focus on the needs of the Arcadia investors. Reinhardt and his sexy little real estate agent, Andrea, are the top suspects. They both have motive. If you hadn't witnessed the murder, he'd be in custody right now."

"What's their motive?"

"The oldest in the book," he said smugly. "Money and revenge. Pay attention, Sasha, you might learn something."

She put up with his condescending attitude to get information. "Tell me all about it."

"Reinhardt's ex-wife was receiving alimony, and she kept digging into his finances, finding bits and pieces he might owe her. She did the same with Andrea."

"They were partners," Sasha recalled.

"It bothers me that Lauren was also working for Westfield," he said. "The autopsy showed that he was murdered. He took a blow to the skull before he fell down the stairs."

She gasped. It was hard to imagine someone killing that sweet, elderly man who loved his cats so dearly. "That's horrible."

"The Denver homicide cops are looking into any connection between that murder and the death of Lauren Robbins. They figure one murder leads to another."

"What could possibly be the motive for killing Mr. Westfield?"

"I don't know. There's some question about a dude-ranch property that Westfield wanted to acquire. Do you know anything about it?"

"I've been there," she said quickly. "Moreno is also interested in buying the dude ranch to set up an ashram for his followers."

"The same property?"

She nodded. "Andrea is the real-estate agent, and I think she was setting up a bidding war between Moreno and her cousin."

"And Reinhardt?"

"I haven't heard anything about him and the dude-ranch property," she said. "It's too far from the ski lodge to be a good development for condos."

"That's good. He doesn't need any more strikes against him." Damien's hand reached toward the screen, preparing to close down their communication. "I should be in Arcadia by three o'clock. When I arrive, we'll make appointments with the CBI. We'll have a nice dinner and a soak in the hot tub."

His face disappeared. Though she hadn't actually told him that she wouldn't be waiting for him at the condo, Sasha was even more convinced that she didn't want to put herself in that position. She might be naive, but she wasn't fool enough to think Damien was interested in discussing her career.

During the conversations she'd had with him over the past few days, he hadn't once asked about her safety. The only time he'd perked up was just now when he talked about champagne and hot tubs. Her brother had it right when he'd said that the condo was a bachelor pad; Damien wanted her alone with him so he could seduce her. The never-forgotten chords of "Trashy Sasha" played in her head.

She closed the computer and looked up at the bobcat on the wall and snarled back at it, baring her teeth. *No way, Damien.* She'd sleep outside in the snow before she spent the night under the same roof with him.

In the hallway outside the office, Brady was waiting for her. Seeing him immediately brightened her mood. Leaning against the wall opposite the office, he squinted down at a small notebook, concentrating hard. For some reason, he was wearing purple latex gloves. Looking up, he gave her a crooked grin. "Either I need glasses or I finally found somebody with worse penmanship than mine."

"Let me see." She held out a hand. "I've gotten pretty good at translating chicken scratches for lawyers."

He hesitated. "This is evidence. I shouldn't let you look at it. Matter of fact, I shouldn't be looking, either."

"Evidence, huh? That's why you're wearing the gloves. You don't want to leave fingerprints."

He held up a purple hand. "I've been carrying a boxful of these around in my SUV for a couple of years. This is the first time I've worn them."

"They're cute."

"That's what I was going for." He held the notebook toward her. "Can you tell what this says? It looks like something about a Dr. Cayman at an office in a southern bank."

She glanced at the scribbled abbreviations. The letters *D* and *R* were in capitals. In small letters, it read "off-s-bnk." She took her cue from the one clear word.

"Cayman," she said, "might refer to the Cayman Islands, a place with many offshore banks."

"I got it." He nodded. "Off-s-bnk. What about the doctor?"

"I'm not sure, but I think that's an abbreviation used by auditors for a discrepancy report, referring to an accounting problem."

"What kind of problem?"

"A discrepancy," she said, "is a difference between reported transactions and actual money. If we could access Lauren's business records for that date, we might have more information."

He snapped the book closed. "Grab your jacket. I need to get back over to the hotel and talk to the CBI agents."

Since the investors' meeting was officially ended, Sasha had no particular reason to hang around at Dooley's ranch, especially since she and Brady would be returning here later. They made a speedy exit through the kitchen door and hiked through the snow toward the barn.

His SUV was parked outside a rustic little two-story log cabin nestled under a spruce tree. "Your house?"

"I never gave you the grand tour," he said. "Well, that's the barn. Over there is a bunkhouse. This is my place. Me and my dad built it when I was a teenager. Tour over."

She climbed into the passenger side of the SUV. "Did your dad live at the cabin, too? I don't understand the whole family dynamic here at the ranch."

"Nobody does," he said. "This property has been in our family for over a hundred years, so it gets kind of twisted around. The bottom line is that Dooley owns most of the acreage and runs the ranch. He's been a widower for seven years but has a lady friend who lives in Arcadia. Dooley has four kids, but only one of them is interested in ranching."

"That would be Daniel," she said, recalling the name from some documents. "And he's married with three kids."

Brady drove along the narrow road toward the front of the big house. "Daniel and his wife have a spread of their own where she trains horses. Their kids are off in college. When he's in town, Daniel works with Dooley. Someday he'll inherit the ranch."

"What about you? What do you inherit?"

"I don't really think about it." He peered through the windshield at the steadily falling snow. "I'll always help out at the ranch, but it's not my whole life. When I was a kid, all I wanted to do was be a rancher like Uncle Dooley. I loved riding and being outdoors. I still do."

His words ended on a pensive sigh. Brady didn't often talk about himself, and she wanted to hear more. "What changed your mind?"

"I want to make a difference." He gave a little shrug.

"Being in law enforcement makes that happen. When people get in trouble, I'm the first one they call."

She thought of the first time she'd seen him, when he responded to her 911 call. His presence had been a huge relief. When she saw his wide shoulders and determined eyes, she'd known that he had come to help her. "You like your work."

"That's why I hate giving up on this murder. I want to make it right."

At the moment, she was less interested in the murder and more focused on the lawman who wanted to solve it. He was so deeply involved in his work that it was an extension of him. Sasha had never felt that way about her job. Sure, she liked the prestige of being employed by a high-power law firm, and the paycheck was decent. But she lacked a passion for the law.

"There must have been something in your childhood," she said, "that made you want to be a deputy."

"I always used to root for the underdog, always took care of the runt in the litter." He tossed her a grin. "If I hadn't become a deputy, I would've been a vet."

"Tell me about your dad."

"He died eight years ago in a car accident. His death was mercifully fast, unexpected. One day he was here. The next he was gone forever. It left me with unanswered questions. I don't think I ever really knew my dad. He was a good man. Quiet. Kindhearted. He loved being a cowboy."

Though his expression barely changed, she felt the depth of his emotion. "And you loved him."

"Yeah, I love both my parents. You remind me of my mom. She's a city gal, real pretty and real smart."

A gentle warmth made her smile. "You think I'm pretty."

"And smart."

At the intersection with the highway, he turned right. On a clear day, the chairlift and the ski lodge would have been visible in the distance. Through the snowfall, she could hardly see beyond the trees at the edge of the road. "Do people ski in this weather?"

"It's a winter sport."

"You never told me why it was so important to see the CBI agents."

"The evidence in the notebook," he said. "I didn't obtain it in the usual manner. I kind of swiped the notebook out of the glove compartment in Lauren Robbins's car, and it's been weighing on my conscience like a twelve-ton boulder."

Obviously, he had already gone through the notebook. "Did you find any clues?"

"The best one is that offshore bank note," he said. "Other than that, it's just random jotting. She only had a few big clients like Westfield and she took them out to dinner and to sports events. Andrea owed her money but not a lot. And she really hated Reinhardt."

"How could you tell that from an appointment book?"

"On his birthday, she sent him dead roses and cheap wine."

Sasha chuckled. "That's pretty funny."

"Maybe for the first year after the divorce or the second, but they've been split up for five years. It was time for her to move on."

"Unless she saw him with her cousin and that triggered her anger." Sasha tried to put herself in Lauren's shoes. Being betrayed by a girlfriend could be painful. She remembered Damien's words. "The oldest motives in the book are money and revenge."

"But Lauren didn't kill anybody. She was the victim."

"I don't know if this helps or not, but Damien told me

that the Denver police have classified Westfield's death as a homicide. And they think it might be connected to Lauren's murder."

"It adds a new wrinkle." He hooked into his hands-free phone. "The sheriff won't be answering his radio. I'm going to try to get him on the cell phone to find out where the CBI agents are."

As they drove the last few miles toward the hotel, she realized that she'd blabbed confidential information. It wasn't a big deal, really. Brady was a cop. He'd know what other cops had discovered.

As Brady drove into the valet parking area at the hotel, he finished his phone call to Sheriff McKinley. He turned to her. "We've got a problem."

"What's that?"

"The CBI is on their way to arrest Reinhardt."

## Chapter Seventeen

Brady rushed into the lavish hotel lobby with Sasha right beside him. Unless the CBI had come up with conclusive proof, he thought the arrest of Reinhardt was premature. His gut told him that Reinhardt was a tough contractor who had earned his millions the hard way and knew that murder was bad business. Reinhardt had already figured out the way to handle his ex-wife. When Lauren gave him trouble, he paid the woman off.

Waiting for the elevator, his cell phone jangled. It was McKinley.

Brady answered. "What is it, Sheriff?"

"We're up here on the concierge floor, and Reinhardt is gone. We've got to assume he's making a run for it. If you see him, arrest him on sight."

Even before he disconnected the call, Brady had a pretty good idea where he would find Reinhardt. When he'd searched for the body of Lauren Robbins, he'd been all over the hotel, but he knew better than to start combing the back hallways and the laundry room. The interior and part of the exterior of the hotel were visible on surveillance cameras, and there was only one man who could make a fugitive disappear from these premises: Grant Jacobson.

He glanced down at Sasha. "Stick close to me."

"What are we doing?"

"We'll know when we get there."

He went to the security offices behind the front desk. In the room with all the camera feeds, he found Jacobson sitting alone, watching the monitors. Brady ushered Sasha inside and closed the door.

"Grant Jacobson, your name came up at a meeting this morning."

"Did it?"

As Jacobson pushed back from the desk and stood, his gaze darted toward his private office at the back of the room. That glance was what Dooley would call a "tell." Jacobson was concerned about something in that rear office.

"Somebody suggested that we should have a private police force to secure and protect the resort, and that you should run it. I had to tell them it was a bad idea. A sheriff's department is different from private security." Brady nodded toward the closed door to Jacobson's private office. "Is he in there?"

Jacobson rubbed his hand across his granite jaw. "You're pretty smart for a cowboy."

"He's not a cowboy," Sasha said. "He's a cop."

"Tell me, Brady. How did you know?"

"It didn't take a lot of brainpower," he said. "I've seen your surveillance setup. The way I figure, you've probably engineered a successful escape from this hotel."

"And why would I do that?"

"Because you know it might be necessary." Brady didn't make a move toward the office. Getting in a fight with Jacobson would be a supremely dumb move, and he wasn't sure he could win. "But the CBI agents made their move too quickly, and you haven't had time to get Reinhardt away from here."

"In another ten minutes, he would have been in the

wind," Jacobson said. "What's the evidence they've got against him?"

Brady took out his phone. "I'll find out."

Sheriff McKinley answered right away. His voice was high and nervous. "Did you see him?"

"Not yet." On the surveillance video screen for the concierge level, Brady watched the sheriff and the two CBI agents searching the rooms on that floor. "Can you tell me about the new evidence?"

"Fingerprints. The victim's purse was with her inside the steamer trunk, and the forensic people found Reinhardt's prints on a couple of quarters in her wallet."

"Sounds kind of circumstantial," Brady said.

"He said he hadn't seen her in months. What are the odds that she's been carrying those quarters around for months?"

That was a valid point. "I'll call you if I find him."

Brady ended the call and turned toward Jacobson. "Reinhardt has some explaining to do."

"Let's talk."

When Jacobson strode across the room, Brady had to remind himself that the man had a prosthetic leg. His gait was steady and determined. If Brady had been in the market for an assassin, he would have put Jacobson at the top of the list.

Using an optical scanner, Jacobson unlocked his private office. They entered the small room that was neatly furnished with a desk, two computers and several file cabinets.

Reinhardt sat behind the desk with his brawny arms folded on the surface in front of him. "I can't believe this. Lauren is reaching out from the grave to make my life miserable."

"Don't blame yourself." To Brady's surprise, Sasha

circled the desk and gently patted Reinhardt's heavy shoulders. "You and Lauren had an intense, passionate relationship."

He shot her an angry glare. "How the hell would you know?"

"As the only woman in the room, I'm kind of the resident expert on this stuff."

Brady was both amused and intrigued by the way Sasha had waltzed in here and taken charge. "What's your evidence, Sasha?"

"It's been five years since the divorce, and they still can't stop poking at each other. He's still paying her off." She looked directly into Reinhardt's eyes. "Not to mention that Andrea looks an awful lot like your ex-wife."

"You could be right," he said grudgingly. "I never got that woman out of my system. She drove me crazy, but there's no way I wanted her dead."

Brady stepped in. Before they all started talking about their feelings, he wanted to get a take on the *real* evidence, namely Reinhardt's fingerprints on the quarters in Lauren's purse. "When was the last time you saw her face-to-face?"

Reinhardt looked at Sasha. "Shouldn't I have Damien here?"

She nodded. "Sorry, Brady. He's right."

"Understood." Brady stepped back. "A bit of advice. Never run away from the cops. It makes you look guilty."

Reinhardt stood behind the desk. "I'll tell you this, off the record. I had breakfast with Lauren in Denver last week. She wanted an advance on her alimony, claimed to be dead broke."

"Did you believe her?" Brady asked.

"Hard to say. She always exaggerated." He looked toward Sasha. "What do you call that?"

"She was a drama queen?"

"That's right. When the bill for breakfast came, she insisted on paying for the tip and calculated the amount down to eighteen percent. She put a couple of coins on the table to show how broke she was."

"And what happened to those coins?"

"I scooped them up and dumped them back in her wallet. Then I wrote her a check for the alimony advance."

That was a simple explanation for the fingerprints. If Reinhardt was lying about his intense relationship with his ex-wife, he was a pretty good actor. It seemed more likely that Andrea would have wanted her annoying cousin out of the way.

Brady arranged for the sheriff and the CBI to meet with Reinhardt right here in the security office while Sasha got Damien on the computer for their session of questioning. He was already on his way in the car, but this situation required his immediate attention.

In the outer room with Jacobson, Brady waited and watched normal hotel activities flitting across the many security screens. From the arriving guests to the maids cleaning up the rooms to the busy kitchens behind the restaurants, this complex was a beehive, a world unto itself. Jacobson was responsible for protecting these people and keeping them from harm.

"Do you like your work?" Brady asked.

"It satisfies me."

His priorities were clear. Take care of the guests, the employees and…the owner. "If I hadn't guessed where Reinhardt was hiding, would you have helped him go on the run?"

"I would have tried to talk him out of it. Like you said, running makes you look guilty."

"What if he insisted?"

"If I believed he was a killer, I'd turn him in. But I think the guy is innocent. And I go with my gut."

So did Brady.

BY FOUR O'CLOCK in the afternoon, the snow was coming down hard. Seven inches had already fallen, and there was no sign of a break. Riding in the passenger seat of Brady's SUV, Sasha had just gotten off the phone with Damien, who was running late and didn't expect to arrive at the condo until nightfall.

She'd managed not to tell him where she was staying, putting him off with a promise to meet with him tomorrow morning at the condo at eight o'clock so they could plan their day. Moreno would be in charge of the investors' meeting program.

Tucking her phone into a special pocket in her briefcase, she leaned back and exhaled a sigh. "That should take care of business for the rest of the day."

"I won't believe that unless you turn off your phone and your computer and unhook yourself from the rest of the world."

"Sorry, I can't. What if Damien needed to reach me? What if something came up at the Denver office?"

"There was a time, city girl, when people weren't on-call twenty-four hours a day."

"I'm not like that," she protested. "I'm not one of those people who are always checking their phones and answering emails."

"Professionals," he said. "That's what you want to be."

A few days ago, she might have agreed with him. She'd always been a little bit envious of the plugged-in people who were so much in demand that they couldn't take two steps without talking on their phone. But she wasn't so sure anymore.

He drove the SUV down the snowplowed road to the big house at Dooley's ranch. Though it wasn't late in the day, clouds had darkened the sky, and the pure white snowfall dissolved all the other colors into shadows. Lights shone on the porch of the big house and at the front of the barn. In spite of the whir of the heater inside the vehicle, a profound silence blanketed the land.

"It's not like this in the city," she said. "Snow means traffic jams and sloppy puddles in parking lots."

"The best place to enjoy new snow is indoors," he said as he drove past the big house to his cabin by the spruce tree, "with a fire on the grate and extra blankets on the bed."

It was the first time he'd mentioned bed, and a shiver of anticipation went through her. They hadn't talked about sleeping arrangements for tonight, and she wasn't sure what was going to happen. Their kisses whetted her memory. She usually didn't fall into bed with a guy until after they knew each other very well. But there was something different about Brady. He wasn't just *any* guy. He'd saved her life. He'd believed in her when no one else did. And she'd be kidding herself if she tried to believe that she wasn't attracted to his six-foot-four-inch frame and his long legs and that teasing dimple at the corner of his mouth.

He parked the SUV inside an open garage at the side of the cabin and turned to her. "I put your suitcase inside this morning."

Looking into his greenish-brown eyes, her heart thumped. "All I have is my briefcase. I can carry it myself."

She hopped out of the SUV into the cold and dashed to the porch, which was covered by the overhanging roof but still blanketed by an unbroken sheet of snow.

He unlocked the door, and they rushed inside. The corporate condo in Arcadia had the sleek atmosphere of a high-class bachelor pad. Brady's cabin was the opposite. It felt comfortable and cozy, and she was glad to see that he didn't share his uncle's fondness for animal heads. The walls were creamy stucco, decorated with framed photographs of landscapes. And there were shelves filled with well-read books and a couple of rodeo trophies. The floors were rugged wood covered by area rugs in Navajo designs. The furniture looked heavy and handcrafted but comfortable with thick wool-covered cushions.

Her suitcase stood by the door as though it hadn't decided whether it needed to be in the guest room or sharing the main bedroom with Brady.

"A warning," he said. "If you want to take a shower, you've got to move fast. My hot-water tank is kind of small."

"I'd rather shower in the morning," she said.

"Me, too."

"Then we'll really have to move fast…unless we shower together."

He met her gaze and then quickly looked away. "That's always an option."

She wandered into the adjoining kitchen and turned on the overhead light. "Should I make some coffee?"

"That'd be great. I'm going to get a fire started."

On the ceramic tile counter, she found a coffeemaker. The necessary beans, grinder and filter were stored in the cabinet directly above. As she went through the movements, she wondered if he was as hesitant and confused as she was about what would happen between them tonight.

It might be up to her to make the first move. Brady was so incredibly polite. He was an "aw, shucks" cowboy with a slow, sheepish grin. If she really wanted anything to happen, she might have to pounce.

The question was: Did she want anything to happen?

Keeping her distance might be for the best. There wasn't a possibility for them to have any kind of long-term relationship with her living in Denver and him being a deputy in Arcadia. Their life trajectories were worlds apart.

After she finished setting the coffee to brew, she went into the front room, where he'd started a fire and placed a screen in front of the blaze. He'd taken off his jacket and hat, tossing them onto the sofa. The sleeves of his uniform shirt were rolled up on his muscular forearms. Still hunkered down in front of the grate, he hadn't turned on any of the other lights in the cabin, and the glow from the fire danced in his unruly brown hair and highlighted his profile.

He beckoned to her. "Come over here and get warmed up."

"That's okay. I'm not cold."

He turned his head and reached toward her. "Come."

His direct gaze sent a tingle of excitement through her. He wasn't asking her to join him. He was telling her. There was no way she could refuse.

Sasha placed her hand in his and allowed him to pull her down onto the handwoven wool rug in front of the fireplace. The warmth from the flames mingled with a churning heat that came from inside as he took her into his arms and kissed her with a fierce passion that she hadn't felt from him before.

His kiss consumed her. A thousand sensations rushed through her body. Never had she been kissed like this, never. She hadn't expected fire from him, but somehow she'd known from the first that he was everything she'd ever wanted.

Sasha surrendered herself to him.

# *Chapter Eighteen*

After a few intense moments, Sasha found herself lying on her back in front of the fire with Brady beside her. His leg was thrown across her body, holding her in place, while he took his time kissing her and unbuttoning her blouse. His knuckles brushed against the bare flesh of her torso, setting off an electric reaction. There was magic in his touch. When he ran his fingers across the lace of her bra, she felt as if she was going to jump out of her skin.

She reached for his chest and grabbed a handful of material. "Take off your shirt."

"I've got a better idea," he murmured. "Why don't you do it for me?"

He leaned back, giving her access to his dark blue uniform. She definitely wanted the shirt off, but stripping him wasn't so easy. Her fingers were trembling so hard that she couldn't get the buttons through the holes. Even worse, there was a thermal undershirt under the uniform. It might take her hours to get rid of all these clothes. Biting her lower lip, she concentrated.

"Hah," she said, "got one."

"Need some help?"

"I can do this." She shoved him onto his back and straddled him while she worked on the shirt. This wasn't the best position for her to maintain concentration. The hard bulge inside his jeans pressed against her inner thigh, and she couldn't help rocking against him. What had ever made her think this man was shy?

As he rose to a sitting position, he grasped both of her wrists in his large hands. "Let me take care of your clothes."

"Do I have a choice?"

"Only if you want me to stop," he said.

"Absolutely not."

While desire had turned her into a total klutz, Brady was smooth; he seemed to know exactly what he was doing as he held her gently against his warm chest. He reached toward the sofa, grabbed a soft woolly blanket and spread it on the rug in front of the fire. Then he stretched her out on the blanket, stroked the hair off her forehead and gazed into her eyes. "Lie still."

"Why? What are you doing?"

"First I'm taking off your boots."

She stared up at the reflection of firelight across the ceiling. Her pulse was rapid, excited. Her senses were on high alert. The crackling of the fire sounded as loud as cannon fire. The scent of burning pine tickled her nostrils.

He pulled off her boots and socks, and the soles of her feet prickled. When he lay beside her, she was grateful to see that both his uniform and his thermal shirt were gone.

Her hands glided over his chest, tracing the pattern of springy black hair that spread across his muscular torso. Touching him gave her much-needed confidence. Dipping her head down, she kissed his hard nipples, and she knew she was having an effect on him because she could feel his body grow tense. Her fingers slid lower on his body. When she touched his belt buckle, he made a growling noise deep in his throat—a dangerous sound that both excited and pleased her.

Before she could reach farther, he had slipped off her shirt and her bra. Suddenly aggressive, he tightened his grasp and held her close. Her breasts were crushed against his chest.

Her mouth joined with his for another mind-blowing kiss. Gasping, she rubbed her cheek against his, feeling the rough beginnings of stubble.

Her clumsiness was gone. She was self-assured and focused. She wanted to explore his body, to learn every inch of him intimately. His male scent aroused her. All man, Brady was all man. And he was hers.

In the back of her mind, she wondered if they should talk about what was happening, to discuss their feelings, and she pushed words through her lips. "What are we doing?"

"I don't know about you, but I'm making love."

"But is this…?" Was it smart? Was it right? Should they reconsider? Should they try to understand?

"It's natural," he said.

And that was enough for her. Her questions and reservations could wait. She forgot everything else. For now, she would live in this moment when they were together, bathed in the flickering light from the fireplace.

His big hands were gentle as he cupped her breasts and teased her nipples into hard nubs. When he lowered his mouth to suckle, a shock wave tore through her. She arched her back, yearning to be one with him.

"You're beautiful, Sasha." His voice was a whisper. "A beautiful woman."

With quick, sure movements, he unfastened her waistband and slid her slacks down her legs. Her white lacy underpants followed. She felt his heated gaze on her body, caressing her from head to toe. And she felt beautiful.

When he lay beside her again, he was naked. She saw

him in firelit glimpses. His long muscular thighs. The expanse of his chest. The sharp definition of muscle in his arms. His rock-hard erection pressed into her hip, and she reached down to grasp him. Her touch sent a shudder through his body.

His arms tightened. She felt his strength and his urgency. As she stroked him, her leg wrapped around his thigh and she opened herself to him. A throbbing heat spread from her core to her entire body.

"I need a condom," he whispered.

"Yes."

"I have one in my wallet."

"Behind your badge?"

He sat up beside her on the floor and pawed through his jeans until he found what he was looking for. When he took her in his arms again, he was sheathed and ready.

He mounted her, taking control, and she arched into his embrace. Before, they had been doing a slow dance of lovemaking. Now the rhythm changed. As he pushed against her most intimate place, she heard the blood surging through her veins. She needed to feel him inside her. When he made that first thrust, she cried out in pure pleasure.

This was better than she'd imagined, better than she had dreamed of. She writhed under him, driven by passion. His hard, deep thrusts went on and on, taking her beyond mere satisfaction.

Sasha wasn't very experienced when it came to making love, and she tended to hold back. Not now. Not with Brady. An uncontrollable urge consumed her, and she desperately clung to self-control. She didn't want these sensations to end but didn't know how long she could hold on. Hot and cold at the same time, every muscle in her body tensed. And then…release. Fireworks exploded behind her eyelids. It felt as though she was flying, that she'd left her body to soar.

Afterward she lay beside him, breathing hard. She felt as if there was something she ought to say but all she could manage was a soft humming noise.

"Are you purring?" he asked.

"Maybe."

"I like it."

BRADY LIKED HER a lot. Making love in front of the fireplace hadn't been a plan or a strategy. He didn't think that way. He had just seen her coming toward him from the kitchen and had wanted to take her into his arms. Why? He couldn't say. Maybe it was because in his cabin, he felt safe and could relax his vigilance in protecting her. Or maybe it was because he wasn't sure how long their passion would last. Every minute with her had to count.

"Are you okay?" he asked.

"The floor is a little hard."

He dropped a light kiss on her cheek, lifted her off the floor, wrapped the edges of the soft woolly blanket around her and snuggled her into the big chair closest to the fire.

"I'll bring you coffee," he said. "Let me see if I remember. A double-shot macchiato with soy milk, right?"

"Or plain black coffee, no cream or sugar."

"I can do that."

On his way to the kitchen, he grabbed his jeans and pulled them on. He was still warm enough from their love-making that he didn't need a shirt. In the kitchen, he filled two mugs and returned to the front room, placing hers on the wooden arm of her chair. Looking down at her gave him a burst of pleasure. She meant a lot to him, more than he would have thought possible after knowing her for only a few days. He hated to think of her leaving, going back to the city.

He carried his steaming mug to the window where he looked out at the snow. Forecasters had predicted the storm would continue through the night and maybe into tomorrow morning, which ought to make the people at the ski lodge happy. The ski slopes had a good base, but more snow was welcome this early in the season.

Taking a taste of coffee, he reflected. So many things were changing. Arcadia was transforming from a quiet backwater town into a destination point. They needed to step up and prepare for new challenges. All the folks that kept urging him to run for sheriff were going to increase the pressure, and he ought to be seriously thinking about taking on that responsibility.

But there was only one thing on his mind: the pretty woman who was curled up in the chair by his fireplace. She was special. Different. When he made love to her, he actually believed that he wouldn't spend the rest of his life alone.

Crossing the room, he turned on a couple of table lamps before he sat on the sofa next to her chair. She smiled at him across the rim of her coffee mug, and the sparkle in her blue eyes brightened the whole room.

"I want you to stay in Arcadia," he said. "Give me a week, and I'll teach you how to ski and how to ride horses."

"I can't."

"Sure, you can. Call it a vacation."

"Maybe later this winter," she said. "It's not like I'm going to the moon. I'll only be a couple of hours away in Denver."

"But you'll be busy with your professional life. You were going to start taking classes."

"I'm not so sure about that." She leaned forward and

placed her mug on the coffee table. Under the blanket, she was naked, and he caught a glimpse of her smooth white breast before she pulled the blanket more snugly around her.

He swallowed hard. "No classes?"

"I don't know if law is the right career path for me. I mean, what if Reinhardt is guilty?"

"What if he is?"

Brady had managed to turn over Lauren's notebook to the CBI agents with a minimum of explanation. They were glad to have a direction of inquiry and would be studying Reinhardt's finances for offshore accounts. More than likely, the murder would be solved when the CBI figured out who had withdrawn enough money to pay the killer.

"If he's guilty," she said, "our law firm would have to defend him anyway."

"That's how the system works."

"How could I represent somebody like that, a person who could commit murder?"

She snuggled under the blanket as though hiding behind the soft folds, protecting herself. Was she scared? Sasha was one of the least fearful people he'd ever met. Her bravado could last for days, which, he suspected, came from being the youngest of five kids. She'd learned not to show her fear.

Gently, he asked, "What are you thinking about?"

"The killer's face." She avoided looking at him. "Shouldn't my memory start to fade after a couple of days? Why do I see him so clearly? The lines across his forehead, the sneer on his mouth, every wrinkle, every shadow seems to get sharper. Is that even possible?"

"Yes."

He believed her. He had suggested to the CBI agents that they arrange for Sasha to look through mug shots.

With their databases and their technology, they could put together a digital array of suspects for her to identify.

They hadn't been interested in his idea. Eyewitnesses were notoriously unreliable, and Sasha had caught only a glimpse of the killer through binoculars. Other people doubted her ability to recall.

But he believed her. Today he would insist on that digital array. "I'll set it up so you can look at photos. He's not going to get away with this."

She turned in her chair to face him. The hint of fear was gone. "Here's what I hate. Why should a lawyer have to defend him?"

Brady said nothing. She wasn't really expecting a response. He sat back and drank his coffee.

She continued, "I know that justice needs to be balanced and every criminal deserves a defense. But I don't think I could be the one who speaks for a guilty person. I'd blurt out to the judge and jury that they should lock him up and throw away the key."

"Are you thinking of changing jobs?"

"Oh, I couldn't. I was really lucky to get this job, and I need the salary. But I'm not convinced that I want to move on in the legal profession."

"Then my work is done," he teased. "I've gotten one more lawyer off the market."

"Are cops and attorneys always adversaries?"

"In theory, we're working on the same side." But he'd had his share of situations when a high-powered lawyer swooped in and got charges dismissed, turning a drunk driver back out on the road or letting a rich kid think it was okay for him to commit vandalism.

"I'd rather track down the bad guys," she said, "than figure out what happens to them afterward."

Before they sank into a complicated discussion of the
law, he asked, "How do you feel about dinner?"

"That depends," she said. "I don't want to go anyplace
else. Do we have to leave the cabin to get food?"

"I've got plenty of supplies right here."

"Then, yes, I'm hungry." With the blanket wrapped
around her like a toga, she rose from the chair. "I should
probably get dressed."

"Don't bother on my account."

He grinned when he suggested that she stay nude, but
he was only halfway kidding. Her nearness and the way
that blanket kept slipping was beginning to turn him on.

She lifted her chin. "Show me where I'll be sleeping."

"You have a choice."

"Show me your bedroom."

He grabbed her suitcase and wheeled it down the hall
to his bedroom—a big, comfortable space with a chair
by the window for reading and a flat-screen television
mounted on the wall over the dresser for late nights when
he couldn't fall asleep.

"Your bed," she said, "is gigantic."

"Extralong so my feet don't hang off the end."

She climbed up onto the dark blue comforter and primly
tucked her feet up under her. Peering through her lashes,
she gave him a flirtatious glance. "We never discussed
sleeping arrangements."

"I want you here. In my bed."

She dropped the blanket from one slender shoulder.
"Let's try it and make sure we fit."

He didn't need another invitation.

# *Chapter Nineteen*

As she drifted from dreams to wakefulness, Sasha felt warm, cozy and utterly content. She loved being under the comforter in Brady's giant bed. As she snuggled against him, his chest hairs tickled her nose and made her giggle.

She should have been tired; they'd made wild, passionate, incredible love four times last night, which had to be the equivalent of running a marathon. But her body felt energized and ready to go.

"Are you awake?" he asked.

She peeked through her eyelids. "It's still dark."

"There are a couple rays of sunlight. It's almost seven."

And she was supposed to meet Damien at eight o'clock at the condo to plan their day. A jolt of wake-up adrenaline blasted through her. The agenda for her day wasn't one happy event after the next. It was the opposite. Damien was sure to be angry about not having her at his beck and call at the condo. The investors' meeting today with Moreno promised to be full of problems since the guru couldn't allow his sterling reputation to be smeared by an inconvenient murder. Oh, yes, and she was still in danger from the killer-slash-ninja.

She tilted her head back and kissed Brady under the chin. "I wish we could stay here all day."

"We could try," he said.

"But it wouldn't work. I can't bail out on my job. And you need to be involved in the investigation." She threw off the comforter and sat up in the bed. Since she hadn't gotten around to unpacking her suitcase last night, she was wearing one of his T-shirts as a nightie. "How long will it take to get to the condo?"

"Half an hour in the snow."

"So I've got only half an hour to get ready."

He sat up beside her, completely naked and not a bit self-conscious. "We'll have to share the shower. To save time and hot water."

She liked that plan but didn't want to rush through a shower with him. Soaping him up and rinsing the suds away should be done slowly and meticulously, giving her the chance to savor every steely muscle in his body. "You go ahead. I'm just going to throw on clothes. I can't be late."

There was only one bathroom in his cabin—a large expanse of tile with a double sink and an old-fashioned claw-footed tub with a see-through circular shower curtain. With Brady in the shower, steam from the hot water clouded the mirrors above the sinks as she splashed water on her face and brushed her teeth.

The awareness that he was naked behind that filmy curtain was driving her crazy. But she was determined to be on time. "Hurry up."

"There's room in here for you."

She groaned with barely suppressed longing. Oh, she wanted to be in that shower. Damien had better appreciate her sacrifice.

"I SHOULD FIRE YOU."

Sasha gaped. She'd knocked herself out to get here on time. She and Brady had entered the condo at five minutes until eight o'clock. Damien had asked Brady to wait outside the front door, which was insulting but necessary to keep the deputy from overhearing any privileged information.

He'd sat her down at the counter in the kitchen, refreshed his own coffee without asking her if she wanted any and made his announcement.

"Why fire me?" she asked.

"This shouldn't come as a surprise." In the absence of a necktie to adjust, he straightened the collar on his gray sweater. "You could have stayed here last night, but you chose otherwise."

She had expected a reprimand, but threatening to fire her was way over-the-top. No way would she let him get away with it. "Are you saying that you'd fire me because I wouldn't spend the night with you?"

"Certainly not," he said in the cool baritone he used to mesmerize juries. "That would be sexual harassment, and I have no intentions toward you other than expecting—no, demanding—a professional performance of your duties."

"But I've been professional," she protested. She'd run the meetings in his absence, recorded them and made sure he was hooked in via computer when his presence as an attorney was required.

"I'm disappointed in you, Sasha. I've gone out of my way to nurture your career at the firm. Some people might think I was expecting a quid pro quo where I scratch your back and you scratch mine, but—"

"Did you lead anyone else to believe in this quid pro quo?" She translated into the non-Latin version: sleeping with him to get favors on the job.

He lifted his coffee mug to his unsmiling lips. "Small-minded people draw their own conclusions when they see an attractive twenty-three-year-old woman rising so quickly through the ranks."

Her jaw tightened. She hadn't been goofing off. As his legal assistant, she'd put in hours and hours of overtime doing research and filing court documents. All her good work was going up in smoke. "You still haven't told me why you'd terminate my employment."

"Let's start with whatever idiotic urge compelled you to spy on the Gateway Hotel through my binoculars."

"That wasn't smart," she conceded, "but the consequences turned out well. Because I witnessed the murder, I could state, unequivocally, that our client was innocent."

Damien shrugged. "I'd be willing to forgive if that was your only indiscretion, but you failed on a more important level. You betrayed the sacred bond between client and attorney."

"Confidentiality," she said.

"Do you deny that you shared information you obtained from me or from one of our clients with Deputy Brady Ellis?"

She couldn't categorically say that she hadn't told Brady about a few details he'd shared with her about the investigation. She knew that she'd mentioned that the Denver police considered Westfield's death to be murder. "I've said nothing that would affect or harm our clients."

"That's not for you to decide," he said. "Confidential means you keep your mouth shut. I partially blame myself for your failure. I should have counseled you about how difficult it can be for attorneys to work closely with law enforcement, especially when the cop in question is a tall, good-looking cowboy."

Her lips pressed together, holding back a scream of frustration. *What a sleazeball.* He was insinuating that Brady had seduced her to get information, which was patently ridiculous. "He was acting as my bodyguard."

"I'm sure he kept his eye on your body."

She couldn't pretend that she and Brady hadn't slept together last night. Nor could she claim a lack of culpability. Damn it, she'd broken confidentiality. She should have known better. And so should Brady.

Her job wasn't the most important thing in her life, but she didn't want to lose it. Not like this, anyway. She didn't want that stain on her record.

Straightening her shoulders, she faced the sleaze and asked, "How can I make this right?"

"I'm afraid it's too late."

"You're going to need my help at the meeting." He had no idea what she actually did to record those sessions and make sense of them.

"You bring up an interesting but irrelevant point," he said. "There won't be any more meetings with the Arcadia investors. Moreno has pulled out because he doesn't want the association with Reinhardt and the murder. Thanks to you, my negotiations are falling apart."

As soon as he spoke, she got the full picture. Damien was setting her up to take the blame for the collapse of the Arcadia partnership and the possible loss of revenue to the firm. He could twist every contentious issue and every argument to look as if it was her fault. Given this scenario, she wasn't just losing the job with the Three Ss. Nobody would ever hire her again.

"I have a proposition," she said.

He chuckled. "You're joking."

"What if I could convince Moreno to come back into the fold? I know he's staying at the dude ranch and he wants to buy that property. I might be able to show him how it would be to his benefit to maintain ties with the resort."

"And why would he listen to you?"

That was a fair question, and she didn't have an answer. For the past couple of days, Moreno had been going out of his way to talk to her. If she stopped and listened, she might be able to change his mind. "I'd like to try."

Damien's cool but slimy gaze rested on her face. Never again would she think of him as handsome or eligible. He was a self-serving creep who, unfortunately, had a vast influence over her future employment. Even if she wasn't working for him, she'd need his recommendation.

"Talk to Moreno," he said. "If you can get him back on board, you can keep your job."

She jumped to her feet. "You won't be disappointed."

Halfway to the exit from the condo, he called after her. "Sasha."

*Now what?* She turned. "Yes, sir."

"Leave the notes and your briefcase."

His words stung. She'd gotten so accustomed to carrying her briefcase that it was like an extension of her arm. Returning to the kitchen counter, she opened the briefcase, took out her personal cell phone and her wallet and placed them in the pockets of her parka.

"These are mine." She also had a small makeup case, but she didn't want to dig through the briefcase to find it. "You can keep the rest. Is there anything else?"

"Be careful what you say to your deputy."

She ran for the door.

In the hallway outside, Brady stood waiting. Too fired up to wait for the elevator, she grabbed his arm and dragged him down the staircase. She charged through the lobby and burst through the exit door. Outside, the snow had given up for the day. Hazy blue skies streaked behind the snow clouds above the condo complex.

It must have been cold, but she didn't feel the chill as she stormed down the shoveled sidewalk. Distance— she wanted to put enough distance between herself and Damien that he wouldn't hear if she exploded. With Brady trailing in her wake, she marched to the end of the sidewalk and climbed over the accumulated snow piled up at the curb. Her boots slipped on the packed ice in the parking lot, but she kept going. If the way had been clear, she would have run for a hundred miles until the anger inside her was spent.

At the next corner, she dug her toe into the snow and climbed onto another sidewalk. Icy water was already seeping through the seams into her boots, which really weren't made for outdoor activities. They were going to be ruined, and she didn't care, didn't care about anything.

Brady caught her arm, bringing her to a sudden halt. "Where are you going?"

"Let go." She wrenched her arm, but he held tight. "Let go of me, right now."

"Talk to me, Sasha."

"I'm in trouble," she shouted. In the still morning light, those words sounded like an obscenity. "Damien almost fired me."

Unsmiling, he asked, "How can I help?"

"You can't. And why would you want to?" She turned on him, unleashing her rage. "You hate my job."

"There must be something we can do."

"You've done quite enough, thank you very much. You're the reason I'm nearly unemployed."

His jaw tensed, and his head pulled back as though she'd slapped him. She knew that she was being unfair. No matter how furious she was, she couldn't blame Brady. Less than an hour ago, she'd been in his bed, in his arms, coming awake from a dream that reflected their night of lovemaking. How could she stand here and accuse him? What was wrong with her?

"Brady, I'm sorry."

"It's okay. Let's get out of here."

He placed his hand at the small of her back to guide her down the sidewalk, but his touch didn't soothe her. She felt empty and alone with no one on her side, no one to help her. She'd been playing with the big kids, and she'd lost.

"I don't deserve to be fired," she said, "but Damien has a valid reason. He accused me of breaching confidentiality when I talked to you, and he was one hundred percent right. I passed on information."

"You never revealed anything that would cause me to suspect Damien's clients."

"Technically, it doesn't matter. I should have kept my big mouth shut."

Her only hope for redemption was to convince Sam Moreno to change his mind and rejoin the Arcadia partnership.

# Chapter Twenty

Before Brady agreed to chauffeur Sasha to the dude ranch to see Moreno, he insisted that they stop for coffee and breakfast. His concern wasn't to feed her; Jim Birch's wife always had something fresh from the oven at the dude ranch. Brady wanted Sasha to take her time and calm down.

Sitting in a booth at the Kettle Diner in Arcadia, he wasn't happy to see her drain her coffee cup in a few gulps. The last thing she needed in her agitated state was caffeine.

He understood why she'd exploded on the sidewalk outside the corporate condo. She was angry. And he knew she hadn't meant to blame him. She'd been lashing out, and he'd been little more than a bystander. Not innocent, though—he couldn't claim that his presence had no effect on Damien's threat to fire her. If Brady hadn't been there to listen to her privileged information, Sasha never would have been in trouble.

The waitress delivered each of them a plate of banana pancakes topped with bits of walnut, powdered sugar and maple syrup.

Sasha tasted and gave a nod. "These might be the best pancakes I've ever had."

"Are you sure they're gourmet enough for you?"

"Is that some kind of dig?"

"I'm just saying that you don't have to sound surprised when the food tastes good. We're pretty civilized up here."

"And a little bit touchy." She gestured with her fork.

"Maybe." He filled his mouth with pancake, not wanting to set off another eruption. One volcano a day was plenty for him.

Her voice dropped to that low, husky alto he'd come to associate with passion. "I'm sorry, Brady. I've already said it once, but I'll say it again. Sorry."

"I'm not mad."

But he was hurt, and he hated that feeling, that weakness. Last night when they'd made love, he'd made the mistake of opening himself up to her. She was more to him than a date or a one-night stand. She was someone he could spend a long time with.

It was pretty damn obvious that she didn't feel the same way. The possibility of losing her job had broken her heart. Picking up a paycheck at a fancy Denver law firm was more important to this city girl than being with him. Fine, he could live with that as long as he didn't gaze too deeply into her liquid blue eyes. He could forget what it felt like to hold her in his arms. He shoveled more pancakes into his mouth, trying to erase the memory of her soft, sweet lips.

"I need a plan," she said. "When I see Moreno, I need to figure out what to say to him. Any ideas?"

"Not really."

"He's been following me around, encouraging me to join his group. I've got to wonder why."

"Could be he's attracted to you."

"Nope, I don't get that feeling from him." She tossed her head, sending a ripple through her blond hair. "A woman knows."

"Is that right?"

"I knew with you," she said. "Maybe it was wishful

thinking, but as soon as I met you, I knew there was chemistry between us."

He didn't want to think about the fireworks when they touched. He focused on the problem at hand. "You've spent a lot of time around Moreno, and you've seen how he operates. How does he recruit his followers? What does he get from them?"

"Mostly money," she said. "People pay a lot for his advice. They think they're going to get rich or become powerful."

"And what happens when they don't?"

She leaned back in the booth and sipped her coffee. "I had a long talk with one of his minions. This guy had given up his job and lost his savings to follow Moreno. I thought he'd be angry. But no. He was even more devoted, more willing to hang on for the next big success. He recruited friends and family members to join the guru."

"Contacts," Brady said. "Maybe he wants to get close to you because of your contacts."

"But I don't know anybody."

"You work at a big law firm," he reminded her. "Moreno might want a connection inside your firm."

She rewarded him with a huge smile. "That's got to be right. In his eyes, having me at the Three *S*s is important. That's where I'm going to start with him."

Her sketchy logic made sense, but Brady wasn't comfortable with it. His gut told him that Moreno was dangerous and not to be trusted.

BACK AT JIM BIRCH'S dude ranch, Sasha was pumped and ready to go. Raw energy coursed through her veins. She felt as if she could convince Moreno of anything. Sure, he was a world-renowned motivational speaker who boasted hundreds of thousands of followers. But she was motivated to get through to him.

Unfortunately, Moreno was nowhere in sight. He and a couple of his guys were out riding snowmobiles and ATVs across the new-fallen snow, taking advantage of a break in the weather. Sasha had no choice but to sit and wait at the kitchen table with Jim Birch and Brady.

Birch leaned forward and rested an elbow on the table-top. With his other hand, he pensively stroked his red mut-tonchops. "I'm going to take the deal," he said.

"Big decision," Brady said. "Are you sure you want to give up the ranch?"

"Moreno is offering a fair price. Not as much as when Westfield was bidding against him. Andrea thinks I could get more, but it seems fair to me."

"And how does the missus feel about it?"

"She's already got her bags packed and has made plane reservations to Florida. It's time we retire."

Though Sasha tried to stay engaged in the conversation, she couldn't stay focused. Under the table, her toe was tapping on the floor.

"We'll miss you around here," Brady said.

"In the summer, we'll be back for visits. But to tell you the truth, I'm not looking forward to another winter in the mountains. Life's too short. Poor old Virgil P. Westfield said he always wanted to retire in the mountains, and now he's dead." He shot Brady a glance. "Folks are saying he was murdered."

"That's what the sheriff told me this morning," Brady said. "The Denver P.D. told McKinley about the autopsy results. The killer clunked Westfield on the head and shoved him down the stairs."

"Did those Denver cops arrest anybody?"

Blake shook his head. "They haven't even got a suspect.

Mr. Westfield was alone in his house when it happened. His body wasn't found until the next morning."

Sasha felt a pang of guilt. She hadn't given a thought to the murders all day. "Was it a robbery? A break-in?"

"The alarm system wasn't on, and the back door was unlocked." Brady focused a steady gaze on her. "They think it was a professional killer."

*Another possible link to Lauren's murder.* A professional assassin had murdered Virgil P. and stabbed Lauren and climbed into the corporate condo like a ninja. And he—if it was only one killer—was still at large. "When did you talk to the sheriff?"

"While I was waiting for you outside the condo."

She gave a curt nod, not wanting to think about those moments when Damien had been running her life through the shredder. She ought to be more worried about her personal safety, but all she could think about was her next job interview when she had to explain why she might be fired. If she told her future employer that she was being chased by a ninja, would it hurt her prospects?

She pushed away from the table, went to the sink, dumped the remains of her coffee and rinsed the cup. Through the window she saw distant peaks etched against a fragile blue sky. Sunlight glistened on rolling fields of white snow, unbroken except for the tracks of snowmobiles. There was no other sign of Moreno and his minions.

She couldn't wait one more minute. Returning to the table, she gave Jim Birch a smile. "Do you have any snowmobiles that aren't being used right now?"

"I was wondering when you'd ask," he said. "You've been as jumpy as a long-tailed cat in a roomful of rocking chairs. It might do you good to get outside and blow off steam."

"That's not a bad idea," Brady said as he stood. "Jim, have you got some heavy-duty gloves we can borrow?"

"You know I do. I keep a stock of everything for the dudes that visit the ranch with nothing more than cute little mittens. Help yourself. You know where everything is."

Finally, it felt as if she was doing something. She followed Brady's instructions as he outfitted her in the mudroom off the kitchen. With waterproof snow pants over her jeans, gloves with cuffs that went halfway up to her elbows and heavy boots that were a size too big, she felt as though she was preparing for a trip to the moon. "Is all this really necessary?"

"Baby, it's cold outside." He studied her with a critical eye. "You should swap your parka for something heavier."

"I'll be fine." She had her wallet and cell phone in her parka. Not that she was planning to use them. "Is it hard to learn how to snowmobile?"

"It's kind of like riding a dirt bike."

With a shudder, she remembered her brother pushing her down the hill outside their house. "The first time I rode a bike, I nearly killed myself."

"I won't let that happen."

Was he beginning to forgive her? Someday things might be all right between them again. But probably not today.

In the dark recesses of her mind, she realized that she might have lost out on the chance to be with Brady. Their relationship had just begun, and it might already be over. She might never make love to him again. She didn't dare to think about that loss. *One disaster at a time.* She trundled out the back door behind him, tromping in his footsteps through new snow that rose higher than her ankles.

In one of the outbuildings near the big barn, Brady showed her a collection of ATVs and snowmobiles. "Jim says he keeps these for the tourists, but I know better.

When he goes out on a snowmobile, he's like a big kid with hairy red sideburns."

"He does have a Yosemite Sam thing going on," she said. "It's ironic that his idea of retirement is to leave this place. So many others, like Mr. Westfield, want to live here."

"Working at a dude ranch is different from visiting."

She sat on a racy blue machine that reminded her of a scooter with skis instead of tires. "Can I use this one?"

"If it has keys, you can take it." He picked a blue helmet off the wall and handed it to her. "You'll need this."

"Why? Am I going to be falling a lot?"

"Count on it."

He ran through the basic instructions, showing her how to use the throttle to give more gas and telling her to lean into the turns.

"It'll take a while for you to get the feel of how fast you should be moving. You need enough speed to go uphill. But you've still got to stay in control. Keep in mind that there are rocks and tree stumps buried under the snow."

She fastened the chin strap on her helmet, started the snowmobile and chugged out the door. As he'd promised, it was fairly easy. By the time they got away from the barn, she was beginning to understand how to ride. As she and Brady went past the corral, a couple of horses looked up disinterestedly and nickered.

Beyond the fences, they hit the wide-open fields. She watched as Brady took off, standing on the floor boards of his snowmobile and flying over the bumps and hills in the field. He let out whoops of pure exhilaration as he swept in a wide circle back to her and stopped, kicking up a spray of snow.

He flipped back the visor on his helmet. "Your turn, city girl."

"I can do this. I'm not a sissy."

"Show me."

As she drove into the snow, the earth seemed to shift under the skis of her snowmobile. She felt out of control and off-balance as she toiled to reach the top of a small rise. And then she went faster. And faster. And faster. The pure sensation of speed hyped her adrenaline as she accelerated over a hill and caught air on the other side. Swerving, she almost turned on her side but managed to right herself.

When she stopped, Brady was right beside her. She flipped her visor up. "This is the best."

"I thought you might like going fast."

"I love it."

"I want to show you a view. Follow me."

"Right behind you, cowboy."

Surrounded by unbelievable, spectacular mountain scenery and revved by excitement, she almost forgot why she was here. She wanted a snowmobile. She wanted to feel like this every day for the rest of her life.

While she and Brady swept across the hills, she lost track of time but still had a sense of direction. The landscape was vaguely familiar. The cliff with the cave he'd shown her two days ago was to her right.

Brady was near the edge of the forest when she saw two other riders coming toward her. It had to be Moreno and his henchman. It was time to put on her game face.

He stopped beside her and flipped his visor up. "I'm surprised you're here, Sasha."

"I've been looking for you." She lifted her own visor. "In the past couple of days, it seems like you've been trying to tell me something. I'm ready to listen."

"You're perceptive," he said smoothly. "I've been trying to get you alone."

She couldn't tell if this was going well or not. With a

determined grin, she asked, "Why do you want to see me? Is it because of my contacts at the law firm?"

"Guess again."

He wanted to play games? Well, fine. She'd humor him. "You can't be looking to me as an investor, because we both know I'm a paralegal with a fixed salary."

"Why would I want to get you alone?"

She glanced over her shoulder toward the forest where she'd last seen Brady. "You want to ask me out on a date?"

Moreno laughed out loud. "I'm a careful businessman, Sasha. I don't like to leave loose ends...or eyewitnesses."

His companion flipped up his visor.

She was staring at a face that was branded into her memory and haunted her nightmares. It was him, the man who had killed Lauren Robbins.

# Chapter *Twenty-One*

From the top of a ridge at the edge of the forest, Brady saw her metallic blue snowmobile trapped between two others. It had to be Moreno. Brady had been looking for him and the minions but hadn't caught sight of them until this moment. The timing bothered him. It was as though they'd been waiting until he was far from Sasha and unable to come to her aid.

He tore off his glove, opened his parka and drew his handgun. He might be making a mistake, but this time he'd go with his gut. Raising his weapon, he fired into the air.

The result was immediate and unexpected. Sasha's snowmobile took off. She raced across the field, headed toward the cliff. *The cave.* She was running for cover.

Gunfire ripped across the valley and echoed. One of the men was shooting at him.

"That's right," Brady muttered under his breath as he fired back. "Focus on me. Forget her."

They didn't come after him. They followed Sasha.

He needed to get to her first.

The powder snow at the edge of the forest wasn't as deep as in the field. His snowmobile shot across the land at top speed. He took a hard jolt and struggled to right himself. If he fell, he wouldn't be able to get up in time to stop them. He couldn't fall, couldn't pause. His bare hand clutching the gun was freezing cold.

But he was making headway. He was within a hundred yards of Sasha when she stopped at the foot of the cliff and leaped from her snowmobile. She scrambled up the path leading to the cave. He didn't know what had inspired her. Hiding in the cave was smart because they couldn't get to her. But she'd be trapped. There was only one way in or out.

He saw her disappear behind the boulder that hid the entrance to the cave. For the moment, she was safe.

And he was closing in. He slid to a stop beside her snowmobile, dismounted and dropped to one knee to aim his handgun. With his fingers half-frozen, he couldn't accurately hit the broad side of a barn, but the other two on the snowmobiles didn't know that. When he snapped off three shots, they slowed and stopped, preparing to return fire.

He dashed up the cliff, following Sasha's path. When he got to the safety of the cave, he'd call for backup. Not to Sheriff McKinley. Unless one of the deputies happened to be close, it'd take too long for law enforcement to get here. He'd call Jim Birch.

Likely, Birch had already heard the gunfire and was wondering about it.

In his bulky snow clothes, Brady squeezed himself through the small opening to the cave. "Sasha, are you all right?"

"I saw him," she said. "The man with Moreno is the killer."

She was using the LED function on her cell phone as a flashlight. In the bluish glow, he saw the fear she'd managed to keep mostly under wraps. He nodded to the phone. "Did you call for help?"

"I've got no reception in here."

He should have figured as much. "Move around. There might be a place you can get through."

She'd already peeled off her extra layer of snow clothes, and he did the same. If they couldn't call out, they'd have to make a stand in here, and they needed to be mobile.

From outside the cave, he heard Moreno's voice. "Are you in there, Deputy?"

"Step inside and find out."

If Moreno poked his head into the cave, Brady had the advantage. While they were squeezing through, he could shoot.

After a moment, Moreno said the obvious. "Looks like we have a standoff."

"Not for long. I called for backup." Brady had his phone in hand. *No reception.* But Moreno didn't know that. "You might as well give up right now."

"You underestimate me. I've gotten out of worse situations than this."

Brady's best hope was that Jim Birch would come looking for them. When he saw the abandoned snowmobiles, he'd know something was wrong. Until then, he'd try to keep Moreno distracted.

"I've got a question for you, Moreno. Why'd you kill Virgil Westfield?"

"The man was in his nineties. His death should have been chalked up to old age. I don't know why everybody got so worked up about it."

*Because he was murdered.* "What did he do to you?"

"He knew too much. When he and Lauren started digging into my financial background to undermine my bid on the dude ranch, they uncovered a few nasty details about my offshore businesses. I was actually impressed.

Lauren was one hell of a good bookkeeper. Too bad she got greedy."

"She tried to blackmail you," Brady said.

"It's about more than just the money. If my finances don't look clean and pure, I lose credibility with my followers. I need for them to believe in me."

"If you conceive it," Brady said, "you can achieve it."

"Ninety-nine percent of the time, it's true. Getting rid of Lauren and the documentation she tried to use against me would have been easy. Her death would have gone unnoticed for weeks if Sasha hadn't been looking through that window. This brings us to the current situation. Something must be done."

The craziest thing about Moreno was that he sounded sane. He talked about multiple murders the way other people made dinner plans.

"I'm leaving you now," Moreno said. "I'll have to take care of damage control and arrange for you to both disappear without a trace. In the meantime, my friend will keep watch outside the cave. Sooner or later, you'll have to come out."

And then, Brady supposed, Moreno's friend would kill them. There didn't seem to be an escape.

STILL HOLDING HER cell phone for light against the intense darkness of the cave, Sasha stepped into Brady's arms and melted against him. Fear had robbed her of strength. Her legs trembled with the effort of merely standing. "I guess losing my job isn't the worst thing that could happen."

He lifted her chin, tilted her face toward his. "I guess not."

Gazing up at him, she saw the dimple at the corner of his mouth. For some reason, that gave her hope. If Brady could still smile, all was not lost. His lips brushed hers, and fear receded another step. He kissed her more pow-erfully, pulling her close against him, and she felt life re-turning to her body. She wasn't ready to give up. Not yet. Not when she had something to live for.

She heard a rustling near the entrance to the cave. Brady must have heard it, too. He turned his head in that direc-tion, lifted his handgun and casually fired a shot, remind-ing Moreno's friend that they weren't helpless.

Her hand glided down his cheek. "There's nothing like facing death to get your priorities straight."

"I was thinking the same thing."

"My job isn't such a big deal," she said. "And it doesn't matter if I live in a city or in the mountains. Other things are more important. People are important."

When she'd been snowmobiling across the field, the threat of danger had become real. And she wasn't think-ing about her employment possibilities or her salary. She thought of him. She thought of long nights in front of the fireplace and waking up with him in the morning. "Brady, you are important to me."

"Same here. You're more important than I ever would have thought possible after only knowing you a couple of days." His breath was warm against her cheek. "I love you, Sasha."

"If I have to die…" Her voice trailed off. "I'm glad we're together."

"Nobody's going to die. Not on my watch."

He gave her another quick kiss and then went into ac-tion, gathering up rocks from the floor of the cave. "Help me out. We're going to pile these up by the entrance. Any-body who tries to sneak in will make a lot of racket."

Still holding her phone, she did as he said. Within a few minutes, they had a stack of loose rock that was two feet high.

"Now what?" she asked.

"We've got to find another way out."

"Didn't you say that you'd explored these caves when you were a kid? You didn't find another exit then."

"I wasn't as motivated then as I am now. You go first. We'll use your cell phone until it goes dark. Then we'll switch to mine."

Losing the light from the cell phone would be terrible. The dark inside the cave felt palpable and thick, almost like being underwater. He pointed the way through the darkness, but she took the first steps, passing the stalagmites that looked like dragon's teeth.

Too soon it seemed as if they had come to the end of the caverns that were large enough to stand upright in. Brady felt along the walls, looking for a break or a fissure. "Bring the light over here."

She knelt and aimed her phone at the bottom side of an overhang. Peering into the narrow horizontal space, she said, "I can't tell if this leads anywhere or not."

"Only one way to find out."

He flattened himself on the floor and stretched his arm into the opening. "I don't feel another rock."

"You can't fit in there. It's barely big enough for your shoulder."

She wasn't claustrophobic but didn't relish the idea of squeezing herself into a narrow space without knowing where it went. "Is there any way to tell how far it goes?"

"No, and that's why I'll go first. I don't want you to get hurt. Sometimes these gaps in the rock lead to other rooms. Sometimes the floor disappears and you fall into a pit."

Reluctantly, she pointed out the flaw in his logic. "I should go first. For one thing, I'm smaller. For another, if I start slipping into a pit, you're strong enough to haul me back up."

Placing the cell phone on the floor, she maneuvered around so she could wriggle feetfirst into the space below the overhang. He laced his fingers through hers, holding tightly as the lower half of her body disappeared into the fissure.

"That's enough," he said.

"There's more space. I can keep going."

"I don't want to lose you. I've barely just found you. If you disappeared from my life, I couldn't stand it."

"I feel the same. And I can't believe that I do. This is happening so fast." She blew the moist cave dirt away from her mouth. "I can count on one hand the number of men I've cared about. And that was after weeks and weeks of dating."

"Fast is good," he said.

"I love you, Brady."

They heard the crash of rocks coming from the front entrance. Moreno's friend had grown tired of waiting. He was coming after them.

Brady yanked her away from the overhang and turned off the light on her cell. Total darkness surrounded them, and she was immediately disoriented.

"Stay on the floor," he whispered.

When she heard him moving away from her, she wanted to grab his ankle and hold on. She curled into a ball. Her hand rested on the side of the cave.

A flash of light drew her attention. Someone was using a cell phone to find their way. It had to be the killer. She didn't see Brady.

The sound of gunfire crashed against the rocks. Two guns shooting. Then one. Then silence.

She pinched her lips together to keep from making any noise. Her heart drummed against her rib cage. The darkness was stifling.

The light from a cell phone flared.

She was looking into the murderer's face. He lifted his gun.

From behind his back, Brady fired first. His first bullet tore through the other man's shoulder, causing him to drop his weapon. The second shot was centered in the murderer's chest. He fell to the floor of the cave.

It was over.

# Epilogue

At the Gateway Hotel, the gala grand opening for the ski lodge was keeping the valets hopping. As Sasha exited the limo Dooley had rented for the occasion, she knew she looked pretty spectacular in her black gown with the plunging neckline, especially since she was draped in a fake fur coat that Jim Birch's wife had given to her. Jim's missus said she wouldn't need fur in Florida, which was where they were going even though the deal with Sam Moreno had fallen through.

Moreno was in police custody, as was his "friend," who hadn't died in the cave.

Everything that had happened after he was shot was kind of a blur. She and Brady had climbed out of the cave into the chilly afternoon light, and he'd put in the call for backup. As it turned out, Sheriff McKinley had already been on his way. Jim Birch had called him when he heard gunfire. The CBI agents had taken responsibility for Moreno's arrest.

She strolled across the red carpet at the entrance with her hand lightly resting on Brady's arm. In his black suit and white linen shirt, he was her best accessory. She was proud to be Brady and Dooley's guest for this event.

When they entered the lobby, Katie Cook rushed toward her and took her hand. "Sasha, darling, how are you?"

She'd never gotten that kind of enthusiastic greeting when she was only a legal assistant. Moreno's dramatic arrest had turned her into a local celebrity. "I'm very well, thanks. Do you remember Brady?"

"The deputy?" Katie squinted as though she couldn't believe this sophisticated-looking man was the rugged lawman who had given them all so much trouble.

He gave her a dimpled smile and a nod. "It's a pleasure to see you, ma'am."

"Dooley's nephew," she said. "Of course, I remember you."

Politely, Sasha asked about the Arcadia partnership and how their negotiations were going, but she really didn't care. She wasn't part of the law firm anymore. Though she'd left two phone messages for Damien, he'd never bothered to call her back.

Katie scanned the crowd, looking for someone more impressive to talk to. Offhandedly, she asked, "What are your plans?"

"I'm going back to school."

"Law school?"

*No way.* Sasha wasn't cut out to be a lawyer. She wanted to help people and to pursue justice in another way. "I'm going to study forensic science."

"Whatever for?" Katie asked.

Brady answered for her. "I'm planning to run for sheriff in the next election. And my first order of business will be to upgrade local law enforcement."

He'd stepped into the role of taking on authority as though he was born to it. Every day she spent with Brady, she found something else to love about him.

As he took her coat, she spotted Damien in his tuxedo. He was standing near the statue of Artemis. "Will you excuse me, Katie?"

"Of course, dear." She was already waving to someone else. "Don't be a stranger."

Sasha looked up at Brady. "There's something I need to say to Damien."

"Do you want backup? I'd be happy to shoot him in the foot or kick his sorry behind."

"I can handle this myself. Like a professional."

She stalked through the lobby until she was standing directly in front of the man she would forever think of as a giant sleaze. When he opened his mouth to speak, she held up her hand to stop him.

"Two words," she said. "I quit."

She spun on her heel and walked back to Brady. By the time she reached his side, Damien was forgotten. She'd never been so happy or so much in love.

* * * * *

# MILLS & BOON®

## Why shop at millsandboon.co.uk?

Each year, thousands of romance readers find their perfect read at millsandboon.co.uk. That's because we're passionate about bringing you the very best romantic fiction. Here are some of the advantages of shopping at www.millsandboon.co.uk:

* **Get new books first**—you'll be able to buy your favourite books one month before they hit the shops

* **Get exclusive discounts**—you'll also be able to buy our specially created monthly collections, with up to 50% off the RRP

* **Find your favourite authors**—latest news, interviews and new releases for all your favourite authors and series on our website, plus ideas for what to try next

* **Join in**—once you've bought your favourite books, don't forget to register with us to rate, review and join in the discussions

Visit **www.millsandboon.co.uk**
for all this and more today!